A PRECARIOUS PROPOSITION

The knock came so softly, so hesitantly, Sean listened again more closely to be sure he'd heard it. This time the rapping was stronger. He closed his hand over his gun. "Who're you looking for?"

"It's Kate," she whispered. "Can I speak with you?"

"A minute, lass." He rose, unlocked the door, then got back in bed and dragged the bedcover over his naked midsection. "Come in."

Kate closed the door behind her and leaned against it. She shifted her feet, lifted her chin, and finally addressed the reason for her visit. "I'm . . . I, uh . . . I want to . . . I have something to say." Her eyes swept over his chest, darted past the covered part of his body to his feet. "I suppose you're wondering why I'm . . . why I've come in the middle of the night."

The girl seemed younger, less sure of herself than when she'd sung earlier for the customers at the Lily. He smiled encouragingly. "Aye. I thought it likely a shamrock hid beneath my pillow."

She ignored his attempt at humor and inhaled deeply.

"I . . . I'll sleep with you for a hundred dollars."

Other *Leisure* books by Velda Sherrod:
A LEAF IN THE WIND

Velda Sherrod

Lord of the Plains

LEISURE BOOKS NEW YORK CITY

A LEISURE BOOK®

August 2001

Published by

Dorchester Publishing Co., Inc.
276 Fifth Avenue
New York, NY 10001

Cover art by John Ennis
www.ennisart.com

ISBN 0-8439-4901-5

Printed in the United States of America.

Visit us on the web at www.dorchesterpub.com.

To
Colleen, Krysteen, and Paula,
Doris and Richard C.,
Majorie, and Jane

Chapter One

The saloon singer wore a ridiculous feather in her hair, the silly ornament the same bold color as the dress that swirled provocatively about her knees. Sean O'Brien focused his eyes on her face. Ivory skin, a generous mouth, a smile to charm every male in the room, eyes wide and filled with laughter. His gaze slithered down to her slender hips, small waist, and full breasts. A beauty and forever a lusty man's dream. It made his mouth water just to look at her.

The first note of her song knifed its way to his groin and stayed there until the piano player danced his fingers up the keyboard in a finale. Only a lass from Galway could sing the old Irish love song with such passion and melancholy.

Hesitating a moment, he stepped away from the bat-wing doors of the Gilded Lily Saloon and flicked a guarded glance over the room. Satisfied with his quick appraisal, he headed for the bar, placed a booted foot on the rail, and nodded at the bartender. "My kind of night, laddie." He adjusted the gray sock-cap on his head, making sure it completely covered his hair. "Yessir, boyo," he said, rubbing his hands together and

9

Velda Sherrod

deepening his Irish brogue until his own father would have blushed in embarrassment. "It looks like a fine night."

The bartender eyed Sean's cap, giving special attention to his customer's broad shoulders. When he met the Irishman's steady gaze, he frowned. "Yeah, a right good night, Irish. And we ain't itchin' fer no fight. Unnerstan'?"

"Right, laddie. And 'tis no fight ye'll be gettin' from me."

"Ain't quite what we've got from your kin in the past. Tore up the place."

"Me Irish countrymen," Sean agreed sagely, "And fightin' men, they are. But me," he added with a hand over his heart, "gentle as a lamb, I am."

"We'll see." The bartender took a rag to the bar. "But remember, I've got an eye on ye."

The piano player beat out another song, signaled the young singer to step up to the piano, then nodded for her to begin. When she opened her mouth, Sean grew hard in inevitable response. What was this fascinating woman doing in the Gilded Lily? You could tell by looking at her that she wasn't a whore. Not even a hundred-dollar whore could look that innocent. His eyes strayed to the men in the saloon, most of them licking their lips in anticipation of taking her to bed. Sean's hands balled into fists. For some irrational reason, he wanted to mess up their faces. After she had finished and the last notes on the piano had died away, Sean lifted his drink in salute. "A beauty and sings like a bird." He set the glass down and thumped his chest in the region of his heart. "Gets me here, lad."

The bartender nodded agreeably. "Nice gel. Don't take much sass from nobody." By this time, he'd apparently accepted the Irishman at his word, that there would be no free-for-all. "Ain't often we git one like her in this place. To tell the truth, cain't remember none. Ain't likely she'll stay that way." His gaze flickered over the room, past the gambling tables, to stop at a door near the bar. "Shore ain't likely."

"What's her name?"

"Kate, she says. Ain't been here long. Nathan Boggs, he owns the place, done hired her on the spot. He likes the new ones, 'specially if they're nice-lookin', if'n you know what I mean."

Sean threw him a knowing look. "Then Boggs must like this one more than the others."

"Reckon all these women looked somethin' like that when they started. You know, young and purty."

"But this one—an Irish lass, perhaps? Hair black as a witch's cauldron. Eyes dark as the Irish Sea. No doubt a Killarney nose. Could be my sister." He winked at the bartender. "Not a pleasant thought, now, is it, lad?"

Sean slid his gaze over her perfect features, down her slight figure to her legs, and up once more to caress her face. Her eyes were fringed with black lashes, and he couldn't determine their color in the flickering light, but probably they were a midnight blue. When she sang, her mouth curved into a luscious pink rose.

Her gaze met his so briefly that only he recognized that she'd acknowledged his presence. A few moments later, as if drawn there by a mysterious magnetism, her eyes sought his again, and on some intimate level Sean felt as though she were assessing him.

She sang two songs, smiled, and bowed to the loud applause before lifting a gracious hand to include the piano player. Intent on refilling his empty glass, the man nodded in the general direction of the audience, and with hardly a glance rose to his feet. He held the back of a chair to steady himself before slouching his way to the bar.

Sean smiled at the girl and raised his glass again. He grinned at the bartender. "I'll be for begging your pardon, barmaster, but I would visit with the lady."

"She ain't gonna pay you no mind, Irish. She don't have nothin' to do with customers."

"I feel lucky, laddie." Sean sauntered toward the piano and settled himself on the recently vacated stool. "Wouldja be knowing 'Londonderry Tune,' lass? 'Tis an Irish song beloved by my countrymen especially around Killarney and Kilkenny and Galway Bay."

The girl looked at him skeptically. "Can you play it?"

"Aye, lass."

"Give me the key."

Sean struck a chord. "About right, you think?"

"Yes. I'm ready when you are."

He ran his fingers over the keys experimentally. "A few sour notes, but we'll improvise."

With a glance and a smile in her direction, he played the melody, waiting for her to pick up the words. When she failed, he supplied the opening lyric. Something magical happened. Kate lifted her head and sang, different words than he knew, but words that fit the music. The sweet, sentimental melody touched every grizzled plainsman, drifter, and cowboy, the only sound a sniffle slipping past an unwary and drunken listener.

The song ended and Sean stood and applauded along with the audience. "You bring tears to their eyes, Kate, girl. Might we give them another?"

When Sean tapped out the opening notes of a new song and looked questioningly at Kate. She gave a regretful shake of her head. "You play well, and I thank you. But Joe's back."

Ignoring the piano player's dark looks, Sean relinquished his seat. "Aye, lass, we wouldna deprive the man of his livelihood, now, would we? As for me playin', I've a mind to believe 'twould take more than a man of talent, a miracle perhaps, to evoke good music from this fine instrument."

"No doubt, sir." Her gaze flicked over him, a fleeting smile, a guarded glance, sizing him up, Sean was to think later. "Will you be here long?"

"No, not long, and that's too bad, since I'd be wishing to hear you sing every day." He walked away from the piano before turning to address her once more. He smiled gently, his gaze caressing her face. "I'll be staying around town a day. Two, perhaps. I've a room at Tascosa's best hotel, so I'll be back. For now, 'tis a good night I'll be wishing you."

But his departure was delayed. A man had emerged from a door near the bar, an entrance almost hidden in the recessed wall. Nathan Boggs. It had to be. The big man himself, Sean thought, not bothering to hide his curiosity. People said Boggs was ruthless. That he crushed those who stood in his way. Some said he traded with the Comancheros. Others said he had been a Comanchero before becoming a saloon owner.

Boggs's thin lips slashed across his swarthy face in a straight line. His eyes narrowed to dark slits as he studied the customers seated at his gaming tables or drinking at the bar.

Sean quickly made his own assessment of Boggs: slippery as an eel, calculating, and sly. Evil. A man to avoid.

Boggs's attention had come to rest on Sean. His expression clearly reflected disdain. "You from around here?"

"Aye," Sean said, wanting to explode a punch into the man's soft belly. "I've a spread southeast of here."

"Long way from home, ain't you?"

"My father's house and my kin are in Ireland. That's a long way."

"Yeah, we've had a lot of Irish trash show up at the Lily. Not enough spuds to go around in Ireland, huh?" Boggs laughed loudly at his own joke. "At the Lily, we'll serve you, providin' you've got the money to pay."

"And it's generous you are, Boggs. I'll spread the word."

Boggs frowned, finally dismissing Sean with a nod. His face changed notably when he stared at Kate. Smiling benignly, he walked toward her. "Kate, you won their hearts. The men love you."

Despite his anger, Sean leaned nonchalantly against the piano. "Two fine musicians you have, Boggs." His casual look took in the entire room. "I don't suppose it's easy to hire a beautiful singer and a good piano player into a place such as this. You must have to pay them well."

Boggs's face turned purple. "Now see here, Irishman, I don't like people buttin' in, tellin' me how to run my bidness. Slurring the Lily."

"I rather thought I was telling the truth."

"Watch your lip, Irishman. I'm an important man in this town." He turned back to Kate. "I enjoyed your song."

"Thank you, Mr. Boggs."

Boggs looked contemptuously at Joe. "Try to stay sober when you're on the job." Turning, he leered at Kate. "You're pretty as a picture, Kate. We're glad you're here. And you're going to be glad you came to the Gilded Lily."

Sean doubted the lovely Kate would be glad very long, if the bartender's words and his own observations counted for anything. Boggs was a bad man to the core. "I say, Boggs, the piano could stand tuning. Some dead keys."

"The hell you say. Why don't you get out of here?"

"Just trying to help." Sean smiled at Kate. "You've a fine voice, lass."

After taking time for one last beer, Sean didn't hang around much longer. He waved a good-bye to Kate, which she pretended not to see, bought a bottle to take with him, then walked the distance to the hotel. In his room he prepared for bed, shedding his clothes and stretching out on the soft mattress.

Tomorrow he'd seek the colonel. With help from the military, perhaps a solution could be reached on the thorny Indian problem. Praying he would not disappoint his father, nor fail to honor his mother, he made plans to drop by his mother's grave on the way back to his ranch. His mother Morning Fawn lay buried in a grove of evergreens, hiding one entrance to the big canyon called Palo Duro.

Sean sifted through his thoughts, letting them settle on the lovely Kate. What downturn of luck had brought her to the Lily? Perhaps in her youthful ignorance, she had chosen the only way open to her. He sighed heavily. Ten years and she'd look fifty. Her eyes would become hard and shifty. After a while, she'd fit into the life of a saloon girl, working for a few pieces of silver, a bar drink, and a chance to ply her trade.

When he thought of Kate swinging her slender hips for a drink of whiskey or a trip upstairs for a paltry coin, he wanted to hit something.

Damn. He rose and poured himself a drink from the bottle he'd brought from the saloon. He didn't want to think of Kate, but her face continued to swim in and out of his mind, disrupting his thoughts as well as his sleep.

Would a kiss from her soft lips taste of honey? Could a man ever forget her touch? Would her body meld in pleasure with a man's? His body had responded to hers at thirty paces. And her eyes had locked with his as if issuing a promise.

The knock came so softly, so hesitantly, he listened again more closely to be sure he'd heard it. This time the rapping was stronger. He closed his hand over his gun. "Who're you looking for?"

"It's Kate," she whispered. "Can I speak with you?"

"A minute, lass." He rose, unlocked the door, then got back in bed and dragged the bedcover over his naked midsection. "Come in."

Kate closed the door behind her and leaned against it. She shifted her feet, lifted her chin, and finally addressed the reason for her visit. "I'm . . . I, uh . . . I want to . . . I have something to say." Her eyes swept over his chest, darted past the covered part of his body to his feet. "I suppose you're wondering why I'm . . . why I've come in the middle of the night."

The girl seemed younger, less sure of herself than when she'd sung earlier for the customers at the Lily. He smiled encouragingly. "Aye. I thought it likely a shamrock hid beneath my pillow."

She ignored his attempt at humor and inhaled deeply. "I . . . I'll sleep with you for a hundred dollars."

Kate *was* a hundred-dollar whore.

He hid his disappointment behind a yawn. "I'm flattered, Katie, but I hadn't reckoned on sharing my bed. Especially tonight."

Desperation flashed across her face. "Don't you want to sleep with me?"

"You're a bonny lass," he said, the truth coming easily as his gaze caressed the ivory skin of her throat and shoulders, not missing the creamy cleavage exposed by the gaudy dress. "And I'd be delighted to, but . . ."

"Then it's settled." Her hands trembled when she started unbuttoning the bodice of her dress. "I want my hundred dollars before we . . . before I . . . I want the money first."

"Kate, best we give a bit of discussion to the subject. I hadn't anticipated—"

"You said you'd be delighted."

"That I did, lass, but I need a mite of time to think about it." But not a lot of time, he thought wryly. Poker winnings earned

15

in Wichita could never be put to better use. He grew rigid.

"I thought men always wanted . . . a bedmate," she finished lamely.

"Rare is the man, Kate, who would say no to such a pretty colleen as yourself, especially if he has a hundred dollars. But I hadn't counted on sharing my bed tonight." He let his gaze drift down to her open bodice. It had been a while since he had enjoyed a romp with a girl, and a very long while since a bounce in the hay included one as beautiful as this one. He could imagine her slender legs wrapped around him, those sumptuous breasts bare against his chest. He made up his mind quickly. "Why me, lass?"

She didn't meet his eyes. "I . . . I choose my partners carefully, sir. Tonight I chose you." Down to her drawers and chemise, she glanced at him. "I thought you would be able to pay."

"That the only reason?"

What started as a serious answer became a grimace. "You looked nicer than the others. Cleaner. I'll not sleep with smelly hide hunters, and definitely no dirty, stinking Indians."

Sean chuckled wryly. "Sure, and I understand the dislike of buffalo killers. But Indians?"

"I hate them."

"Mind telling me why?"

She shrugged. "They kill people. Burn homes. Kidnap babies."

"Your baby?"

She frowned. "Heavens, no."

"Then . . . ?"

Kate glanced down at her feet. "Let's not get into an argument about it. People talk about such things in the bar."

But that wasn't all, Sean thought, wishing he could argue with her. No doubt she had heard such stories from the men who came to her bed. "I suppose some Indians do those things. But not all."

When she removed her chemise, her breasts rose high and firm, their crests centered in primrose pink areolae. Her hands fluttered up to cover them.

16

The gaze she turned on him met his without wavering, but she couldn't hide the tremble in her voice. "Indians are mean. Given the chance, they kill white people." She put a nervous hand to her hair and smoothed back a tendril, the action inadvertently provocative. "Where's the money?"

"What am I paying for, lass? The hundred dollars. What does it buy? Half the night? All night? Thirty minutes?"

Kate hesitated. "Half the night."

Sean smiled lazily. "Too expensive for half a night."

"What do you think is right?"

"A hundred for all night."

Considering, she opened her mouth to speak, closed it, and took a deep breath before making up her mind. "All right."

"But I'll not be paying to sleep with a log. Response, I would have. Response or nothing."

She shifted her weight from one foot to the other. "Yes. Of course, response. I'll . . . I'll do that. Respond, I mean."

"Take off all your clothes, lass." He reached for his pants, removed some bills, and handed them to her. "A hundred dollars for all night. That's the bargain." And it would be a bargain at twice the rate, he thought in amusement.

Grabbing the money, she counted it and knelt to place it in her shoe. "Until five o'clock in the morning." She loosened the drawstring and let her drawers slide to the floor.

He sucked in his breath. Naked, she was beautiful, perfect, exquisitely made, with high, sweet breasts and slender hips, a dark triangle where her thighs met. Her face had become a delightful rose color, which he dared hope signaled a need to match his own, but he seriously doubted that. Desire, raw, wicked, and discriminating, centered in his groin. He threw back the cover. "Come to bed, darlin'," he said huskily. "We're wastin' the night."

When he stretched out his arm for her to lie beside him, she glanced at him, her eyes wide. "I want to do this right, you understand. Earn the hundred dollars. So if I'm not . . . if I'm not responding the way you want, just tell me and I'll . . . I'll consider it."

17

He drew her close, one big hand gently covering her breast. "No wrong way, lass."

She shivered. "Yes, of course. Right."

Nuzzling her throat, he whispered against the clear, beautiful skin, "Cold?"

"A little."

He brushed kisses along her cheek. "We won't let you stay cold, darlin'. How did you get to Tascosa, Katie?"

"I rode the stage."

"Where are you from?" His teeth nipped at her earlobe, his mouth moving on to sample her mouth.

She wiggled away and looked at him accusingly. "You didn't pay for my history."

"How much more would it cost me?" Laughing a little, feeling his gray eyes warm with tenderness he circled her breast with his palm, his thumb rubbing the pebbled bud. "But if you haven't put a price on it, I think your history might wait for another time. Kiss me, pretty Kate."

"Yes." She turned her face to his at the same time his hand slid down past her stomach to the soft thatch between her legs. She gasped. "Oh . . . oh, my."

"Aye," he whispered. "Aye." He rose to his elbow, tenderly brushing her lips, kissing the corners. Her mouth remained closed, and he ran his tongue over her lips. "Widen a bit, Katie, darlin'." When she complied he didn't hesitate, but plunged into the glory of her open mouth. As his da would have said, the luck of the Irish had finally caught up with him.

Luring her into the passionate journey, Sean moved slowly. "No need for haste, lass. When making love, we don't measure the time." Tender and wistful, he told her of the excitement she had brought to his bed, laughing a little as his ragged breathing increased. He was glad she neither stained her nipples, as some saloon girls did, nor smelled of cheap perfume. Soap and water came to mind as he stroked a bare shoulder. "I've a feeling it'll be a short night."

"Am I . . . do I . . . please?"

He nearly choked. "Aye, darlin'." His hands roamed slowly over her body, caressing, pausing to enjoy the gentle thrust of her breast. His tongue flicked out to lave the crest. "God, yes," he whispered before his mouth closed over the luscious nub.

At her gasp, he raised his head. "Did I do something you don't like?"

"No, oh, no," she said breathlessly. "I like what you're doing. Truly, I do."

He'd been promised an honest response, but hadn't expected this much honesty. When a tiny sound escaped her, it gave an incredible surge to his already burgeoning desire. Lowering his head, he buried his face in the valley between her breasts. "Lovely."

"They told me men were usually . . ."

"Aye, Katie, that we are," he said, his voice husky. It was apparent she hadn't been long in the profession. "Would you be for telling me who these people were?"

"Doesn't matter."

"Doesn't matter at all." Sean continued his exploration of her body, murmuring solicitations, all the while drawing her closer. Her skin was ivory satin, her lips a soft cherry pink. "Especially doesn't matter when I'm holding such perfection. Touch me, darlin'."

"What?"

He took her hand. "Hold me, lass."

Her fingers feathered around him, then remained still. "Yes."

He guided her in the way. When she responded, he groaned. "Aye."

Encouraged, she continued caressing him until he covered her hand again. "No more. Best wait until the second time for such pleasure." The fragrant smell of her, the honeyed taste of her would be with him forever. He rimmed her lips with his tongue before gently urging them apart again. A faint whisper touched his ear—his, hers, he couldn't be sure. "Aye, lass. The best is yet to come." Perspiration beading his forehead, his big body poised for the joining, he rose above her. "Now, sweetling?"

Katie choked back a sob. Her body was worth a hundred dollars. Only a hundred dollars. What if Maureen learned that her sister had sold her virtue for money? Would Maury be grateful? Or feel disgraced?

Fearing her tears would betray her agony, Kate reminded herself that Maureen was worth any sacrifice. Besides, she couldn't turn back now. A flash of panic rippled through her as he centered himself over her. What came next? "I'm . . . I'm of a mind."

Sean lowered himself until his body barely touched hers. He worked at going slowly; he wanted them to reach the mountaintop together.

"Don't remember desiring anybody quite so much, Katie, sweet." Breathing tender words into her ear, forgetting he had paid a hundred dollars for the privilege, he thrust into her. He felt the shattering of the barrier, heard her whimper become a sob. *God.* The enormity of what he had done staggered him, but it was too late. He closed his eyes and let the pleasure of the moment wash over him.

When his shudders subsided, he stared down into her wide-eyed innocence. He had bedded a virgin, and her helpless cry rang in his ears. Had she thought he could penetrate her body without his knowing? Abruptly another thought sneaked slyly into his consciousness. He had bought the night.

Why not take what he'd paid for?

Nay, he wouldn't let that happen again with this girl. His joy in their lovemaking now weighed like lead on his conscience. "Are you all right, Katie?"

Tears clogged her voice. "I'm . . . I'm all right."

God help him, he still wanted her, craved the sweetness of her mouth, needed to bury himself in her softness. Growling his mortification, he plowed his hands into her hair and lifted her face to within inches of his own. "Why me, Katie? Bloody hell, why me?"

"I need the money." She sniffled and wiped her tears away with the back of her hand. "I couldn't go to bed with any of the men at the saloon, money or no. Two were half-breeds. I couldn't bear to do . . . to do this with an Indian."

Frowning, he leaned away from her toward the bedside table. His bandanna was convenient, and he handed it to her. "Blow."

She grabbed the red neckerchief and blew her nose. "Thank you," she said primly, and handed the kerchief back to him.

"You're welcome." Sean kissed her cheek. "Remember, Katie, Indians fight for what they consider to be theirs. Most of us would do the same." His gaze caressed her. "For a legitimate reason, I'd have given you the hundred dollars without taking you to bed."

"I'll not be beholden to anybody. Never."

Something inside him clawed to undo what had been done, and he knew he'd carry the weight of the night's enjoyment for a long time. He almost snarled. "A hundred damned dollars, Kate. Why was it so bloody important?"

"I've told you already. You didn't pay for my history."

"Stay at the saloon and Nathan Boggs will have you in his bed. He has a history, Kate. Girls come and go there. If you keep saying no to him, you'll be out of a job. Or it's something worse you'll be getting. In time, lass, you'll move on to other saloons, and eventually to other men."

She used the hem of the sheet to wipe her cheeks again. "No, no, no. I had to have the money. But I'll never sleep with Boggs." She met his gaze with a steady look. "When I knocked on your door, there was so much I didn't know about . . . you know . . . about doing this with you. And I've more to learn, but there will never again be a price paid."

He didn't need this kind of responsibility, didn't want it, had enough on his shoulders without adding one damned thing, especially not the loss of this girl's innocence. He shook his head wryly. "It wouldna have been me tonight, lass, if I had known. A mistress of the night I thought you were. I'd not bring a virgin to my bed without commitment. Against my honor, you see. Wasn't there another way to obtain the money?"

"No other way. And I thought about it over and over." She nodded her conviction that hers was the only choice. "I don't know about such things, but I hope you got your money's worth."

"Aye, lass. I hope the prize was worth the sacrifice." He

clenched his jaw. "But 'tis more than just your coming to my bed. Or the money. I was part of the decision. And I should bloody well have had a say. Did I hurt you?"

"No."

"Tell the truth." Using a finger, he gently turned her face toward him. "The truth."

Her gaze slid past him. "A little when you . . . you know."

Sean exhaled slowly. "Yes, I know."

Why was he picking on the girl? It was himself with whom he was angry. Obsessed with lust, he'd closed his eyes to the obvious. He'd known from the moment she came into his room.

She was inexperienced and courageous, and he'd taken her at the expense of his conscience.

Mindful of his nakedness, he clutched his shirt to cover his most private parts, rose, and went to the washstand. In moments he was back. He knelt beside her, a damp towel in his hand. "Let me."

Her face flushed crimson once more. "I'll do it myself."

"The idea of hurting you bothers me, lass. I wanted you to feel the joy—something I'd like to feel again with you. But it isn't likely, I think." He stared hard at her. "But you felt no pleasure, did you?"

"Doesn't matter. I'm not planning on doing it again with anybody else, unless of course I get married, which isn't likely. As for what we did together . . . after a while, I didn't mind."

"Didn't mind, Kate?" He rolled his eyes. Heaven had opened to him. For her—nothing. No pleasure, joy, or delight. "I'm sorry."

She must have sensed her poor choice of words. "I liked it when you kissed me. When you put your arms around me. Your hands were . . . were . . . I liked the way your hands made me feel. The nice things you said."

A rueful grin played about his mouth. "Keep going, lass."

"I didn't know what to expect, that it would hurt, or what my asking would do to you." She lowered her eyes to his chest and cast a fleeting glance downward, then just as quickly looked up, her cheeks a lively pink. "Only of the hundred dollars."

A whimsical smile briefly curled his lips. "Honesty sometimes stings. But it's what I asked for, and 'tis honesty I'm hearing."

"Mama always said I'd tell the truth if it paralyzed the pope."

"Well, the pope may be in more danger than he knows, unless you guard tonight's secret well."

Kate continued as though she hadn't heard him. "I'd like to sing in nice places. Like in a church. No saloons. And to be paid more than just a few dollars. If I were paid what I think I'm worth, tonight would never have happened."

"I understand. You've a wonderful calling." Her father should have put her in a convent, where she would have been safe from men like him. "You've training, I think."

"My mother." Dully, she looked past him. "And my father before he died."

"Your mother dead also?"

"No."

He recognized that the topic had reached a dead end. "Where did you learn the Irish songs?"

"My grandmother, my father's mother, was from Ireland. She's dead now."

"Life's not easy, lass. And maybe 'tis harder for a woman."

"Most women would agree," she said bitterly. She played with the hem of the cover. "I don't suppose I pleased you, the way some other woman would have."

"Ah, Katie. It was a beautiful experience."

"Are you just telling me that?" At the shake of his head, she gave him an unsteady smile. "I'm glad I chose you."

Laughing, Sean cradled her face and kissed her. "I'm glad you chose me." Privately, he thought otherwise before remembering she would have selected some other man who might not have appreciated her lovely body as he had.

"Do you want me to go?"

"Stay until the hotel occupants are in. It isn't talk about you we'd be wanting." He put his hands behind his head. "Question is, what now?"

"You've paid for all night."

He closed his eyes. *Maybe someday, Katie, me girl, I'll collect.*

"True enough. And probably for a lot of sleepless ones."

"I don't like owing anybody."

Katie, full of anger, bone-deep honesty, and a passion that simmered just below the surface, was so beautiful a blind man would be drawn to her.

After a while she slept, her breasts rising and falling easily with each breath. He wasn't so lucky. He stared into the sickly light of the room, his uneasy thoughts forcing sleep out of his reach. Sometime later, he slipped his arm under her head, pulled her close to him, and closed his eyes.

Kate studied herself in the mirror. Her looks hadn't changed, but inside she was a mess of conflicting thoughts and feelings—all a result of the previous night she had spent with the Irishman. No doubt her sins already showed on her face. Milton Scruggs, her mother's new husband, a wild-eyed, podium-pounding preacher, would think so. His ideas of right and wrong were habitually etched in the forbidding frown he wore. His judgment of others started at the end of his nose and included everybody. When she considered Milton, somehow her rendezvous with the Irishman didn't seem so bad.

She hadn't asked the stranger his name, nor had he supplied one, but he had been gentle and kind, even understood why she had come to his room.

His dark gray eyes haunted her, as did the memory of the rest of him. He had worn the cap, his hair neatly tucked beneath it, the one he'd worn at the Lily. His steadiness was surprising, but it was his quiet confidence that set him apart from the miners and drifters.

He was tall and lean, his stomach flat, his biceps bunching each time he lifted his arms. She remembered his mouth, a warm, laughing mouth. And when he kissed her, funny things happened to different parts of her body, exciting things, deliciously sinful things.

For a moment she longed to feel again the sweet agony she'd known in his arms. She walked to the window in time to see

24

him canter on horseback down the street. He moved with the gait of the big stallion he rode, his shoulders erect, his gaze directed on the road ahead of him. Abruptly he turned and looked up at her window, then lifted his hand in salute. How had he known she was there?

After she'd spent the night with him, she'd gone to her own small room. He'd not asked her for more favors after their coupling, but cuddled her close until she slept. Sometime after five o'clock, he'd awakened her, given her a chaste kiss on the forehead, and told her good-bye. "It was a beautiful night, Katie. It's doubtful I'll ever know such a night again."

He had watched her dress, his head propped on his elbow. "I've never known anyone as beautiful, Katie. If you ever need me, I'll come."

"Not likely," she had responded. Nodding her good-bye, she had slipped away before the other hotel guests awoke. She'd crept to bed flinging herself down and burying her head in a pillow. She hadn't been proud of the few tears that fell.

The owner of the Tascosa Hotel rented this room to her for a reasonable price, an amount she'd thought unreasonable at first. The Irishman probably looked on her as one of Nathan's gray doves that frequented the place. Kate pursed her lips. Depended on the definition, she supposed. But she had made sure her sister could get away from Mama. And Verlin and Milton.

Kate prayed Maureen would receive the hundred dollars before becoming Verlin Digby's wife, or Milton had his way with her. Mama's beloved Milton had had his eye on Maureen from the time she'd sprouted breasts. Not that Mama would ever admit it. In her eyes her husband could do no wrong. He was perfect, a man chosen by God to save sinners. Kate couldn't stand him, with his wispy salt-and-pepper hair, bony face, and crooked teeth.

Counting on her fingers, Kate added up the days it would take before Maureen could slip away and catch the stagecoach. Several more before she could get to Tascosa. If all went as planned . . .

If Milton didn't discover the letter . . .

Velda Sherrod

If Mama didn't take the money . . .

If Maureen had more courage than a goose . . .

At thoughts of her sister, Kate forced back tears. Maureen's gentleness was no match for Milton's hypocrisy. Mama had refused to see Milton's lecherous glances at both her daughters, how he managed to touch them at every opportunity. Kate could remember the revulsion she felt when he placed a wet kiss on her cheek, barely missing her mouth. She'd wanted to throw up.

After Papa, how could Mama be drawn to such a hypocrite? *Man of God—ha.* In the pulpit his eye was always on the collection plate. At the church door he bowed and scraped, admiring the simpering matrons while respectfully addressing their husbands. Extolling the beauty of chastity, he playfully patted the young girls, admonishing them to stay sweet and charitable and virtuous.

At home he was mean and spiteful, making no effort to hide the ugly side of himself except from Mama. The haunted look in Maureen's eyes showed her fear and revulsion of her stepfather. To make matters worse, Mama was determined to marry Maureen to Verlin, and let no opportunity pass to shove Maureen in the man's direction.

Viewed by the town's matrons as a worthy catch, Verlin was twice Maureen's age. His sandy hair barely covered his pate. His pale blue eyes were separated by a long beaklike nose. His mouth was a thin straight line. Kate could hardly bear to look at him, and as for her sister marrying and going to bed with him—it was unthinkable. Kate knew she had to get Maureen away before her sister did something desperate.

Kate thought of her own position at the Gilded Lily. If the Irishman was correct, she could expect unwanted advances from Nathan Boggs. She'd noticed Nathan eyeing her, his gaze always centering on her bosom. Because of Maureen, she'd sing until Nathan made it impossible to remain.

Perhaps if she sang well enough, the customers would insist he keep her, in which case she could warn Nathan to leave her alone or she would move on. Feeling better, she dressed and made her way downstairs, prepared to run errands before appearing at the Gilded Lily.

She met the Irishman at the door to the hotel. Dark and tall, he touched the brim of his hat and hesitated a moment, his eyes searching hers. Then he nodded and walked on. He stopped at the desk, where he spoke a few words to the clerk and asked for his mail. Moments later he'd climbed the stairs, his spurs clanking as he disappeared down the hall.

Kate gave her chin a pugnacious lift. The man might at least have passed the time of day or inquired of her health. Of course, he could be thinking of her reputation, since they both had rooms at the hotel. Or maybe he thought she'd cheated him.

Truth be known, he probably thought she was a harlot.

Head up, she sailed off down the street. No point in rehashing the previous night's happening. The deed was done.

But somehow she knew the Irishman didn't think she was a whore.

She walked a little faster. Hurrying from one store to the next, she soon completed her errands and marched on toward the Lily. If people wanted to judge her, let them walk in her boots.

When she arrived at the Lily, Joe was already at the piano, head bent, fingers hovering over the keys. She changed quickly into her usual gaudy costume and, with a last pat to her hair, strolled to the piano. "Joe."

He glanced at her without raising his head. "You shoulda come earlier so we could practice. I might not know how to play what you want."

"I'm early, Joe."

"Yeah. Guess I'm just complainin' because my head is threatenin' to bust."

Kate looked at him sympathetically. "Maybe you should—"

He grinned mockingly. "Yeah, I should, but I ain't a roarin' drunk yet. Close, maybe." He glanced down at the instrument. "This old piano's been around since Noah loaded the ark. Seems like the thing gets more bad keys all the time. Or could be my playin' gets worse."

"Why doesn't Mr. Boggs get the piano tuned once in a while?"

"I ain't aimin' to ask 'im. I wouldn't advise you to."

Laughing, she glanced about her. "Suppose our customers would know if the piano were in tune?" She looked toward the office door. "Where is everybody? Is Mr. Boggs here?"

"Oh, Boggs is here, all right. Prob'ly countin' his money. The tarts are still sleepin'."

Kate turned away so he couldn't see the flush rise to her cheeks. After last night, she wasn't a lily-white virgin herself. "Shall we begin?"

Joe played the opening notes of a ballad they both liked, frowning when he struck a bad key. "Might as well." He looked past her and muttered a curse word for her ears alone. "Here comes Boggs, best known for his compassion, even after he sticks a knife in your back."

One pants leg tucked into the top of his shining boots, his red velvet vest showing his gold watch chain to advantage, Nathan beamed with good humor. He chewed on a lighted cigar and advanced to within a few feet of her.

"Katie, honey. You're rehearsin'. I'm glad to see you're serious about your singin'."

"Thank you, Mr. Boggs."

"Call me Nathan. I've a feelin' we're going to get along fine."

Her heart sank to her shoes. "I am glad you think so." She forced a bright smile. "Well, now, Joe and I had better get on with the practice." If the Irishman's prophecy was true, being around Boggs would be like fighting off Milton. She'd have to be on constant alert to watch out for his hands. When Boggs's gaze slid down her body, her smile faltered. The Irishman had recognized the truth: Nathan Boggs wanted her.

Sean tied his horse to the hitching post and made his way inside. "I've an appointment with the colonel, lad. Ye might mention my name: Sean O'Brien, late of County Mayo, Ireland, the Emerald Isle. Urgent business."

Moments later he was ushered into the presence of Col. Peter Collins, commander at Fort Cooper. "Come in, come in." The colonel stuck out his hand, at the same time motioning with his head for his aide to leave the room. He beamed his welcome. "Sean O'Brien, you were a very young lad the last time I saw you. How's your pa?"

"Getting older, but sends warm regards, sir."

"Honorable man."

"He's skeptical about the project, Colonel. But he has personal reasons for wanting to see it succeed. As do I."

The colonel rolled a cigarette, licking the paper with his tongue. "If it works, maybe it will prove to a lot of naysayers that the Indians and whites can live together peaceably."

"There's mutual distrust, sir. By limiting the project to one band, perhaps the plan stands a chance. It might even catch on. Of course, I have to convince my grandfather."

"I think Stone Wolf will listen, Sean. He's intelligent. He's also a sly old fox."

"Aye, but so far no treaty has worked, and I doubt it ever will. Too many whites are moving west, Colonel. It's too big an area to control."

"But if we try for a workable solution among a few, Sean, perhaps more will follow."

Sean was willing to give it a chance, but he doubted they'd have much success. "Aye, sir."

"You know that if the whites get wind of this, they'll call you a traitor and probably hang you."

"If the Comanche hear, they'll bury me in an anthill up to my eyebrows."

The colonel drummed his fingers. "Risky either way." He leaned forward. "You can still back out."

Sean shook his head. No, he wanted to do it for his mother, for his grandfather, for the children he hoped to have someday. "No, I'm in for the draw."

The colonel nodded his approval. "You are a brave man. If our plan succeeds, many people will owe you their lives."

Sean shrugged, uncomfortable with the praise and responsibility the colonel offered. "Let's discuss the details."

The two men talked for a long time. Finally the colonel rose. "Then report back to me as soon as you see any visible results.

"Aye, sir." But Sean harbored grave doubts as he hurried out the door. He was uncomfortable hiding his true identity. Half Irish, half Comanche, he was what the whites called a breed. He was proud of his ancestry. His grandfather, wise old Stone Wolf, chief of a small Comanche band. Morning Fawn, his kind and gentle mother, who had died when he was small. Little Crow, his friend. And of course Da, his Irish father, back home again in Ireland, who encouraged his half-breed son to use his unique background to seek peace, while at the same time cautioning him of the dangers inherent in trying to walk in both worlds.

The whites despised the Comanche.

The Comanche hated the whites.

And he, Sean thought in disgust, was caught in the middle.

A short time later, Sean guided his gray stallion toward his ranch, a sprawling spread southeast of Tascosa, a distance of a hundred miles or more. He rode leisurely, his eyes on the sky, the skyline, and occasionally on the shortgrass. To break the monotony, he talked to the horse.

"A long ride, Ghost. And I've a notion burning in my breast that I'd discuss with you, providing you're in a mood to listen. It's about Kate. All the women who've gone before have long since faded from my memory, leaving only the sweet Irish lass who sings like a nightingale. Kissing her was as close to heaven as a man's likely to get. I keep hearing her wee whimper. Makes me want to stroke her breasts and see passion suffuse her face." He sighed. "Stay away from a virgin, Da used to say, and if you can't stay away, marry her."

Marry her!

The thought pummeled his mind like a fist to his gut. So she was small, beautiful, and Irish. And innocent. It wasn't as though he'd pursued her. She had come to him. She had taken off her clothes, and his self-control had deserted him. No matter what Da said, he couldn't have stopped. He almost groaned. Given half a chance, he'd do it again.

Disgusted with himself, uncomfortable with his thoughts, he lifted his gaze to the horizon. Thin spirals of smoke rose along the southeast ridge. "I've a strong feeling it's trouble, Ghost.

Could be a campfire, of course. We'd better investigate."

About an hour later, he rode upon a scene of destruction. At least ten or twelve wagons lay overturned and smoking, their contents scattered about on the ground. The occupants had made a valiant effort to circle the wagons, but they hadn't been successful. Carnage was everywhere. A baby lay lifeless in the arms of a young woman he could only guess was the child's mother. A young man, not much beyond a stripling, lay face-down in the dirt, a Comanche arrow buried in his back.

Chapter Two

"Mother of God," Sean whispered, hurrying from one victim to another. Not one had been left alive. The Comanche had ambushed the wagons, killing all the people, including the babies. Often the Comanche took prisoners. There was no way to know if that had happened here.

Grotesque in death, men, women, and children were sprawled over pieces of furniture, spread-eagled over the dry prairie grass, even draped over wagon wheels. A chant to ward off evil spirits filtered through his mind, dragging cold dread with it. Now all hell would break loose again. The whites would want to kill every Indian in the country, whether they were guilty or not. And they could count on the Comanche fighting back.

Sean rummaged through the wagons until he found a pickax to loosen the hard, dry dirt. Each swing eased the nagging ache in his gut but did little to hasten the burial. He had to prepare a final resting place for the victims. His Catholic upbringing required it. Resting a moment, he studied the landscape carefully. Only sagebrush and tumbleweeds met his eye. The wind kicked up dust, swirling it about his feet. His first choice for interment was a woman lying in a pool of blood, an arrow in her chest. His nostrils flared at the smell. Rage, hot and red and stifling, shot through him. How in hell could the plan he and the colonel had put together ever work?

When he stooped to pick up the body, he heard a sound, no more than a sob quickly squelched. Somebody had suffered through the slaughter and remained alive? *God!* Unless they'd been buried up to their necks.

Cautiously he laid the body down near the shallow grave, and in one quick movement drew his gun. The snippet of noise had come from the dry creek bed on his right. Dreading what he might find, he strode to the thicket of salt cedar lining the bank.

Sean paused. With his gun at the ready, he pulled the cedar branches back. Surprise furrowed his brow. Huddled together, a black man and a small white girl stared up at him. The man rose, still holding the child's hand.

"The gun isn't necessary, mistuh. We're all that's left, the child and I, of the wagon train headed for Oregon." The man spoke in the softly articulated words of an educated Southerner. He put his arms around the girl and pulled her closer. "You could use some help to bury the dead, suh. I'd be glad to help."

Sean extended his hand. "Sean O'Brien."

"Coleridge, suh. Call me Cole. And this is Afton Shepherd. She's nine years old. The Indians murdered everybody they saw." Nodding toward the empty hole Sean had dug, he lowered his voice. "You've prepared a place for her mother."

Afton, unwilling to look at the open grave, focused on some faraway horizon. She glanced at Sean, her eyes still glazed with terror. "They killed Papa, too. Shot him with an arrow. Here." Whispering, the small girl pointed to her throat. "They killed Marian. Marian was my best friend." Her voice became high, and much as she'd recite a litany, she chanted, "Mama's dead. Mama's dead." Then she broke into tears. "My mama's dead."

Realizing the little girl bordered on hysteria, Sean knelt in front of her. He pulled her to him and stroked her thin shoul-

33

ders. "I'm sorry, child. You've witnessed a bad thing. And you and Cole were lucky to have gotten away yourselves." He comforted her until she turned from him; then he stood and threw an expectant look at Cole. "How did you escape?"

"The mastuh told me to keep an eye on Miss Afton. See that she was safe." Tears glistened in his dark eyes. "I would have done it anyway. When the noise started, he yelled for me to hide her. I grabbed Afton and ran to the ditch. We hunkered down." He motioned with his arm. "And I pulled the shrubbery around us."

Sean didn't try to hide his admiration for the black man's resourcefulness. "That took courage, Cole. You saved two lives, yours and the girl's. After you've learned to live with the grief, you and Afton will get along fine." He didn't really believe that, but he had to give them some hope. What could he say to the child that she would understand? "A bad thing happened here, Afton. You'll need to keep on being strong."

Afton's face twisted in agony. "Mama and Papa . . . the Indians killed them. I only have Cole now."

With effort, Cole spoke sadly. "Afton and I are obliged for your kindness, suh."

"Wish I could be of more help." Sean motioned toward the smoking debris, scattered personal possessions, dead bodies. God, he had to get away from this pain, if but for a few minutes. "I'll check the area. Somebody may still be alive." Sean walked from wagon to wagon, fighting the horror that filled his breast, eventually finding his way back to where Cole stood with the girl. "Well, Cole, it won't be easy for you, but we need to get to the business of burying the dead."

The two men worked together, changing from pickax to shovel and back again. Grunting and straining to break hard ground, they finally placed the last of the corpses in a common grave. The girl stood nearby, never venturing far from Cole. Sean smiled at her. Her stony gaze met his briefly before she turned away.

"Cole, we've a problem." Using his sleeve, Sean wiped sweat from his face. "I'm on my way to the Shamrock Ranch, a good seventy, eighty miles. What about you and the child? Where will you go?"

"We've no place to go. When the war ended, Mastuh Shepherd had nothing left. The plantation had been burned to the ground. The slaves had run away or been turned away. There was no food to feed them. Several white families and a few black folks headed west to the Oregon territory." He looked at the smoking wagons and his voice fractured. "Then the Indians came."

"Might be we could say a prayer, Cole," Sean said, not wanting to prolong the man's agony.

"Of course, suh." When Sean nodded for him to go ahead, Cole pulled Afton to him and bowed his head. "Oh, Lord, we . . . we . . ." His shoulders shook as he groped for words. "Mistuh O'Brien, suh, would you . . . ?"

"Yeah, Cole, I'll try." He leaned on his shovel. "These are bad times, God. Give comfort where it's needed. And spare us more spilled blood." Somehow he got through it and said amen.

"Amen and thank you, suh."

Sean nodded, then asked the question uppermost in his mind: "What now, Cole?" His heart wasn't hard enough to point out the dangers inherent in their present course to the Oregon territory.

He tried to smile, but the ugly truth was that Negroes, Irishmen, and Indians, including half-breeds—especially half-breeds; look at Quanah Parker—were about as welcome as smallpox at a tribal powwow. Sooner or later Cole would have to make a decision—turn Afton over to authorities in some town, or hide her away from prying eyes. The latter would be impossible, and Sean felt a stab of sympathy.

"I keep going over it in my mind, Mr. O'Brien, thinking I'll come up with an answer. Or a direction. Nothing so far."

Things were tough everywhere, Sean knew. Lord, he had enough to worry about: peace between the Indians and whites, his ranch, trying to live up to his promise to his father.

And Kate. The biggest worry of all. She was no longer inexperienced, but close. Still so innocent. And he'd left her in the clutches of a violent and evil man. As many times as he reviewed his options, he had yet to find one that was satisfactory. He had stolen Kate's virtue and repaid her with a lousy hundred dollars and desertion. He knew he would go back to help her—even if his conscience hadn't demanded it, he would have been unable to resist his longing to see her again, to hold her once more.

And now it looked as though he would add Cole and Afton to his list of worries and responsibilities. He couldn't leave them here. Cole would be lynched if he were found alone with a white child.

The black man hesitated. "Mr. O'Brien, perhaps we could walk along with you. Until we reach a town?"

"And then what? Afton would not be allowed to remain with you. The townsfolk would be outraged."

Startled, the girl looked quickly at Cole. "But you have to stay with me, Cole. You're all I have now. Slaves have to stay with their owners."

"But I'm no longer a slave, Miss Afton. Mr. Lincoln freed us."

Afton tugged at one of her blond braids. "Pooh. How can he free you? You don't belong to Mr. Lincoln. Mama said so. She said old Abe was a meddler."

"Perhaps so, but I'm no longer a slave."

Afton stamped her foot. "You can't leave me." A worried look followed swiftly. "You won't, will you, Cole?"

"I don't know, Miss Afton. We'll have to think of something."

Sean made a hasty decision. "We'll head toward the Shamrock. Maybe one of us will have an inspiration." He strode over to where his horse was waiting and picked up the reins. "We'll be taking turns riding with the girl on the Gray Ghost."

"I can walk, Mr. O'Brien, and when she gets tired, I can carry Miss Afton."

"Perhaps," Sean said mildly, "but we'll both be walking and riding, lad. I'll mention it to the Ghost. Ordinarily, he's a bit uppity with strangers."

For the first time, Cole smiled his relief, his teeth flashing white against his dark skin. "I'll give him proper respect, suh. I surely will."

At first the child rode alone, Cole beside her, one hand steadying her. At Sean's insistence, he finally mounted behind her. "I'm not comfortable, suh, seeing you walk."

"We'll change places in a while." Sean carefully avoided the yucca, cacti, and tumbleweeds. Just as studiously he tried to avoid thoughts of the future. What would happen to Afton and Cole? What would he do to help them? His dismay increased as the day progressed. More responsibility. More pain and suffering. More frustration.

To distract himself, Sean questioned the black man about his past. "You don't speak like a slave, Cole. Former slave," he amended.

"Mastuh Shepherd brought me into the big house early. I was taught the ways of the white folks."

"Who taught you to speak like them?"

"The mastuh taught me." Cole smiled. "And I learned well."

Sean stopped in the shade of a tree near a stream. "Did he teach you to read?"

"Yes."

"I thought teaching blacks was illegal in the South."

"It was."

"Then why did he . . . ?" Sean glanced at the black man. "Wasn't it odd that he'd teach you?"

"The mastuh was different."

Sean realized he'd have to work at getting Cole to talk, if he were to learn anything about them. "And Afton? Can she read and write?"

"Yes." Cole spoke quietly, not loud enough for Afton to hear. "Mastuh and I taught Miss Afton. He recommended I do it on the sly."

"Why?"

Obviously uncomfortable, Cole didn't respond for a moment. "Her mother didn't want me to teach her. I . . . she didn't like me."

"Why not?"

"She said I was a smart-alecky nigger."

Sean grinned. "Are you?"

Nodding, Cole laughed. "I expect I'm a bit smart-alecky, suh."

"My home here in Texas is the Shamrock. A nice little spread—around a hundred thousand acres. I inherited it from my father. Our ancestral home is near Galway Bay. My father lives there now."

"In Ireland. I've read about it."

Sean chuckled at this information. Coleridge was a bundle of surprises. "O'Briens are from County Mayo. And a prolific bunch we are. I've cousins, aunts, and uncles in most every part of the world. As the first son in my family, I inherited the Shamrock." He laughed again. "I also inherited all the lads who care for the cattle. Cowboys, they call themselves."

"Who runs the ranch when you aren't there?"

"I've a foreman, a crusty fellow and a bit of a hothead, but he knows the business of ranching in this country."

"How many . . ." Cole paused. "How many of these cowboys do you have there?"

"What with cowhands moving on to greener pastures, the newcomers with their families, and Mexicans coming up from the south, the numbers change often."

"I've been thinking . . . Could you use another pair of hands? I've no knowledge of ranching, but I know farming. Besides, I can learn. I'd work hard. That way Miss Afton would have a home." He spoke earnestly. "Otherwise, I don't know what will happen to her."

"We'll see. In the meantime, let's feed the wee lass. I've jerky enough for her. You and I . . . we'll have to wait."

"Thank you, suh. I hope she'll eat something."

Sean glanced at the child slumped in the saddle, her head lowered. "She's not going to have an easy time of it."

"I know. The hurt goes deep."

Sean doubted they could find a family who would take the girl in and make her a family member. More likely she'd become a servant, close to a bondservant, much like a slave.

An impossible situation, Sean thought, at the same time glad it had been he who had found them instead of others he could name. The black man's life would have ended. And the girl? He shuddered at what would have been her fate if the Indians had found her.

Worse still if it had been the Comancheros.

With no urging, thoughts of Kate returned again and again to plague him. As they made slow progress toward the Shamrock, he found himself reliving his night with her, enjoying her smile, her sigh, her touch. He berated himself for taking a virgin to bed, but knew that, given the same circumstances, he'd do it again. With even more certainty he knew Boggs would pursue her, first with promises, then with bribes. If neither of those snares succeeded, he'd use force. Sean's frown deepened. Why had she taken such desperate measures for a hundred dollars? Why did he keep remembering her blue-black hair? Her mouth? Her naked body?

Her innocence?

The thought of Boggs running his hands over her, kissing her, drove him crazy.

Luck of the Irish! Bloody hell!

"Kate, you're pretty as a picture." Nathan Boggs smiled indulgently. "Sing good, too, honey. Real good." His gaze played lazily over her breasts. "We haven't had anybody as pretty as you at the Lily in a long time. You're going to be glad you're a part of our little operation."

"Thank you, Mr. Boggs." Afraid he could read her thoughts, she turned her face away. His oily features and lascivious smile nauseated her. "You've been kind."

"I could be a lot kinder, Kate." He poured wine from a crystal decanter into a delicate stemmed glass and offered it to her. "A whole lot kinder."

Kate shook her head. "Not when I'm going to sing, Mr. Boggs." She glanced around uneasily. How could she leave without creating a scene? And if she made it this time, what about the next?

She looked past him at the paintings on the wall. Boggs had spared no expense in furnishing his office. The desk, a ponderous rolltop, was large and elaborately carved. A leather couch rested comfortably against one wall. Two matching overstuffed chairs, conveniently separated by an ornate mahogany table, were slightly worn.

A mesquite log blazed in the stone fireplace. The room, suffocatingly close, smelled of cigar smoke, burning firewood—and incense, of all things.

The effect was overpowering and much too cozy.

"I couldn't possibly ask for more consideration than you've already shown." He had come uncomfortably near. "Now if you'll excuse me, I'll get back to work."

Nathan ran an exploratory finger along her cheek. "Sure, Kate. We can talk later."

Butterflies danced in her stomach. Kate backed away, pivoted, and hurried through the door. Once in the saloon, she sighed in relief, squared her shoulders, and walked sedately to the piano. She was still in control. But how long would it be before Nathan Boggs made it impossible to remain at the Gilded Lily?

"I'm sorry to be late, Joe. Mr. Boggs wanted to talk to me."

"I'll bet. Soon he'll want more than talk. You ain't the first one to be invited into his office. Won't be the last." Joe struck a discordant note on the piano. "You ain't out of the woods, my girl. He'll catch you one of these days. Won't be nothing you can do. Oh, you'll yell, all right, but nobody will hear you. They'll all be too busy."

Kate shuddered. Joe made it sound so ominous. The Irishman had also warned her of Nathan's intentions, and his predictions were coming closer and closer to fulfillment. "I'll try to protect myself."

"Oh, you won't get by with that. Nathan's not always gentle. In the beginning, maybe." He glanced at Boggs's office door. "The man ain't likely to make an exception in your case."

Maureen just had to be on the next stage.

She tried to hide how scared she was. "Joe, let's rehearse the new song." She hummed a little of the tune. "Pretty melody."

An hour and a half later, Kate stood outside the door of the saloon marking time until the stagecoach arrived. Once it rounded the corner, she didn't wait for the creaking vehicle to come to a stop, but ran along side it trying to see inside. "My sister didn't come?"

The driver looked at her from the top of the coach. "Nobody come except two gentlemen."

Disappointment clouded her eyes. "Did you bring any mail?"

"Yup."

She waited, her nerves on edge. "I'm expecting a letter."

Reaching in a pouch, he drew out an envelope. He looked at it closely. "A woman's handwriting." He jumped to the ground. "Postmarked Missouri. Know anybody in Missouri?"

Kate all but snatched the letter from his hand. "Yes. Yes, I do." She whirled and swept her skirts aside to hurry across the street.

A quick glance assured her the letter was from Maureen. Questions flooded her mind. How much longer would she have to wait? Had Maureen changed her mind? Kate shook her head to dispel the negative thoughts. She had paid dearly to protect Maureen, sold herself to the Irishman, and would forever be a whore in his eyes. Raw pain sliced through her. With effort, she forced her thoughts back to her sister.

Maureen would have to slip away when Mama and Milton weren't watching. She was such a namby-pamby. If they caught her, Maureen would give in and do whatever they told her. Always fearful when harsh words were spoken, she'd never learned to handle confrontation. But, Kate thought wryly, she couldn't say that for herself. She'd always been too quick to speak.

Seized with the need to be alone when she opened it, Kate stuck the letter in her reticule and quickened her pace toward the town stable.

The liveryman smiled at her. "Howdy, Miss Kate. Ol' Barney's waitin' for you. I think he enjoys these rides as much as you do."

"I love Barney, Mr. Sanders. I look forward to the rides like a thirsty person craves water."

"I can tell." He nodded while helping her upon the sidesaddle and then handing her the reins. "Hell of a way to ride a horse, if'n you don't mind my sayin' so. Indian women got the right idea."

Disdain curled her lips into a mirthless smile. "Right, Mr. Sanders," she said, her words mild considering the way she felt about Indians. "Maybe one day I'll buy myself some men's pants to wear."

He chuckled. "Or a squaw's buckskin dress."

A squaw's dress . . . never. She bit her lip to keep from saying something she would regret and nodded good-bye to Mr. Sanders.

Kate rode out of town and headed south a few miles before turning to follow a clear stream to a grove of cottonwoods. On either side of the creek, salt cedar vied with willow and undergrowth for a spot near the water. It was a wonderful place to be alone. A place to think and to plan for Maureen. To get away from the festering problem with Nathan Boggs.

She dismounted and settled herself in her favorite spot, a grassy area beneath a great cottonwood. Anticipation made her heart beat a little faster, and she held the letter to her breast. As soon as Maureen got to Tascosa, they would leave, maybe go to San Francisco. For a moment the Irishman's face swam across the surface of her mind. It wasn't likely she'd ever see him again. Her spirits took a nosedive.

But she and Maureen had to get away. Boggs had begun his campaign in earnest. Each time he touched her she broke out in chill bumps. And once he laid eyes on Maury, saw her innocence and angelic face, no doubt he would go after her as well.

Kate shuddered. Afraid of Boggs herself, she would be twice as scared for her sister. Anytime Boggs looked in Joe's direction, Joe's face blanched with fear. The saloon girls walked on tiptoe when Boggs sauntered through the door. Only the Irishman hadn't been intimidated by him. For some reason that didn't surprise her. He laughed easily, made love tenderly, and, like Papa, was strong.

His touch had been arousing. He had pressed her against him, and even though his gray eyes smoldered, he had taken the time to be gentle. His kisses had incited longings she'd never felt before. His hands had explored her body tenderly, making her ache for his caresses.

He'd known their coming together had hurt. He'd rocked

her in his arms and told her he was sorry, called her a sweet lass. He probably tells that to all the girls he makes love with, she thought sourly. His face appeared frequently in her mind, and at the most inappropriate times. *I'll not forget;* he'd said. Neither would she.

Maureen's note was short and to the point. It had no date.

Dear Sister,
Thank you for the money. Verlin Digby and I are getting married in a few weeks. Mama says the wedding will be real nice, and the hundred dollars will come in handy. I'll wear a white dress. Mrs. Pratt will play the organ. I wish you could be here.

Verlin is a big contributor to the church, and Milton likes him.

I hope everything is fine for you. I'm glad you like your job. Thanks again for the money.

Your loving sister,
Maury

Kate stared at the words. So Milton liked Verlin. No surprise there, since Verlin was a consistent contributor to the church collections. After several minutes the truth sank in: Mama had guided the pen as surely as if she'd held it in her hand. Kate began to laugh. She laughed and laughed until her howling gave way to deep, heart-wrenching sobs.

A virgin, her sister could wear white at her wedding. What color, Kate thought mutinously, could she wear appropriately, honestly?

Scarlet, of course.

Control returned slowly, and Kate brushed at the tears on her cheeks. Her emotions spent, she sank back into the grass, pillowing her head in her arms. She remembered how vulnerable Maury had always been, her eyes enormous, her fear equally large.

They'd felt so alone when Papa died. Increasingly protective of Maury, Kate had tried to shield her little sister from Mama's strident tongue and quick backhand. For Maury, Kate defied

43

Mama, dodged the ever-ready open palm, and later challenged Milton.

Maury depended on her, Kate thought wearily, and even though she had promised her sister she would send for her, Mama and Milton had bullied Maury into marrying Verlin before Kate could keep her word.

Kate closed her eyes against the awful truth. She had offered all she had to fate in an effort to protect her sister. She had failed. Only one person knew the price she'd paid, but that person loomed larger in her mind than anyone else, including her sister. The Irishman. Anger stirred in her. No doubt he'd already forgotten her name.

As a boy, Sean had looked on the ranch with mixed feelings. He had had some of the most fun and rewarding experiences of his life learning to ranch. He had also never worked harder. Da had never spared him; he'd wanted his son to learn everything about ranching. His father, Irish to his blue-blooded toenails, knew little about ranching, but loved how different it was from farming in Ireland. As a young man he had come to the States to learn more about life in the wild west.

Da had acquired the ranch and with advice from Malachi stocked it with whiteface cattle. He'd fallen in love, married an Indian maiden and a year later sired a son. He'd stayed in America for ten years until tragedy struck, and he had taken his son and fled back to his homeland, leaving Malachi Malone to run the big spread. The bandy-legged cowman had not failed him.

Once he had recovered somewhat from the death of his young wife, Da had returned to his Texas ranch many times, staying three months, six months, once as long as a year, always bringing Sean with him. Not only had they lived at the Shamrock, but they had also traveled with his mother's tribe. His father had wanted his son to know about all of his heritage. He'd never failed to remind Sean, "Stone Wolf is your grandfather, your mother's father. Respect him."

Stone Wolf had taught Sean the way of the Indian, to use a bow and arrow, to hunt, to become a Comanche brave, and

Sean had learned to revere the old man and his wisdom—and to love him.

Who was more to blame for the bloodshed, the Comanche or the whites—atrocities by the Indians or brutality by the whites? His father had watched the clash of the two peoples with such anxiety that Sean, wanting to please him, had decided as a young boy that someday he would return to the Shamrock and make a permanent home there. And Sean had done just that. He had no regrets, only brief and isolated moments of homesickness for Ireland, especially when he saw the carnage left from battles between whites and Indians.

He had always loved the Shamrock and the more nomadic lifestyle of his mother's people equally. And recently he had decided it was time he tried to act as an instrument for peace between his mother's people and the whites. He knew Da had harbored such hopes long before his son had arrived at that decision.

His mother's death would have been incentive enough.

He'd been ten years old when his father had carried his mother's bruised and lifeless body into the house and placed it on the bed. He remembered his mother's lovely face, the strangulation marks around her throat, her torn clothing, how he'd been overcome by despair and bewilderment. His father had attempted to comfort him, but only time could really start the eventual healing process.

Now at his father's advanced age, Sean knew Da would never set foot on the ranch again. As in all things relating to the ranch, he relied on his foreman to steer his son in the right direction. And Sean listened with growing respect. Malachi knew the ranching business, shortgrass country and the white-face cattle that grazed its prairies.

"What do you think, Malachi? Will the market hold?"

"Cain't say, Sean. Everything's up in the air now that the war's over."

Sean nodded his understanding. " 'Twas an unpleasant period for the States. Still is, I suppose."

"Ireland, too, I imagine, considerin' the potato blight. Your pa didn't seem to be affected much."

"We were better off than most, but everybody suffered."

Since they were speaking of suffering, now would be a good time to discuss the new arrivals at the Shamrock. Sean was fairly sure Malachi didn't approve of them. The foreman also appeared unconcerned that Coleridge and Afton had no place to go and no money to support themselves, that their very difference in color could spell disaster.

"About Cole and Afton, Mal. What's your opinion?"

Malachi glared at him. "My opinion don't mean sicc 'em where them two are concerned. I'm sure as hell they'll be stayin'."

"Cole earns their keep. Besides, where would they go?"

"Let 'im figure that out for hisself. He's got Abe Lincoln to thank for his predicament."

"And the child?"

"Prob'ly she ort to be in a orphanage. If'n you keep 'im around, I'd watch 'im, Sean. Steal you blind, right down to the horns off the cattle."

Sean winced at Malachi's description. Working to make himself indispensible, Coleridge conducted himself as a gentleman, a fact doubtless noted by his foreman and thereby deemed a threat. "I'm not for letting them starve, Malachi. We'll find a permanent place for them at the Shamrock. He'll earn his pay."

"That girl—she's spoiled, Sean. Worst I ever seen."

"Aye, spoiled, all right, but I'm thinking she might grow out of it," Sean said mildly. "She's only nine years old. She still has maturing time and needs grieving time."

The foreman sniffed. "What she needs is fer somebody to take a hick'ry switch to her backside. And that black man shore ain't goin' to."

At that moment Coleridge came out the door, carrying a pan of ashes he'd taken from an upstairs fireplace. He nodded respectfully. "Morning, suh." Lowering his head, he spoke softly to Afton, who had followed him.

"Hello." Afton's lips formed a straight line.

"Have you had breakfast, Cole?"

"Yes, suh."

46

"If that's what you call it." Afton sniffed. "I've had better. Whoever heard of beefsteak and eggs for breakfast?"

Again Coleridge said a few words, then looked up and smiled. "A fine breakfast, and we're grateful."

They walked some distance before Coleridge emptied the pan. Their words weren't distinguishable, but Afton's imperious stance gave a clue to her feelings.

"See what I mean, Sean? It just ain't natural fer a girl to git by with that kinda talk. And there she is follering that nigger around."

"Nigger is an ugly word."

"But that's what he—"

"No."

Malachi thrust out his chest and took a deep breath. "It's your ranch and you can do what you want, but I'm tellin' you—"

"Then it's settled."

Muttering, Malachi stalked toward the barn, head down, shoulders hunched. Along the way he kicked at a rock, missed, and tried again. He was still mouthing as he closed the door behind him.

Well, he'd handled that little problem with the skill of a schoolboy, Sean thought resignedly. Fortunately, Malachi wouldn't carry a grudge, at least against him. The bantam-size foreman was usually fair in his assessment of a man, but having been reared in the South, he looked upon Negroes as property—as if one man should ever own another. As if color had a bloody lot to do with character. That included Indians.

Truth was, Afton needed a mother.

And Coleridge? The man remained a mystery.

Sean pondered the circumstances of Coleridge's relationship to the child. The black man was patient with her but not subservient. That he cared deeply for her was an understatement. His sepia-colored face softened each time he looked at her.

By the time the evening meal was served, Sean had almost forgotten the morning's incident. He sat at the head of the table and eyed the food—mounds of it: potatoes grown at the Shamrock, beef off the range, gravy to feed the county.

"Good evening, lass." Sean smiled at Afton. "And what kind of a day did you have?"

Afton glanced at Coleridge, who had remained standing. "Good enough, I guess."

"Aren't you eating with us, Cole?" Sean addressed the black man with a smile of invitation.

"Oh, no, suh. I'll help with the table."

"Cole never eats with us," Afton said disdainfully. "He's not supposed to. Negroes eat in the kitchen."

"We have different rules here, Afton. Cole is not a slave. What's more, his color is of no importance. He will sit down and eat at our table."

"Oh." Afton threw down her napkin and scrambled out of her chair. "Cole, have Juanita bring a tray to my room."

Sean spoke softly. "You're excused, Afton, but there'll be no food brought to your room. Sit down, Cole."

"But suh . . ." He glanced at Afton. "I don't mind—"

"Sit down, Cole. I make the rules here. Run along, Afton."

"But I'm hungry."

"You should have thought of that."

Her eyes filled with tears. "But . . . Cole always waited table. And I'm really hungry."

"Doesn't Cole get hungry?"

Afton looked startled. "I suppose . . ."

"You're willing, then, to have Cole sit down with us?"

She nodded, her gaze fixed on the floor. "I guess so."

"Good. He can sit beside you."

Not to be totally outdone, Afton looked at the black man. "All right, Cole. But watch your manners. Mama was dead-set against anything or anybody interrupting a meal."

"Of course, Miss Afton. I'll be careful."

"Good."

Later, Sean was never sure who had won. In the end, he decided it had been a draw, Afton having had the last word. The young girl was as passionate against Negroes as Kate was against Indians—the child heartlessly taught, Kate driven by hate. He wondered again from where Kate's strong feelings stemmed. He suspected some tragic incident in her past was responsible for her present views.

How would the Lily's songbird feel if she discovered she'd spent the night in the arms of a half-breed?

Kate adjusted the neck of her dress. Why had they cut it so low over her bosom? And short! The garment barely covered her knees. She was almost certain the men sitting closest to the stage could see up her dress.

Tonight the whole Gilded Lily, men and music alike, made her nauseous. Her dark mood hadn't lifted since she'd read Maureen's letter. How could her sister let herself be maneuvered into marrying Verlin Digby? Of course, Mama would be overseeing the wedding with Milton at her shoulder to approve each decision.

The hundred dollars would provide Mama with a fine dress and Milton with a new coat to impress his parishioners, and Maureen could kneel at the altar in a white dress and veil.

Mama would be overjoyed at her own elevation in society as the mother of Mrs. Verlin Digby, the wife of one of the town's leading citizens.

As for her other daughter, Minnie Scruggs showed a surprising lack of interest. She sent no word of love, nor that she missed her older daughter, no concern for her well-being, nothing about the money. Maybe she was afraid to ask how Kate got the money.

Unknowingly, Mama was wise.

Kate glanced at the saloon entrance. Framed in the doorway, his hands on the swinging doors, was the man who'd made Mama's dreams come true. He smiled and waved, then walked toward the bar. He wore the same gray sock-cap, the same scuffed boots. But this time he wore a deerskin jacket that couldn't hide the gun sagging against one hip.

Ire bubbled in her veins. He might well have come over to speak to her before heading for the bar. Or have given some indication his wave was for her. He could have been saluting Joe, for God's sake.

She chose a rousing, raucous song always popular with the

49

men and sang lustily. When it was over, the men clapped loudly and long, stamping their feet and whistling. She didn't look in the direction of the bar, but she knew when the Irishman came nearer.

"Hi, Katie. And how is the Lily's pretty songbird?"

"Fine," she said coolly, nodding to Joe to begin a new song. When she finished, the Irishman was still there, clapping his hands and whistling like the rest of the men.

"Lovely, lass." He smiled at her. "And might you be having a drink with me?"

"I don't drink alcohol, sir."

"Then sit a moment with me."

In spite of herself, Kate found herself walking with him toward a table in the back of the room, one that gave them a bit of privacy. He drew out a chair and seated her.

"Everything well with you, Katie?"

"Well enough."

He covered her hand, holding it more tightly when she would have moved it away. After caressing her fingers, he lifted her palm and kissed it. "Boggs giving you problems?"

"A few." She glanced in the direction of the office door, unable to hide her apprehension.

"He hasn't made any demands. Yet."

"Will you tell me when he does?"

She frowned. "What does it matter to you? You don't owe me anything. I knew what I was doing that night."

"But I didn't, you see. And that makes all the difference." He looked at the ornament in her hair. "Do you need anything? Money?"

"No." Self-consciously, she put her hand up to touch the gaudy yellow flower. "I suppose this thing's kinda—"

"Ridiculous," he supplied, smiling at her. "I like your hair without it—all shiny black and wavy. Which parent provided you with that inheritance?"

"My mother has red hair. So does my sister."

"I'd be thinking you got your mother's disposition." His gray eyes met hers. "Right?"

"You're asking for my history again."

He gave a negative shake of his head. "Just trying to understand you better, lass."

"Why?"

"We shared a special night."

"So?"

"We're no longer strangers. Our lives have touched." He stroked her cheek. "We'll never be quite the same again."

Heat suffused her face. "You're saying I'll always be a—"

He covered her mouth with his hand, gently blocking the ugly word on the tip of her tongue. "No, lass, we both know better than that."

Tears threatened, and she ducked her head to hide them. "What's done is done."

"Aye." Smiling encouragement, he spoke softly. "Want to talk about it? Why you needed the money? Your plans?"

She shook her head. "I don't want to talk about anything—money, plans, the saloon. Nothing."

"Go home, lass."

Her anger was instant, suffusing her face with crimson. "Mind your own business, Irish. I'll never go home."

He kept his voice mild. "And Boggs?"

"I can handle the situation."

He doubted she could handle Boggs. "I had business north of here. Now I'm on my way back to my ranch, the Shamrock."

"How far is that?"

"From Tascosa?" He thought a moment. "Roughly a hundred twenty-five miles."

"Why stop in Tascosa at all?"

He tucked a tendril back from her face, his knuckle skimming her cheek. "I came to see you."

"Why?"

"You're important to me."

Irish blarney, she thought, and refused to respond to his charm. "Right now I've got to go. Joe's back at the piano."

"Would you be singing an Irish song, Katie? And might you be singing it just for me?"

Her voice neutral, her face hiding her feelings, she nodded. "I might."

"And a bit later might you be wanting some air?"

She shrugged and stood, looking around for Boggs, then toward his door. "I've been known to."

Sean relaxed. "I'll be outside."

"In about an hour I'll be headed to the hotel."

"For sure, I'll be headed that way myself about that same time."

An hour and a half passed before she appeared at the bat-wing doors. He waited until she'd gone to the end of the boardwalk and would be taking to the open street, before stepping up beside her. The moon scooted from behind a cloud and flooded the street with light, then just as quickly hid again. Sean took her arm and drew her into the shadows.

"Katie, you've been on my mind."

Just words, she told herself, and answered in what she hoped showed the right amount of disinterest. "You've been on mine a few times. At the moment, I can't remember why."

He winced, but managed a chuckle. "You wound me, Katie." He stroked her cheek, then drew his fingers along her throat. "You're beautiful."

She leaned away from him and inhaled deeply. When he used that tone of voice, it made her insides go crazy. "Did your business go well up north?"

"So-so, I guess." Sean stepped closer. He let his hands slide down to her waist, then back up under her breasts. His fingers itched to caress their fullness. He lowered his voice. "Katie, I've been thinking. We get along well"—he smiled—"even if I am a dimwit at times." He hoped she'd understand that he was talking about their night together, and his ignorance in not recognizing her innocence. "We were lovers. Why don't we get married?"

Hurt, joy, pride, bravado, anger, pain—each emotion flicked over her beautiful face.

"I don't even know your name, and you're proposing marriage."

"Sean O'Brien, at your service, lass."

She spoke as if she hadn't heard him. "You think I'm a fallen woman. One time in your bed and I'm a whore, and you think you're the cause of it. And your conscience hurts." Her voice was tinged with sadness. "Someday, I'll meet a man who will love me, and I will love him. I'll tell him about my night with you. He won't think I'm a fallen woman. Nor will he think he'll be doing the manly thing by keeping me out of a whorehouse. He'll know I'd never let that happen. Good night, Irish."

Chapter Three

Kate wanted to hold her nose. Would she ever get used to the stale smells of the saloon? The odor of unwashed bodies and the sickening smell of whiskey were always there. The gambling tables were full. Smoke shrouded the room. The Lily's lack of charm grated on her nerves worse than usual because her eyes burned from lack of sleep.

The night before, she'd curled up on the bed, too miserable to get under the covers. Sean O'Brien had offered marriage—as though he was paying off a debt. As though his lily-white conscience just couldn't bear to have one taint, one irrepressible sin, such as deflowering a virgin, staining his Irish soul or the sheets.

Why couldn't he have said he found her attractive and couldn't help himself? That bedding her was the supreme moment of his life? Perhaps he would have lied a little bit—said maybe he was falling in love with her.

Sighing, Kate rubbed her temples. No time to cry over lost virtue. She was the one who'd gone to Sean O'Brien, and he'd paid what she had asked.

He'd been disturbed that he'd taken her innocence, believing she'd tricked him by coming to his bed. The only one she'd tricked had been herself. She remembered too well the hunger in his eyes, the taste of whiskey on his tongue, and how his big body felt against hers. His beguiling Irish brogue still lingered in her ears. She hadn't counted on the magic of his hands on her body, or the thrill of his mouth on hers. She hadn't known such feelings existed between a man and a woman.

She sighed and tossed back a wayward curl. Always there was the hundred dollars to consider, making all the difference.

If she'd used one ounce of common sense, Kate told herself repeatedly, she'd have known Maureen would never see the letter first. Not with Mama around. As for the money, once Milton got his hands on a hundred dollars, with a little sleight of hand, he'd have it in his pocket. Regardless of its origin, regardless of its true intent, Milton would twist the facts to fit his needs and keep every cent.

The sound of Joe's playing reminded her it was time to sing, but before she could rise from the chair, Boggs called her name. The piano music stopped abruptly. Boggs stood in the doorway of his office, his face wreathed in smiles, his eyes almost hidden beneath bushy brows. How could he see with all that excess skin over his eyelids? Kate managed to contain an involuntary shudder as she recognized Nathan Boggs for what he was: a repulsive man bent on a conquest.

She had news for him: neither he nor anyone else would have access to her bed—ever—unless she wanted him there. It would be her decision.

His silky summons was soft and oily. "A word with you, Kate, girl."

Joe's voice was low, meant for her ears only. "Be careful Kate. He's not a man you want to be alone with for long. I'm sorry I can't interfere, but if I go chargin' in where my nose don't belong, I'll be unemployed and lookin' for a place to hide."

"Don't risk your job. If he's planning to entice me to his bed, he'll have to rethink his strategy."

"If you ain't out in a few minutes," Joe whispered, "I'll find a reason to rap on the door. Not that I'm coming in, understand."

"No. I'll handle Boggs myself." She tilted her chin upward and walked primly toward her employer, her greeting courteous, if a little stiff. "How are you, Mr. Boggs?"

"Come in, girl. We have a few things to discuss." He ushered her inside and closed the door. "Why don't we have a glass of wine? I know you don't drink when you sing." He poured two stemmed glasses to the brim. "But tonight you don't have to sing. You deserve some free time."

"But I like to sing."

"I know. And it shows. But tonight we'll relax in front of the fire. Get to know each other." He led her to the sofa. "Sit down and take the weight off your beautiful legs. And here's your wine, sweet Kate."

Sweet Kate indeed! Nathan Boggs was as smooth as a snake-oil peddler. "Joe's waiting for me. We've had requests for a couple of songs and need to practice before the house fills with customers."

Boggs's gaze slid over her bare shoulders. He ran a stubby finger along the smooth skin of her throat. "The piano player works for me, Kate. Remember, I decide who does what at the Lily."

"Of course, Mr. Boggs."

Confident of victory and all smiles, he motioned her to sit, then plopped his heavy body down beside her. "Kate's a nickname. Right?"

"My name is Kathleen."

"Folks live around here?"

It was like staring a cobra in the face, she thought, and despite the break in her breathing she managed to smile. "Missouri. Not far from Independence."

He drummed his fingers on the arm of the sofa. "You and the Irishman . . . anything between you?"

"I'm not sure what you're asking, Mr. Boggs. He's your customer." Could Boggs possibly know about the night she had spent with Sean? "Once when Joe took a break, the Irishman played the piano while I sang."

"And that's all?"

She'd been singing in the saloon long enough to recognize that lascivious glitter. "That's all."

Boggs leaned toward her, his arm settling possessively about her shoulders. "I wouldn't want the Irishman to have special privileges."

"I don't understand what you're saying, Mr. Boggs."

When she started to rise, he stopped her. "We'll let it go for the time being. You're mighty pretty, Kate. I've looked all my life for a girl like you. Now I've found one right here in my own place of bidness." He chuckled. "Hard to believe." He tried to pull her toward him.

Kate brushed his arm away and stood. Arching an eyebrow, she let amusement curl her lip. "Really, Mr. Boggs . . ."

"Sit down, Kate. Every girl likes attention, and I can give you a lot more than that." He pulled a long, slender box from his pocket and opened it. "This necklace reminds me of you."

She sat on the edge of the couch, clinging to the hope that her true feelings didn't show. Thoroughly frightened, she was nevertheless determined not to let him know how uncomfortable she was. She glanced at the gaudy bauble. Even with her limited knowledge, she knew the stone was a fake. "It's beautiful, Mr. Boggs, but—"

"Then it's yours. And call me Nathan." He loosened the clasp. "Turn your head a little. Toward me, honey."

"Mr. Boggs, I can't accept the necklace." To ease her blunt refusal, she smiled. "It's far too expensive. Now I really need to get to work."

His voice was cold. "Kate, we've got more to talk about."

She headed toward the door. "I'm paid to sing, Mr. Boggs. That's all."

"Look, little canary. Maybe you've forgotten, but I'm an important man in this town." Beside her now, he tapped his chest. "I pay your wage." He pinned her with one arm and grasped her breast with his hand. "A kiss, Kate."

Kate didn't move, nor did her gaze waver. "Mr. Boggs, I'm not interested in romance with you or with anybody else. And

57

I don't accept expensive gifts from a man." She pushed his hand off her breast. "Any man."

Boggs's face turned ugly. "Innocent as a baby, ain't you? Nobody ain't never touched you. Never even been kissed. You ain't foolin' me."

"I've never tried to fool you, Mr. Boggs."

"You're a teaser, and I'll tell you straight off, teasing don't go over with me. Never did." Anger bloated his face. He forced her back toward the couch, his breathing heavy. "All you have to do is cooperate a little, and this argument never happened."

"Let me go." Filled with outrage, she pushed against him and raised her voice. "Let me go."

"Keep your voice down, girl. Remember, I can make it difficult for you. And damn near impossible for you to get a job." He tore at her clothes, managing to hike her dress past her thighs. He slipped his knee between her legs and tugged at the fly of his pants. Lust heated his face and turned it purple. "I take what I want, Kate."

Anger, like a snake, coiled in her breast. It struck with a force she didn't know she possessed. She slammed her knee into his crotch, heard his high squeal, and watched dispassionately as he grabbed himself and doubled over. She gave him an icy stare. "Don't go to the trouble of firing me, Mr. Boggs. I quit."

He coughed, and forced strangled words from his white face. "I'll get you, canary. I'll make you sorry you were ever born. No place you can hide. No place in hell that I won't find you."

In a matter of seconds Kate had straightened her clothes, patted her hair into place, and marched through the door. Working to control her breathing, she gave Joe a conspiratorial wink. "I'm leaving, Joe."

"What about Boggs? Is he mad?"

Kate nodded. "Mad as hell."

He smiled at the profanity. "But you survived."

"I convinced him to let me alone. With my knee."

Joe directed a long, straight look at her, his bony face serious. "It's not over, you know. He's not one to give up. All the others—the ones before you—they either gave in or gave up. Most of them gave in. They had no place to go. Sooner or later, bad things happened to 'em." Whispering, he kept his head down, his eyes glued to the keys. "Get out of town as quick as you can."

"What about the other saloons in town? I might get work at one of them. The men in Tascosa like my singing."

His eyebrows went up before he shook his head. "I am warning you. People are afraid of Boggs. That includes saloonkeepers and piano players all over the panhandle." He stuck out his hand, his eyes straying to Boggs's office door. "Hurry. Leave Tascosa. If I don't see you again, be careful."

"God, Joe." She took his hand in both of hers. "You make it all sound so . . . so bad. How do you know about this?"

"Rumors, Kate." He opened his mouth to speak, closed it, then shrugged. "Just rumors."

She squeezed his hand, draped a shawl about her shoulders, and darted out the door. Moving along the darkened street, she hugged the building walls. Joe's words echoed in her ears. How long before Boggs got word to other saloon owners? How long before he came after her? The other women, what had happened to them?

Her outrage at Boggs became bone-jarring fear. Thank God she had a little money. She couldn't afford to be without a job for more than a week, but at least she had enough saved to get out of town.

Sean had judged Boggs correctly. All he had wanted was to get her into bed. And worse, she now sensed that the saloon owner possessed a really malicious streak. She wondered if he would use any means to get revenge.

What had Joe started to say before changing his mind? She shivered. Maybe she didn't want to know.

Oppressive and still, the night now felt cold and charged and fearful. She increased her pace, her usual healthy confidence taking flight. The metallic ring of a spur and the grunting gasp of harsh breathing brought her to attention.

Someone was following her.

The wind kicked up, playing tricks with her saloon dress, whipping it around her knees. Quickening her steps, she hurried on, only to have the jingle of spurs continue at the same pace as her own footfalls.

The moon floated behind clouds, leaving a sooty darkness in its wake. One store showed a faint light far back in the interior, but no one appeared to be there.

She changed her course and jumped from the boardwalk to the street. The thud of her pursuer's boots hitting the ground confirmed that he had done the same. She flicked a glance over her shoulder. A tall shadow loomed to her right. Her mouth became desert dry. What if she pivoted and confronted him, demanded to know why the hell he followed her? It didn't take long to dismiss that thought.

Oh, God! He was so close, he had only to reach out to grab her. Did he plan to rob her? Rape her? Had Boggs decided to kidnap her, or simply to frighten her?

Panic lent her wings. She broke into a run, her reticule beating against her thigh. When her shawl slipped from her shoulders, she didn't stop to retrieve it.

Only a little way to go. A bit farther and she'd be safe.

But so far.

With a last surge of speed, she made it to the hotel porch. She screamed and darted up the steps, expecting any minute to be attacked from behind. What if he hurled himself at her, preventing her from screaming again?

But the man didn't follow.

Once inside, she leaned her back against the door. Nausea choked her, rising in her throat to leave her mouth raw. Grasping the handrail, she groped her way upstairs. In the safety of her room, after checking to be sure the door was locked, she sank wearily onto the bed.

Who? And why? A Lily customer? She doubted it. A drifter? Unlikely. It had to be one of Boggs's men. He'd not wanted to catch her—just scare the daylights out of her. Boggs would want the privilege of hurting her himself.

With trembling fingers, Kate unbuttoned her shoes and replaced them with a pair of worn boots. Shivering, she removed her gaudy saloon costume and drew on a modest high-necked dress. From there, she went about the business of gathering her belongings. She folded the saloon dress and carefully laid it on the bed. She walked to the window.

Slowly, not really wanting to see below, she eased aside the curtain. A shadow moved at the corner of a building. Kate didn't deceive herself. Nathan hadn't been playing with her. Either she went along, or she'd be sorry. Well, she had no intention of going along. Sean had said that if she ever needed him . . . That time hadn't come yet, at least not the way he meant it. Turning to the water stand, she lifted a pitcher and filled the bowl. Cupping her hands, she splashed her face with cold water. The small mirror attached to the wall returned a chilling glimpse of her white face.

Now that she knew where she stood with the saloonkeeper, she'd handle it. She wasn't sure how, but she'd think of something. As for Sean O'Brien, whatever had happened between them that night, the change in her that followed, the longing . . . well, in time she'd handle that, too.

Maybe not the way she'd like.

But she was still in control of her life, including all its bumpy upsets, and it was infinitely better than being back in Missouri with Mama and Milton.

Wearily, Kate sank down by the window and waited for daybreak. At least her rent was current, so she didn't need to wait to see the landlady before she left. She had to get out of town before Boggs knew she was gone.

With the first hint of light, she grasped her bundle of belongings and hurried toward the livery barn. The owner of the stable saw her coming and stood in the doorway, his face showing concern. "Howdy, Miss Kate. You're out early."

"I want to buy Barney, Mr. Sanders. And a man's saddle."

The liveryman nodded. "Barney's a good horse. Long, good legs, big body. About four years old. Be willing to sell, ma'am, if'n you're willing to pay. As for the saddle, I can't say I blame you. Ridin' astride is a whole lot more comfortable, I'd think."

After some haggling, they agreed on a price. "Don't understand why you'd want to buy 'im. You'll just have to turn around and let me take care of 'im."

She gave the liveryman a weary smile. "I suspect you know, Mr. Sanders."

Nodding sadly, he patted the horse's smooth rump. "Sooner or later something always happens. The girls go—somewhere. You're lucky to get away."

"Mr. Sanders, I'd appreciate it if you'd forget the direction I take out of town."

"Always had trouble with directions. Sometimes I git turned around so bad, I cain't tell north from south."

Kate stuck out her hand. "You're a good friend."

"Be careful, Miss Kate. The wind is particularly bad today." And with this final warning, the livery owner turned back toward the stable.

Once on the outskirts of Tascosa, she guided Barney toward the stream where she usually rode, a good three miles away. It was dangerous country. If she followed the creek, she'd be able to stay off the main road. Maybe Boggs's men wouldn't be able to follow her tracks.

Hiramville would be a good place to start. The town lacked the wildness of Tascosa—a blessing if she could get a job. She patted her reticule containing her savings, making sure she still had the money. She swiveled in the saddle to look behind her. If Nathan Boggs turned more vengeful, where could she hide? She remembered Sean's warning that Boggs could make it tough for her. She hadn't realized how tough.

She rode for several miles before the harsh wind grew worse, and it soon became a gale. She ducked her head against the gusts, finally choosing a secluded spot on the lee side of a bend in the stream. She tied her horse to a strong shrub, curled into a ball, and prepared to wait until the weather died down.

The wind howled through the cottonwoods, snapping at branches, hurling dirt and grit in all directions. Occasionally Kate turned a desolate gaze on the appalling landscape, but mostly she kept her head covered and her eyes closed. The weather began to calm down eventually, and Kate felt exhaustion overtake her. She hadn't gotten much sleep the night before, and just gathering the courage to leave Tascosa seemed to have sapped the last of her strength. She just needed a few moments sleep.

Stiff and uncomfortable, she awoke after what must have been hours. Slowly she raised her head. The sun shone in her eyes, blinding her, and she had to blink the surroundings into focus. The outline of several men on horseback swam into view. Her peripheral vision included others. God, she was surrounded by Indians.

She stifled a scream and scrambled to her feet. Terror froze her blood. What could she do? Run? Her horse was too far away. It was a silly thought anyway, when there wasn't a chance in ten thousand she could succeed. If the Indians were friendly, their garishly painted faces did a convincing job of hiding their neighborliness.

She held out a trembling hand in a gesture she'd heard was a show of friendship. "Sure hope you speak English, because I can't speak Indian. I'm Kate—I sing at the Gilded Lily Saloon in Tascosa." No point in saying she had run away. "Maybe you've heard of me." She licked her lips and looked with hope from one to the other. "I sing there at night. Mostly ballads and the like. I'm glad to have met you, but it's getting on toward suppertime. After that, I'll head for the Lily, so I need to hurry." She gave a scared little laugh. "Can't be late for work, you know."

She made a headlong rush toward her horse, and none of them followed—until she mounted. One Indian, the leader, dressed in a breechclout and carrying a spear with feathers tied to it, motioned for her to ride out. They hadn't understood a word she said.

Kate gave a decided negative shake of her head. She wasn't about to go peaceably. "Sorry, fellas. My job comes first."

Her heart beating wildly, she sucked in a short breath and kicked Barney in the flanks. He lunged forward, but not fast enough. The leader, his face lined with streaks of ocher, reined his spotted pony forward and jerked the reins from her hands. He grunted a command to his warriors and urged his mount forward. Her own horse followed. Terrified, she clung to the saddle horn.

"Look, you . . . you Indians," she yelled, "you'd better let me go. They'll miss me at the Lily and come hunting for me."

The man leading her horse paid no attention. The others were equally impassive. She was alone among the hated Indians of the West. The trick was to not look scared. When tears threatened, she raised her voice. "Hey, you ugly painted savages, taking me with you, is . . . is bad medicine."

Single file, the Indians moved along the trail, their expressions hidden behind streaks of yellow, blue, and black. Because she had to follow, hysteria jolted her, rising like gorge until she gulped it back. Whatever happened, she intended to stay alive.

Sean slipped into his Indian persona as easily as he donned his Irish cap. His mind closed to his white heritage, and once again he was Grayhawk, son of Morning Fawn, grandson of Chief Stone Wolf, brave, fearsome. . . .

Comanche.

Leaving the Ghost, his white man's horse, to guard Midnight's mares, he mounted the half-wild black stallion. It had been a long time since he'd ridden his prize animal, and he had thought that it might take a little time for the horse to get used to him again, but he was in for a surprise. Midnight not only remembered him but actually seemed glad to see him.

From the stallion's back he surveyed the landscape. Hidden Valley had served him well, Grayhawk thought contentedly. He had discovered the valley before he left for Ireland on one of his innumerable trips across the ocean and back. He'd run in a few mustangs, among them Midnight, then a few more, until he'd acquired a sizeable herd.

Tucked away in one of the ravines, the valley was rich and verdant, and would be difficult to find, even if one knew of its existence—a perfect place to hide his herd until he could make permanent arrangements. At stud someday, Midnight would be known by everybody in the ranching business.

Grayhawk leaned forward and patted the animal's neck. "I've missed you, too, good friend."

The high-strung stallion, ever sensitive to the gentlest pressure, tossed its head only once when guided away from the lush green of the hidden valley. Hawk spoke apologetically. "You'll have to forget the ladies for a while, Midnight. I'm sorry, but the Gray Ghost will have to take over your duties with the harem." He spoke quietly, his words low and guttural in the language of the People. "He's as big around as you but not as handsome. Nor does he stand as tall. At nearly seventeen hands, you spark attention wherever you go. Soon I'll take you and your lady friends home to the Shamrock."

He growled deep in his throat when he sighted a footprint, the boot track of a white man. Someone had found his valley and his horses. Aware he couldn't spare the time to track the intruder, Hawk held his anger in check. Gray Ghost would not make it easy for the man to take him, but the mares wouldn't stand a chance against a seasoned horse thief. Hawk laid aside the temptation to dwell on such a happening. He would just have to return all the more quickly to collect the herd. Knowing there was little else he could do at the moment, he turned his mind to the task before him.

"My grandfather Stone Wolf is an old man now. His grandson's arrival will give him pleasure. But no doubt he knows already that I am coming."

Stone Wolf's eyes were sharp. They could see where others could not, in the smoke of his pipe, the flow of the clouds, the visions in his dreams. Hawk wondered what type of future his grandfather saw for the People. Hawk knew guns bartered from Mexican traders would delay the white men for only so long. Time was running out.

Hawk sighed heavily. How much longer could the Comanche be a nation? Hawk vowed again to protect his mother's people as long as he could. And to stop the massacres when possible, whether white or red led the charge. He and the colonel had defined their plan as friendly. A good word here, another there. They both believed establishing trust between the white settlers and the Comanche was the best way to achieve peace.

Deftly, Hawk reined the big black through the canyons surrounding his valley. As he rode, he let his gaze shift over the rugged terrain. His head filled with priceless memories of a carefree childhood spent roaming these serpentine trails. He had always doubted the whites were aware of the valley's existence. Today that had changed. He had found the imprint of a boot not his own.

Who had found his valley?

Riding north, he adjusted the leather band around his head and the gray hawk's feather projecting from it. He bared his chest to the sun, his deerskin pants covering his thighs and legs, worn moccasins protecting his feet.

He had fifty miles to go to Stone Wolf's campground in the Palo Duro canyon. During the winter months, the canyon provided shelter from the cold, wild game for food, and pasture for the tribe's horses. His people had been camping there for hundreds of years.

As Midnight carried him closer to his Indian heritage, Hawk's mind pondered the events of the past few weeks, settling on Kate.

He had never felt responsible for a woman before. Bloody possessive, to be honest about it. Sometimes he imagined himself back at the hotel making love to her, losing himself in her. Just as often he remembered her hesitant smile, then the funny little laugh that usually followed. How expressive her eyes were. She had yet to be afraid of men, including Boggs. Mildly concerned, but positive of her ability to handle the saloonkeeper, she had shrugged and dismissed any threat as ridiculous.

"I needed a job," she had said, chuckling softly. "Mr. Boggs gave me one. If he wants more than that, he'll have to find another singer." And then she'd squared her shoulders, defiance evident in her Irish-blue eyes. "I work cheap but it won't always be that way. As for the other, Boggs can find someone else to indulge him."

Brave words, but foolish. What Boggs wanted he got—one way or another. But he wouldn't add Kate to his possessions. Hawk would never allow that to happen. He planned to go back for her.

Why, Hawk wondered, was she so angry when he suggested

she go home? Had someone broken her heart? Anger sparked and surged through him. He was her first lover, and by primitive thinking she belonged to him. Secretly, he thought of her as his woman. She had refused his offer of marriage, but he knew a way to change her mind. An unbidden smile stole across his face. He just needed the opportunity.

He became aware of the wind provoking an eerie wail through the canyons. The mournful sound echoed his own apprehension. He must convince Stone Wolf to control his braves; then he and the colonel could encourage trust through trade between the whites and Stone Wolf's band. That would be a beginning. The Comancheros, that ragged bunch of wily outlaws, would have to be dealt with. Was Boggs involved with the Comancheros, as rumor suggested? Hawk tensed at the thought of the unsavory saloonkeeper. If anything happened to Kate at his hands, Boggs would pay.

Hawk willed his thoughts to silence, wrapping himself in the stillness and waiting for tranquillity to enter his soul. Dismounting, he drank from the stream and staked his horse. Lifting his head, his face upturned, his eyes closed, he heard the slurring cry of a hawk and felt the flutter of a wing against his cheek.

He waited long, his arms raised in supplication, aware of a muteness bound to the shadows. He had hoped for direction, perhaps a consciousness of what lay ahead. Nothing came to him—only Kate's lovely face twisted in fear.

Despite her assertion that she could take care of herself, his concern for her intensified. He would have to return for her as soon as possible. He had left her this last time only because of the timetable he and the Colonel had arranged.

Weary at last, he made his way to the base of a gnarled cottonwood to sleep, to dream until morning ushered in patchy fog and fine mist. He awoke, washed himself in the cold water of the stream, and gathered mint leaves from along the bank to crush against his chest.

With a few muttered words to his horse, he mounted and once more headed toward the Comanche campground. Memories crowded in to greet him. He recognized the next bend in the canyon, the narrowing of the stream, the rocky gorge where the water backed up during a rainstorm. He could still remember the excitement of seeing the stream turn into a heaving, pulsing monster, churning its way between the cliffs.

The names of friends teased him—Gray Dog, Spotted Owl, Red Rock. Did they still remember those days as fondly as he did? And his friend Little Crow? Would Crow recall the day they had exchanged blood beneath the giant cottonwood on the banks of the Red River? Would he still call him brother?

Hawk rode bareback, in the way of the Indian. Soon he'd enter the Indian campground and arrive at his grandfather's tipi. What would Stone Wolf think of Kate?

Uneasily, he wondered what Kate would think of Grayhawk. Would she freeze and turn away? Be so frightened she'd faint? Somehow he knew Kate wouldn't faint. He sensed that her hatred of Indians was too great to do anything but fight. Silently he cursed. How did he think he could truly convince her to marry a half-breed?

He followed the stream until well past midday, when the sun had started its descent. At last he saw the tipis, yellow in the fading light. Everything was as he remembered.

Hawk acknowledged that his heart beat faster. Stone Wolf had an uncanny way of predicting what the future held. He would feel his grandson's presence as he had done in the past. But would he know a woman had entered his grandson's life?

Prompted by old habits, he looked down the line of tents to the place where he and Da had always erected their home. They had placed it a distance from the center of the village—symbolic, he supposed, of the boundaries that separated them from the others. Da had learned early to ignore the jibes of the braves. He had proved himself a warrior on many occasions: the war with the Pawnee, the chase of the buffalo. He had married the daughter of the chief.

Hawk acknowledged the nostalgia that tightened the muscles of his belly, but not by so much as a blink would he betray his emotion. It was the Comanche way.

His tipi was in place, its blue-striped entrance flap facing the stream. At Stone Wolf's direction, it must have been erected in anticipation of his arrival. His grandfather's visions had not dimmed with age.

With a slight pressure of his knees, Hawk guided Midnight through the village. Women stopped their work at scraping buffalo hides to watch him. On their knees close by, small girls bent on learning the skills of their mothers watched wide-eyed as he rode by. The village became quiet.

At the flap of Stone Wolf's tipi, Hawk stopped and slid off the back of his horse. He met the eyes of the men nearest him. The braves neither responded nor stirred. Lifting the flap, he went in to greet his grandfather.

Inside, the tipi was warm from glowing coals contained in a small circle of rocks. Stone Wolf sat cross-legged on the floor, his pipe in his hand. He had grown older, the lines in his face deeper, his hair almost white now. Without looking up, he puffed on his pipe.

Hawk remained standing. It wasn't his place to announce his presence. His grandfather knew he was there.

Stone Wolf spoke. "I wonder why my grandson stands when he could sit."

"Your grandson would not presume to show anything less than the greatest respect for Stone Wolf and his wisdom." Hawk spoke in the language of the People. "Therefore he would not sit unless invited to do so."

"Since he left his people to cross the great waters, my grandson has become a man wise beyond his years. It was not always so. Sit, grandson."

Hawk chuckled. "I've grown older, Grandfather. I'm not sure of the wisdom. But Stone Wolf hasn't changed. He would sport with his grandson."

The old man took another puff on his pipe. "As always, Stone Wolf is glad to see his grandson."

"My father bade me to convey his regards and also his respect. As I do."

Stone Wolf nodded his acceptance. "The People remember your father well." He handed the pipe to Hawk. "Why have you come?"

Taking one puff before handing the pipe back, Hawk

glanced around the tipi. How many times had he sat here silently listening to the wise words of Stone Wolf as he counseled with other chiefs?

A new buffalo skin, softened by the hands of his wives, hid the floor where his grandfather sat, his legs crossed. An old bow lay next to the entrance flap. His grandfather had been a great hunter.

"Grandfather, the white man descends in numbers. Always westward, threatening the land of the People. The Comanche must learn to live with him."

"The white man speaks from both sides of his mouth."

Hawk bowed his head. "We must try, Grandfather. My father believes that if Stone Wolf would lead his people to be friends with the people of Colonel Sullivan's fort and the ranchers in the area, if the two people could become good neighbors, it would set an example. Perhaps we could have peace."

"How can I influence my braves to forget their anger, when they see the destruction of their villages, their women raped, the children killed, the buffalo dwindling, all due to the white man's greed?"

"I don't know. But killing the whites is not the answer. Stone Wolf is old and wise. A great chief. The spirits speak to him. They whisper secrets your grandson cannot hear."

"The spirits whisper much. Always they speak of the death of the Comanche as a people."

"But we must try, Grandfather, to forge a friendship with the colonel and his men. And in time, all the whites. I'll act as a negotiator—give my life, if necessary, to save our people."

"I'm an old man. I can't hold back the night. Just as the sun once rose for the Comanche, so will it rise for the white man."

"We must try for peace," Hawk argued desperately.

A long silence hung in the air before Stone Wolf spoke. "Yes, we must try."

"Thank you, Grandfather. I'm glad, as my father will be glad. As my mother would have been."

"How will we carry out this task? Will you remain among us?"

"First, the plan must stay secret. Only you and I and the colonel will know. I'll go from the white man's world to my grand-father's people and back again. Planting seeds of friendship. Warning against attacks from either side."

Stone Wolf puffed his pipe. "You will be in grave danger. The Comanche are warriors."

His father had given him a harsh and exacting task. All for a love interrupted between an Indian girl, who died at the hands of a white soldier, and an Irishman who had loved her, married her in the way of the People, and given her a son. He refused to feel guilty if the plan didn't work, Hawk told himself for the hundredth time. Just as he'd tried not to feel guilty about Kate. After all, he'd asked her to marry him—and gotten a firm re-fusal.

Chapter Four

Maureen still couldn't believe she'd finally made the break. She'd stolen away from Mama and Milton, left Missouri behind, and was headed for Texas and a home with Kate. Fanning at the dust wafting in from the coach's open window, Maureen bit her tongue to keep from singing. She had slipped away in the night and begged a ride on the wagon train to Fort Leavenworth. Once in Kansas she'd bought her fare to Tascosa and settled back to ride the stagecoach all the way to Texas. She couldn't wait to see Kate again. Whenever she felt her nerves were about to get the best of her, she thought of her sister to bolster her spirits.

She'd never so much as talked back to Mama, and she'd always hidden from Milton to avoid his unwanted attentions, although lately it had become more and more difficult. But as the date of her wedding to Verlin drew closer, she'd known she had to do something drastic. She absolutely could not marry Verlin. She'd rather die.

It had been pure luck to find the hundred dollars, and even though the money was hers, she felt like a thief for taking it.

Mama and Milton always made her feel guilty. She had Kate to thank for the money, as well as for giving her the courage to leave. Courage—she had so little of it.

Maureen smoothed her dress, her only dress, grateful it matched the hand-me-down poke bonnet she wore over her rebellious red hair. Now and then she cast a surreptitious glance at the young man in the seat across from her. Andy. He said his name was Andy Bennet.

From the time their trip began in Fort Leavenworth, he hadn't bothered to hide his admiration, nor fail to speak it loud enough to be heard over the shouts and curses of the stage-coach driver. Verlin's attentions had been so watered down that the words could have come from a tree stump, for all the impression they made.

"We're on the last leg before we get to Tascosa. You excited?"

Maureen smiled shyly at the cowboy before lowering her gaze to her lap. Andy had the bluest eyes, and a wonderful laugh that seemed always on the verge of erupting. "I'll be so glad to get there."

His grin deepened. His flirtation was delicious in a forbidden sort of way and fed her heart, which was starved for attention. "You gonna live with your sister?"

"Yes. I can hardly wait."

In the beginning she hadn't been sure she should be talking to a stranger, but they'd been riding together forever. What had started as an exciting adventure to escape Mama and Milton had begun to loom as a fearful ride into the unknown—until Andy joined her on the stagecoach. He had lessened the fear. Now she was scared again, up to her eyebrows. He wouldn't be staying in Tascosa.

Maureen felt a warm rush of pleasure when he looked at her, which was most of the time. As the journey took her closer to her destination, she realized how much she liked him.

"How long will you be staying in Tascosa? Several days?"

"Naw, not long. I'm going to that big canyon called the Palo Duro, maybe a hunnerd miles south. Spotted some wild horses down there. Just plain lucked into 'em grazin' in a sheltered valley. Mustangs. One, a big black stallion. Their leader, I 'magine. Yessir, I'm gonna round 'em up and make me a bunch of money."

"What if the horses belong to somebody else?"

Andy grinned at her, his eyes crinkling at the absurdity of her question. "Then I mustn't take them, must I?"

"Will you?"

"How am I gonna know whether they belong to somebody if they don't wear a brand, honey?"

"I don't think you should call me 'honey.' "

Laughing, he leaned toward her. "Well, now, just how long should the acquaintance be before I can call you something besides miss?"

Nobody had to tell her. Maury knew her face was crimson and suspected her voice would betray her. "We haven't been introduced properly," she said.

"You're hell on proper, honey."

"There you go again."

Andy frowned. "Look, we've been with each other day and night for a lotta miles, and we may not see each other again. Ever. Besides, from here on in, it's just you and me. I'm right glad about that. Felt like shouting with joy when the woman and her little boy got off at the last trading post. Reckon now we could forget what's fit and rightful and just be easy with one another?"

She didn't want Andy to think she wasn't friendly. Besides, he was probably right. They might never see each other again after they parted in Tascosa. The thought brought a sinking feeling in her stomach. Not wanting him to see her disappointment, she glanced out the window. "This is a big country."

He smiled at her and leaned forward, one sandy eyebrow raised. "Can I call you honey now?" When she nodded, he took her hand and caressed it between both of his. "Yeah, Texas is big. So're Kansas and Oklahoma. But, honey, when I get some money, I'm gonna have me a little spread in the southeast corner of Colorado. Or maybe up in Montana. Gets pretty cold, I've heard, but I'm not afraid of work, so I guess there's no need to be afraid of the cold."

"Montana's a long way from here." It made her feel lonely just thinking about it.

"Yep."

"I'll be living in Tascosa. If you should come back that way sometime, you could stop by. I'm sure people in Tascosa will know my sister, Kathleen Hartland. I don't think the town is very big."

"Gotta get my horses first." He lifted her hand to his lips and kissed the tips of her fingers. "After that, I'll look around for a wife."

After she got over the shock of his lips on her hand, she worked at hiding her feelings behind a change of subject. "My sister is a singer at a place called the Gilded Lily."

Surprise spread over his face. "Yeah, think I've heard of it."

"You have?" she asked eagerly. "You've been there? Have you heard Kate sing?"

He hesitated, took his hands from around hers, and leaned back against the seat, his gaze focused on the outdoors. "It's been a while."

Disappointment clouded her eyes. "I suppose when you've been as many places as you have, you forget."

"Yeah, been lots of places." He pointed at the landscape. "Wild country. Indians, Comancheros. Shady characters, drifters, hide hunters. They're all out there. Texas is a state in the Union, but some say Texas is a state of mind. Law ain't come yet, leastwise nothing you can count on. Can't be too careful, I reckon. 'Specially women."

She knew he'd deliberately changed the course of the conversation. Unable to hide her indignation at some implied reflection on her sister, she glared at him. "It must be a nice place. My sister lives in Tascosa. And she's a proper lady, sir."

He held up his hand, at the same time shaking his head in denial. "Naw, I ain't sayin' nothin' about your proper sister. I'm talkin' about this part of Texas."

By the time they arrived in Tascosa, they were talking little and laughing not at all. Maureen cast doubtful glances at the forbidding terrain, the sparse grass and mesquites. What if Indians swooped down on them? Massacred her and Andy? Kate would never know. And what if Kate no longer lived in Tascosa?

It was early evening in Tascosa when Maureen stepped down into the sandy street, her eyes darting up and down the ugly storefronts, coming to rest on the Gilded Lily Saloon.

Maureen covered her mouth with her hand, while fears like wasps buzzed around in her midsection. Judging by its shabby exterior, she found it hard to believe that Kate had made enough money singing in this saloon to send a hundred dollars to pay her sister's way to Tascosa. Did she still sing at the Gilded Lily? Had she ever sung in such a place?

Turning, Maureen met Andy's perceptive gaze through a glaze of tears. "Well, we're here."

"Want me to go in with you?"

She gave a negative shake of her head, then, reconsidering, nodded in the affirmative. "If you don't mind."

"Don't mind a'tall." Andy took her arm, piloted her through the door, and waited until their eyes adjusted to the gloom. Across the room, a lanky scarecrow of a man didn't glance up, his long, clawlike fingers hovering over the yellowed keys of an ancient piano.

Andy urged her in the direction of the piano player. "Sir?"

"Place ain't open yet. On the other hand, if you got a request, make it. Hell, I might even be able to play it." His gaze swept over Maureen, his bloodshot eyes widening when they focused on her face. He rose unsteadily, put out a hand to balance himself, and made a dogged effort to stand up straight. "My God, girl. What's your name?"

The man was drunk, a condition that didn't appear to hamper his piano playing. "My name is Maureen Hartland." She inhaled deeply. "I'm Kate Hartland's sister. She wrote me that she sings at the Lily."

The inebriated scarecrow placed a wavering finger to his lips, but too late, a voice sounded behind him. "Well, look who we have here. Kate Hartland's little sister. You sing, darlin'?"

Hawk stood outside his grandfather's tipi and watched a scouting party arrive amid the shouts and laughter of women and children. The braves rode slowly, looking neither right nor left, their backs straight, their legs dangling, their prisoners limping and staggering along beside them.

When they got to the middle of the village, one Indian, obviously the leader, kicked his prisoner with his foot, and the groan that accompanied the blow was clearly not that of a man.

Hawk shuddered, muttering a disgusted "Bloody hell." A young woman, no more than twenty-one or twenty-two, sprawled on the ground, her face buried in the dust. She struggled to raise her head.

Little Crow poked at her with the blunt end of his spear, and the woman staggered to her feet. She rasped a few curses through dry, cracked lips. Attempting to swallow, she gave up and made a feeble attempt to shake her fist.

Too exhausted to stand without swaying, she brushed her hair out of her face and gave her audience a glimpse of scratches and bruises. "Water. Give me water." She ignored the sneers and jeers, and it was clear that only her strong will to survive managed to keep her on her feet. Barely conscious, unable to focus, she still mouthed her contempt. "Damned . . . evil heathens. Give me some water."

Hawk sucked in his breath and forgot to exhale. *Kate!* Beautiful, beguiling Kate had been reduced to a half-alive captive asking for a drink of water. *God.* Where had Little Crow found her?

"Little Crow," Hawk muttered in the language of the People. "My friend has returned victorious."

Little Crow stared at him for several seconds before he smiled. "Blood brother. Grayhawk has returned to his people."

"When I left, Little Crow was a boy, learning the ways of a warrior."

"And the Hawk was not so tall."

They made the sign of friendship, Hawk hiding his anger and anxiety. Feigning indifference, he sauntered forward a few steps, an exaggerated interest replacing his passive features. "The woman is ugly."

Little Crow nodded. "She will make a good slave."

Velda Sherrod

Too bad Abe Lincoln's Proclamation hadn't reached the Comanche. Hawk shook his head. "I see under the dirt. The woman belongs to me."

Angrily Little Crow slid from his horse. He swung his spear threateningly. "She is mine. My wife is pregnant. I need a slave."

Hawk had no intention of giving Little Crow even the smallest margin of doubt, even if it meant scoffing at Kate's beauty. "The woman is weak. She will not live long."

"Long enough," Little Crow said coldly, his gaze going from Hawk to his prisoner.

Fists and blows and starvation had left their marks on her, but beneath her exhaustion, her fighting spirit remained; a flicker proclaiming courage still raged in her beautiful breast.

He watched her try to take in her new surroundings, then give up and close her eyes. If she remained with Little Crow, in six months she'd be half-dead from starvation, beatings, and exposure.

Hawk folded his arms over his chest in the classic Comanche stance and waited. He counted on Kate's being too disoriented, too near collapse to see or think clearly. If she should see beyond his Indian personality, which he doubted, maybe she'd know to keep her mouth shut. He had a strong suspicion she would make no allowances in his favor.

Her shirt hung in shreds. Her skirt was ripped and torn, exposing her lovely long legs. A bare shoulder showed streaks of blood, and a bruise, like a dark shadow, smudged one cheek. He longed to take a knife to Little Crow's throat.

"The woman belongs to me," he said in a growl.

"Little Crow brought the woman here." Stone Wolf studied his grandson. "Why would Hawk claim her?"

"She could be carrying my seed." He stepped forward, his legs apart, his eyes narrowed. "My seed."

Little Crow raised his chin. "Hawk comes back to the People claiming to be Comanche. He is not Comanche. He is white eyes. A liar."

Quickly Hawk drew his knife. "Will Little Crow challenge a Comanche warrior with such words?"

Before the fight could begin, Stone Wolf held up a hand. "If she belongs to my grandson, why did he not bring her to his people?"

Hawk smiled. "The soldiers came, but not before I laid claim."

Several braves laughed, and Hawk joined them.

Glancing at his captive, Little Crow maintained his threatening posture. "We have only Hawk's word."

"The word of a warrior."

"Little Crow has brought Hawk this woman." Stone Wolf's face was unreadable. "Has my grandson considered taking a Comanche maiden?"

Hawk struggled for a suitable answer. "I've traveled many places since I left the People. I have no wife, nor have I had the opportunity to take a Comanche bride. I've met many women. None that would make a good wife." He threw a disinterested glance at Kate. "This one is dirty and ugly. She carries my son. Otherwise it would not matter."

With a nod, Stone Wolf expressed his understanding. "Then Hawk must pay."

Little Crow looked at Stone Wolf, his eyes still glaring his anger. He focused a covetous gaze at Midnight. "I will take your stallion."

With a slight movement of his body, Stone Wolf agreed. "The black stallion. Hawk must give the great horse he rides to Little Crow in payment for the prisoner."

If he hadn't been so worried about Kate, he'd have challenged that "luck of the Irish" hogwash. He sighed in disgust. "The stallion is a fine horse, more valuable than the frail woman. I must think on this."

Stone Wolf shook his head. "Anger in the breast festers. We will settle the matter now."

"Is the woman worth a horse?" Little Crow sneered. "Do you still want to trade?"

Hawk walked around and around Kate, as though making up his mind. He shrugged off her dull glare, doubting she could see him. Until she spat at him. He suspected that only her terror kept her on her feet. She shifted, her blurry gaze scanning the faces around her, coming to rest on him.

He froze. Would she recognize him? If she did, could she control her temper? Would she believe him if he told her he wanted only to put his arms around her and tell her to leave the worrying to him? Doubtful.

"I will do it, but only because I have no son."

"If it is a girl will Hawk want the horse back?"

Hawk made one more slow turn around Kate. At last he nodded. "She will bear a son. Little Crow will not lose his stallion."

Hawk clamped down on the cold anger filling his chest, at Kate for getting herself caught, at the Indians for capturing her, and at Little Crow for taking the finest horse a man could ever expect to own.

Silent now, both men waited for Stone Wolf to give the final word. "If Hawk would have this captive as his wife, we will bind them together." He glanced at the sinking sun. "Soon the sun will go down. The woman and Hawk will appear before Stone Wolf. Campfires will be set. The People will dance and bear witness. Stone Wolf's words will unite Hawk and his woman. They will live three days in the ceremonial tipi. Little Crow will take the horse."

Little Crow, no longer interested in the woman, took triumphant possession of the valuable animal. His eyes glinted in laughter. "The fine stallion is mine. Hawk made a bad trade."

Shrugging, Hawk glanced at the woman. "A horse for a son. A good trade."

Satisfied that he had come out ahead in the transaction, Little Crow took the reins. When he prepared to mount, Midnight bared his teeth and shied away. "Hawk has trained his horse well."

A few words from Hawk and the big beast allowed the Indian to lead him away.

Briefly, Hawk stared after them. If he pulled off this charade, he should be awarded the Medal of Honor. "I'll take the woman to the tipi before the ceremony."

Again, Stone Wolf studied his grandson. "It's not the way of the People, but neither is it the way of the People to claim the prize of another. Little Crow has been awarded the stallion.

Hawk will wait to take the woman to the ceremonial tipi."

After the war party had dispersed, Grayhawk stood with Kate and his grandfather. "When the sun goes down, the woman should wash in the stream."

"Yes," Stone Wolf said, a gleam in his eye. "As you say, she is dirty and ugly."

His grandfather clearly harbored doubts about his story of Kate carrying his son. Hawk knew he couldn't jeopardize his agreement with his grandfather, any more than he could fail the colonel. Also, and with certainty, he knew he would never desert Kate again.

He would marry her in the way of the People, and in their eyes, she would be his wife. As his wife she would be afforded some measure of protection within the tribe—a tribe among whom she would have to live for the moment. There was no other way. He could not reveal that he had lied to his grandfather.

For now, he had to maintain his Indian persona. Kate must not recognize him yet. He longed to tell her, to ease her stress. But he was not sure she could handle any more shocks at this time. Besides, he wanted to explain the situation in the privacy of his tipi, not here in front of his grandfather.

Hawk gave a mental shake of his head. What had he gotten them into, himself and Kate, besides more trouble? From the moment she'd been brought into the Indian camp, she hadn't stopped fighting. Feeble and only half-conscious, she had yet. to cease struggling against her captors. A true Irish lass. He'd give his life for her. After all, he was her first lover. She was his Kate. Soon she'd be more. She'd be his wife. The thought did not displease him.

Two Indian women pointed toward the stream. When Kate didn't respond, they took hold of her arms and made a noise for her to come with them. "Damnation," she whispered, staggering in the direction they led her. Her mouth was so dry she could hardly make a sound. Dazed by exhaustion and lack of water and food, her body a mass of cuts and bruises, Kate clung to consciousness by sheer will. Anything, she thought, to be away from that wretched heathen who had kidnapped her.

When they reached the stream, the Indian women went through the motions of undressing, pointing first at her and then at the water. They pantomimed bathing, no matter if the sun had dropped over the edge of the prairie. Limping, she stumbled a few steps forward and sank to her knees on the bank. Kate cupped her hands and drank greedily. Water had never tasted so good. After washing her face, she made circular motions with her hands. "If I'm to bathe, you'll have to turn around." She swayed. "I need privacy."

They appeared puzzled, then turned and looked behind them. One spoke in her own language, slowly at first, then building to a shriek. She sent a nervous glance over her shoulder.

If she hadn't been so weary, Kate thought miserably, she'd have had a few words in exchange. "Think I'm putting a hex on you? Wish I could, including your half-naked relatives. I despise Indians. They're dirty, mean, crueler than animals." Numb in mind and body, her teeth chattering, she took one step forward. She glanced in the direction of the Indian women, but they had disappeared.

Kate thought dully of escape, of running toward one of the ravines, and as quickly put it out of her mind. Somewhere nearby, somebody watched her. Besides, how far could she get with no shoes, no food, no horse? What had they done with Barney? Bone-weary, fatigued to the point of exhaustion, she wanted only to lie down. To rest. To close her eyes and sleep. To forget for a little while what awaited her.

When the women reappeared, Kate peered at them through a gray haze. Shaking with cold, she shivered into her torn and bloodstained clothes and ambled in the direction they pointed. They led her to a tipi and, too near collapse to argue, she staggered inside.

They removed her clothes, smoothed tangles out of her hair, and bound the heavy mane with a rawhide thong. Moments later they dropped a green deerskin dress over her shoulders. One of the women her eyes flat and cruel, held out moccasins of the same color as the dress.

Hysteria bubbled up in her. They probably planned to make her a blood sacrifice. She sank to the floor. "I've never been keen on fringed buckskin," she said with a sigh, "but I appreciate the moccasins. And clean clothes." Too tired to stand, she glanced at their impassive faces.

They made a few unintelligible sounds and backed out of the tipi, their voices gradually fading. Overcome by weariness and the warmth of the tipi, she curled into a defensive ball and closed her eyes.

But rest was not to be. One of the women, the tall one with the cruel eyes, returned and none too gently nudged her backside. Kate snarled a curse before easing her sore body to a sitting position. "What?"

She held out a bowl of steaming food. Kate lunged for it and devoured the sustenance without hesitation. It mattered little what she ate, only that she survived so that one day she could get even.

She'd heard stories of ways the Comanche killed their captives. Now she prayed they were exaggerated. If the tales were true and it was to be her fate, she hoped her death would be swift.

Her left thigh had turned blue with colorful patches of green and purple, and her leg ached all the way to her heel. For that matter, her insect bites, scratches, and sore ribs all hurt or itched. She flicked a weary gaze toward the women.

"What now?"

The women looked at each other and with grunts and signs motioned her to follow.

Did Comanche women watch at bloodlettings? What about run-of-the-mill forms of torture? Like burning at the stake? She tried again. "This dress . . . where am I supposed to wear it?"

Ignoring her question, the women made motions for her to fall in behind them. Anything was better than waiting for fate to catch up with her. When she attempted to stand, her knees wobbled, throwing her against her captor. The woman struck her hard across the face, bruising her cheek and sending her to her knees. Blood dripped from the corner of her mouth.

"I'll get even," she vowed, her mouth barely opening around

her split lip, her threat lost in the pounding of the drums. "I'll remember you, ugly one."

Her blurred vision stayed with her all the way to the tipi where the old man from earlier waited. She mingled prayers and curses with feeble threats of vengeance, all muttered under her breath.

Darkness settled gradually over the village. Mothers watched her with expressionless faces; their children, silent and curious, peered shyly from behind them. Warriors stared at her, their hideously painted faces grotesque in the fading light.

Dressed in a long feathered headdress, the old man observed her approach. Next to him lounged the dirty savages who had kidnapped her. Her strength fading, she turned a weary eye on the man she'd named Savage.

Ramrod straight, dressed in buckskin pants with fringe, and wearing beaded moccasins, he hardly glanced at her. That was fine with her. His face was streaked heavily with blue and white stripes. His coal black hair had been braided into two plaits and hung down on either shoulder. Not as ugly as the kidnappers, he was certainly a clown. And probably had cloven hooves. She tried to concentrate, to hang on to her sanity. Surely she'd imagined it, but in the brief glance he flicked her way, his mouth had softened. She must be hallucinating.

Relieved of their duties, the Indian women stepped to one side, leaving Kate alone. The old Indian, the one she assumed was the chief, beckoned her forward. *Oh, God.* The drums had stopped.

She stumbled close enough to see the chief's deep wrinkles and the ancient wisdom in his tired eyes. Mesmerized, unable to turn from his hypnotic gaze, she remained still.

He studied her, looking into her soul, she was to think later. He spoke to Savage with words, shrugs, and motions.

Savage moved to stand beside her, never taking his gaze from the old man.

Chanting, the chief waved a hand encompassing the breadth of the canyon, slowly stamped his feet against the earth, and turned his face up to embrace the dark sky. A minute passed, then another, before he cast a glance at the two of them. He

84

beckoned them forward, took Kate's hand, and placed it on Savage's palm. He looked long at Savage. At last, the chief, or whatever he was, bowed his head twice as though giving a blessing. The drums started. Bonfires lighted. Soon shrieking began.

Perspiration trickled down between her breasts. Kate stared at the fires. Did they plan to burn her in some barbaric ritual?

The braves formed a circle, stamping their feet in time to the drumbeat. Round and round they shuffled and pounded the earth, howling their unearthly cries. The women soon joined them. The old man and Savage, who still held her hand, remained with her. Too exhausted to think clearly, she drew away, only to hear Savage mumbling a word or two. She recognized the command in his voice. A few minutes later he joined the dancers. His cries soon mingled with theirs.

When he returned, he walked back to where the old chief stood, the repulsive Indian who'd kidnapped her ambling along beside him. The two men talked in low tones, occasionally nodding in agreement, sometimes laughing. Neither glanced in her direction. When the man walked away, Savage strode to her side. Using his thumb, he wiped the blood from her mouth.

"Stay away from me," she mumbled, too spent to raise her voice.

When he led her to his tipi and raised the flap for her to enter, she balked. She didn't know what came next, but she had no intention of making it easy for him. In her hesitation she stumbled over her feet and would have fallen if he hadn't caught her and cradled her body against his. She made no protest. She was too tired.

Savage carried her through the entrance and eased her down to the buffalo skin covering the floor, then sank beside her and pointed to the food bubbling on the coals. When she didn't move, he motioned for her to serve the food.

"You may be a Comanche lord," she muttered, "but I'm a singer. Singers don't make good serving maids. Unless you decide to do something drastic like cut off my ears. In that case, we'll negotiate."

85

Velda Sherrod

The man's face remained in the shadows, his big chest and arms bare, bronze in the flickering light. He grunted, pointing and speaking in guttural utterances she supposed were the Comanche tongue. He hadn't understood that she wasn't a servant. She dragged her weary body toward the pot.

She squinted at him, trying to bring his face into focus. "This one time, but don't get comfortable with it."

After they ate, he motioned her to sit near him. Fear blanked out all thought except to protect herself. She shook her head dully. "No."

He moved with the ease of a cat to squat beside her, his face still in the shadows. He brushed tendrils of hair from her cheek tucking the strands behind her ear.

Another man had fingered her locks and praised their shine. Would that man remember her? "Are you saying you like my hair, or that it will make a nice souvenir to place on a pole outside your tipi?"

His features were hidden behind the paint and shadows, but nothing could hide that magnificent body. He cupped her cheek with his palm and murmured something soft, almost musical, and she relaxed a bit. At least he hadn't picked up his tomahawk. When he motioned for her to take off her dress, she immediately tensed again. Her heart pumped faster, but she still had the presence of mind to shake her head. His eyes became narrow slits, and once more he gave a one-word command. How should she handle this new threat?

"Look, Savage, I don't sleep with Indians," she said wearily. "It goes against my upbringing, especially since a band of them killed my father."

His hungry gaze met hers. Kate glared, but deep inside something fluttered and quickened, something half-remembered; then, like a wisp of smoke, it was gone.

He stared at where the dress molded to her breasts. His eyes met hers and something hot and vital and inexplicable passed between them. Stunned, Kate scooted away from him, bewildered by her feelings and the flash of triumph in his eyes.

"Stay away from me, Savage." Fury sizzled through her. "I'll never be an Indian squaw."

He pointed at her and smiled. "Comanche wife."

"No. White woman."

"Wife," he repeated.

Her stomach twisted into a knot. In a matter of hours and a ritual ceremony, in the eyes of these Indians, she'd become, God forbid, wife of this bloodthirsty Comanche. *Never, never, never.* When she married, it would be because she loved the man, and he loved her in return.

Now it was too late.

Chapter Five

When the sun dropped over the rim of the canyon, night came quickly. As nearly as she could guess, it was about nine o'clock, a long time until dawn. Kate followed the movement of the Indian from the time he stood until he raised the tipi flap and disappeared into the darkness. He still wore the ferocious blue and white stripes down his cheeks and across his forehead.

With a jerk of her shoulder, Kate reinforced her determination to fight every step, survive any way she could. She looked around for a weapon. With no idea of what to expect from the big Indian, she wanted to be ready. His broad shoulders, black hair, and bronze skin went a long way toward proclaiming him a savage, until she remembered his gray eyes. It could mean only one thing: he was a half-breed, and probably the fiercest of all.

Maybe he wouldn't come back. She wanted desperately to lie down, close her eyes, and sleep. With her nerves on constant alert, she doubted that could happen. The fire had burned low and she shivered, as much from anticipation of the savage's return as from the chill.

Abruptly the tipi flap was flung open and the object of her speculation stood framed in the entrance. She let her gaze roam upward and took a hard blow to her belt line. The Indian, his face free of the bizarre blue and white paint, wore the compelling features of—

The Irishman.

"Oh, my God." She'd been rescued. That thought evaporated as quickly as it appeared. The Irishman hadn't breached the Indian stronghold with plans to save her. He was an Indian, a Comanche savage.

He was one of them.

Tears filled her eyes, and she brushed at them angrily. "What the hell is going on? What're you doing here? Does that old white-haired man, wrapped up like a sausage in a biscuit, know you play white man when you're away from here?"

He squatted beside her. "The old man, Kate, is my grandfather. He's also the chief and deserves respect."

"He's an Indian. And I want to go home." *Home!* She didn't have one, but he couldn't know that Boggs had run her out of town. Her anger seethed and boiled. To think she had trusted this turncoat. "You do plan to get me out of this band of bloody savages?"

"It isn't that simple, Kate."

Kate screamed in frustration. "Then tell me, for God's sake."

"Look, darlin', try to keep your voice down. The camp will hear."

She didn't lessen the sting of her words, but she did lower her voice. "What will they think? That you're beating your new squaw?" The glow from the fire briefly illumined his face. The man was beautiful. Magnificent. She sniffed. "What about the fires? All the demons of hell couldn't have made more noise. The old man, your grandfather? He mouthed some gibberish, stamped the earth, and shook his fist at the sky. I was dressed in an Indian costume and held hands with you like we were sweethearts on our way to a church social. What was going on?"

His lips twitched in amusement. "Stone Wolf recognized you as my wife and told the village to do the same."

"I'm nobody's wife."

"In the eyes of this village, you're my wife. If you want to get out alive, you'll remember that." He spoke blandly, his gaze roaming lazily over her face. "Later . . . perhaps we can find a way."

Face it, she told herself. She had been joined to a Comanche brave in some kind of clang-and-clatter ceremony. A Comanche brave she had thought was Irish. A Comanche brave to whom she had sold her virtue. If tears would help, she'd cry, but she doubted she'd get any sympathy. Bitter anger rose to the surface, and she braced against the inevitable shame that would surely follow. In her wildest nightmares, she'd never have dreamed that she would end up at the mercy of an Indian—and certainly not one who knew of her greatest shame. Sullenly she acknowledged that she might have to endure it, but she wouldn't make it easy for Tascosa's guest savage.

"What's your Comanche name?"

"I'm Grayhawk. Sometimes just Hawk."

"A predator safe with a family of predators."

He shrugged. "We're all predators in one way or another."

"I have the most astonishing luck. First the Indians kill Papa. I leave home, and Nathan Boggs hires me to sing and thinks that includes his bed. I run away in time to be captured by Comanche braves. And unless the sky falls in, I'm doomed to share a bed with an Indian who claims I'm his wife."

"You shared my bed before, Katie, and you said some nice things about what we did."

The fire flickered, throwing his shadow against the tipi wall. Somewhere in the canyon, a coyote wailed his mournful cry. "My judgment wasn't the best that night."

His answer to her admission was to cradle her face. "I didn't notice, darlin'. What I remember was your sweet kisses."

The Irish lilt was back, lulling and mesmerizing her into his arms. "Forget it," she said as forcefully as her jumping nerves would allow. "That was a business arrangement."

He smiled, his gaze caressing her mouth. "Money got involved along the way, but business . . . not the way I recall it." He brushed his lips over hers. "And I've a good memory."

Kate heard him murmur something, beguiling even in Comanche words. When Kate could get her body back under control, she glared at him. "If this is a rehearsal for what's to follow, you can cancel the show."

He let his hands drop and sat on the floor with his legs crossed. "From the moment I first saw you, I've had you on my mind. I've a need for you, Katie, and it won't go away."

Now he'd done it, he supposed, but best to get it out in the open. Let her hear about his feelings right from the beginning, for whether she wanted to believe it or not, in the eyes of his grandfather and his people she belonged to him. She was distressed and terribly angry, in the way of any true Irish woman. He couldn't blame her. For that matter, he was perplexed himself. Kate had complicated his life, his mission, and his standing in the eyes of his grandfather. But it still didn't change the way he felt. He wanted his hands on her body and his mouth on hers. He wanted to dip into her sweetness, taste the glory of it. He wanted whatever she had to give, just so long as it was in his arms.

He smiled at her, glad she couldn't go far until he had a chance to make her laugh, maybe sigh when he wrapped himself around her. Above all, he wanted her safe. The only way to make sure was to lay the cards on the table. He covered her hand, discovered it was cold, and brought it to his lips. "Katie, the Comanche have a long history. They came to this area many seasons ago, discovered the horse, and made their home here. They traveled the land, not assuming ownership of it, but understanding it was necessary for survival." His voice rose and fell; he sometimes seemed to be letting his Irish ancestors guide his tongue, but often borrowed from his mother's people. He did not hide his pride in the tribe of his grandfather. "They were successful. Until the white man came."

"They're barbarians. You may be, too. Probably are. Stop staring at me."

"I like looking at you, especially when you're mad." He touched her hair. "You're beautiful. And courageous, I think, to come through what you've endured. Now we must make use of your bravery."

Velda Sherrod

"And that means sharing your . . ." she began, then hesitated, her face turning pink. "Sharing your sleeping arrangements."

"I'd like that. And you would, most likely." Her mutinous glare deserved a chuckle, but he wisely held off. "If you should change your mind just a bit, remember, darlin', I'll be here. At least most of the time."

Her head jerked up. "Where are you going?"

"I have work to do that will take several days. Then I'll be back to share our home here with Stone Wolf and our people." His eyes met hers. "And you."

"But the Indian who captured me, wanted to make a slave of me, what's to keep him from taking me back?"

"We made a fair trade. He'll honor it."

"What trade?"

The transaction still irritated him, losing Midnight. Not that he wouldn't do it again—he would do almost anything to save Kate. "My horse."

"You traded your horse for me. I'm worth the price of a horse. I'm overwhelmed."

"Midnight is a fine animal. One of the best." He kept his face straight. "Not every woman would bring such a high price. I said to Little Crow, 'Midnight for an ugly woman.' He agreed."

"Oh you, you . . ."

"Had to do it, and it was a good trade. If I had said my Kate is beautiful, he would have asked for more horses. Instead I got a beautiful Irish lass with eyes as blue as cobalt and a body made for loving." Lust was forever with him when he was near Kate. "She sings my country's songs with a tremble in her voice, and could sing a lullaby with the same devotion." He nodded his acceptance of the situation. "No, lass, I'm a good horse trader."

Fearing her explosion would douse the fire, he tossed a few sprigs into the flames. "You can help the women with chores. Learn to make jerky. Clean a buffalo hide." When her face turned crimson with anger, he hid his laughter behind a benign smile. "I'll ask my aunt, my mother's sister, to show you. She's old and wise."

She snarled at him, her voice low and vicious. "Look, you

uncouth barbarian, I'm not an Indian. I'm not a slave, and I don't want to learn to skin a buffalo. What if you had ideas of your own about how your life was to be lived, and you were put in the room with a woman you barely knew? She tells you what you'll do—if, of course, you want your life to be spared. And what if you had a feeling in your midsection that she considered that you and she were married? No choice in the matter, you understand. Wouldn't you be upset?"

He yawned, lay down, and closed his eyes. "Would depend on the woman, I think."

"Is that all you can say?"

"Let's sleep on it. And if you've a mind to, you can get close to me."

"Ha. If I've a mind to."

He smiled at her, his eyes warm, his voice husky. "Lie with me, Katie. I want you. I think you want me."

Her eyes grew large, shining with something close to tears. "I can't sleep with an Indian."

Chuckling, he lay down again. "Would you consider an Irishman?"

"No."

"The time will come, my Katie, when it won't matter whether I'm Comanche or Irish."

Dawn crept in around the flap in the door and where the poles crossed in the tipi top. Kate woke with her head pounding like a runaway mustang headed for the wild. "What comes next? Do we make our own morning meal? If so, where's the cupboard?"

Hawk yawned and tossed aside the blanket covering them. "No cupboard, darlin'."

"When and what do we eat? Or do we go chase a rabbit?"

"I could kill a rabbit, if that's what you want. I'm good with a bow."

"I'll bet. You're also good with a lie."

"Lower your voice, Kate," he said mildly. "I lied to save your life."

"What did you tell them?"

Velda Sherrod

"I told them you carried my seed."

"What?" Her voice became shrill. "You told them I'm pregnant with your baby?"

"Otherwise you'd be a slave to Little Crow's wife. She's heavy with child. It wouldn't be an easy job."

She grasped the buffalo robe and tugged it to her chin, then carefully aimed a fist at his handsome nose. "Oh, you."

"Bloody hell." Hawk dodged the force of the blow, but it grazed his ear. "Kate, darlin', I needed something to make them believe you belonged to me."

She pointed a finger at him. "You get me out of this place. You hear? Now. This minute."

"Katie, it isn't that easy."

Along with the roaring in her ears, she had trouble breathing. The man she thought of as Irish was a half-breed Comanche who posed as a rancher, played the piano, had even offered marriage to protect her virtue.

Marriage.

Kate stifled the desire to pound the floor in frustration and disappointment. "What now?"

"We could lie together a bit. Or a whole lot, if that would suit you."

"You're out of your mind."

Before she could back away, he had her in his arms, his mouth an inch above hers. She braced against the impulse to put her arms around his neck. "Irish blarney," she said, pushing against his chest, "mixed with Comanche mumbo-jumbo."

"Can't you think of anything beside my blood relatives?" His frustration ended in a snarl. "Damn it, Kate." He eased his voice down to a soft whisper. "Give us a chance. Lie with me now. Let me love you."

She caught herself before she could lean into him. "I'd make a terrible wife, Irish. Just take me out of here."

A few words and an easy shrug, what she later referred to as his Comanche parley manners, constituted his answer.

Face it, she told herself. She had been united with a Comanche brave. "I don't want to be a wife." She looked at him, beseeching him to understand. "It just wouldn't work."

He caressed her chin with one finger. "How do you know? When I kiss you, I can feel you tremble." Then he added, chuckling, "Before you growl at me."

Enveloped in bands of steel, Kate couldn't move. She could feel his warm cheek against hers before he took her mouth with his. Heat surged through her, unexpected and utterly devastating. She didn't move, couldn't have moved if she had wanted to.

"You see, my Kate, we could be good together."

"I don't want to be your wife," she said nervously. "I wouldn't know in the morning whether I'd wake up in bed with an Indian or an Irishman."

"Neither, Katie. You'd wake up with your husband."

"Since that won't happen, let's go see your aunt. I'm hungry."

Hawk released her, stood, and helped her to her feet. "Aye, the first rule for a new wife is to stay busy." He grinned. "In her man's arms, if possible. Making his life comfortable comes second."

When she was dressed, he strode in front of her to his aunt's tipi, his breechclout brushing his legs as he walked.

The old woman's name rolled easily off his tongue. "Pia. Mother, I bring my wife to learn the ways of the People. Will you teach her?"

"Does she want to learn?" Her tired eyes moved to his face. "She is white. She will dislike Indian woman's work."

Hawk nudged Kate closer, an arm around her waist. "She is hungry, Mother."

The old woman nodded and looked down at the cornmeal mush she shaped into bread. "She will work then."

"Teach her to prepare food. Then show her to make soft a buffalo hide. The things women know." A quick glance told him Kate paid attention, her eyes going from Pia's face to his. "My wife is smart, Mother. She will learn quickly."

A hint of amusement appeared briefly in the old woman's eyes. "A frog jumps when prodded."

Inwardly Hawk winced at the comparison. "Teach her, Mother. Before I leave to ride north, I'll kill a deer and leave it at your tipi."

Velda Sherrod

Pia finished shaping the cornmeal and stood. "I will teach her the proper way to tan the hide. Come now, and we'll eat."

Later, after leaving his aunt's tipi, he guided Kate toward the stream. "When you have a problem she will help you." He bent and cupped his hand. "The water is sweet and clear from a spring. By the time the stream stretches a hundred miles, it has grown many times this size. You can bathe here when you like. No one will harm you."

Kate's reaction surprised him. "Hawk," she whispered, her voice perilously close to tears. "The women hate me. You've forgotten how they kicked and pinched me yesterday when I was forced into their camp. They'll kill me when you're gone."

"Your status has changed, Kate. You're wife to the chief's grandson. Stone Wolf would not let anything happen to you."

They spent the afternoon going from one task to another. "You must learn to start a fire. The nights are cold, especially when you sleep alone. Did you notice how the tipi became cool before I added wood to the flame? Perhaps not," he said, wrinkling his brow in thought. "You were snug against me." He leaned over and kissed the nape of her neck, once more the glib Irishman. "I kept you warm."

She remembered those words when she woke that night, shivering. The cold crept in like a ghostly breath and turned her hands and feet to ice. Chill bumps rose on her skin. Hawk said he had kept her warm the night before. She'd give him another opportunity tonight, when she could stop her teeth from chattering. She inched over until her body touched his. It was like backing up to a furnace, she mused contentedly. A moment later a thought spun giddily through her head: what if he became aroused? How would he behave? Could she stop him? Speculation lent a fuzzy feeling to the middle of her stomach—and other places. He didn't move, and she drifted into sleep. When she awoke, she was snuggled in his arms, his breath against her cheek.

Cautiously she peeped out beneath slitted eyelids. Cozy. She should slide away, but she was too comfortable to do it. A slight movement behind her said he was awake. She started to rise, but he had other ideas. Holding her gently, he whispered near her ear, "Good morning, darlin'. And would you be wantin' a kiss before breakfast?"

"I'd prefer coffee."

"No coffee, Katie, but 'tis a fine morning. My arms wrapped around a beautiful Irish lass, her body snug against mine. Gives me pleasant imaginings to go with last night's dreams."

She didn't move when he brushed a hand carelessly over her breast. "Do we have grasshoppers and duck eggs for the morning meal?"

"No grasshoppers, lass. Unless you really want them." He rose above her, laughter alive in his eyes. "Do you?"

"Of course not, you . . . Indian."

He toyed with her hair, watching a curl wrap around his finger. "Hatred is ugly. So is bigotry, my Kate."

Kate flounced over to her stomach and stared into his face. "I'm not a bigot. Indians killed my father. Indians drove me through mesquite, yucca, and cactus. Indians refused me even a drink of water. That's just what they've done to me. You think I should love them?"

"In time, perhaps. But make love with only one." He laughed and tweaked the end of her nose. "A dream of mine, but I've a notion 'tis not to be. At least not this morning."

"Then we're back to breakfast."

He tossed away the buffalo skin that covered them. "I'll be leaving soon. There's much to be done today. We'll eat; then you'll spend time with Pia. I call her Mother at times. At others, Pia. She's actually my aunt but I think of her as a mother. In between the two, I think."

It was mortifying not knowing anything and being told what to do, she thought grumpily, but she couldn't help but be impressed with his regard for his aunt. "You could take me home and give the old woman a rest. She'll hate teaching me as much as I'll hate doing it."

"She has no daughter. Her children and husband were killed by the Cheyenne."

Kate sucked in her breath. "How horrible to lose everybody in your family. I'm sorry," she mumbled.

"You can help her at the same time she helps you. It works best that way, my Kate."

Possibly, she thought despondently, unless it was by an Indian woman, in an Indian camp, buried in a canyon. They maneuvered through the tipis to where Pia worked outside her home tending a fire. The meeting was much like the previous day's exchange. They dipped into a pot and called it breakfast, then walked out into the sunshine and met a cool and gusty headwind.

"Mother, I'll ride out for the deer," Grayhawk told the woman.

Pia answered by nodding, her eyes directed to an old cottonwood where a rabbitskin lay stretched on the ground. "No deer, maybe antelope."

Grayhawk smiled at Kate. "I have a wife but no horse. Grandfather has lent me an Appaloosa until I can get horses of my own." He gripped her shoulders lightly. "It will not take much time to find antelope, lass. Deer a little longer." With that parting word, he broke into a loping run toward horses grazing half a mile away. A few moments later, and with considerable misgivings, Kate watched him ride out of camp, his long legs dangling on either side of a spirited stallion.

When she turned back, Pia handed her a scraper, a piece of flint made sharp by much use. She pointed a clawlike finger at the hide and motioned for Kate to begin. It didn't require much imagination to know what she was to do with the rock.

"All right, Mrs. Pia, since I have nothing better to do for a while." The old woman didn't glance at her. "I'm a singer. Or was. My employer wanted more than songs, so I departed as fast as Barney, my horse, could take me—right into a party of Comanche braves. A couple of nights ago you held a howling powwow just for my benefit, and I went home with a half-breed. Now I'm employed as an apprentice hide tanner. Just between us women, life's full of surprises."

Pia grunted without looking up. She continued her vigorous scraping until Kate was sure the old woman's arm would fall off. Her own back hurt, her hand cramped, and she was sick to death of the smelly rabbitskin. She glanced around the camp, at the women busy at tasks similar to hers, caring for their children, watching boiling pots, carrying wood, while their men stalked around doing nothing. Absolutely nothing. The braves nodded to one another, pointed, sometimes talked loudly; some slept or leaned against any available tree.

Fear tingled up her spine when she saw Little Crow eyeing her from his place in a circle of men. She threw a sidelong look at Pia and met the old woman's careful scrutiny. A slight shake of her head was all Kate needed to keep her eyes on her task.

After a while she sat back on her heels and pointed to herself. "Kate." She pointed at the old woman and raised a questioning brow. "You? What are you called?" She knew the older woman's name from Grayhawk, but could think of no better way to establish some means of communication.

Pia placed a stubby finger against her own chest. "Pia."

Smiling that they'd made some progress, Kate repeated after her: "Pia."

Pia returned the smile, exposing missing teeth. "Kite."

"Close enough, Pia."

The rest of the afternoon they learned to know each other. When she thought Pia was not looking, Kate glanced in the direction Hawk had taken. Nervous that he wouldn't be back when night came, she scanned the path out of the camp more and more often as the day progressed.

Her eyes alight with humor, Pia spoke softly. "Kite." She mumbled several words in her own tongue, rocked in the manner of riding a horse, then waved toward the afternoon sun. Slowly she lowered her arm toward the horizon.

Kate puzzled over the old woman's actions. "Hawk will be back soon?"

The old woman had gone back to her task and did not act as though she'd heard. Moments later, Hawk rode into the village, a deer thrown across his horse's rump. The animal had been gutted. Hawk let it slide to the ground before dismounting.

"The deer I promised, Pia." He did not look at Kate. "It's yours now."

"My son remembers well. His mother would be proud."

Velda Sherrod

Hawk spoke in his mother's tongue, the guttural sounds coming easily from his throat. "I honor my mother's sister for troubling herself with teaching the way of an Indian woman to this homely white woman."

Pia barely nodded, her gaze going to Kate. "She works hard, but she is clumsy yet." For a moment, amusement lit her face. "She will be prettier when she isn't so clumsy."

"I ask the patience of one who is old and wise."

She shrugged. "Bring your wife back in the morning."

"Thank you, Mother."

Kate looked up from her place beside the skin. "I've got blisters from raking that hide scraper all day. What did Pia say about me?"

"She says you watch for my arrival." Shadows smudged the ivory skin beneath her eyes. Her fascinating mouth, curved to fit with a man's, drooped at the corners. When she didn't explode in Irish fury, he tried again. Anything was better than the despair in her eyes. "You're pretty, Kate, even when you're dirty and smell like a dead rabbit."

She didn't disappoint him. "Bloody hell. I haven't spent the afternoon at tea."

His gaze caressed her fascinating mouth. "Let's bathe in the stream," he said soothingly. "I'm covered in dirt and blood."

"Like most Indians."

"Deer blood." Her often-repeated disparaging references to Indians, mostly to him and the Comanche, disturbed him. "I killed the deer so Pia would have food. And," he added slyly, "so you'd have something to do tomorrow."

"Oh, you . . . I wish you had to clean and tan that detestable hide."

"Woman's work," he said grandly, thumping his chest. "Comanche brave kill deer. Feed hungry belly." He chuckled. "For now, let's go bathe in the stream."

Her lips formed a narrow line, but she nodded and started out ahead of him.

He chose a spot downstream, secluded and deep enough to submerge in. Soapweed grew handily along the bank. "We won't be bothered here."

"I'm not undressing in front of you and the whole camp."

"Kate, darlin'," he said, using all his Irish charm to coax her, "nobody will see us. As for me, I know every inch of that lovely little body."

She scrunched up her mouth, but the ire had gone out of her words. "Makes no difference to me if you've memorized the freckles on my shoulders; turn around while I take off my clothes."

"Aye, Katie, there's nothing to bring to memory but skin smooth as satin and the color of ivory. Makes a man's mouth water just to run his hands over it."

She made a twirling motion with her hand. "Around, please."

Dutifully he turned his back to her. "A husband has the right to look at his wife when she bathes."

"I'm not your wife, but we won't argue. The water is wonderful."

Hawk shed his clothes quickly and belly flopped into the water, splattering her face and hair. "During the winter, when ice forms, it gets a little cold."

Her hands came up to push her damp hair out of her face. "You don't really go in the water then?"

He squelched the impulse to gather her slick body into his arms and kiss her until she begged for mercy—or something more he was prepared to give her. "It's true. Bathing becomes less important then. Probably the reason we have a certain smell about us. But you'll get used to it."

Kate drew a quick breath before she caught on that he was teasing. "Pia wouldn't be pleased if she could hear you," she said archly. "She'd probably say you were thinking like a white eyes."

"Pia knows that when a man and a woman are sparring, no matter their color, that they'll spit and hiss and wrestle, but eventually they'll close the tipi flap and love each other crazy." He ran a finger over the swell of her breast. "Like we'll be doing, my Kate."

He hoped she'd melt into his arms. When her lids grew heavy, he congratulated himself that she was experiencing desire equal to his. Instead she smiled provocatively. "Unless you don't mind losing, I wouldn't gamble on it."

He gambled. His hand closed gently over her breast. His thumb caressed the peak, and he was pleased when it became hard. He took a chance and covered her mouth with his. "Katie, Katie," he whispered, drawing her against him. "Oh, my Kate, we'll be good tonight." With his lips pressed against hers, he deepened the kiss and tossed caution to the wind. "Come back to the tipi," he whispered huskily.

She caught him unaware, her knee to his groin.

He was thankful she wasn't tall enough to do much damage, glad the water lessened the blow, but he saw no reason not to grasp the opportunity to gain sympathy. He'd even mix in a little guilt.

He clutched himself and gasped, then moaned and blinked several times to show he was wounded. "Lass, would you un-man me?" he said in a groan. Rewarded by the pained look in her eyes, he leaned against her and put an arm around her shoulders. "Now I must ask for help to the tipi, darlin'."

"I'll put on my clothes," she said uncertainly. She frowned and urged him toward the shore. "Could you lie down on the bank? I didn't really mean to hit you so hard."

"Aye, lass. I can rest a bit while you dress."

As she quickly donned her clothes, he eased his breechclout on to cover himself, then, with his arm around her, limped toward the tipi. He stumbled once, his hand sliding up under her breast. When she didn't resist, he waited until they reached the entrance of the tipi before slumping against her. He managed to close his hand possessively over her breast.

Startled, she threw him a suspicious glance. "You can lie down now."

"Aye." He lay down on the floor and half closed his eyes. "Would you bring me a drink of water, Katie? Perhaps lie with me a bit?"

"Of course." She dipped the hollowed-out gourd in the stone basin. Turning, she knelt down beside him and dashed the water in his face.

"Mercy, Kate," he said, sitting up quickly, spluttering and wiping the water out of his face. "Now you'd be for drowning me."

She had her hands on her hips. "You lying renegade. I didn't hurt you that badly."

"But you could have, my Kate," he said whimsically. "You didn't really want to hurt your man, now, did you?"

"My man, yet."

"And who else's, I should wonder?" He inched closer until she had to look up to see his face. "I'm going to kiss you, darlin'. Could you forgive me long enough to cooperate?"

When he pulled her to him and fitted her body to his, her eyes grew large and a flutter pulsed at her throat.

"Look, Hawk." Speaking in little nervous phrases, she braced herself against his chest. "I don't know whether I hurt you or not. I'm ignorant of these things. But I'm not . . . you're not my—"

He didn't let her finish. He cradled her face, and words soft as summer rain rolled off his tongue. "Katie, darlin'," he whispered, "would you be denying a kiss to a starving man?"

Before she could answer, a shout drove him back to earth.

Chapter Six

Hawk moved easily to the entrance of the tipi, listened, then mouthed, "I'll be back." When Kate started to speak, he shushed her with a shake of his head. When she frowned, he was back at her side. "I doubt it's serious, lass, so don't be afraid. Don't go outside."

She leaned close to him so that she touched him, and her eyes went to his face. "But what if something terrible happens? To you?"

He touched her hair and smoothed it. "I like having you worry about me. But you must stay here and be quiet."

"Oh, fiddle. I'm going with you."

Before her eyes, his face changed to stone. His hard hands closed around her wrists. After a moment of tension, he eased her away, his eyes seeking and holding hers. "You will do as I say," he said, and went out the door.

Tonight she'd learned there was a point where he was invulnerable, where her charms fell short of persuasion. Never before had she realized how much a part of him was Indian. When he spoke the low, guttural language of the Comanche, he adopted the mannerisms of his people. When he spoke English, she could expect the Irishman, charming and teasing his way into her heart . . . into people's hearts.

She ran a shaky hand through her hair. She didn't debate whether to follow him or stay in the tipi and hide. She had only one choice: to crawl under the buffalo rug and pray he didn't get an arrow to the chest. With her luck, she'd follow him outside and some brave would mistake her for the enemy and ricochet a tomahawk off her back.

So far she'd heard nothing. Then loud voices broke the silence. Horses snorted and stamped, and above it all she heard Hawk's voice rising and falling. Shortly after, there was the sound of retreating hooves. She sat on the floor, wrapped in the buffalo rug, and waited and worried, absently working to free her hair from its braid.

Hawk appeared quietly, stopping at the entrance to look down at her. "A scout brought news of a sortie several miles north of the camp. It looks as though the troops are now headed away from us. It is nothing to worry about, unless they change their minds and come back this way. We'll stay ready." With the grace of a cat, he sank down beside her and grinned. "Now where were we?"

Inadvertently, he had shown her a way, given her an opportunity to go back to her own people. At the same time, something inside her quivered at the thought that she'd never see Hawk again. "You could take me to the soldiers, and I could get back to civilization."

"No." He looked tired and disappointed. "You're safer here than you'd be with a bunch of soldiers."

Kate wondered if he spoke the truth, or if his bias was showing. She'd heard tales of soldiers being callous toward women, but suspected the women were of loose virtue. "I've never heard of a decent white woman being assaulted by a soldier."

"You're not white anymore, Katie."

"What?"

"You're Indian. Comanche."

"No, no, no. You're wrong. I'm a white woman from Missouri."

Sadness clouded his eyes. " 'Tis late, lass. Better we leave discussion till morning."

Would the soldiers treat her badly, as Hawk seemed to think? After her experience with Boggs, she found herself more apt to believe Hawk's words. Besides, she realized with surprise, she trusted Hawk. He would not let anything bad happen to her if he could help it. "I suppose the camp has gone back to sleep."

"Aye, it's time for us to do the same." He lay down and opened his arms. "Come, Kate, the wind is blowing hard. I promise I'll keep you warm."

"I'll bet," she said, and her pulse fluttered, as it always seemed to do when he used that tone.

Turning away from him, she took off her dress, folded it, and placed it near. A surreptitious glance told her Hawk's eyes were closed, so she lay down in her camisole and drawers. They were torn and frayed, held together by strings stripped from a cactus. What would she do when the pitiful garments were no longer wearable?

Her thoughts were interrupted when he turned to his side, propped his head on his elbow, and eyed her speculatively. "After we're lovers, my Kate—not that we aren't already— you'll have to get rid of those . . . those . . . undergarment things."

"The undergarment things stay on. And we aren't lovers, nor are we going to be lovers," she said matter-of-factly.

"Aye, lass," he said, his voice serious, "it's wanting me, you are. Sooner or later you'll admit it."

"What is this? Indian fortune-telling?"

"I'm Irish as well, and we lads from the green isle feel pain when our womenfolk speak so. After all, you and I have known pleasure in each other's arms." He muttered something in his mother's tongue.

"What did you say?"

He leaned forward and kissed the cleavage between her breasts. "I said we'll know it again."

Kate waited for her heart to settle back to its normal rhythm. "You're terribly sure."

"Aye. Tonight would be a fine time to begin." He touched

his lips to hers, brushed them in a teasing kiss. "You see. You like what I'm doing. And you'll like it more as we go along." One instant he was tender, cajoling, murmuring endearments; then in a lightning flash he captured her mouth.

The jolt hit with a wallop. Sinking into the kiss, she wound her arms around his neck. After a while she sighed. "No more."

He shrugged and turned his back. "Should you change your mind, Kate, darlin', it will be all right if you wake me."

She mumbled under her breath, "Highly unlikely." She was tempted to move closer, to touch him, feel his warmth, but if he was still awake, he'd think she wanted to begin again. And she wasn't sure she'd want to stop him.

She closed her eyes and went over the tasks awaiting her in the morning. Carrying wood. Hauling water. Scraping hides. On and on. She yawned. Why didn't the women rebel? Tell the men they could do the backbreaking work themselves?

White women worked as hard. Washing, ironing, cooking, gardening, caring for children—the list was endless. They must care a lot for their husbands. Was it the same for Indian women?

Hawk woke her the next morning with a tiny kiss. When she didn't respond, he rolled her to her back and kissed her noisily. Several seconds passed before she remembered to push him away. He didn't move very far. His eyes were warm, reminding her that he knew how she felt, and that he felt the same.

"It's morning, you . . . you savage." He had an incredible mouth. "Time to get up."

His lips curved slowly, enticingly. "Time to make love, Katie, lass. And 'tis a fine way to begin a morning."

God forbid. She really wanted to. "I wouldn't know."

He kissed the end of her nose. "Your words pain me more than you realize, for I know it's truth you speak. But someday you'll know a different truth." He grinned and rolled to his feet. "I plan to be there when that happens."

"Humph." She needed to think beyond the fascination of gazing at his body, naked as the day he was born. She kept her

107

eyes above his waist and shook her head at his absurd lack of modesty.

"Does my nakedness bother you?"

The man could read her mind. "I don't have to look, so why should it?"

His grin erupted into a chuckle. "Oh, my Kate. I never miss a chance to look at you." He leaned over and kissed her ear. "Your nakedness bothers me overmuch."

She refused to argue the merits of propriety over indulgence. Especially when she knew he was teasing her, easing her toward blurting out her true feelings in a moment of pique.

"I admit that your nudity makes me uncomfortable."

"Good." He went about dressing in long deerskin pants and moccasins. "We're even. In the meantime, I'll be out today with the braves. The scouts found buffalo near the canyon rim."

In the days that followed she saw little of him, except when he arrived at night too tired to do little besides eat and sleep. With legs bare to the thigh, young women rode in behind the hunters, the slaughtered buffalo on travois. Hawk told her there'd soon be a big feast.

He took one animal to Pia. The hide he presented to Kate. "The great buffalo hunter has returned, fair Kate, and brought you a fine skin. 'Tis for tanning." He smiled broadly. "I know your heart is glad."

She made no effort to hide her distaste. He teased her, knowing how she loathed animal skins. "I'm sure you know what's in my heart. I hate the damn—" She bit her tongue. "I dislike buffalo. Their skins are so big."

"Then tonight," he said gallantly, "I shall bring a rabbit."

With an occasional trip for water to break the monotony, Kate divided her time between carrying wood and scraping at a skin. Pia's occasional grunts and nods encouraged her to keep on; besides, she didn't know what she'd do if she weren't busy. Idleness would be unbearable.

At the end of the week Hawk told her good-bye, and she recognized his reluctance. No smile warmed his eyes, only a sadness at leaving. "I must go, my Kate. A week, possibly longer. Ten days, even two weeks. You will stay with Pia in her tipi. If you need anything, speak to Stone Wolf."

"We don't communicate."

He didn't try to hide his irritation. "Damn it, Kate. Try to talk with him. Use the same means you use to communicate with Pia."

The quaking inside her began again. It wasn't that she was afraid of the chief. After all, she had been joined to his grandson, was his wife, and by Comanche law belonged to him. But with Stone Wolf her innermost thoughts were exposed. He could see into her heart, where she wrestled with the truth that she had begun to care for Hawk. "Where are you going?"

"I've business north."

"I'll bet," she scoffed, trying hard to hide her dismay. "What business north . . . you aren't going to join in a raid somewhere?"

"Nay, lass, you know I would never do that. 'Tis truth you're hearing. And important." His voice became at once cajoling and tender. "Do you think I would leave such a lovely colleen for even one night if I had a choice?"

" 'Tis blarney I'm hearing," she mimicked without being conscious she'd done so. "Why can't you take me home?"

"In time, darlin'."

She didn't want to appear too anxious, too eager for his return, but the words were out before she could stop them. "What if you don't come back?"

"I'll be back." He grasped her shoulders and pulled her rigid body to him. "Nothing, Katie, absolutely nothing can keep me away. Remember, don't go far from camp, and leave only if Pia is with you."

His words ringing in her ears, she watched him ride away. "But what will happen to me if you don't come back?" she whispered.

Seeing him leave left her dry-mouthed and frightened. She reminded herself that she had only to participate in the daily workings of the camp, the simple chores relegated to the women. But she couldn't ignore the undercurrent of suspicion directed toward her by the women, and even more so by the men, most noticeably by that horrible Little Crow.

Hawk rode upward toward the rim of the canyon, winding through evergreens and sagebrush. Misgivings mixed with his gloom. He hadn't had the heart to tell Kate that Little Crow had asked that she visit his tipi. Little Crow had reminded him that they were blood brothers, that brothers shared their wives. "Brother loves brother," Little Crow had reasoned. "A brother knows that if his brother dies, nobody takes his place. He gives his brother what he can. A brother lends his wife. A gift. When braves go raid, it is the same. A brother can sleep with a wife. It is the Comanche way, brother."

"She wouldn't understand," Hawk had argued. "Whites don't share wives."

Little Crow touched his chest with his fist. "We are Comanche. If you were killed in battle, I would take her. She would be a favored wife. She would have her own tipi. She would not have to work hard." Little Crow held up two fingers. "I have two chore wives to do the hard work."

Hawk used his most persuasive voice. "I'm convinced my blood brother will honor my wishes."

"Perhaps my brother will change his mind and send his wife while he is away." At Grayhawk's negative answer, Little Crow strode away, muttering an insult common to Comanche men: "How many enemies have you hidden from?"

The concept of sharing Kate brought Hawk's blood to full boil. If she were provoked, she'd find a way to stick a knife in Little Crow's heart, a thought that lightened his spirits somewhat. He'd done all he could to make her safe—warned her not to take chances, like going too far from camp, admonished her to remain close to Pia and Stone Wolf. He did not think she would contemplate running away. He had tried to make sure she understood that if she were caught attempting to escape she'd be beaten, tied to a tree, and starved until he returned. It worried him that in his absence he would be unable to protect her better.

Her courage and humor and passion had convinced him

he'd found the right woman. For the rest of his life, he wanted her beside him, loving him.

His lie to his grandfather disturbed him. He had told Stone Wolf that Kate was pregnant. A Comanche woman was not prolific, usually birthing no more than two babies, rarely three or four. Highly prized, the coming of a child brought rejoicing to the tribe, and he knew Stone Wolf looked forward to the birth of a great-grandchild. A boy, preferably, but a girl would also be cherished.

What a kettle of fish. To keep faith with his grandfather, he had to seduce Kate. So far Kate didn't have a problem saying no. Reluctantly he put the possibility of making love with her out of his mind.

He turned his thoughts to the meeting with the colonel. A day and a half separated him from the place he and the colonel had agreed on, each traveling an equal distance: Dusty Flats, a tough little town where a few stores and a saloon tried to meet the needs of the cowboys, ranchers, outlaws, and riffraff from everywhere. He and the colonel had chosen well. Neither of them would be known.

Sadly, the wagon train massacre would have to be discussed. Unsure of how the old soldier would react, Hawk debated telling the colonel about finding Cole and Afton. Was there some rigid law the colonel would have to follow in resolving the problem of a white child—a girl at that—being the responsibility of a black man? Most Yanks—to say nothing of Southerners—would find the situation intolerable.

Another problem gnawed at him. When could he take Kate from the camp? Where should he take her? To his ranch? He told himself she was becoming more attached to him. His touch was becoming important to her, especially if she were caught off guard. Whatever her resistance to their union, he fully intended to wear down her objections.

The last time he'd kissed her, he realized something was not quite as it had been, that they were closer to bedrock emotions. His Comanche pride had led him back to his mother's tribe. It was the luck of the Irish that had led him to Kate.

Hawk turned his attention to the present, the ride before him, boring only to the indifferent and uninitiated. Sagebrush had colored the prairies purple, a sign of rain, old-timers said. He glanced up. Not a cloud in the sky.

Evergreen dotted the landscape like stiff, lonely sentinels. Occasionally he spotted an old pronghorn leading his harem to a different grazing ground. When the antelopes saw him, they bounded away on their matchstick legs. Further on he interrupted a rattler warming in the sun, but before the diamondback could coil, Midnight shied away.

"Glad you're watching out for us, laddie. A man gets careless with so much open space."

He wasn't bothered by the solitude. In fact, the quiet provided time to sort out his thoughts, make some decisions. At a secluded spot he changed clothes, becoming once more the glib and laughing Irishman, Sean O'Brien from the Emerald Isle. At a hidden recess between two great boulders, he tore aside tumbleweeds to uncover his saddle.

Once more a white man, he rode into Dusty Flats, and like any tired and parched cowboy he headed straight for Maggie's Saloon. He swung his leg over the saddle horn and dropped to the ground. Inside, he clunked his way to the bar, his spurs keeping time with each step. "Whiskey, friend barmaster. I've a dry mouth and a big thirst."

The bartender nodded. "Whiskey comin' up."

Sean glanced at the broad mirror behind the bar, spotted the colonel, and gave a slight nod. He hooked a foot over the boot rail and picked up his drink. "Good barmaster, here's to all the Irish in this fair land."

"Gittin' to be a lot of 'em. Big drinkers, too."

"Aye, sir. Some are great drinkers and take pride in it."

Unprepared for the colonel's elbow jab, Sean watched his glass spill whiskey over the bar. He shook his head irritably. "In this saloon, it seems a man with a thirst is apt to stay that way."

"Pardon me, cowboy. Didn't mean to interfere with a tired man's drink."

Sean looked him over scornfully, beginning with the colonel's head and slowly moving down to his feet. "Aye, pardon accepted. Never been one to argue with the military."

As if searching for a particular person, the colonel turned to look behind him. "I've a meeting scheduled, but I'd like to buy you a drink for the one I spilled."

Leaning his elbows on the bar, Sean nodded to the bartender. "Make it a double, lad."

The colonel signaled the bartender to hand him a bottle. "Might as well sit while we get acquainted."

They chose a corner table, and the colonel placed the bottle in the center. He kicked a chair back and sat down. The colonel lowered his voice. "Anything happening?"

"Aye, and it's bad. A war party attacked a wagon train. Killed everybody. Guess you know that, though."

"I heard." The colonel filled their glasses. "Had my men look into it. Forty-three people, including the babies."

Sean felt the old sick feeling that always followed when he heard of some heinous crime committed by his people. Red or white, it was all the same. His voice was low and harsh. "Stone Wolf says his braves didn't attack the train."

"Doesn't matter to people hereabouts. One Indian's the same as another." The colonel tossed back his drink. "The military's mad. Somebody got into the army's horses. Took most of them. Hell of it was, nobody heard a thing. Major Jeffers is mad enough to take on the whole Indian nation."

Without meeting the colonels' eyes, Sean nodded. A man couldn't keep from admiring an Indian's skill in adding another man's horses to his own herd. "Indians like horses."

"A fracas went on at Adobe Walls recently. Quanah and his braves got into some kind of a struggle with a few cowboys. The cowboys got lucky. Nobody was killed, and Quanah had to retreat, unusual for him."

Sean shook his head and sighed. Quanah Parker was another half-breed like himself. His mother, Cynthia Ann Parker, had been stolen by the Kwahadi band under Naconi. She grew up and Naconi made her his wife. Now, their son, Quanah was giving the whites a fit. Whether Quanah or another chief, it was always the same. The Indians made trouble, followed by reprisals by the whites. The next time the reverse would be true; it was a vicious cycle.

"At present, Stone Wolf has his braves under control, but I don't know how long that will last, sir. If the whites could hold off for a while, see that the two peoples could work things out, something might come of our plan."

"We won't give up on peace, Sean. Trust me. As long as I have a say, we'll keep trying. But the wagon train massacre, everybody killed . . ." The colonel studied his drink. "Doesn't help, Sean."

After some thought, Sean made up his mind to take the colonel into his confidence. "Not everybody died. A black man and a white girl child escaped. They hid in a salt cedar grove. Colonel, if the news gets out it will be a shame. A black man and a white girl together. Sure as there's a blarney stone, Cole, the Negro would get strung up to a cottonwood. I don't know what would happen to the girl."

The colonel gave the unusual situation some thought. "Well, we've got Lincoln's Proclamation that says Negroes aren't slaves anymore. How do these two get along together?"

"The girl's about nine years old. She claims him for a slave. Seems her daddy gave him to her. Cole doesn't seem to mind and is devoted to her."

The colonel gave a negative shake of his head. "About the time you think you've heard it all, something else comes up. Where are they now?"

"At my ranch. Where they'll stay, I suppose, until something better comes along."

After sipping his drink, the colonel summed it up neatly: "Unlikely, son. Folks may have a guilty conscience where slavery's concerned, but they don't necessarily want the races mixing."

The same could not be said for Indians. The Comanche freely took what they wanted, including women and children. Some captives a brave kept for himself, to act as a wife, a slave, or sometimes even a son. He sold the ones he didn't want; race figured very little in the decision. "You're right, Colonel. And Cole is aware of this situation."

"Does your grandfather still think there's a chance for peace between the Comanche and the whites?"

"I can't say, sir. But my grandfather is an honorable man. He'll keep his word."

"People in Tascosa want the military to handle the Indians. Nathan Boggs, the saloon owner, is stirring up trouble. He's whipping up the hotheads. Tells them to shoot every Indian on sight. Funny thing, though—he never mentions joining in or leading a posse."

"Stone Wolf says his people didn't attack the train."

"Boggs has done a good job convincing people that the only good Indian is a dead Indian."

Sean adjusted his cap. " 'Tis a feeling I have that Boggs wants to keep people stirred up to cover his own tracks."

"Yes, but so far we don't have proof."

"Sooner or later, Colonel, we'll have proof."

"You're right, son. In the meantime, Boggs is wrecking our plan." The colonel poured himself another drink. "I've set some things in motion. Like getting Louella to speak a good word at her teas and church. My wife's good at that. I told her we've got to get along with the Indians or an awful lot of people are going to die."

"I've been mapping a route to take me around the panhandle. I'll be doing the same as Louella, only at saloons and taverns." He laughed. "Comanche women don't have teas."

"We'll have to see if Louella makes progress."

"Sir, whites sneer at Indians. Indians scorn whites. Each side hates the other. I wonder if time is the only thing that will settle the problem."

The colonel leaned back in his chair. "Won't hurt to hurry it along," he said mildly. "Do your best to keep Stone Wolf's band out of trouble. And you'd better keep the black man and the child for a while, or I'm afraid we'll be adding the Negro to the casualty count."

"I'll do that."

The colonel finished his whiskey, then stood and held out his hand. "Have a safe trip, cowboy. Glad to have met you." Under his breath, he muttered, "Stone Wolf. That old man's the

115

only hope we have in this area. See if you can get him to influence Quanah."

After the colonel went back to the bar, Sean mulled over their words. Where did the whites plan to begin their annihilation of the Indians? Was the whole area becoming involved? He studied the people in the saloon. One way to get information was to question a whore. For some reason, men opened up to a whore.

Putting on a wide smile, Sean sidled over to one of the more intelligent-looking saloon girls. " 'Tis a nice night. On such a night, a cowboy just naturally wants to spend some time with a comely colleen," he said, and added with a wink, "such as yourself."

"What does that mean?" She eyed him suspiciously. "You said I was comely."

"Aye. The word means pretty."

The girl giggled. "And that's me?"

He was glad his Kate was not present. She'd never have understood that he was only gathering information. And he surely would not appreciate having to explain that he had selected the youngest whore and, in his opinion, the least jaded. Some might say she was the prettiest.

"Come sit at my table." When he had her seated, he poured whiskey into a glass and handed it to her. "Now, pretty colleen, tell me about yourself. I've a hunger to hear you speak."

She tossed back the drink and held out her glass for a refill. "My name is Jewel. Mama said when I was born, I was a perfect little gem."

"Sure, and I can see that. The men here must think the same."

She giggled. "Yeah, they like me. To tell the truth, more men ask for me. Makes the other girls mad."

"Jealous, don't you imagine," Sean said, encouraging her.

"Sure they're just jealous. But I guess I am prettier. . . . I'm not braggin', you understand. It's just a fact. Anybody can see that. Why, the other night a gentleman come in. He wanted a girl. The best-lookin' one, he said." Waving her drink, she preened a bit, sloshing her whiskey in the process. "He chose me. And he had money, that guy did. Give me a lot more than I usually get."

"Is that so?" Sean was glad the girl didn't seem reluctant to talk. "Have any Indians come to your . . . uh . . . couch?"

Jewel threw back her head and gave a loud, raucous laugh. "If a Indian walked in here, somebody would take off his dirty scalp."

"There's talk then?"

"One of my regulars said some men was forming . . ." She hiccuped, daintily covering her mouth. "He said people was getting fed up with the damned redskins. He thinks we ought to kill them."

Sean lifted his glass to hide his distaste. "Does he now?"

"He said," she whispered conspiratorially, "that men all over the place were fixing to kill 'em all."

Sean felt his heart sink to his boots. "But what if most of the Indians are peaceful?"

"No such animal." She waggled a finger, her eyes narrowing. "They want to kill us, so we're going to kill them. We'll show 'em. That's what Jim . . . Forget I called his name. A woman in my profession has to be careful not to give names of the men she"—she struggled to find the correct word—"she entertains."

"I understand, Jewel. Your profession calls for secrecy. I'll not mention it." He gave her an admiring look. "And I'm sure your customers appreciate that about you, that you don't bandy their words about."

Jewel frowned in concentration. "I ain't acquainted with that word. Bandy."

"You don't gossip."

"Oh, no. That's what I told Jim. I ain't no gossip."

"Did Jim—"

"I told you not to mention his name."

"There're lots of Jims, Jewel," he said mildly. "Where does Jim think this battle with Indians will start? Here in Dusty Flats?"

"Yeah, and Tascosa."

Sean emptied the bottle into her glass. "Where else?"

"Boggy Creek. Somebody said they had a massacre up there and folks was really, really mad."

After telling Jewel good-bye, Sean rode out of Dusty Flats as night was falling, waiting until he was some distance away before urging his horse into a gallop. Kate. He had to make sure she was safe. If the disgruntled whites found the camp and rode in with their guns blazing, they'd be blind to a white woman. They wouldn't know her from an Indian woman. And they wouldn't care as long as she was living among the Indians.

Kate knelt by the stretched deerskin and picked up her scraper. It made her back hurt just to look at the smelly hide. Instead she watched the morning sun peek over the canyon rim and streak the cliffs with slashes of sunshine. She was glad that much of the day, she and Pia would work in the shade. She almost groaned aloud as she thought of the backbreaking scraping left to do on the deerskin today. She longed for a change of clothes, a dress she could call her own, not just someone's old castaway.

She and Pia were not yet friends, but they had become more respectful of each other, learning to work together. The old woman had shown her how to shape and cure the hide, mumbling disapproval or encouragement in the same tone of voice. She smiled occasionally and had laughed aloud when Kate slipped and landed on her face. Kate had given her a feeble smile in return and wiped off much of the grease, but the smell had stayed with her, even after she washed in the stream.

Pia came out of her tipi and walked close enough to inspect the deerskin before nodding and saying good morning. She used the word *eat*, a word Kate had taught her, and pointed inside.

Smiling, Kate followed her. She sank to her knees near the small fire bedded in a cluster of rocks, and inhaled. She had learned the contents of the pot by watching Pia prepare it, and her appetite had increased to the point where she could eat as much as her teacher. After she had filled her stomach, she said, "Good," in the ancient woman's tongue, a word Pia had taught her. "Very good," she added in her own language.

"Gude," Pia said, "gude." She bobbed her head. "Bury gude."

"Yes. Very good. Now I'll go to work."

"Wok."

"Sure, why not?" Kate said good-naturedly.

All day, with frequent respite times, they worked at the deerskin. Kate took increasing pride when Pia showed her the process to make the skin soft. Kate did her best to show her gratitude. She used the few words she knew in the Comanche language, and added English words when she struggled.

She worked and sang and soon attracted a few children. As more came, their mothers joined them, sitting expressionless, their babies and small children forming a circle. Kate pretended not to notice, until one small girl, her hair in short braids, came and sat close enough to put out her hand.

Lonely to distraction, Kate laid her scraper aside and gathered the child in her lap. She did the only thing she knew: she sang to entertain—songs from her grandmother, ballads from her father, and a few bawdy songs from the Lily. The children scooted closer, their mothers edging up when they thought she wasn't watching.

Before Kate could begin again, Pia pointed at the deerskin, then shooed the audience away. "Wok," she said, and took up the scraper tool.

Soon the song session became a morning ritual, and with it Kate earned the women's bashful smiles and the children's exuberant laughter. A few days later, upon returning to her tipi after breakfast Kate found a pair of doeskin moccasins, buttery soft and fringed, placed at the entrance to her tipi. She had no idea who might have placed them there, as following Hawk's instructions, she spent the nights with Pia. Unable to resist their appealing comfort, though, she slipped on the beautifully made footwear, taking them off only at night to sleep. She did not allow herself to consider how she felt about accepting gifts from Indians.

When the deerskin had been completely cleaned and softened, Pia used grunts, gestures, and a few English words to tell Kate that a wife was responsible for her warrior's clothing, as well as her own. Kate should make a garment for Hawk.

Kate's first thought was to let him fend for himself. She'd worked too hard and too long to provide a garment for a man

119

who couldn't make up his mind whether to be Indian or white. But when the time came, she found herself doing as Pia had instructed, cutting, shaping, questioning, until she had fashioned a jacket. Not the neatest, nor the best fit, she supposed, but it earned Pia's approval. She beamed—not very brightly, Kate thought, but it was enough of a beam to keep her going. Occasionally she wondered if Hawk would wear it.

For all her effort, and the progress she'd made, she waited impatiently for him to return. He was her only hope for getting back to civilization. And despite her best intentions, she missed him. Even as she damned him for making her feel lonely, she couldn't help watching the trail leading into the camp, looking up often to scan the rim.

Stone Wolf emerged outside his tipi several times a day, sometimes to smoke, other times to pass words with the men loitering about camp, or to watch them gamble or wrestle. Frequently he stopped to correct a young brave engaged in making a bow. And then there were times she'd look up and there he'd be observing her, his blanket around his shoulders, his hair in two long gray braids tied with pieces of rawhide, hanging on either side of his head.

One day Pia nodded for her to approach him, and Kate dutifully rose to her feet. Hawk had demanded that she respect his grandfather. Now, looking into the ancient face lined with wrinkles, the steady look in his eyes, she understood why. She wrapped her arms around herself to still her trembling hands and met his probing gaze.

Not knowing what else to do, she bowed her head. When she looked up, she saw amusement in his eyes. He pointed toward the trail, turned his head to rest on his palm, and closed his eyes. Then he lifted two fingers.

"Hawk will return." She followed his example by placing her palm against her face and closing her eyes as he had done. She held up two fingers. "In two nights."

Stone Wolf smiled and moved away, paying no further attention to her, and Kate had no choice but to go back to work. At last, she had communicated with someone besides the children and Pia. The women who gathered to hear her sing each morning said nothing to her directly, nor made any attempt to communicate, besides the small smiles in response to her singing. Possibly they were waiting on her.

Tomorrow she'd make an effort. Papa used to say it was better to have the goodwill of a cur than to curse it.

Papa would have been efficient either way. Friendly, if given the chance, willing to help when needed, and more than adequate in cursing a blue streak. She felt the loss of her father anew. It slammed her chest, and once more the old hatred rose to color her cheeks. How could she ever feel anything but the blackest enmity toward these people?

Grayhawk nudged his horse into a lope. He wanted to see for himself if Kate continued to spit at him. How had she gotten along with his aunt? Most of all, he longed to see that she was safe. He had spoken to Stone Wolf about his conversation with Little Crow before he left the camp. His grandfather had smoked his pipe, finally meeting his eye. "It's the Comanche way. A brother cares for a brother. He gives all he has, including his wife, to his brother when he leaves on a mission or to fight an enemy." He puffed on his pipe. "It's not the way of the whites. Your wife carries a baby. Little Crow must leave her alone."

God. There it was again, the need to make love to Kate. He couldn't disappoint his grandfather by revealing that he had lied to him. He couldn't take Kate without her permission. She adamantly refused his advances, and he didn't want her unless she was willing. Such wishful thinking sent a bolt of lust straight to his loins.

By the time he reached the camp, the sun rested comfortably on the horizon. He relaxed in the saddle, letting his horse find its way down the trail to the canyon floor. His arrival caused no stir. He rode in quietly, unsaddled his horse, and slapped it on the rump to send it racing toward the herd, then lugged his equipment to his tipi. He was the only man in camp with a saddle. He'd won it with four sixes in a card game. If he were forced to hurry Kate from the village, they could ride better and faster if she were in a saddle.

The tribe was gathered around a fire; a few warriors danced to a drumbeat. He stepped out of the shadows and sat cross-legged beside Kate, chuckling at her start of recognition. He nudged her and kissed her cheek. "Did you miss me, darlin'?"

"Like I'd miss a case of measles." But she smiled.

"Ah, Katie, love, you make me happy when you look at me so. And 'tis the truth. You've never been away from my thoughts." He leaned closer. "I've a gift for you."

"What is it," she whispered, "a battle-ax?"

"The last thing I'd bring. You could slay the enemy with a look."

"It hasn't worked so far."

"Perhaps you would do as well with that glorious laugh."

Her face became serious. "I've learned to soften hides. I've made friends with the children, and . . ." She threw him a side-long glance. "I have a gift for you."

Tenderness filled his heart. "Ah, my Kate, you did think about me."

"Don't let it go to your head, Savage. It was Pia's suggestion. I'd have used the skin for myself."

He laughed. "Honest Kate. Even when her honesty threatens the pope."

"Pia and I became friends, sort of. At least she didn't pinch me. She taught me to cook. I now know the mysteries of that pot that seems to be always boiling."

"Ah, love, I can hardly wait until you share this knowledge and achievement with me."

"You're laughing at me."

"No, lass, never at you."

His gaze swept the circle of dancers and met Stone Wolf's knowing look. With an almost imperceptible nod, he acknowledged his grandfather's greeting. "Kate, the party may go on for a time yet. If we leave now, they'll never miss us." He rose and helped her to her feet, leading her toward their tipi. "I want to be with you, Katie, darlin', just you and me."

Inside the tipi, he gathered her in his arms. "I've had you on my mind, thinking that when I returned you'd greet me with a kiss." He didn't give her time to answer. "Lie down and I'll help." When they rested on the animal furs, he held her body fitted against his and covered her mouth, his lips brushing over hers, deepening the kiss when she started to respond. His breathing became unsteady, and he roamed his hands over her back, easing upward under her breasts. He could feel her heart pounding against his chest.

"I want you, my Kate," he whispered low in his mother's tongue, mumbling his longings against her mouth. "Like I thirst for water, like my need to breathe." He switched to English. "It was a long trip, Kate. Longer because I was away from you."

"Then why didn't you take me with you?"

He caressed her breast. "I needed to travel fast." He frowned down at her. "Katie, you've never mentioned the Gilded Lily once since you've been here. Did Boggs bother you?"

"He made the situation complicated. I chose to leave on the advice of the piano player. You remember Joe?"

"Aye. What did he tell you?"

"That if I didn't intend to go to bed with Nathan, I should leave town."

"What did he say would happen if you didn't?"

"Joe didn't say much, but he clearly indicated I would be in grave danger if I stayed in town after rejecting Nathan's advances. I got the impression that Boggs is a very dangerous man."

"Aye. He is, lass. I don't want to scare you, but on this last trip I heard rumors that would lead me to believe he barters girls for guns with the Comancheros. Thank God, you got away."

"Out of the frying pan . . ."

"Aye, lass. Into my arms." His mouth grew hungrier. He skimmed his lips over her face and throat. "Kate, love . . ."

"I'm not . . . I can't lie with you, Hawk. I'd be betraying Papa." Her eyes clouded. "You should have seen his body. Burned black."

He sighed in frustration. "But I had nothing to do with that, Kate."

"You're an Indian."

"I can't argue with that." He reached for a package he'd

tossed near their pallet. "Here's the gift. I asked McDougal at the trading post to order boots for you the last time I was there."

She claimed one of the boots, turning it over and over in her hands. "It's been a long time since I've had boots like these. You were nice to think of me."

Nice had nothing to do with it. He'd hoped for a kiss. More than one. "You needed them, and so I brought them."

Throwing her arms around his neck, she pressed her soft mouth on his, started to draw away, but then changed her mind. "Thank you, Hawk."

Startled, he opened his arms to her. On the long ride back she'd filled his mind. He hadn't expected the spontaneous pleasure he'd seen on her face when he sat down beside her at the fire. Now that he had her body warm against his, he wanted to keep her there. "I'll remember to bring a gift every time I return from a trip."

Disappointment darkened her eyes. "Will you be leaving again?"

"Yes, but not tonight, love."

"Oh, I almost forgot. I made this for you." She held up a jacket made of deerskin. "Pia seemed to think I should make a garment for you. She showed me how to treat the animal hide and sew together the different pieces. It was a lot of work, but it is the first coat I have ever made."

He hadn't the heart to tell her that the Comanche viewed the deer as having much power in love affairs. Pia must have laughed when she encouraged Kate to make his jacket. He'd have to thank his aunt with another skin, possibly from a buffalo, to keep her warm during the winter when the wind blew cold from the north. But most assuredly she'd get another deerskin.

"The jacket will keep me warm."

"Will you really wear it, Hawk?"

He cradled her face and kissed her mouth. "Aye, lass, I'll wear it." The gentle kiss grew hungry. No woman had ever affected him the way Kate did; he longed to hold her, make love with her, see her smile. She'd lost weight, he thought dimly, running his hands over her body. "I think you did miss me, darlin'."

She glared at him. "Now, don't go putting words in my mouth. Just because I kissed you to thank you for the gift doesn't mean I'm going to bed with you," she said, adding primly, "if you know what I mean."

He hadn't thought he'd ever long to see anger flash in her eyes, but he'd also forgotten how beautiful she was when something riled her. Laughing, he shook his head. "As much as I want you, I'd never take you for granted."

"Well," she said, somewhat mollified, "as long as you know the rules."

He'd like to take the bloody rules and toss them into the creek. "I know the rules, my Kate," he said wearily, and closed his eyes. "Perhaps it's best we rest."

She responded by snuggling up against him and promptly drifting off to sleep. As tired as he was, Hawk had a harder time relaxing with Kate's body pressed enticingly against his.

When Kate awoke the tipi was warm. A small fire burned low in the rock pit. Hawk stood naked, his magnificent body seeming to fill the tipi completely. Yawning, she stretched her arms above her head. "Why are you up so early? The men I see around the camp do little but lounge around, talking and playing games, when they aren't demanding some woman to wait on them. They're too lazy to work."

He frowned. "You're quick to judge, Katie. The whites have the military who stay ready to fight. When they aren't fighting, they're gambling, tumbling girls, or loafing. Comanche braves do the same. If the camp is attacked they go into action."

"They could bring water from the creek," she argued, "while they're waiting around combing their hair. They take time to paint their faces."

"The military shine their shoes."

"I suppose an Indian would draw that comparison," she said archly.

He drew on his pants and leggings, his muscles bunching when he stepped into his moccasins. "I must see Stone Wolf this morning. Will you be here when I come back?"

"I learned to boil stew meat while you were gone." She slipped her dress over her head. "Pia said, as nearly as I could tell, that she'd teach me which plants to add. Of course, I'll have to go with her to learn where . . ."

"Katie, you're rambling."

"Oh, God, I know. I'm afraid you'll leave again. I have Pia to talk to, but it isn't the same." She blinked back tears. "You've no idea how lonely it gets."

Hawk closed the distance between them, his voice soft and flowing. "Aye, I know. 'Twas a long ride, and I thought of you all the way. I want you, my Kate. Seems that's the only thing I can think of these days."

With effort, Kate forced her gaze from the mesmerizing look in his warm gray eyes. "There's too much difference between us. When I get the chance I'll leave here."

"Only when I say. In Stone Wolf's eyes, you're an Indian now. You're my wife."

"I'm not a damned Indian," she said furiously.

"Where did you learn to curse, Kate? At the Lily?"

"Papa was fluent in profanity," she said, blurting the words. He was so close, he'd know she was trembling.

He burst out laughing and pulled her against him, his amusement fading the instant his mouth, hot and demanding, covered hers. Despite her determination, she sank into the kiss, unable to push him away, lulled by skilled hands that caressed and kneaded. When he centered his hardness against her, she recognized a tiny moan as her own.

"Has the time come, lass?"

"What?" she said, her vision coming back into focus. She pressed her hands against his chest, shocked at the need he'd fanned to a blaze. "The time?"

"No, 'tis not to be this day," he said, frustration straining the muscles in his neck. He murmured something unintelligible and ran his fingers through his hair.

What was the matter with her? Why couldn't she think? Why was he angry with her? When she could get her breathing even again, she met his irritation with her own. "I'll not deny I liked having you kiss me. But that's all. Go talk to Stone Wolf."

He bolted for the entrance. "Hell, yes, I'll talk to Stone Wolf."

"Hell, yes, I'll talk to Stone Wolf," she mimicked once he was through the door. She gave him time to get to his grandfather's tipi before marching out into the sunshine. She washed her face in the stream, considered bathing and washing her hair, but then decided Hawk might want to bathe in the evening. This time she'd take off her undergarments. After all, he'd seen her naked before. The more she thought about it, the more appealing the decision became.

She wanted to see his eyes turn from a clear gray to dark with stormy desire. It gave her a feeling of power knowing she could do that to him. Of course, it was also like playing with fire. She thought she could handle it, though.

Their tipi was clean. The scent of smoke from the fire lingered, but no stale food smells nor odors of unwashed bodies permeated the air. She sighed. There was nothing left to do but work until Hawk finished talking to his grandfather.

Chapter Seven

The sun's rays filtered through the trees, dappling the area with gold. The stream gurgled its way past the camp, going south. And those lords of the air, the hawks, sailed lazily on thermal currents arising from the canyon floor. Idyllic, Kate thought, sitting back on her heels, unless the task was as backbreaking and odious as the cleaning of hides.

Always the children came as soon as they saw her arrive. They sat in a semicircle, their hands in their laps, their eyes focused on her. "I wonder, kids, if you know that I'm learning one job at a time? This detestable chore is the hardest because I never get through. The hides smell. They're greasy. Finish one and there's always another. So far I've learned to scrape, cook a bit, and carry water. Impressed? I was afraid not."

One small boy, more daring than the rest, made a humming noise to attract her attention. He was unabashedly naked, as were most of the boys who surrounded her. A few of the little girls swayed in place, as though anticipating the music of her voice.

Bored to distraction, Kate made an elaborate bow, or at least as much of one as she could manage sitting down. She was center stage, and her audience was made up of children. "You've come to hear me sing? First you must learn to say *sing*." She repeated the word, then pointed a finger at them. They didn't respond. She tried again, humming, then motioning for them to do the same. Nothing. But after several more attempts she was successful. She pointed a finger at them. "If you want me to sing, say so. Sing."

"Shang," they shouted.

"Good. Now we understand each other. Little ladies and gentlemen, I shall start with a tune I sang at the Gilded Lily. Your mothers need not worry. The words are fine for kids. Wouldn't make much difference, would it? You nor your mamas know the meaning anyway."

When their mothers came and sat on the ground nearby, she nodded to the children. "I see you've invited your mamas." She waved a friendly hand. "Good morning, ladies. Welcome to the party. Sorry I'm not prepared to share a cup of tea. I would, on the other hand, be glad to share my scraper."

As usual, they were reluctant to talk. "What? No friendly greeting this morning? Did you leave your lazy, no-good, renegade husbands asleep?" She tilted her head. "No? Doesn't matter, I suppose. They can sleep leaning against a tree. Which is where they spend most of the day."

She sang all the verses of "Greensleeves" before pointing at the children. "Sing."

"Shang," they yelled.

From the corner of her eye she caught a glimpse of the ugly Indian. Hawk called him Little Crow. She had a few choice names for him herself, none of them complimentary. He raked her with flat, black eyes, lingering overlong on her breasts.

Kate inhaled sharply when he pointed to the piece of rawhide wrapped around his forearm. He slid his hand down suggestively, then pointed at the rawhide and then at her. God, he had stolen a piece of her deerskin, and he wore it, a sign that he desired her. She attacked the deerhide, scraping as hard and fast as she could. He'd shown unwanted attention before.

She was scared. Suppose nobody was around and he assaulted her?

Suppose she screamed for Grayhawk?

The tipi was large and decorated inside and out as befitted a chief. An elaborate headdress of eagle feathers hung suspended on a small pole cut from a willow. A fire burned steadily in a bed of rocks, and near it was a ready stack of buffalo chips. Stone Wolf had two wives to take care of his needs. One was older, almost as old as the chief himself. He had taken her when she and Stone Wolf were very young. The second wife appeared young enough to be his granddaughter. Both of them adored their husband.

As always, Grayhawk was amazed at the thrift of movement his grandfather displayed when in serious discussion. Stone Wolf sat with his legs folded, his pipe balanced on his knee. At regular intervals he lifted the pipe to his mouth, puffed three times, and replaced the pipe to its former position.

The smoke spiraled upward toward the opening where the tipi poles intersected, serving as a kind of chimney. Hawk waited for his grandfather to share his thoughts. He'd learned as a child that the old man would not tolerate so much as a sigh of impatience. Like the smoke slowly seeking ventilation, important discussions took time and many puffs from the pipe.

"Tell me about your meeting," the old man said.

"I met with the colonel, Grandfather. Neither of us had good news to report. Afterward I rode to several communities near the town of Dusty Flats. There's grumbling among the whites, tales of atrocities by Indians. Always they say 'Kill the Injuns.' "

"We're a proud people, grandson. Our ancestors roamed this land. Now the white man comes in great numbers. He wants the land. He will take it."

"Grandfather, I listened in the saloons. On the village streets. Talked with strangers. Always I added a word here, another there to support my mother's people. If I said too much, they called me an Injun lover. There's talk some will take the law into their own hands. Come after the Comanche to kill them."

Pain appeared in the old man's eyes. "Such words are carried in the wind."

"Grandfather, if the soldiers come and find me here, and also my wife, the plan the colonel, you, and I have put into place will be ended. My usefulness will be over. The whites would call me a traitor and try to kill me. Stone Wolf's braves would no longer trust me. They'd call me a traitor as well. Sooner or later they would kill me."

"You must go while there is still time. Take your wife. When my great-grandson is born, bring him to see me. Go quietly. There will be fewer questions to be answered."

Hawk knew he'd been dismissed, but he had one remaining point to make. "At this time Stone Wolf's band would do well to get out of the big canyon." Hawk knew he couldn't push his grandfather, but he had to make him see the danger. "If the whites find the camp, our people will be cornered like foxes in a den."

"I will think on it," Stone Wolf said. He made a slight motion toward the door. "When you go again and talk to the white men, tell them our braves are not guilty of attacking the wagon trains."

"Who, then? Quanah?"

Stone Wolf shrugged. "Quanah Parker is a brave leader. He leads his warriors on the warpath."

"The military can't catch him."

Stone Wolf nodded again. "He has a while longer."

Hawk knew his grandfather would consider the tribe's actions carefully before coming to a decision about moving his people.

Opening the flap, Hawk stepped into the sunshine. The day was pleasant, the wind a soft breeze. He scanned the area looking for Kate and found her near the creek, working a skin pegged to the ground. She sang softly to an audience of children as she scraped. From a short distance away, women watched, their dark faces inscrutable. Hawk's heart ached at the sound of Kate's beautiful voice.

Little Crow leaned indolently against a tree, his gaze fixed on Kate, his legs crossed at the ankles. He wore beaded moccasins and his breechclout. A rawhide band encircled his forearm.

Hawk read Little Crow's mind, and what he found filled his breast with a deep and abiding anger and premonition: someday he'd have to kill his blood brother.

Making sure he had his fury in check, he came up behind Kate just as she finished her lilting tune. The sun's rays had turned her ivory skin to pale apricot and glinted her dark hair with streaks of red. When she stretched her arms, her dress moved enticingly across her breasts.

"Would you be giving the rest of your day to your lover?"

"I don't have a lover."

Aye, but you will. "Then let us consider a way to change that circumstance. Will you spend the day with a brave Comanche warrior?"

"Comanche warrior, is it? What's his name?"

"Grayhawk. A loving predator."

"Goodness, I didn't know such a one existed," she said primly.

Enjoying the little flirtation, Hawk smiled at her. "Aye. He does."

"Sounds more like an Irishman to me."

"Again, aye. A combination. And a heart that beats as one."

"Back to what we'll be doing today, if I decide to go with you, of course."

"I've a place to show you. It will find favor with you, I think."

"Sure. Anything would find favor if it got me away from working this skin." She got to her feet. "Even gathering buffalo chips."

"We won't be needing buffalo chips. But we will need a horse, and Stone Wolf has lent me one."

"We'll ride double?"

"Aye, lass, bareback, with you pressed against me." He grinned at her. "Your arms around my middle."

"Real cozy. Would Stone Wolf lend his grandson *two* horses so we could ride more comfortably?" she asked slyly.

"I would never interrupt my grandfather's meditation with such a request. He has many things on his mind."

"So have I," she said with a sniff. "How to relieve monotony would top the list."

He flashed her his best Irish smile. "I know an excellent and charming way. Let me show you, darlin'."

"I'll bet you do," she said, "and I've a notion what that would be."

"Aye. Any colleen with an ounce of Irish blood has a wonderful imagination. Tell me your fancy, lass."

"Humph," she said, her tone clipped, "it wouldn't be the same as yours."

"Would you care to wager, Kate Hartland?"

To his amazement, she laughed. "How would you know whether I answered honestly?"

"Because," he said tenderly, "my Kate always tells the truth." He moved closer to her and took her hand as they walked toward their tipi. "Your pulse is racing. Are you afraid you'll remember your fantasy when I kiss you? For I warn you, I fully intend to kiss you."

She cleared her throat. "I'm not afraid of you. Or your kiss."

"I'd not want you afraid, my Kate."

When they reached the tipi, Hawk went in first. "Wear your leggings, darlin'. Otherwise your legs will get sore rubbing against the horse's side."

"I've always had to ride sidesaddle. A silly custom, I must say."

"Silly," he said, "especially if the woman has pretty legs."

"The rule must have been made by a woman."

He nodded agreeably. "With short, fat legs."

Her laughter joined his. After donning proper dress, she made ready their food. "Pia gave me pemmican. She gave me to understand that you liked it. I think she thought I might want to make it."

"And did you?"

"Never crossed my mind."

Smiling hugely, Hawk looked down at her. "What else did Pia teach you?"

"You mean besides how to tan a deerskin, make your jacket, start a stew with deer meat and toss in the right weeds?"

"The right weeds?"

"Some weeds are poisonous. But I suppose there's no need for an Indian man to know that. He eats when he is hungry, and it is his wife's duty to have prepared what he likes. All he has to do is sleep."

Hawk shrugged. "He has more to do than that. Loving his wife demands some of his time."

"If he has a wife," she said, her eyes warming to the debate.

He winked at her. "Aye, and it's lucky I am."

They left the tipi and walked downstream to where Grayhawk had tethered a horse before going to talk to his grandfather. "We'll ride bareback. I'll get on first, then help you to mount behind me." He could only smile as her arms went around his waist, tightening when he urged the horse forward.

Her clutch grew stronger the farther they went, her breasts pressed against his naked back. He grinned his appreciation, but knew better than to share his thoughts with her. He pointed toward the northwest. "See the top of the tall sandstone cliffs on your left? That's where we're going."

"How far is that?"

"Hard to say. Five miles. Maybe more."

By the time they'd covered half the distance, Kate complained about her bottom, assuring him it would never have feeling again. "There's something to be said for saddles."

"Aye. A saddle is a good thing, but at present we don't have one. We'll rest now, and let you recover. Slide over the horse's rump. That will be easiest." He waited until she was on the ground. "Riding bareback is a skill the Comanche learned when they tamed the horse. Walk around a bit, and then we'll ride on."

After they were under way once more, Kate brought the subject up again. "Are you saying all Comanche women have calluses on their backsides?"

"Not if they hold on to their man while they ride and think about sharing a blanket with him when they stop."

Her arms abruptly relaxed, and he urged the horse into a trot. She jerked in response, then clung tighter, bouncing up and down with the rhythm of the horse. "I'll get even, you crazy

Irish Indian. I'll put toads and lizards and poison berries in your stew."

"To ride in such a way shows a woman she needs her man." He reached back to pat her thigh. "But we're almost there, love. A few minutes more. See how the cliffs block out the sun? How would you like to spend the night under the stars, lying in your husband's arms?"

Kate groaned and rubbed her hip. "I don't have a husband. But at the moment, that plan doesn't sound so bad if it means I won't have to ride again for a while. I may change my mind when feeling comes back."

"It's an obstinate woman you are, Katie," he said, chuckling. "Beautiful but obstinate." He drew the horse to a stop, threw his leg over the animal's neck, and slid to the ground. He held out his arms invitingly. "Come, darlin', your man is willing and waiting."

"Is that an invitation to share your blanket, or to help me off this horse?"

"Both, Katie, love. But first things first. I'll help you down and steady you until you can walk easily. Then we'll discuss the other."

"Nothing to talk about. I'd love a drink of water."

"There's a spring of fresh water close by. It feeds the stream. As soon as you feel like it, we'll walk over there."

After they rested, Hawk pointed to the top of the cliff behind them. "That's where we're going. We'll sleep in a cave."

Kate looked at the steep path upward and moaned. "That's straight up. You mean we're going to climb those rocks up there?"

"Aye, lass, that we are. With a little help from our horse."

After drinking and washing their faces, they walked back to where the horse grazed. "Katie, hold on to the horse's tail. He'll pull you up. I'll be at his head to guide him."

Some time later they reached the cave, and Kate staggered forward to sink to her knees in the warm sand. "I hope it's easier going down."

He led the horse toward an evergreen shrub. "After I secure the horse, I'll scout the cave for snakes."

135

Openmouthed, Kate stared at him. She nodded. "It'll be easier going down."

He flushed the cave interior with the limb of a mesquite and motioned her to come back. "Our home is free of bobcats and snakes."

"That's comforting. My opinion of the Indian male has risen," she said, adding innocently, "somewhat."

"I've more surprises, Kate." He took her hand and led her to the edge of the open space in front of the cave. He slipped his arm around her waist. "Sit down to look."

Kate gasped at the scene below her. A narrow rocky gorge backed the water up for half a mile, forcing the stream through the narrow opening to rush down the canyon floor. Farther on it evened out, becoming once more a mannerly stream. "It's wild and beautiful," she said when she could get her breath.

"Da and I stood here many years ago, when I was a boy. A rainstorm had turned the creek into a roaring monster. It uprooted trees, tossed logs, and tore at the cliffs like a great, evil beast."

"Were you scared?"

"Aye, but I never admitted it to Da." He pointed across to the thick vegetation on the far side. "Fall will soon be here. Frost will nip the leaves and turn the cottonwoods yellow. Indian summer, the whites call it. A big yellow moon shows up. And for a time the prairies will be warm and awash in goodwill. A harvest moon."

"What name do the Indians give it?"

Shrugging, he smiled at her. "A Mexican moon, when the Comanche steal Mexican horses. The Mexicans say Comanche moon for the same reason."

"Is this the truth?"

"Aye, lass. Before the raid the Indians pay homage. They form a circle of rope or rawhide, whatever they have. In this magical moonlight, they smoke and pray the rope will take many horses."

"And does it?"

"The Comanche are great thieves, especially of horses. Any objects of nature—a sunset, a glorious morning, an ancient cottonwood—all are tribal deities. The people pray to them."

"Do you believe these deities hear?"

"Aye, my Kate. They hear." His eyes gleamed with laughter. "The Comanche have many horses."

"They surely do. A canyon full of them. But I doubt their gods have anything to do with the theft."

He shrugged. "Who knows?"

"It's beautiful here, but autumn is wonderful most anywhere."

"There's an ancient sadness about it, Katie. All living things must die. The Indian carries this feeling inside his breast." He knew she was not ready to look at what he carried in his heart, his hopes and fears. "I'll tell you more one day."

The cave was high above the canyon floor and gave them a pulse-hammering view of the area. Kate noticed small angular notches leading down, chipped into the cliff wall. "I believe you when you say all things die—especially Indians, if they used these notches as a way down."

"These steps were cut a hundred years ago. Maybe more. Comanche, Kiowa, Cheyenne. They all camped here at one time or another."

"Did they start at the bottom and work up, chipping away as they went? Or from the top and work down?"

"Both, likely."

"Hard to believe. Do your people come to this cave often?"

"They don't come at all. The story goes that an Indian maiden leaped to her death from this spot. My people are superstitious. They stay away."

"Why did she jump?"

"She was in love with a young brave. Her father gave her to an old Indian for ten horses."

"Her father sold her," Kate said indignantly. "How awful."

"Well, kind of a bride's dowry in reverse."

Kate leaned back on her elbows. "What happened to the girl's sweetheart?"

"I can't remember the rest of the story."

"Probably took three more wives and forgot the maiden."

He toyed with her hair, running his fingers through it. "Not

137

if she were as beautiful as you, my Kate. No man could forget you. You're pretty in the Indian dress. You walk so gracefully. It sets the fringe in motion in the most becoming way."

"Still trying to turn me into an Indian."

"I'd never change you, darlin'. But I suspect you're already part Comanche."

"Then God forgive me." She stood and circled back to the cave. "Where will we sleep?"

"In each other's arms under the stars, unless it rains."

She glanced at the cloudless sky. "There's lots of room out here. You can sleep there. I'll sleep here."

"You're afraid, Katie, afraid I'll kiss you."

"Ha. I'll have some say about that."

"True. I'll not kiss you unless you want me to, love. But it's all right if you ask me." He went about the business of building a fire. "The wind brings in the cold. The cave never really warms during the day."

Later, after the sun had disappeared from sight, Kate agreed with his prediction. She drew the blanket close around her and eased up to where the small fire had turned to coals. She dozed, awakening with a start. Hawk wasn't in sight, and her nerves sparked to attention. She glimpsed him at the edge of the cave lying flat and watching the canyon floor.

His glance said he knew she was awake. He placed a finger to his mouth, warning her not to speak, and by sliding his hand in the manner of a snake, he beckoned her to come to him. Minutes later she lay beside him. He placed an arm around her shoulders and pointed down to where a campfire burned. A group of men lazed around the blaze, too lacking in concern to stake a lookout. Laughing, talking, cursing, they shared a jug, passing it from one to another.

"Comancheros," Hawk whispered close to her ear. "Either they're waiting for Indian traders with their captives, or they plan to stay there until morning."

"They're a mangy-looking lot," Kate said in a low voice, watching a man lurch to his feet and relieve himself just beyond the circle. "What if they decide to come up here?"

"It isn't likely they know the cave is here. If they do, they won't want to climb the cliff. Especially if they're drunk."

"Are they white men, Indians? What?"

"White and Mexican. An Apache there on the left. Comanches to the right."

"Comanche?"

"Aye," he said, sorrow heavy in his voice.

"Joe said . . ." She waited expectantly. "You remember the piano player? Joe said the Comancheros pay the Indians for the captives they bring in." She shuddered. "Women and children, the Comancheros sell them. The women to Mexican bordellos. The children into slavery."

Once more the Irishman, he tugged her close to him, brought her hand to his mouth, and kissed the palm. "Don't worry, darlin'; your man will protect you."

Kate was surprised that she had no hesitation in accepting his promise as truth. "You're making a joke. But you won't have to protect me if we stay hidden."

He brushed his lips over her hair. "I want you to see me as a hero."

"But not tonight with the Comancheros below us."

"I can think of other ways. Pleasurable ways."

Before she could answer, a shout came from below, and half a dozen men rode in and dismounted. Kate felt her mouth go dry. "What are they doing?"

"Can't tell yet." There was tension in his voice. "Boggs is with them."

"Oh, my God," she whispered. "It's true what they say, that he trades with the Comancheros."

"Seems so."

"Will you tell the military?"

"Aye, and soon."

"Joe told me I was in danger." Rage grew inside her, filling her breast, clogging her throat. "He's a bastard, Nathan is. He ran me out of town because I wouldn't go to bed with him."

Hawk closed a firm hand over hers. "Katie, should there be a time when you're in danger and I'm not with you, hide here. I'll come to you."

Somehow she knew he would.

She leaned forward and scraped dirt off one of the small, chipped steps. "I'd hate to imagine climbing down using these formidable little footholds to make a getaway. Thinking about it makes my stomach go crazy. I couldn't do it."

"You could. You're strong. Stronger than you give yourself credit for."

Kate shrugged. If he thought her strong, so much the better. The time would come when she'd have to escape from the Indian camp. Away from Pia and the children.

And Hawk.

"I give myself credit for running headfirst into trouble."

She'd have to search her heart for what mattered most in her life. Only when she was free and back with her own kind would she know. Out of the blue, the thought slammed into her midsection: she wanted his touch, his lips on hers.

"You've courage, Katie," he said tenderly. "Looks like the party's over. Now we can sleep. Together?"

She eyed him warily. "Nothing's changed. Same rules here as in the tipi."

He answered gruffly, "Sure, and some rules never change. But eventually this one will, and I'll spend the nights loving you. There's a spirit here in this place, powerful and benevolent. I feel it smiling on us. Lie down and sleep, Kate. I'm a patient man."

The next day they rode into Stone Wolf's camp about noon. The children saw them first and ran toward them, shrieking and laughing and calling her name. "Kite. Kite."

"Oh, my God," Kate said, a break in her voice. She pushed off with her hands, slid over the horse's rump to the ground, and set off running. In a flash she had a small boy up in her arms. "Hawk," she screamed, "hurry. Hold him up by his heels. Hurry. He's strangling."

The child couldn't breathe, his face already blue. The moment Hawk had the little boy upside down, Kate gave a quick squeeze to the boy's middle. She knelt beside him and ran her finger into his mouth. "Something's lodged in his throat. I can touch it with the tip of my fingernail."

"God, please," she whispered, praying as her finger stretched to reach farther into his throat. She managed to wiggle the object, pressing her fingernail around its hard surface and easing it forward.

Hawk, his hands around the child's ankles, assured the boy he'd soon be fine. "Your father will be proud to see his son so brave."

She heard him add his prayers to hers. And, as if in answer to their supplications, a rock, small and round with a vicious little hook, fell out of the child's mouth to the ground.

The small boy gagged and struggled, and Hawk turned him upright. "Breathe, lad, breathe." He was rewarded when the boy sucked in a lungful of air.

Kate caressed the young face. "You're going to be fine, fella." Tears dribbled down her cheeks. "He's going to have a very sore throat, Hawk."

"You saved his life, lass."

"Both of us, I guess." She took an unsteady step toward their tipi. "I feel a little sick to my stomach."

"Wait, and I'll go . . ." He didn't finish. Little Crow strode toward him, sunlight emphasizing the fierce look on his face. He moved through the huddled children to where Hawk stood cradling his son. Tenderly the father gathered the child to him and comforted him by placing the small head on his shoulder. He did not look at Kate, but directed his gaze to Hawk. Nodding once, he turned and hurried to meet his pregnant wife.

Grayhawk exhaled, letting his breath out slowly, a little at a time. Little Crow would never thank a woman, but he could thank her brave. And Hawk thanked the Great Spirit, the Holy Mother, and all the patron saints. He could let his blood brother live.

Kate had saved Little Crow's life by saving the warrior's son.

The next morning, Hawk found Midnight staked outside his tipi.

"Sure and it's welcome you are, big black. 'Tis a reunion I hadn't expected." When Kate walked out, he beamed at her. "Because of you, my darlin' Kate, I have Midnight again."

Kate patted the horse's neck. "A pretty good trade, it seems to me. A child's life for a horse." A scowl crossed her expressive face, lingered, then faded slowly. "It could have been different."

"Don't think of what might have been, lovely Kate. We have our horse. He has his son."

"I had trouble sleeping last night."

"Aye, lass. Such a problem I have myself every night, sleeping beside you." Much to his amusement, she chose to ignore his comment. She moved away from the tipi, walking in the direction of the stream, and looked back over her shoulder at him. "I'll bathe, I think, while the village is busy and I have you as a lookout."

He wanted to tell her how wonderful she was, but she didn't give him time. "One of God's blessings, bathing. I'll wait for you by that old cottonwood." He pointed at the ancient tree. "Been there a hundred years or more."

"I'll treat it with reverence," she said, "if you promise to stay there."

He walked the distance to where the tree still held on to its yellow leaves, their edges rimmed in brown. Little Crow waited for him, not moving as Hawk approached.

Hawk nodded, and was rewarded with a nod in return. "The boy?"

Again Little Crow nodded, and pointed toward the stream. "My brother's white wife is very brave. She saved my son's life. My brother is very lucky to have her. I respect his wishes not to share such a wife."

Hawk's relief was so great he leaned against the tree. "My brother understands."

"I have three wives now." Crow placed his hands on his stomach. "One carries my baby, but I will share the other two with you. Anytime."

"My blood brother is generous." He had seen Little Crow's wives. They were no temptation. "I'll go now. My wife has finished her bathing." He had no intention of apprising Kate of his blood brother's generosity. He hoped she would never learn of the danger Little Crow had presented.

* * *

The following morning Grayhawk walked outside to a flurry of activity. He sighed his relief. Stone Wolf had made a decision: The tribe would move elsewhere for the fall. When the weather changed to cold winter winds and snow, and the threat of invasion by the military ground to a halt, his grandfather would lead his people back to the protection of the big canyon.

"What's going on?" Kate appeared beside him and turned cobalt eyes up to his. "They're taking down the tipis."

"Stone Wolf is moving his camp," he said briefly, not wanting to go into an explanation of why it was necessary.

"But why? And where?"

"I don't know yet. Possibly Tule Canyon southeast of here. It's easy to get out of in case there's an emergency." He smiled at her, caressing her with his eyes. "If that's where he's going, the place is close to Shamrock Ranch."

"Then I'll soon be . . ." Her eyes shone. "I'll be leaving."

Was she so anxious to be rid of him, or just the company of the tribe? Hawk wasn't sure he wanted to know the answer to that question. "First you need to take down the tipi."

"And what will you be doing?"

"I have arrows that need feathers."

She looked at him as though trying to determine whether he was teasing. Her next words indicated she had decided to judge him as sincere. "Necessary, no doubt, when you kill a buffalo. How far can you shoot an arrow?"

"If the wind isn't too strong, three hundred yards."

"Accurately?"

He grinned. "That's the reason I need the feathers."

"How do we get the tipi and utensils to the next campground?"

"Travois." He took her hand gently, raised it to his lips, and kissed it. "Nothing to it."

"What's a travois?"

"Two trailing poles, one tied on either side to a horse. A skin is attached between the two. The women pack the tipi and household utensils on it."

"Just dandy. The woman not only build the house and tear

143

it down but move it to the next location as well. And, once in the new location, they have to put it up all over again."

"It's the Comanche way," he said, laughing.

"How do I get the thing down?"

He was pleased she didn't argue. He'd have been hard-put to explain. "As I've told you before, Pia is a woman of great wisdom."

"It's not blasted wisdom I need. It's a man with a strong back."

She needn't have worried. When they reached their tipi, two women approached and, without a word, began the process of dismantling their dwelling. "Why are they doing this? Did Pia send them?"

"The tribe knows you are ignorant of how to take down a tipi. The women come to do it for you. You're a heroine, Katie."

Kate looked with awe at the two women, one standing on the shoulders of the other, as they removed the top strip of rawhide that held the tipi together. They worked rapidly and efficiently, their conversation carried on with each other in short, guttural phrases.

"I've never been a heroine before."

"The village considers you one."

"I guess I don't have to worry anymore when they start a fire," she said lightly.

He didn't meet her eyes. "If they'd had burning at the stake in mind, you'd no longer be here."

"I suppose not." The two women laid the poles on the ground and without a word left as silently as they'd appeared. "When you have a chance, thank them for me. Better yet, thank them for yourself. I don't see the tipi as figuring in my future."

"Temporarily, darlin', we move with the band."

"Do we walk?" She threw up her hands in disgust. "Of course. The women do."

"Not all the women. You can ride the travois. The horse. Or behind your man on Midnight. Your arms would be about him, your face pressed against his back, and you'd caress him with kisses to his back." He smiled tenderly. "Come, Kate, walk with me beyond the creek. I'll put kisses on your mouth. My hands will roam your lovely body. We'll find a mossy spot beneath a cottonwood, and . . ."

She brushed her hair back. "And?"

He ran a finger down her cheek and tucked a tendril of hair behind her ear. "When we return, love, we'll have memories to last forever."

"Irish blarney," she said without conviction.

Patience, Hawk told himself. To win over the most skittish filly required patience.

The camp moved out on signal, following Stone Wolf mounted on a piebald gelding. Warriors rode bareback, their naked legs dangling on either side of their horses. Alert to danger, they carried spears and quivers filled with arrows. Mothers trudged along, their babies on their backs like small sacks of grain, tiny faces peeking out to view the activity.

The very old rode travois. Able people walked, including the children. When the small ones grew tired, they were hoisted to the backs of gentle mares or mules. It was all very efficient, very purposeful.

During the long, arduous journey through sagebrush, yucca, mesquite, and native grass, autumn eased in with tired winds and shorter days. The travelers labored in a southeasterly direction, trading a deep, long canyon for one more shallow with fewer ravines, less protection from the blasts of winter, but it would be easier to fade into the prairies if the camp were threatened.

Kate made a bonnet of her ragged underwear. She had discarded her modesty for relief from the sun, she informed Grayhawk, and shook her fist at him when he laughed.

"Charming, Katie. 'Tis feminine and daring."

She trudged along beside Midnight. "You said Indians were thieves. They're liars, too."

"Nay. Who could lie to a beautiful Irish lass whose dark eyes sparkle with laughter? Whose cheeks are like satin? Who shields her fair skin from a fierce and relentless sun?"

She stared at him and shook her head. "God. The blarney rolls off your tongue like blather from a Yankee drummer."

145

Hawk threw his head back and laughed. "You've a way of keeping a man grounded. Come, love, ride with me. You can ride in front. Midnight won't mind."

After a moment's hesitation, she nodded. "For a short way. The women will think I'm not strong enough to make the trip without help."

"You shouldn't worry about such things. You've been Comanche for only a short time." He didn't give her time to react. Within seconds she sat in front of him, her legs astride Midnight's broad back. "You're more comfortable, I think, but your headgear interferes with any Irish endearments I might want to whisper in your ear."

Placing the sack of pemmican she carried on the horse's neck, Kate relaxed against Hawk's broad chest. "Whisper away. I'm not taking off my bonnet. When I get a job singing again," she said softly, turning her head to brush his lips with hers, "I don't want to look like an Indian."

"But until then . . ."

Abruptly Hawk forced her head back and took her mouth. There was nothing gentle about it, and because she couldn't turn from the siege—nor did she want to—her heart catapulted into a pounding fury. The kiss went on forever. She opened her lips to the dance of his tongue, her own mating with his, her insides a mass of jelly. "Yes, yes," she whispered.

When the kiss ended, he moved a hand up to caress her breast. "Damnit, Kate, why couldn't you pick a time to seduce me when I could do something about it? Midnight's back is broad, but hardly the place."

She had no answer. Her action had sprung up spontaneously.

They arrived at Tule Canyon, walking down its sloping trails to the canyon floor. In a short time, and from years of experience, the women turned the camp into a home—temporary but sufficient. Kate sighed in relief when two women came to erect the tipi she shared with Hawk. She thanked them herself, smiling and bowing.

Once the tent was up, the women accepted her words of

appreciation with hardly a glance. "I must have overdone it. Doesn't matter," she told their retreating backs. "I'm grateful from the top of my head to the bottom of my blistered feet."

Later, lying in bed, she told Hawk about her attempt to thank the women. "I'm not sure they understood. I did everything but kiss their hands."

"They knew, darlin', but with the proper inducement tonight, I'll be sure to tell them tomorrow, just in case there was a misunderstanding."

"Proper inducement?"

"I want you, lass. Aye, 'tis a terrible longing."

Kate closed her eyes to the same terrible longing.

Chapter Eight

The camp bustled with activity. Women hurried from one task to another, carrying wood, stirring cooking pots, talking, and laughing. Children appeared to be afflicted, running in circles like puppies chasing their tails. As Kate walked by each tipi, she spoke greetings in her mangled Comanche. Sometimes she received only a stare in return. More often the women answered in their own tongue, now and then adding Kate's name, wanting, she hoped, to assure her they were including her. In the few short weeks they had been at the new camp Kate had started to feel the women were more friendly toward her.

She followed a trail to the stream, adjusted her deerskin tunic, and knelt to scoop water in her palm. Before her hand reached the water, her face was mirrored briefly, fading away in nauseating waves. Her insides convulsed and gorge rose in her throat. She grabbed her middle and groaned. She fully expected to vomit, but the sickness ebbed, and she lay down on the grassy bank. After a while she splashed water over her face and neck. What in the world had brought on such a feeling? She must have picked the wrong weeds to put in her cookpot.

She needed to talk to Pia so she wouldn't make the same mistake again. As soon as she was sure she could stand without staggering.

Overcast with a few low-lying clouds that promised rain, the sky rocked when she looked up. Most mornings she felt at peace here. Today was the exception. All she wanted to do was make it back to the tipi and lie down. Without warning, her privacy was shattered. Brown Wren, a young Indian girl, scurried over the rocks toward the stream, her water pouch in hand. When she saw Kate, she stopped and stared. Kate almost groaned. Of all the young women in the camp, Wren was the biggest gossip. Even with her limited grasp of the Comanche language, Kate knew from watching and from Pia's hand gestures that the smallest bit of information could be woven into a story and carried from tipi to tipi with the speed of a wild mustang. Just as in a small town, along the way, the tale would gain with repetition, fabrication, and invention.

Mustering a smile, Kate greeted Brown Wren and was given a smile in return. Wren hesitated only a moment, then quickly filled her water pouch and escaped up the hill. Thanking her lucky stars she hadn't vomited, Kate lurched to her feet and walked unsteadily up the hill to the tipi she shared with Hawk.

After a while she felt better, as if she'd never had the bad moments at the stream. The same thing had happened twice before in exactly the same way. The morning would start well, but then the nausea would come, hang around briefly, and then just as quickly as it had come, leave her topsy-turvy stomach at peace. Only to reappear again the following morning.

Morning sickness.

She counted back two months and caught her breath. The first month she'd blamed the trauma she'd been through. But the second month, already two weeks past, was a different story. For one glorious moment, she felt a wild and uninhibited joy.

She carried Hawk's baby. Gently she placed her hand on her stomach. A baby grew there. Warmth spread over her. Then cold, hard truth stabbed her breast, and questions rolled in like

149

tumbleweeds. How could she tell Hawk? What would his response be? Would civilization be kind to her and to her part-Indian child? She should be crying and wringing her hands, and all she could think of was the baby she carried under her heart.

She went outside to work on an ever-present skin.

A short time later the children clamored around her, touching her and smiling, getting as close as they could. When Little Crow had dragged her into camp—a million years ago, it seemed—the children had watched her from the safety of their mothers' skirts. Now they followed her eagerly, chanting, "Shang, Kite. Shang, Kite, shang, shang."

She gave up and joined in their contagious laughter. Sinking to the ground, she sat cross-legged and motioned the children to join her. They flopped down, making a semicircle, the smaller children pushing to the front. "Kite, shang," they all yelled, until she lifted her hand for them to stop.

"All right, little urchins, I'll sing, but not for very long. I've a few chores of my own this morning, namely to find out why the camp is abuzz. Excitement is in the air. Campfires are set to be lighted. Food is being prepared. You'd think it was Christmas." She choked back laughter. "On second thought, maybe All Hallow's Eve."

"Shang, Kite."

"So you keep the knowledge to yourselves and make me wait to learn the secret. For that you get one song, two verses. No more."

She sang, but her mind was on her baby.

What caused the camp fervor? Had they captured an enemy and planned to torture him? She shook her head, refusing to spoil the day with such depressing thoughts. Instead she'd try to enjoy the morning and the children.

Ignoring her own promise to sing only one song, she sang several, repeating when they begged. She finally turned a deaf ear to their wheedling. "Go back to your mamas, you little rogues. I've things to do."

What had turned the camp into a beehive? *Pia! Of course.* Pia would know what was going on. And Pia was her friend.

Friendly, anyway. Perhaps because she looked on Kate as Hawk's wife. Or, Kate thought, perhaps because she enjoyed seeing a white woman learn the agony of being an Indian. Whatever the reason, Kate realized that after working side by side with Hawk's aunt, she had formed a grudging respect for the old woman that increased with each day's passing.

Kate recalled the mistakes she'd made preparing hides. Pia had never once shown impatience or annoyance. She'd smiled often, clucking or chuckling at Kate's mistakes, showing her again and again how to stretch a hide, the slow process of tanning, where to find the proper food plants, and how to prepare and cook them.

When she reached Pia's tipi, Kate called her name softly, not wanting to attract attention. She heard nothing and tried again. At the third try, Pia poked her head out the entrance and motioned her to enter. Hawk's aunt went back to preparing food for the cook pot. Kate had learned enough of Comanche ways to wait until Pia was ready to talk; otherwise she knew she might as well be talking to herself for all the response she would get.

Kate sat quietly, observing her surroundings. The only light came from the hole at the top of the tipi where the poles joined, and from the flickering blaze beneath the boiling pot. Several strips of rawhide were in the process of being woven into a belt. Pieces of bone, probably buffalo, lay lined up near the tent wall, no doubt to serve as stirring spoons. Small, colorful rocks formed a circle, almost like a necklace, to the left of the entrance. Pia had attempted to satisfy her need for something beautiful with these pretty stones. In all likelihood, when they changed camps, Pia would leave them. Hawk had said the tipi furnishings were sparse for a reason, namely because transportation was limited to a horse or dog, or a woman's back.

Pia's home was clean, smelling only of wood smoke and boiling food, not always true of other tipis, Kate had found, her knowledge limited to fewer than a dozen tents.

At last Pia paused and looked at her. "Kite, we talk."

"What's going on in the village?" Kate used gestures to encompass the camp, and with her limited Comanche made Pia understand. "What's all the excitement?"

"Big feast," Pia said, her mouth curving into a gap-toothed smile, her face wrinkling into leathery folds that almost hid her eyes. "Men bring deer, antelope. Eat much meat." She waved her arms and thumped the pot with the long bone she used for stirring. "Beat drums. Play games. Gamble. Dance. Good time, Kite."

Kate smiled at the excitement in Pia's eyes. With hand signals, and using Comanche and English words, Pia described how the People went about preparing for such an activity.

"Dress up." Preening and twisting, Pia put her hands on her hips and strutted around the tipi. "Good time. Eat and eat. Buffalo, deer, antelope, rabbit."

"Nothing like a party," Kate said, laughing. She continued to sit, enjoying Pia's company until she feared she'd overstayed her welcome. Pia had said nothing about a captive being asked to the festivities, so Kate supposed she'd remain in Hawk's tipi. "Food smells good," she said, doing her best to make Pia understand. As she usually did when nothing more needed to be said, Pia nodded, her gaze fixed on Kate's face. The old woman smiled.

Kate said good-bye and stepped outside. Her heart turned over at the sight of Hawk astride Midnight. Tall and straight, he rode bareback, his long legs dangling on either side of his magnificent steed. A gutted deer lay draped over the back of the packhorse. She met him with a host of questions.

"Yes, tonight there's a celebration. Give me time to tether the horses, and I'll tell you about it. Meet me at the tipi."

He called something out to Pia, his guttural words coming too fast for Kate to understand, but she imagined they focused on the big deer he dumped at his aunt's door.

Kate waited impatiently inside the front of their tent. Why hadn't Hawk told her of the party, so she could have prepared? She was sure the women would be expected to cook food. When Hawk made an appearance, she didn't hesitate. "Are we invited?" She frowned and tried again. "Am I invited?"

He kissed her lightly, his arms encircling her in a bear hug.

" 'Tis a party, lass. As for your being invited . . . Whither I go, wife, thou goest."

"A Comanche quoting scripture," she said, scoffing.

He gave her a lopsided grin. "Aye, lass, Indian or white, I'm considered a scholar of the good book."

"Where did you study, I wonder?" She couldn't keep the mirth out of her voice. "The Comanche School of Scalping?"

"Nay, Kate, speak kindly. My father is a good Catholic. He made sure I went to Mass and was familiar with the catechism."

"Your explanation is accepted," she said, shrugging, "since I've no way of knowing."

"Now. Where were we? Oh, yes. You were in my arms, and I was kissing you. I remember distinctly that you liked it and wanted me to continue."

"As Mama would say, you're a sight. First you quote the Bible and then lie like the devil."

Hawk burst out laughing. "Make an honest man of me, darlin'." He drew her into his arms and kissed her face, letting his lips drift down to her throat. When she didn't resist, he splayed his hands over her back and, after nudging the neck of her dress aside, kissed her bare shoulder. "Already I'm beginning to feel truth and veracity creep into my soul." His voice became husky with tenderness. "Aye, lass, the longer I hold you, the stronger these qualities become."

Kate knew she should back away from the mesmerizing sound of his voice and the pressure of his lips. But her erratic pulse pounded its way through her body, and she couldn't hear for the thunder of her heart. "I doubt—"

"Never doubt, my Kate. Passion is a lovely thing between two people." He continued his gentle stroking, ravishing her with soft, persuasive words and murmured endearments until her body was afire. "Aye, lass, now you'd be wanting me."

Sanity returned slowly, but made an appearance before she threw caution to the winds and her arms around his neck. What magic was he weaving that drew her to him with such irrepressible urgency, that lured her to respond to his sweet torture? His muscular body exuded raw power and strength, and she couldn't deny she wanted to be in his arms. It seemed her body and mind were always at war.

She tugged his hands from around her waist and closed her eyes to his hurt and questioning look. "The party. Remember?"

"You've the devil's own means of inflicting pain, Kate. Have you no heart?" He stalked to the entrance. Gone were the sweet talk and the soft whispers. He spoke in short, clipped sentences, each word stamped with roughness. "The celebration begins this afternoon and goes on all night and into tomorrow. People sleep a little, usually around dawn. A big campfire is lighted. Everybody dresses up. There are games, dancing, drums. The women prepare the food."

"If you had told me, I would—"

He ignored her, continuing his explanation of the festivities. "Pia will prepare our part of the food."

"Sporting of her," Kate said, dryly. "And why didn't you ask me?"

"You'd prepare a pot? I'm surprised, Kate."

She saw the conflicting emotions that crossed his face, and then his sudden wry grin. "The pot would be, too, I imagine."

Following his brief flash of amusement, the storm returned to his gray eyes. "Women's work is important, whether you like it or not. I had no idea you'd want to contribute to the preparations."

"Some compliment, but if that's what it is, you can save it. I thoroughly dislike women's work, at least the kind Indian women are required to do. On the other hand, I'm inclined to do my part when necessary." She certainly wouldn't have voluntarily added to Pia's responsibilities. "You said everybody would be dressed up."

When he turned disinterested eyes on her, neither kindness nor tenderness showed in his face. He let his gaze wander over her hair. "Braid it if you want to; it's your hair. Indian women usually plait one braid to the side. As for clothing, wear whatever you have. I'll go in the jacket you made." He lifted the flap and stepped outside.

She had seldom seen Hawk even mildly annoyed. Today he was angry with her, and she was uncomfortable. He knew how she felt about his claiming her as his wife, and yet he persisted in calling her that. Members of the tribe considered Hawk her husband, and she was forced to admit she felt pride in the respect he received. One part of her wanted to tell him they were having a baby. But what if she had the chance to go back to her white world?

Left alone to nurse her newly recognized responsibility, and to wrestle her guilt at nearly succumbing to his pleas and regretting that she hadn't, she started plaiting her hair. She wished she could forget his kiss. It was most irritating to be left feeling the way she did, and no doubt he knew that. Angrily, she took her frustration out on her hair, pulling and tugging it into a long, fat braid.

The revelry began with a loud pounding of drums. The smell of burning wood mixed with the pungent odor of cooking food and the ever-present scent of evergreen. Indian women passed back and forth carrying vessels of stone and hide and placing them on flat-topped boulders forced together to form a crude table.

The smaller children screeched and played as if school were out and they had nothing to do but push and shove, roll on the ground, and taunt each other. In an open space, teenage girls with sticks in their hands fought hard to drive a deerskin ball to a designated goal. Heavy with decorative beads and dangling pieces of colored glass, their showy garb rattled and clacked as loudly as the girls' groans and shrieks. The game was fast, and the young women played skillfully.

The young men shunned the girls' games and strutted to the beat of the drums. Their ornaments—colored stones, pieces of bone, beads, and feathers—were braided into their hair. Some had two or three rings in one ear, as many as five in the other. Most wore breechclouts.

Kate threw a quick glance at Grayhawk. Today he was Comanche from his headband to his moccasins. She could tell he was still irritated by the set of his jaw. Smelling of mint, he wore the jacket she'd made for him, his big shoulders straining at the leather and appearing even broader. He wasn't the only one who was mad. She had some complaints of her own, and being held against her will ranked number one. No doubt he was showing the camp what an unsatisfactory wife she was, one who didn't properly care for her man.

Her man!

Disgusted at where her mind had taken her, she clung to her anger. Clearly he wasn't ready to be friendly. Well, she wasn't either, even if she couldn't help but marvel at how handsome he was.

And why was he astonished that she'd want to bring food? After all, she was a member of the camp and spent every day working at tanning, stretching, and cleaning those wretched odorous hides that had begun to make her stomach roil. Any change would be welcome, and that included tonight's party. It surprised her how strongly she wanted to be recognized as part of the community. She told herself it was only because she had worked hard over the last few weeks and deserved to be able to join in the celebration.

In all of her life Kate had never seen anything to compare with the festivities. Women came dressed in their finest, their skirts fringed at the hem, some with poncho-style tops serving as blouses. Skirts and tops were laced together at the waist and decorated with paint and beads, while matching leggings and moccasins completed their outfits. They were mesmerizing to watch, as each woman had weaved her own colorful pattern into the pieces she wore.

"Where do they keep their Sunday clothes?" Kate asked Hawk, as much to draw him out as to gain information. He'd been so grim, so unlike himself.

Hawk walked beside her, unbending enough to answer questions, but his flat tone indicated that he still nursed his irritation. "In a rawhide, envelope-shaped wardrobe case that has a fold-over flap."

"How long are you going to be mad at me?"

"Nay, Kate, I'm not mad at you. A lass has the right to say no," he said, adding judiciously, "if she really means it. Which I don't think you do."

The truth was, she wasn't sure herself. She eyed him questioningly. "If we don't sleep together, will you find someone else?"

"Not as long as you're in my bed."

"But you would take another woman? Say, in her bed?"

"I'm a man, Kate."

"What kind of an answer is that?" Fuming, she stopped. When he turned to wait for her to catch up, she placed her hands on her hips and glared. "Even when you call me your wife you'd go to another woman?"

He lost his stern countenance and worked at hiding a grin. "Would it matter?"

"As long as I'm in your tipi, I'd appreciate your not flaunting . . ." She paused and searched for the right word. "Your infidelity," she said defiantly, an unpleasant lump lodging in her throat. Especially now that they were having a child together. But if she were honest, she had felt such twinges before and been uncomfortable.

"And if I should just talk to one?"

"Have you . . . would you go to a woman's tipi . . . ?" The conversation had become unbearably painful. "Have you . . . here in camp?"

"Katie, are you sure you want to ask me such a question?"

She rolled her eyes heavenward. "Yes. Or I wouldn't ask."

"In that case, I'll be truthful." He looked very solemn, but his eyes were filled with laughter. "Never. Before you came or after."

She eyed him suspiciously. "When you were gone, did you . . . did you . . . ?"

"Did I what, Katie?"

"You know what I mean." She knew she was acting like a jealous wife, and foolishly as well. Her face reddened. "You do, don't you? Know what I mean?"

"No." He scratched his head and looked puzzled. "I guess you'll have to ask me straight out what you want to know."

Blast the man. It was like pulling teeth to drag the answers out. "Would you go to another woman?" The nights he was gone, had he spent them in another woman's arms? The thought of Hawk making love to someone else, his hard body naked, warm, and sated, curled around someone else, was too painful to dwell on. "Well, would you?" she asked irritably.

"Would I go to another woman's bed? Only if she's as beautiful as my fiery Kate."

How had she ever gotten herself involved in this conversation? No matter; she had to know, even if his answer might be painful. "Have you found such a person?"

"There's no other like my Kate." His gaze swept over her before settling on her mouth. At last he smiled. "Not in the entire universe."

Somewhat mollified, Kate turned her attention back to the gathering. "What are the men and women doing in the small circles?"

"Gambling," he said briefly, and moved on to where Pia had placed her cookpot. She hovered over it, stirring and tasting. She barely looked up as they approached.

"Mother, we're grateful you prepared food and included us in your generosity."

Pia answered him in the Comanche tongue. "I did not think your squaw could learn the ways of our people so rapidly. Perhaps she should have brought your food to the revelry."

"She learns easily."

The old woman nodded, her gaze fixed on Kate, while her hand still held the stirring bone. "She works hard, but she'll not be Comanche right away."

"Why do you think this, Mother?"

"She may be your wife, but she's also a captive. Kite does not like being a captive." Pia focused questioning eyes on his face before filling a wooden bowl and handing it to him. "Does she like being your wife?"

He shrugged. "Who knows the working of a woman's mind? I hoped you could tell me."

Pia gave her head a slight shake before ladling food into a bowl for Kate. She let her gaze rest on Kate before turning back to Hawk. "She is a woman. Don't you share a bed?"

Hawk sighed. The conversation was not going the way he'd hoped. "I've never shared my bed before."

"You blame her for this?"

"I place no blame on her or myself."

"But you're not pleased with her?"

How had he ever thought talking to one woman about another would provide answers? The Fates must have been laughing to put Kate in his path. "More than pleased, Mother. I feel . . . I'm strongly attracted."

"Give her time. It is not an easy thing to be a captive. Our ways are not her ways. Be patient with her. She will need it," she mumbled, shooing them away with her hand.

Patience. Time. He'd give Kate both. After all, what choice did he have?

Kate watched them intently, her gaze going from one to the other. Hawk and Pia talked too rapidly for her to follow, but she was sure she was the topic of their conversation. Once they were out of hearing, she stopped him. "What were you saying to each other? I know it was about me."

"Aye. Pia said you learn quickly. She prepared the food this time, but in the future she thought you could handle the responsibility."

Kate couldn't suppress a small feeling of pleasure at the older woman's unexpected praise. Satisfied at least enough to relax, she pointed at a group of men, women, and children, all listening as one old Indian entertained them. Soon, using words and gestures, another man joined in. "What's going on there?"

"They're telling war stories. How they fought the Cheyenne, and how many of the enemy they killed."

"Do they tell the truth?"

A grin slashed his mouth, and at her puzzled frown he broke into a chuckle. "They're putting together a history to leave to their children. They've told it a thousand times, and will go on telling it that many more. They'll blur the difference a bit between history and yarn, and as a cook enhances with a dash of spice, a storyteller enriches with fantasy. 'Tis a pleasant way to spend some time, especially if the story is a good one. Not so different from the ways of the Irishmen. I heard many a tall tale at my da's knee."

"He has the attention of his audience; even the young men are interested."

"The young braves most of all. They learn what to expect from the enemy, what is expected of themselves. They learn how to be men, warriors."

Kate shuddered. "They learn cruelty at their papas' knees."

"Aye," he said, bitterness entering his voice again. "So do white children. The difference is in the rules. Once the red and white understand that, perhaps they can get along with one another."

"It means a lot to you that they get along?"

"It means everything. These are my mother's people. I've lived with them. I love them. But I learned to respect them from my father." He ran his fingers through his hair before looking pointedly at her. "I care about the world we pass along to our children, Kate."

Our children!

The thought was not as repugnant as it once might have been before she'd lain beside Hawk in his tipi and known his touch, the taste of his kiss. Never a Comanche baby . . . but Hawk's baby? She glanced at him, at his strong profile, and pictured holding his son. She had to remind herself over and over why she couldn't care for this man.

Hawk was Comanche.

Sensing that their conversation was as painful to him as to her, Kate tugged him to a circle of men and women sitting around a buffalo skin. Occasional laughter mixed with harsh words broke the attendant silence. One brave angrily pounded the earth. "What are they doing?"

"Gambling," he said, slowing his stride, intentionally guiding her in a different direction. She strained toward the group, tugging him along with her. "Can we watch? Please, Hawk."

Hoping to distract her, he hung back and pointed toward a field where young boys were engaged in a mock battle against the Cheyenne. "Don't you want to see how boys get to be braves?" Anything to get her away from the gamblers. "Comanche boys start early, learning and playing war games."

"Later, Hawk," she wheedled. "Besides, gambling's a game."

He gave in stiffly. "If you must, then let's go. Step softly. Let's not attract attention."

They eased up quietly and sat down close enough to see. After watching for several minutes, Kate pulled his head-down and whispered, her lips close to his cheek, "Keep me informed as to what's happening. Who's winning. Who's losing."

He braced himself against the temptation to turn his mouth to hers and forget anyone else within a hundred miles, forget what she'd done to him this morning, forget he'd stayed in a sweat for an hour afterward. He'd never known such feelings with anyone else, and he'd told himself again and again that his passionate need for her was exaggerated. But just as he knew the truth about himself, he also knew the truth about Kate. She wanted to lie in his arms, but her stubbornness always got in the way. He'd never force her. The decision to make love with him had to be hers.

Lost in his thoughts, he smiled at her. "What were you saying?"

"Who's the winner? The loser? I can't tell from here. Look, Hawk. They never look at the ugly man on the west side of the circle. When he speaks they ignore him."

Here it came, what he'd feared when she insisted on following the game. "He's mean. Cruel to his wives."

"How many does he have?" she asked.

Determined to be brief, he planned to answer only one question at a time. "None. He had two until recently."

His blunt words seemed only to heighten her interest. "What happened to them?"

How could he explain to a young white woman something so repugnant? "He killed them."

"No," she said under her breath. "Both of them?"

Hawk shrugged and tugged her braid over one shoulder. "Kills Often said they were unfaithful."

Several tense moments passed before she could speak. "And nobody stood up for them?"

"Aye. The women were sisters. Their family tried to reason with him. Offered him gifts, but he refused."

"And they did nothing to stop him?" She was silent a moment. When she spoke again, her voice carried above the gamblers' chatter. "If I'd been a relative, I'd have strung him up by his toes for the buzzards to feed on."

Hawk clapped a hand over her mouth. "Not so loud, Kate; we're attracting attention."

"You'd think their father would put an arrow through him."

"The marital bond is stronger than the blood bond." Hesitating a moment to gather his thoughts, he muffled his words with his hand, speaking sparingly, his eyes on her face. "Katie, darlin', white men killed their wives farther back than we have records. Remember Henry the Eighth? He cut off the heads of his wives. Bluebeard had his way of ridding himself of wives he didn't want."

"Bluebeard? A likely tale. How do you feel about Kills Often and other husbands murdering their wives?"

A lump of tenderness formed in his chest. "Katie, darlin', I may want to turn you over my knee, but to harm you . . . Nay, girl. I want only to make love with you."

She looked relieved, and then grinned wickedly. "Well, in either case, you should know that I have a dangerous left punch."

Sudden wailing broke through the quiet. The gamblers ignored the woman's groaning and continued to play without looking up. "Why is Kills Often laughing?"

"He won. He gets Big Bear's sister."

"God. Big Bear bet his sister. You must be mistaken."

Hawk rose and helped her to her feet. "Afraid not," he said impatiently, a scowl crossing his face. "Big Bear lost all his property. His horses. His tipi and everything in it. A mule. He had nothing left to bet. In desperation he bet Red Morning."

"It's enough to give wives and sisters nightmares."

"Kills Often can't get a wife, so he took the only way open to him: he gambled and won. Let's go watch the young braves shoot their arrows in competition."

Shuddering, Kate stumbled along, trying her best to keep her teeth from chattering. After walking a while, she had her stomach under control, but the party had lost its excitement. She desperately wanted to return to the quiet of their tipi. Let the

Indians live by their customs. She would never be able to.

But could she live with Hawk, a man who was half Indian? At this point, she couldn't honestly answer.

By the time darkness came the fires blazed cheerfully, and the celebration became noisier and more boisterous. The drums increased in volume. The young men and women chanted their songs and danced to the drumbeat. The dancers, men on one side, women on the other, stood a short distance apart. When the beat began, a brave selected a woman, placed his hands at her waist, and waited until she gripped him the same way. Then they moved in joyous abandon, round and round the fire, their friends outside the circle laughing and shouting and encouraging them all to go faster.

Hawk smiled at Kate and drew her into the circle. "Shall we, Kate?"

"I don't know how," she protested.

"It's not complicated, lass. I'll teach you."

A musical voice rose on the night air, the words lost in the beat of the drums, the rhythm drawing them into the cluster of dancers. Soon Kate moved naturally, letting Hawk show her the way. The pace quickened, and the ones applauding increased the sharp slap of their palms.

The drum continued to beat, but after Kate and Hawk had made many rotations, Hawk took pity on her. "Time to rest a bit, darlin'. Else you'll be calling me names in the morning."

"And it's thankin' ye I am, Master Hawk," she said, chuckling at her own attempt to imitate his Irish accent.

A woman came out of the darkness, planted herself in front of them, and held out her arms. "Dance with me, Grayhawk." Smiling provocatively, she drew her skirt to her thigh. She thrust out her breasts and moved her hips seductively to the beat of the drums. "I promise I'll not stop dancing till the drums quit. Nor will I stop anything else you might have in mind."

Kate's eyes narrowed. "What did she say, Hawk?"

"She wants me to dance."

"Tell her to find her own partner."

"I'm sorry, Morning Dove."

Crooking a forefinger, Morning Dove beckoned him before reaching down to take his hand. She pouted and pulled him forward. "Kite is tired. Morning Dove is not. Only a Comanche maiden knows how to dance with a brave."

When Kate jumped to her feet, the drums stilled. Silence as deafening as the noise settled over the revelry. "Look, you ill-mannered harlot. Keep your hands to yourself. I don't lend my man."

Hawk struggled to hide his delight, and the camp burst into raucous laughter. "Morning Dove is teasing you, darlin'. She knows I'm your man."

"Humph," Kate said, controlling her anger with effort. "There's no difference between Comanche humor and their practical jokes."

"Grayhawk's squaw has fire," a masculine voice yelled.

"She has a baby in her belly," another volunteered.

Hawk didn't translate. He didn't want the camp to see a riled Kate take aim with a fist.

The music started again, and Morning Dove laughed and undulated back to the group she'd left. The drums pounded their beat, and the dancers swung into the rhythm. A brave tried for Hawk's attention, and Hawk ignored him. Little Crow was not popular with Kate. To him, Little Crow was no longer a threat. Hawk smiled at Kate. "Time to dance, Kate, with your man."

She refused to meet his eyes. "When I said those words, it was to let that strumpet know she couldn't get by with rudeness."

"I understand," he said mischievously. "A woman has to guard her possessions."

"You're not my possession, nor are you my man. The words just slipped out," she said lamely. She placed her hands at his waist in the manner he had done. "Let's dance."

It was a splendid celebration, Hawk thought, easily the best he'd ever attended, but it would go on all night and tomorrow and into tomorrow night. His brow was beaded in sweat, his hair wet, his feet beginning to ache. A tantalizing smile bracketed his mouth. "A fine dance, Katie, love. Aye, the very best.

But it wears a man down. Would you be for going back to the tipi and resting a bit? In your man's arms, of course."

She tilted her chin and gave a shake of her head. "My man. The words already come back to haunt me. And yes, I'm ready to leave."

Laughter, jeers, and a few ribald jokes that Hawk made no effort to interpret followed them as they attempted to sneak away. Let his Kate think what she would; perhaps she thought their friends were bidding them good night.

Kate began undressing, stopping when she saw him cover the small fire with a container of sand. "What are you doing? By morning we'll be frozen stiff."

His eyes glittered with mischief. "I usually wake up that way," he said, adding hastily, "when the fire burns down, of course."

"I didn't know. You always seem warm to me."

He hid a chuckle. "Aye, warm when your body is close."

Eyeing him suspiciously, she started once more to take off her clothes, yawning as she loosened her skirt. "Must be past midnight."

"Don't take off your clothes. We've other plans for the night."

Surprise spread over her face. "With our clothes on?"

Laughter accompanied his words. "Aye, lass. The night is not always for sleeping. Sometimes it's for traveling," he whispered against her hair, "or loving."

She didn't move away but fixed him with a hopeful glance, her eyes wide and expectant. "We're leaving the camp, aren't we? Where are we going? You aren't taking me to Tascosa?"

"Nay, lass. We'll not play into Boggs's hands. To the Shamrock. My ranch. There I'll know you're safe."

"What will Stone Wolf think when the camp wakes up tomorrow and we're gone?"

"I've spoken to him." Hawk thought of his conversation with his grandfather, the old man's graciousness, his understanding. "And I listened."

"And he gave permission?"

"Aye. Come back, he said, when the baby is born."

"When the baby's born."

He splayed his fingers over her stomach, gently caressing as

165

he gazed down at her. "Aye. We must begin soon."

She backed away from him. "Tonight?"

"What's wrong with tonight?" he asked harshly, hoping his voice hid his longing and impatience. "Or last night? Or the night before?"

"I don't understand why we're leaving," she said, her breathing shallow. "And why now? Because you told Stone Wolf I'm pregnant?"

"Bloody hell, Kate. We're leaving. I lied to my grandfather. I told him we were making a baby. I'd like to keep my word, should the occasion ever arise. Which I doubt."

"There's one thing you've overlooked."

"Aye, and you'll hasten to tell me."

"I didn't invite myself here. And I made no promises to Stone Wolf. As for making a baby . . ."

It took him by surprise, the shine in her eyes that he finally realized was tears. They trembled on her lashes and eased down her cheeks. "What the . . . ?"

Her voice trembled. "None of your business, you . . . you Indian."

Transfixed, Hawk stared at her. His Kate, who hadn't paled before Little Crow when he had dragged her across the prairie, who had demanded food and water, knowing she'd be refused, Kate who worked at tanning skins because she wanted never to be dependent on anybody, was crying.

He put out a tentative finger to lift one of the teardrops and bring it to his mouth. Salty. Kate's tears were salty. The same could be said of her spirit.

"I don't know why you're crying, Katie. I thought you'd be glad to leave." He had never wanted her more than at this moment, her soft, moist lips tempting and tormenting him to ravish them.

"I want to go," she said, her voice unsteady. "After all, who wants to spend her life in a Comanche camp knowing some of the men may have killed her father?"

"Right," he said roughly. "I can't think of anybody, certainly not a white woman the Indians treat like a queen. Or the children who want her to sing. Or an old woman who treats her like a daughter." Impatiently, he flung an arm in the direction of the bedcovers. "We'll need blankets. Fold the hides so we can tie them over the horse's rump. Several miles down the canyon we'll come out on the prairies, where the wind is freer, stronger, and cold. Fill the parfleche with jerky. All you can stuff in it." He looked around at the sparse furnishings of the tipi, and with a silent oath turned abruptly and headed toward the entrance. "We've a way to go before morning comes and while the tribe is still asleep."

"Why are we going at night?"

"I didn't think you'd want to tell the camp good-bye." True words, but not the real reason they were stealing away like thieves in the night. If the military came, the soldiers would see him as an Indian, and the plan the colonel had carefully orchestrated would be lost in savagery. Hawk would likely lose his life. And what would happen to Kate? How had he gotten himself in such a tangled web?

Bitterly, he led the way to the horses, his fists clenched, fighting a private war that threatened all those he loved—and himself.

167

Chapter Nine

When they reached the horses, Hawk dropped the buffalo robes and drew Kate to him. In the waning light he let his gaze skim over her face, hoping for a pause, a bit of reluctance at leaving the village. Would she forget the shouts of the children, the smiles of the women? In the night would she long for the touch of his hand on her breast, or his thigh against hers, thinking the caresses unintentional? "Go quietly, lass; we wouldn't want to disturb the others. They wouldn't understand."

"Why not?"

"In their eyes, you've become one of us."

He heard her inhale. "I'll miss them. Not all of them, you understand. And I surely won't miss the hard work."

"Aye, lass. For that I'm glad as well."

Her breath fanned against his cheek, igniting his desire to have her content in his arms, to be his wife, moving from his Indian world to his white world, happy in either because he was there. He decided to tell her the whole truth.

"We wouldn't want to explain why we're leaving. That you want to leave. And that I'm afraid of a raid by the military.

Going now, we'll avoid having to make those difficult explanations."

"I can't believe the soldiers wouldn't honor a white woman."

"I consider this a wise move. I am worried that one day a spy will find the canyons at a time when Stone Wolf has his band here. They will ride in with their rifles and handguns, shooting and killing everyone, even children. They'll take you for a Comanche. And now we'll talk no more about it."

She leaned closer to him, pointed toward the coat covering the buffalo skins, and spoke barely above a whisper. "What are you doing?"

"The white man's slicker has many uses. Protection from wind, the cold. I picked this one up at a trading post." He glanced at the starless sky. "In this case, the slicker will keep the buffalo robes dry in case of rain." He lifted her onto the back of the horse, then wrapped the hides and tied them on behind her. He tossed one robe over her shoulders and tucked it about her. "You'll need it near morning." Satisfied that she was ready to travel, he threw himself onto Midnight's bare back and, holding the reins of the mare, started up the trail. Black night enveloped them, bringing the unmistakable smell of rain, and with it a latent sense of danger.

He didn't consider himself superstitious, not the way some of his Irish countrymen invoked the protection of saints against noises they couldn't explain. But the omens given Stone Wolf? Aye, those Hawk believed, and because of them he relied on his intuition. He gave one last glance at the fires lighting the tipis and urged Midnight forward.

The feast was in full swing and would go on until the tribe was exhausted or a rain drove them inside. Earlier in the day, Hawk had said good-bye to his grandfather. He had explained that the time for him and Kate to leave had come. It had not been easy to tell Stone Wolf of his plan to take Kate away. He spoke of his fear that the military would find their village and take her back to her people. He explained to his grandfather that white women who had spent time with the Indians returned to a harsh and cruel life. "She'll be a target for slurs, Grandfather."

The old man had agreed, only reiterating his earlier request that Hawk bring his great-grandson to see him. "Before I die," he had said, and without meeting the man's wise old eyes, Hawk had promised. They had talked again of the camp's location on high ground far enough away from the stream that, should a heavy rain occur, the tribe would be safe. They talked of the soldiers, and of the whites in their haphazard rides over the prairies, finding the camp. It was just a matter of time, Hawk had told his grandfather. "The soldiers come closer and closer. One day they will ride in. We must work with the colonel."

The parting was sad and solemn.

No longer willing to dwell on their leavetaking, Hawk studied the task uppermost in his mind: getting Kate safely away. He was unable to see more than a few feet ahead of them and was forced to rely on hearing and memory. If they were to find the sheepherders' adobe hut before the rain set in, he'd have to depend on Midnight's surefootedness, his instinct, and his eyesight in the dark, traits that would help lead them to the cabin.

As they traveled, the stars disappeared and a great black cloud muttered threateningly. Broad sheets of light flashed from its heavy underbelly. The storm drew nearer, occasional streaks of lightning cutting through the sooty darkness. At such times Hawk had glimpses of remembered sandstone walls that now served as points of reckoning. A strangely shaped rock, an ancient cottonwood, curves in the stream, all became sentinels pointing them toward the ravine and the sheepherders' cabin.

Clumps of evergreens bowed and swayed in a whirling dervish not unlike the dance of the Apache. Mesquite trees shimmered their lacy leaves and exposed their black trunks to the lash of the gale. When rain began with big, fat drops, he knew they were in for a cold, wet journey.

Hawk spoke softly. "Kate, we've a way to go. The rain will get worse. Can you hear me?"

"Yes, I hear you. I just can't see you until the lightning shows me you're still there."

He'd always be there for her, for despite her denial, she was his woman, his Kate. "We've come a few miles. I'm not sure how many. Maybe five. We should reach a certain ravine soon, and from there it's about half a mile to the cabin. Uphill all the way, I'm afraid."

Depending on Midnight's ability to choose his way carefully, Hawk gave the horse its head. He looked behind often to where Kate hunched over the saddle horn. Flashes of light revealed her white face. As usual, she was too stubborn to complain, but he was sure that, given half a chance, she'd have a few choice words to fling about.

The sporadic fall of raindrops changed to a hard, driving rain, pelting them relentlessly. The trail had become a journey in mud. When the storm hit, it struck with the ferocity of a great, dark bird, swooping, shrieking, slicing the sky with a forked beak of lightning.

Hawk's concern for Kate became intolerable. "Kate, can you hear me? Are you all right? Damnit, Katie, answer me."

Her voice sounded faintly. "I'm cold. My feet are frozen. My hands have no feeling. Otherwise, I'm fine."

"You're brave, darlin'. The rain's getting worse now. I'm going to hurry Midnight along, so hang on tight. You hear me?"

"I hear."

The farther they went, the harder the rain fell, and the heavier the clouds became. A dazzling flash of lightning, a rumbling growl of thunder, and above the fury, a distant sound that froze the blood in his veins—an unforgettable roar not unlike the agonized bellow of a great, wounded beast thrashing its way to safety in the depths of the ocean.

A cloudburst on the floodplain. A hard-driving rain that poured its runoff into the stream, transforming the stream into a monster.

Hawk faced the fact they could be washed away, and the pitch-black darkness paled beside the fear welling in his breast. They had so little time, not enough for him to dismount and go back to reassure her. Perhaps not enough time to reach the cabin. He kept calling out to her, making sure she was still with him. "Kate, can you hear me? Hang on, darlin'." As his ears became accustomed to the fury of the storm, he heard her faint answer.

171

Hoping she had a firm grasp on the saddle, he kicked Midnight in the flank. The big horse surged forward into a gallop and the mare followed gamely, both animals instinctively aware of the danger. Hawk swiveled to look back. Kate clung to the saddle horn, her body almost level with the horse's back.

In the precious little time left, he had to get Kate to safety, straight ahead toward the great wall of water roaring toward them. If he had reckoned correctly, the ravine was less than half a mile from where they were.

The dense black vault above them split with a dazzling fork of lightning, and the whole canyon lay vividly clear. A quarter mile, maybe less, lay between them and safety. Midnight lengthened his powerful stride to great, ground-eating leaps, taking Kate's mare with him. And above the crashing and roaring, the rumble of water became louder.

Unsure at first, Hawk recognized the break in the cliff walls. His despair gave way to hope. If they could make it up the slope and then to higher ground, they had a chance, puny at best, but a chance nevertheless. Bending low over Midnight's neck, he praised the horse, thanked him for being his friend and for risking his life to save them.

The big animal responded. He heaved them upward, his great haunches bunching to find purchase. Slipping and sliding, he carried them forward, every foot a step farther from death. Again and again, Hawk screamed at Kate to hold on, willed her to hang on, and between curses, prayed fervently she gripped the saddle horn so tightly she couldn't possibly fall.

He could hear the hungry slurping of water growing wilder, louder, more threatening. Midnight climbed, carrying them up and up above the burgeoning stream. At last they were on high ground, Hawk thought, out of the way of the flood, but he couldn't be sure. He wiped the rain from his eyes, waited for a flash of lightning, and made out the lofty niche where sheepherders had had the presence of mind to locate their cabin. Hawk blessed them again. If he'd had another hand, he'd have made the sign of the cross.

Tension eased from his shoulders. He could breathe again.

Kate would be safe in the weather-beaten hut, and as soon as he could get a fire started, she'd be warm.

He swung his leg over Midnight's neck, jumped to the ground, and hurried back to where Kate huddled in the buffalo skin. He couldn't determine which looked more dejected, the mare or Kate.

"We made it," he exulted. "We made it, honey. We're safe."

"Safe," she whispered. "Oh, God, safe."

"I'll help you down."

"My face is frozen. Hands too cold. I can't let go of the horn."

Seeking to loosen her fingers, he gently pried them away, drew her feet from the stirrups and pulled her down. With scarcely a murmur, she sank into his arms and buried her face against his chest. He held her tenderly, promising she'd soon be warm, that he knew she was hungry. He wiped the water from her face and lifted her into his arms. Slogging through mud and rocks and little rivers of water, he carried her to the cabin.

Below them, the torrent struck with the force of a locomotive, crashing and booming and shaking the earth, blasting its way down the canyon and devastating everything before it in its wild rampage toward the sea.

Kate shuddered in his arms and pressed closer. He thought of their terrible brush with death, of the village with its tipis spread along the banks of the normally placid stream. Once in a hundred years, Stone Wolf had told Hawk, when Hawk played around his knees, a terrible flood struck the canyon. A great water surged through the canyon, tearing at its cliffs, taking everything that got in the way. His father had spoken of such a happening, Stone Wolf had said.

Hawk peered through the rain at the faint outline of the cabin. Tonight must have seen the end of the hundred years. His people were safe downstream, their tipis on higher ground. This time he thanked the Great Spirit.

He kicked the adobe door open and stepped inside the pitch-black cabin. The place smelled musty, but it was dry, and that was the main thing. Working to get his bearings, he set Kate on her feet with the admonition to lean against the wall until he could get a fire started. When she began to protest, he silenced her with a few words and a significant glance. "I don't know who's here, or what you might stumble over." He heard nothing further from her.

Spotting the wood box, he also found some of the new matches that could be lighted by scratching the head. "Once I get a blaze going, it won't take long for you to get warm." Kneeling, he glanced at her over his shoulder. "Are you all right?"

"Yes. Not so cold now."

The fire caught and soon cast a flickering light, exposing the rustic interior. On one side a bed, laced with strips of rawhide, sported sacks of straw that served as a mattress. A crude table held center stage, a bench on either side. Chairs with rawhide bottoms had been placed near the fireplace. Nobody had been here for a while, but the last person to use the place had filled the wood box.

The sheepherders who had built the adobe had constructed it to last.

Kate remained against the wall. She'd freed her hair from its braid and allowed it to hang limply about her shoulders. Now and then she'd shudder and pull the robe more closely about her.

Rising from starting the fire, Hawk went to her. "Take that chair next to the fireplace. I'll give you a hand."

"You don't have to worry about me. I've been cold before."

"I know, lass, you can handle it, but there's no law that says I can't lend a hand."

"Thanks. To be honest, I can't help thinking about any animals that might be hiding here."

Hawk chuckled. "It's animals that's bothering you, is it?"

"What kind . . . ?" She gave a shake of her head. "I don't think I want to know."

"I'll have a look. The floor's dirt. Dirty as you'd expect."

"Usual with dirt floors," she said dryly, and he laughed.

After scouting the corners, he told her the house was free of varmints. "You can shiver just at the cold now."

"Thank God the place is dry, and," she said, shuddering, "we're out of the storm."

He hadn't the heart to tell her how close they'd been to death, how Midnight and the mare had barely gotten them above the water in time. The surefooted animals had saved them. "Let me take off your wet boots." She protested that she could remove the boots herself, but he caught a heel and tugged. He placed both boots near the fire.

Taking her right foot in his hand, he massaged warmth into her cold toes, noting how small her feet were, how perfectly shaped. He gently transferred his attention to her left one and knew from her face when her feet lost their throbbing and stinging. He continued his ministrations awhile longer and then rose. "I'll take care of the horses and bring in the buffalo robes. Who knows? Maybe they stayed dry."

Outside, the rain showed no signs of letting up. He drew Midnight and the mare to the lee side of the house, where the adobe backed up to a rocky ridge, and where there was more protection from the driving rain. He stroked the mare's neck. "Poor beastie, you've spent a miserable night following your stallion." He turned to Midnight, patting his wet forehead. "Look after her, laddie; she's a good match for you. I've such a one inside, but I've a notion your chances are better than mine."

After checking the animals for cuts and bruises, he made wild promises that when the storm was over and morning came, he'd see they had food. He had no notion of how he'd keep his word, but he'd bloody well give it a try.

Inside once more, he shoved the door shut and fastened the latch. "A hell of a storm, and it shows no sign of letting up."

Kate looked at his hair plastered to his head, then down to where puddles had formed around his feet. "Come dry yourself by the fire." She grinned. "You're getting the floor muddy."

"Just got here and you're nagging already," he said, chuckling. "I expect you're hungry. I'll get the pemmican."

"Woman's work."

"Aye, woman's work. When your boots dry we'll make different arrangements."

An iron cookpot, not as large as Pia's, hung from a hook on the fireplace. A few broken pieces of pottery served as bowls. Sparse but adequate, Kate thought, as she made a visual journey about the room, hoping they wouldn't have to spend much time here. Surely the rain would be gone by morning.

Her gaze collided with the bed. They would sleep there, both of them in the small bed. Closer than the pallet they'd shared in the tipi. So close their nude bodies would be touching all night. Her heart started its racing, pulsing, hammering beat, warming her in outrageous places too private to mention. She could not—must not—be tempted this night.

"More pemmican?"

Kate lifted her eyes to his and shook her head. "Pemmican isn't my favorite food."

"Only when you're hungry and cold and have nothing else is pemmican good. If you're ready we should go to bed. The rain is still coming down. Harder, if anything."

She was tired. Her muscles ached. But she was warm and dry and no longer hungry, at least for pemmican. "I wish we had jerky."

"That's for breakfast."

She told herself she could relax. She was no longer in danger of starving or drowning. Hawk had steered them through the harrowing experience, and when death seemed certain, he'd led them to the cabin. At the time she could think only of the baby, and Hawk, who, unaware that their child grew in her stomach, had risked his life. For her.

She had escaped the incessant and never-ending hard work, and was heading back to a civilization where she belonged. For some reason, knowing she'd cut her ties with members of the camp didn't bring the elation she'd thought it would.

Away from Hawk.

It should have made her happy to know that in a short time she'd never have to share a pallet with an Indian, to bathe in a stream, to cook in one big pot, or to scrape a buffalo hide. She'd never see the sun slide over the rim of the canyon, hear the chant of the children, or lie at night beside Hawk.

The fire flickered, and she glanced up. He had stripped his

jacket over his head and loosened the rawhide tie that held up his pants. He stood naked, a bronze savage who'd cheated the flood, had challenged nature in one of her terrible tantrums. With help from the fire, she could see his hard, gray eyes.

"Bedtime."

She curled her toes, stared at the fire, and then looked back to him. "Yes." It wasn't the first time she'd seen him naked, but each time she was amazed at his body, at the power and beauty of it. She wanted to slide her hands over his sleek chest. Tonight it was just the two of them. No Stone Wolf, no Pia, no children, no Indians. "Yes," she said again.

"If it's worried you are about what I might do to you, you can put your mind at ease."

No, she wasn't worried, not about what he would do, but of the direction her treacherous body might lead her. Worried? With her body clamoring for his touch, all fatigue gone, every nerve aware? This raw need had plagued her since the night in the hotel room. It haunted her dreams. It spawned restless desires. These new feelings had come when she should have been remembering and thinking about Papa. How the howling savages had tortured him to death. But the memories were fleeting, replaced by nagging thoughts of satisfying her needs, of Hawk's arms around her.

She stood and laid the buffalo robe aside. She had shed her damp clothes already, while Hawk was outside tending the horses. Now she was as naked as he. The trick was to walk tall, get to the bed, away from those probing eyes, lie down on the straw mattress, and cover herself. Perhaps he'd ignore her and want to sleep, but she doubted it, sure that he harbored desires similar to her own.

After carrying her in and removing her boots, he'd made no move to touch her. Nor did he now. To wipe that frown from his face, she supposed, would take an act of God.

The act came sooner than expected: a flash so intense, so eerily bright, it flooded the room with an unholy brilliance. Shrieks followed, a crash, an earsplitting boom. Sobbing in terror, Kate hurled herself into his arms. She clung to him, shuddering, her face buried against his throat.

"Oh, Hawk," she cried. "Oh, God. What's happening?"

He clasped her tightly, murmuring encouragement, assuring her the storm would pass, that she was safe and needn't worry. Because he was there.

Stretched to the breaking point, Kate locked herself in his arms and refused to move. Gradually she became aware of his naked body and of her breasts pressed against his chest, of the changes taking place in them both. He lowered his head to search her face, and whatever he sought, he found, changing swiftly from comforter to lover.

He adjusted her nude body, cradled her hips against his, and took her mouth. Growling deep in his throat he tasted and demanded. And because she was unable to turn away, she followed blindly, meeting his need with the same primal insistence. The throbbing, blazing, naked feel of him, skin against skin, pounding heart against pounding heart, took away all thought but the escalating demands of her body.

His skillful hands found her breasts and caressed them. His thumbs stroked the crests to hard pebbles. His mouth followed, scorching a trail to lave each in turn with the same intense attention. Trembling, her defenseless body responded. She made a weak attempt to move away and met his eyes.

"Stop me if this isn't what you want," he said, his voice hoarse.

She couldn't think, didn't want to think. All she wanted was to follow his lead, trusting blindly that where he led them would satisfy this terrible and desperate need.

"Tell me, Katie. Tell me yes."

Katie tried to dredge up the words to say no, to confound him with them, bewilder him as he confused her, but no sound came, not even a whimper. After a struggle, she gave up with a tiny, almost imperceptible movement of her head. "Yes," she whispered.

Helpless to slow the tide, she sank into the wonder of it, responding to the invasion of his tongue, the delicious scrape of his hands over her breasts. In the powerful grip of desire, she strained to breathe, pulling his head down, drowning in the molten steel of his eyes, the taste of his mouth.

"Aye, lass," he mumbled, lifting her effortlessly and carrying her to the bed. He nipped at her lip. " 'Tis a beggarly place, but we'll make do."

"Aye," she whispered. And again, "Aye." She smothered a moan in the onslaught of his mouth. In the far recesses of her mind, she goaded her conscience, acknowledging that he was Indian. Comanche. The enemy.

Struggling with honesty, she willed herself to pull away, to distance herself from the force that rendered her helpless, but its claim was too intense and too delicious.

Body against body, flesh against flesh, heart against heart. When he thrust into her, she rose to meet him, her gaze focused on his face, the furrow fierce between his eyes. Her mind allowed no thought except this thundering, indescribable need.

He seduced her with lavish endearments, breathing them against her mouth, her cheeks, her throat, words to encourage, words she didn't recognize. "I want to please you," he whispered, "ravish you until you're aware only of my mouth and my hands. I want to hold you in my arms and press my body against yours. I want to fill you, and have you know the wonder of it all. Aye, Katie, I want to give you that."

She felt the wonder, feared she'd drown in it. She took and took all that he gave, and in the loving, gave in return. Her body rocked to the rhythm of his, higher and higher, until she was sure she could go no further. Panting, calling his name, she strained for what eluded her.

"Reach for it, darlin'," he rasped harshly, his lips against her mouth, his ragged breath against her face. "I'll take you there."

And she reached, moaning, climbing, going up and up until there was no peak left, only the searing heat before the explosion. Wild, raw, it catapulted her into a dizzying pool of sensation. And she was glad when he joined her, shuddering, pouring himself into her.

Later, after she'd given in to the delicious lethargy that followed, she wondered at the powerful greed that had prompted their giving thoughtlessly, each to the other, and ultimately satisfying themselves.

Hawk shifted to lie beside her, covering them with the skin.

179

He propped his head on his elbow and looked down at her. She knew he searched for answers, but she had none for him. And none for herself. When he drew her limp body to him, she gave in once more to the comfort of his arms.

"It's time to sleep, lass," he said huskily.

Hawk awakened first, his body curved around Kate, her hair tickling his nose. He buried his nose into the tangled mass, inhaling the faint fragrance her hair always seemed to have. All warm acquiescence last night, she had given and given, melting into him, matching her own need to his reckless demand.

Would she wake with warm remembrance in her eyes? Or would the memory be hateful to her? The storm had passed on during the night hours. Below them water still boiled and churned, blocking their leaving by way of the stream, and while that was the shortest way to the Shamrock, it would be impassible for days. Better to take the trail up to the rim and run the risk of a confrontation with the military or with Indians from another tribe.

It was barely light and already Kate was stirring in his arms. He had cradled her small body during the night, and this morning his hands still sought the delicious silky feel of her. She shifted to meet his eyes. Hers were cloudy and tempered with anger.

"Morning, lass. Sleep well? I know the bed wasn't what you'd call comfortable, but it was dry."

"Humph."

"The storm passed during the night. Dumped more water than Texas usually sees in a year."

"Humph."

He held on tightly, but anger started in his chest. It spread rapidly over his body, heating his face and clouding his mind. After last night, how in hell could she spoil everything?

"I guess you didn't sleep too well?"

"I slept just fine."

He watched her out of the corner of his eye. She looked temptingly soft and pink, her shoulders bare above the robe she clutched to her chin. Despite his frustration, the sight of her got his blood circulating. "Maybe you just need a cup of coffee."

"Tea will do."

"Well, I hate to tell you, but we're out of both." So she wanted a fight this morning. Well, his foul mood would match hers. He was ready to go the full ten rounds. She had flung herself at him, and what was he to do but go along? It was true that he hadn't lost control as she had. At least not then. It was also true he'd taken advantage of the thunderbolt's crash. And true that after he had his arms around her, he couldn't have stopped loving her if the cabin had washed away. "Perhaps you'd settle for jerky?"

She turned toward him, her gaze clashing with his. "You know what I'm thinking, and it isn't about the damned jerky."

"Well, now, since I'm not a mind reader, would you care to share those lovely early morning thoughts with your bedmate?"

"No," she said archly, "I wouldn't."

"I suppose you're going to say last night was a mistake. Should never have happened."

"That's right. It should never have happened. You know how I feel about Indians."

"Firsthand, when it comes to this one." She was a fine one to talk, throwing herself at him, all quivering flesh, her face flushed, wanting him the way he wanted her. His temper rose along with other parts of his body. "Especially about this one."

"I'm not calling you names. Just Indians in general."

"Damnit, Kate, I can't help it if I'm an Indian."

He saw her blink rapidly to force back the tears. *Bloody hell.* He didn't want to make her cry. He wanted to hold her in his arms and make love again, slow and easy and satisfying. He wanted to see her face when he helped her toward the summit, catching her when she tumbled down.

He'd worried all night, wondering how she would wake up: angry or loving, snarling or acquiescent? From the look on her face, she'd never smile at him again. And as for lying with him, her mind on making love, her body soft and yielding—that was a memory to dredge up at inopportune times, like right now.

181

Throwing back the buffalo robe, she stood a moment, her face white and strained walked to her clothes, and began putting them on. "About your being an Indian, I have nothing further to say."

"That shows great understanding," he said mockingly. "In the meantime, I'll check outside, take care of the horses." He slammed the door behind him.

The rain had washed away part of the hill. He could only marvel at the whirling, churning monster that swirled below him. They were alive today thanks to Midnight. Last night he wouldn't have given two cents for their chances.

Using his most respectful tone, he thanked Midnight and the mare, running his hands over them, making sure he hadn't missed any cuts or bruises the night before. The skies had cleared without a cloud in sight. The sun winked its way over the horizon and promised a beautiful day. Much of the water had formed gullies and drained into the whirling torrent below them. The rocky hillside was firmer than he'd expected. He walked a way toward the rim, dodging loose boulders that had washed down, some big enough to knock a hole in the cabin. Once again he was overwhelmed at how close they'd come to death.

He trudged back to the door, wiping his feet on the rocks as best he could. Kate sat before the fire, running her fingers through her hair. She didn't speak or look at him. Because he couldn't think of anything to say, he went to the wood box, took out a couple of logs, and placed them in the fireplace. "Looks passable outside. We can leave when you're ready." He couldn't resist. "Unless you'd like to spend another night."

She twisted in the chair to look at him. "Be reasonable."

"Reasonable, is it?" he said, slapping his forehead. "Reasonable."

Her eyes narrowed, sliding from his head to his feet; then to his utter surprise and for no plausible reason that he could think of, she laughed.

"From reasonable to humorous," he said. "What next?"

She burbled with forced laughter. "I'm twenty-two years old, and . . . have lived enough for two lifetimes. I have two choices:

to laugh or to cry. No, make that three. I could always scream. Because of my mother's determination to marry me to the town's richest boor, and my stepfather's unflagging efforts to molest me, I ran away. Sang in a saloon for enough money to provide food and shelter, sold my virginity to pay my sister's way to Texas, became threatened by the saloon owner, captured by Indians, became an Indian wife and went to bed again with an Indian who claimed to be an Irishman."

His voice demanded that she listen. "The Indian you describe is also an Irishman. I'm proud to be both. As for the times you spent in my bed, you came to me willingly. The first time for money. I would have given you the money for the asking. The second time you came because you wanted to." He watched her long, tapered fingers continue their slide through her hair. "The third time, Kate Hartland, will be the same."

"There won't be a third time."

"Aye, lass," he said gently, "you can count on it; there will be a third time. And after that a fourth and a fifth. Maybe not tomorrow nor the day after. But you'll come, searching for a place in my arms."

"You're so sure."

He leaned toward her. "You've been there once, Katie." His voice was low and mesmerizing. "You found joy. And you won't forget."

"Humph."

"I take it the subject's closed." He grinned at her, enjoying the changes in her expressions as she threaded her way through the challenges he'd tossed her. "Best we be on our way."

"Will we go down to the creek the way we came up?"

"The canyon's filled with water." He went about folding the buffalo robes. "You might have told me about your sister."

"I've never liked being dependent. Owing somebody. When we were growing up, Mama would give us something, Maureen and me, and in return we were expected to repay it in ways she wanted. She was determined I'd marry Verlin Digby. When I refused, she made sure Maureen would marry him."

"So Maureen is married to this man, even though you sent her a hundred dollars to get her away?"

183

"Maureen always did what Mama told her."

"But you couldn't."

"No. With Mama, she and I always ended up shouting at each other. Maureen wouldn't do that. She was too scared. Especially after Papa was killed and Mama married Milton."

"Did Milton make . . . Was he . . . Did he make improper advances?"

"Every chance he got. We tried to tell Mama the kind of man he was, but she wouldn't listen. She said he was a man of God. She alway believed him when he said that we had encouraged him to touch us."

Hawk shook his head. Such a plight for two young girls. Fate had thrown one of them in his path. He believed strongly in fate. "How did you get away?"

"Mama was away, and Milton came into my bedroom when I was dressing. He started tearing at my clothes, accusing me of inviting him to do things to me. We were wrestling when Mama came in. She called me names. She said I should marry Verlin right away, before I got into trouble."

"But you couldn't do that. This Verlin. How did you feel about him?"

She gave a mutinous toss of her head. "Verlin? He was twice my age. Not exactly a young girl's dream. Mama liked him because he owned Digby Mercantile, the biggest store in town. Milton liked him because he was a big contributor to the church."

"And later your mother chose Maureen to take your place as Verlin's wife."

"Actually, Verlin's a good man, but . . ." Her face turned a delicate shade of pink. "I could never have gone to bed with him."

"And Maureen?"

"Maury doesn't have a backbone. Even after I sent her the money, she let Mama talk her into marrying him."

"You hear from your mother?"

"Not once." Pain etched its way across her face, haunting her eyes. "I'm in such a state. Everything I believe in has turned upside down. I loved my father so much, and his death was such a terrible blow. For all I know, your kin may have killed Papa. I feel like a traitor. I've been in your arms. More than that, I threw myself into them and spent the night there."

For a fleeting moment she had allowed him into her private world of despair. Her story was not a new one, nor very original, but because she was Kate, his Kate, he felt her anguish as if it were his own. He told himself he couldn't change what had happened to her, but as long as she stayed with him, he'd protect her from men like her stepfather and Nathan Boggs.

"Try not to dwell on it, lass," he said, kneeling beside her, "or you'll let the pain drive away the pleasure."

"Ha. Pleasure. Pain. One always comes with the other. What's the difference?"

"Living is good. The bad things you can't change you put away and forget." He kissed her tenderly and smiled. "If you can't forget them, tell them to me and I'll make them go away."

She sighed. "I wish it were that easy."

"Think now about getting to the Shamrock and meeting the people who live there. There's the foreman, Malachi; and the cowboys; Juanita, the cook; and Anna, the housekeeper. Gertrude the upstairs maid. And a couple of new additions, Coleridge and Afton, a black man and a young white girl." He hesitated at telling her about the massacre of the wagon train.

"Please don't coddle me. I'm not a child."

"Wouldn't consider it," he said lightly, getting to his feet, "but we need to be on our way. We've several miles to go, and a muddy climb ahead of us."

The climb proved less muddy than he'd expected, since there was a rocky trail straining upward, leading to the canyon rim. Where the rain had washed the prairies, the sun splashed its rays over the grass and sagebrush, spilling tiny liquid diamonds. It was a rare day.

A good day, he thought, one that had started badly but had turned into a balmy autumn promise of better things ahead. When he turned, Kate met his look with a scowl. Color had not fully returned to her face, and he shrugged at his hasty assessment. He still had her with him, and after last night, who could tell? Maybe he'd keep his word to Stone Wolf after all.

Chapter Ten

As Sean led the way up the narrow trail, and her horse followed obediently, Kate examined the Irishman. He had reminded her to call him Sean now that they were no longer among the tribe. The name change wasn't difficult to remember. After all, Sean was the name she had known him by when she sang at the Lily. They had started the ride in a friendly enough manner, Kate thought as they climbed out of Tule Canyon. Both were aware of the stiffness, the wariness that followed the change in their relationship.

He began the day in clothes that allowed him to enter the white man's world without question, shirt, jacket, pants, boots—rancher's attire. His hair was tucked under a cap, its jaunty angle making it dip ever so slightly over his right eye. Gone was any vestige of his Indian identity.

An Irishman even to the song he bellowed, he looked back frequently, and to outward appearances forgot the morning's unpleasantness. She wished she could do the same, but the previous night lingered in her mind, too disturbing to be dismissed with a song. She had no defense. Her body went out of control. And her mind? *Ha.* She lost it in his arms, swallowed up in a delirious, sweet madness.

When he addressed her this morning, it was the Irishman with his lilting voice who sought to charm her and succeeded far beyond his dreams. Had the pattern been set? Knowing the feel of his mouth, the lure of his body, would she yield again and yet again to his gentle persuasion? To that lovely glory? The mystery of it?

Was he correct in saying she'd come back to his arms, not once but many times? Would her head rule her heart, or would her heart dictate? Now that she carried a child, what should she do? Stay at the Shamrock until she had money enough to leave? Soon her condition would be obvious, and since the child was his also, how would he feel at her leaving?

She'd had a frightful time this morning, hiding her nausea. All she'd wanted to do was to lie down or maybe die.

"Why don't you sing with me, Kate? On such a morn, sing-ing's a calling sent from heaven to bless travelers on their way to wherever they're going." He looked at her closely. "You're not still angry, are you, lass?"

"My head is full of conflicting thoughts. I'm wondering what comes next in this crazy, mixed-up world."

"And can you change it by worrying?" At the shake of her head, he chuckled. "Then why worry?"

What could she expect at Sean's ranch? She had no clothes, no money. The boots on her feet had been a gift from him. She'd had pitifully little when she left the Lily.

With Pia, she'd spent time making the top and skirt she wore now, a replacement for the tattered attire she'd arrived in. The remainder of her time had been used to do chores and, of course, to make Sean's jacket. After removing it last night, this morning he'd tucked it in with the buffalo robes. A shoddy piece of work, she thought morosely, when compared to ones made by the Indian women. She should have learned more about the care of skins before attempting to make a garment for him. But then she hadn't been born into this world to be-come Comanche.

Although her clothes said differently, she thought ruefully as she looked down at the Indian garb she wore. Her doeskin skirt, long-sleeved jerkinlike top, and leggings all did nothing to proclaim her white. Outwardly their positions had been reversed: Sean was Irish; she was Comanche. And they were headed toward civilization.

The climb to the rim of the canyon had been steep, and they'd been forced to go single file, but when they reached the top, the sun had jumped over the horizon to bathe the prairies in golden sunshine. Sean beckoned her forward so they could ride abreast.

"The Shamrock is a full day's ride from here. When you get tired, we can stop and rest." Fun sparkled in his eyes. "Don't be afraid to speak up."

No, she wouldn't be afraid to speak, nor had she ever been, but one disturbing thought after another tumbled through her mind. After last night and their conversation this morning, she wasn't ready to talk about the baby, to discuss their future, to empty herself of her beleaguered thoughts.

"I'm sure I'll impress those present at the Shamrock with my Indian dress."

"Kate, darlin', I had McDougal at the trading post order clothes for you when I picked up your boots so you could ride to the Shamrock in style, but I never got back to get them. I'm sorry."

"No need to be. Once we're there I'll make some clothes. At least a change."

"Aye, whatever you say." But his frown said he wasn't happy about it. He turned abruptly and halted his horse and hers. "Katie, there's something you must know, something that is important and must be addressed."

From the look on his face, whatever he planned to tell her was serious. "I'm here. Tell me."

"I have to trust you, Kate."

Puzzled, she watched the strain appear about his eyes and mouth. He was so serious, so intense. "Yes," she said, dreading his answer. "What . . . what is it?"

"Nobody at the Shamrock knows I'm part Comanche, except Malachi. He knew my father and my mother before I was born.

It's very important that people coming to the ranch—guests, servants, cowboys—consider me an Irishman."

She sighed in relief. What he was asking did not affect her. She had only to give her word. Before she could get her breath, her confidence shattered. If anyone found out about his ancestry, his life as well as hers and the baby's could be in jeopardy. She wanted desperately for her voice to be steady. "Mind telling me why?"

He hesitated overlong, finally answering her question. "A military man and I are working toward bringing about some kind of a lasting peace between Stone Wolf's band and the whites in the area. The idea is that if the two groups can get along here, the strategy could spread to other bands and other tribes. Not," he said bitterly, "that we've had any success to this point."

"If the whites find out, they will likely kill you."

"I'm afraid so."

"And the Indians? Stone Wolf?"

"My grandfather," he said, pride seeping into his voice, "is wise to the plan. He's lending his support."

"And his braves? His warriors?"

"They know I'm half white."

Kate read between the lines, her heart setting up an uncomfortable pounding. "But the Indians don't know of the plan, and if they find out, they'll kill you."

He broke into a grin. "I knew you'd understand, darlin'."

"Crazy Indian." She tried to smile and failed. How could he joke about something so serious? "What will you tell people at the Shamrock about me?"

"I've been giving that some thought. I'll tell them I rescued you. That you were—"

"For heaven's sake, don't say I was scraping a rabbit hide to make a cap."

"Picking berries. I'll say you were picking berries and I happened by."

"And Stone Wolf's braves stood around and watched us ride away."

Sean smiled broadly, enjoying himself. "When you put it that way, maybe it's not the best plan."

"Say I slipped away at night and you found me before the Indians could put out a search party."

"Aye, that's better, and believable. Now let's forget all about it."

But she couldn't forget. She could see through two sets of eyes. Indian and white. He had put his fate in her hands, and she wasn't comfortable with the arrangement. What if she had a slip of the tongue, and because of her Sean lost his life? What if somebody recognized her from the Gilded Lily, and Boggs came looking for her, seeking the truth about her relationship with Sean and finding he was part Indian, parading as an Irishman? Such thoughts cut her to the quick.

Once again Sean was the engaging host, pointing out places of interest, a gnarled tree, a distant hill, a buffalo wallow, even educating her on the merits of the short native grass. It came as a surprise to her, this possessive feel for the land that he shared with her.

"Shamrock acres, Kate. Wide-open pastures beneath the very vault of heaven."

She was incredulous. "Your land? All of this?"

"Aye." He laughed exuberantly, and made a magnanimous sweep of his arm. "The whole bloody lot of it, lass."

She was surprised that he owned so much land, but then it appeared worthless. Miles and miles of nothing but sagebrush and tumbleweeds. Now that she'd soon be back where she belonged, with people of her own kind, she could work for a wage. If Sean were not in a position to pay her, perhaps another rancher, one more affluent would. She'd make new clothes, apparel big enough to hide her condition a while longer. Very soon she'd leave and make a fresh start somewhere, get a job singing. If she had to, she could pretend to be a widow and teach, maybe in California.

She had to do something. The Shamrock, as he so lovingly called his home, would be a place to begin. She should have been elated at the prospect of leaving, getting out on her own. Going to San Francisco. Maybe Denver. But something had happened to her mind. She needed to clear her head. To go anywhere away from Sean carried none of the excitement she'd had when she left her home in Missouri.

She glanced at Sean. He'd metamorphosed so completely into his Irish personality, she had no trouble making the change along with him, and wondered if the reverse would be true should a return to the Indian village ever happen.

For the last time, she swiveled around in the saddle and looked behind her, searching for a farewell glimpse of the cabin. Only its chimney was visible, and regret made a fleeting nudge in her breast. Regret for what? The night in his arms? The intimacy of the cabin? She didn't know, and searching too closely made her uneasy. The sun warmed them, chasing dawn's early chill, and leaving last night's lovemaking at their backs. A new day, a fresh start, and Sean the Irish Indian was riding beside her.

He had been in a spin to get away this morning, so she'd elected to forgo braiding her hair, and as they rode a breeze tangled it about her shoulders. After a halfhearted attempt to tame it, she gave up in disgust and let it fly.

"You've lost the battle, Katie, and it's a fine thing seeing your lovely hair swirling about your face. Like silk, it is, with shiny streaks that catch rays from the sun. Perhaps you'll be wearing it so at the Shamrock?"

She shivered. How did she know how she'd wear her hair until she came face-to-face with the people? She had no idea what went on at a ranch. Were the people like the ones she'd known in Missouri? Or, since this was Texas, would they dress and act like the cowboys who stopped at the Lily to drink themselves into idiocy? She hadn't an inkling of what to expect. "We'll see."

"Aye, and we've a way to go yet. Perhaps we'll ride in by late afternoon. Whenever you want, we can stop and rest. There's no law says we have to be there at a certain time today. We've invited a state senator and his wife and a few others up for a few days. By the time they get to the ranch, you'll have some new clothes. Thank God for Malachi. He took care of any last-minute arrangements and will have the ranch looking its best

Velda Sherrod

for the guests. They should be visiting for a day or two."

"What will they think, these people who work at your ranch, when you bring in a dirty, bedraggled woman dressed in Indian clothes?"

"Interested, for sure. I'm wondering how you'll feel when we arrive there?"

Embarrassed, she thought, especially when curious eyes looked her over, and she had to be helped out of the saddle because her back end was without feeling and her face sunburned to the color of salmon. Would people at the Shamrock laugh when they saw her? After all she'd been through, she was convinced she could handle whatever came. But, she thought as she straightened her shoulders, women liked to look their best when they went into a new situation. Give her a new dress cut to style, a nice pair of boots, a chance to arrange her hair, and she could rub shoulders with royalty.

They traveled on and on until she ached with fatigue. Her throat was parched, her back hurt and her bottom had grown to the saddle. An occasional bout of nausea added to her misery. "How much farther?"

Sean, fresh as he was when he arose, smiled encouragingly. "You'll see the ranch house when we top the next hill." He waved in an easterly direction. "Tell me, lass, have you ever seen more beautiful country?"

The man was mad. "It's certainly . . . different," she said, trying her best to think up words to express an admiration for this wild expanse of desolation.

"Aye, Katie, once you saw it, I knew you'd fall in love with it. A homecoming, that's what it is. Only Glenmorra, my home in Ireland, is more beautiful. Ireland. An island, lass. Green as a shamrock. One day I'll take you there to meet Da. And all my kin." He paused. "I'd like that."

Would she like that? To go home with Sean? He talked as if they would have a future together, but she hadn't made up her mind. God, there were so many things to consider, and now the baby was on the way.

They topped a hill and Kate had a partial view of the ranch house. Men worked at something, going from barn to barn,

192

corral to pasture. There was even a blacksmith shop. Bending and stooping, two people worked in the big garden. A black man raised his head now and then to address a small white girl. It was all so big, so busy, so frightening, but the garden scene could have come straight from a farm in Missouri. It melted her heart. Any minute now, Papa would come barreling down the road cracking his whip and shouting over the heads of the horses. Making a show, Mama always said, but Kate knew better. He'd been so glad to see them. He had laughed and laughed, calling their names, and telling them their papa had come home to see his girls. She'd been thirteen then.

She was twenty-two now, and was no longer that young girl. Too much had happened, including her night in the sheep-herders' cabin. She hadn't been able to separate the night there from thoughts always in the back of her mind. Before her lay the Shamrock, and she was struck dumb. A tree-lined stretch of road led to the largest house she'd ever seen, big as the courthouse in her hometown. It sprawled in all directions, including up, and sprouted chimneys from everywhere. There were fifteen at least, she thought, rising in the stirrups to see them better. The second floor claimed a wraparound balcony partly visible from the road and decorated with ornate black ironwork. She counted the broad steps, ten of them, leading from the driveway to the entrance, where light gray shutters framed long, narrow windows. Two tall urns held plants that bloomed in great red clusters.

The place was overpowering.

Sean's low curse said he wasn't pleased. "Senator Platt came early and brought an army with him."

"You don't like him?"

He spoke grimly. "He's a senator. We'll be civil."

Embarrassed that her skirt exposed her bare legs to the thigh, and that smoothing her hair helped little, she waited for Sean to dismount. He was busy laughing and waving, caught up in seeing the people gathered in front of the house. "Great folks, Katie. Let me help you down." She started to protest, but as weary as she was, she was afraid she'd fall on her face in front of the crowd. Not that such a thing would be anything new.

After all, her first appearance at the Indian camp hadn't been auspicious either.

Once her feet were on the ground, she struggled to maintain poise, meeting the questioning looks of the people Sean introduced her to, nodding as he called each by name. He gave a questioning glance at a man dressed as a cowboy. "And your name?"

"Bonham, Mr. O'Brien. I'm one of your riders."

"Then why aren't you working?"

"Well, I . . . since I was workin' here and all, I figured this was a good time to meet you." He turned his gaze on Kate, then let it travel slowly down to her boots. "And Miss Hartland." From his clenched fist, she could tell Sean stifled an impulse to bloody the man's face. Instead he ignored Bonham and moved on to present the others to her. Few of the faces were friendly. She would have to be doubly careful not to betray Sean's confidence by calling him Hawk in front of these carnivores. Not only would his plan with the colonel be ruined, but he'd be surrounded by enemies.

She held his life in her hands, and his trust tore at her heart.

Besides the children, only a few acknowledged his introduction. Some of the older people, especially the women, refused to look at her or to speak.

Someone spoke in a loud whisper. "Did she live with a Comanche tribe?"

"She looks dirty enough."

"The braves probably liked her."

Another voice held suppressed laughter. "She's brown as a squaw. Hard to tell the difference."

Sean's face said he heard them. He introduced her to the senator's wife, and Kate met the woman's hostile stare with a nod and a thin smile.

The senator appeared at loss for words, but that condition didn't last. "Miss Hartland, is it? Nice to meet you, Miss Hartland. Know you're glad to be away from them rascally Comanche. A bad lot. Bet you've got a lot of interestin' Indian stories."

"Indians are an interesting people, sir." Conscious of more

sly remarks, she excused herself and ignored further attempts by the senator to draw her into conversation.

A harsh female voice broke into the conversation. "Miss Hartman, did you go without clothes or did you always wear Indian garb?"

"She wore clothes. Her name is Kathleen Hartland, and she's tired from a long journey." Sean's voice was firm, with a hint of belligerence. "I'm sure you'll excuse her."

Kate knew she would remember Sean's face always, a veritable thundercloud. He took her arm protectively and escorted her inside. He had been so happy to be home, to show her the Shamrock, but he hadn't reckoned on the senator and his followers being there, spewing their sly remarks and insults. She wished fervently that she had a place to go other than remaining at the Shamrock. At the moment the paucity of opportunity was overwhelming. Following Sean's lead, she held her head high and marched through the great doors.

The house was grand. Overwhelming. The floors were marble, the ceilings high. Broad windows gave a view of rolling prairies that stretched forever. A wide, curving stairway complete with carpet and a polished railing led to the second floor. And she'd had the ridiculous idea that Sean might not be able to pay her for the work she hoped to do here.

"Kathleen, this is Anna, the housekeeper." He nodded in the direction of the stairway. "Anna, take Miss Hartland upstairs and acquaint her with her room. Find someone, maybe Lena, to help her with her clothes and hair."

He turned a tender gaze on Kate. "Be comfortable, Katie. You're home."

Home? Comfortable? The man must be joking. With all the scowling people staring at her as though she were a Comanche renegade, she was supposed to get comfortable? And with this harridan leading the way. Surely, Sean hadn't noticed Anna's instant dislike of the female guest he'd brought home, or he'd never have asked her to see to Kate's needs.

Kate trailed Anna up stairs, noting the woman's rigid back. No doubt, she felt her domain had been sullied by the dust of a Comanche woman. The severity of the housekeeper's black dress emphasized her large hips, a small white collar drawing attention to her scrawny neck. When she squared her shoulders, her meager breasts made hardly a bulge.

She looked back once, her scornful gaze flickering over Kate, a sneer narrowing her thin lips. "If your hands are greasy, please keep them off the handrail. We've just polished the wood."

Kate did not bother to reply; she refused to let this woman bait her.

She trailed Anna upstairs. At the end of a long hallway, Anna stopped and thrust open a door. "Your room. You'll find everything you need." She waited for Kate to enter, her disdainful gaze sliding down to Kate's dusty boots and back up again, not missing a single dirty detail. "Lena will not be available tonight. She's busy helping the senator's wife. Dinner is at seven. There'll be guests. If you want to bathe, I'll send up a tub."

If you want to bathe! Of course she wanted to bathe. "Right away, please," Kate said, barely short of being imperious. If Anna wanted to be disagreeable, Kate thought archly, she'd give the woman full cooperation.

The room smelled deliciously of flowers. A great canopied bed, enhanced by a gold, ivory, and blue spread, occupied the center of the room. An Aubusson rug covered the floor. Earlier she'd noticed an Aubusson tapestry downstairs.

Opulence.

"Mr. O'Brien said you'd want clean clothes. I've placed them on the bed."

Putting on a wintry smile, one she'd successfully used to quail the fainthearted at the Gilded Lily, Kate glanced at the woman. "Good."

She refused to give Anna the satisfaction of seeing her apprehension, her dread at meeting the guests. On the journey from Tule Canyon, she had never once anticipated such an ordeal, where servants insulted friends of the family. After what she'd survived, she'd never appease anyone or apologize for anything, not her appearance, her need to bathe, her position in this household. Nor would she scurry around looking for places to hide. She couldn't believe Sean had known she'd get such a reception.

Anna busied herself opening drawers and laying out linens. When the door slammed, Kate didn't bother to look up.

A short time later two young men, probably in their teens, arrived bearing a tub and, not long after, steaming kettles of hot water. They looked at her curiously, one muttering a few words in Spanish and exchanging smirking glances with his partner. She didn't thank them when they went out the door.

Throwing off her mud-spattered clothes, she sank chin-deep into the warm water. She sighed blissfully and closed her eyes. Such heavenly luxury. She inhaled deeply, ducked her head under the surface, and came up dripping and searching for soap. Mouthing a small oath, she looked around her. Anna had deliberately placed the bar out of reach.

Kate dripped her way to the bedside table, got the soap, and backtracked to the tub, trailing water all the way.

No doubt Anna would tell the servants about the woman upstairs who'd messed up the floor. Kate could see it all. Anna would raise imperious eyebrows, look down her long nose, and wonder aloud about a woman who arrived with only the clothes on her back—and those, mind you, befitting a filthy Indian woman. What, Miss Anna would demand to know, could decent women expect?

Courtesy, Kate wanted to shout, courtesy that had been in short supply since her arrival. If Anna's ungracious welcome was a sample of Texas hospitality, Kate mused, too comfortable to move, then she'd been led amiss by a couple of well-mannered Texans, namely Joe, the piano player, and Sean O'Brien, the rancher.

The water cooled, and reluctantly Kate rose and looked for a towel. There was nothing within reach, Spying a towel neatly folded and out of reach, she splashed her way out of the tub, ignored the wet tracks she made, and dripped her way to the bed. If Anna wanted something to crow about, Kate Hartland would cooperate.

Kate rubbed her hair briskly, loving the squeaky-clean feel of it, and walked to the dressing table. She found a comb that

Anna had so thoughtfully placed in a drawer, worked the tangles out of her hair, and, using pins found far back in another drawer, fashioned her long and heavy mane as best she could.

She dressed in the gown Anna had carelessly tossed on the bed and studied herself in the handsomely carved mirror. The dress was a fashionable wonder of silk, satin, and taffeta the color of her eyes. The bodice wrapped around her middle perfectly. In another month she wouldn't be able to wear it. The off-the-shoulder neckline exposed bare shoulders and a generous amount of cleavage. Sweeping the floor in a whirl of taffeta, the skirt made a lovely rustling sound. The shoes were blue satin and matched the dress.

Surprised at how well everything fit, she had no idea whose clothes they were, nor where they had come from, but she was determined to thank Sean for providing them. Undoubtedly she'd hear snickers when she went down in her borrowed finery, but she trusted Sean enough to believe that he'd never be party to such ungracious behavior.

The house was splendid, and since arriving she'd been wide-eyed with wonder. Never for a moment had she anticipated anything so grand. Sean had never mentioned wealth to her, his own or his father's. What would Glenmorra be like, if ever she should go there?

Thankful she still had time, she disrobed and sank gratefully into an overstuffed chair. Maybe she'd take a little nap and forget what lay ahead at dinner tonight. After all, there was plenty of time to dress later.

Sean leaned against the corral fence and watched Malachi roll a cigarette. He'd used a meeting with his foreman as an excuse to get away from his noxious guests. "What do you think, Mal?"

"About what?" Malachi asked, his innocence as false as his teeth. "You speakin' 'bout the gel?"

"Of course I'm talking about the girl. I'm also talking about how she was received by the household staff. About the senator, his wife, and the hangers-on he brought with him. Did you notice how they looked at Kate?"

Malachi nodded with a slight dip of his head. "Who could help it? Wonder what Miss Kate thought?"

"I'm not sure she was aware."

The old man looked at him as if he'd grown two heads. "She didn't miss a thing, son. Not a damn thing."

Sean sighed. He'd been lying to himself, telling his conscience she hadn't seen the hostility. How could he help, aside from kicking the good senator in the butt and advising him to take his ugly wife and the fawning entourage and go back to Austin? The colonel had thought—nay, hoped—that Sean's playing host to the senator, speaking softly of reconciliation between white and Indian, and encouraging the government to participate would help bring about a solution to the Indian problem. So far the plan he and the colonel had laid out had only stirred up dust.

"What do you think, Mal?"

"My honest opinion?"

"Yeah, Mal, an honest opinion."

"Well, since I've been foreman of the Shamrock, and that's been a while, I've seen some purty gels. And I'd say Miss Kate's purtier than most. Eyes big as cow pies."

Exasperated but hiding a grin, Sean kicked the corral fence. "I'm aware she's beautiful, Malachi. I can see that for myself. But the other . . . the welcome-home to a white woman who's lived with Indians?"

"Plumb nasty, Sean. Them gumment people woulda been nicer if she'd been a shore-nuff Comanche gel. And a Indian gel wouldn't stand a chance with that bunch of harpies. It's too bad they got here 'fore you and Miss Kate. She could've had on different clothes."

Sean nodded his head in agreement.

Malachi held his cigarette between his thumb and forefinger. "One of Shamrock's cowboys told ever'body here that he seen her walking with Stone Wolf's band along the breaks in Tule Canyon."

"Who?" Sean wanted to kill the man. Hang him, shoot him, bury him in an anthill. "How did he know right away today that Kate and the woman were the same?"

"Name's Seth Bonham. Hired on about three weeks ago. Said he could tell right off she warn't no Comanche. No Indian woman ever walked with her head that high, he told Mike Smith. Or swayed her hips that graceful-like. Hell, Sean. You'd think the sumbitch knew her by name."

Sean clenched his teeth in frustration. He hadn't liked Bonham the moment he had laid eyes on him. And he didn't need Bonham to tell him Kate wasn't an Indian. That she was pretty. Or that she walked like a dancer. He wondered if—nay, feared—the man had come from Tascosa and recognized Kate as the former singer at the Gilded Lily.

"Know where he worked before he came to the Shamrock?"

"Said he held a job as wrangler at the Seven Cross. We knew some of the same people."

"Is he any good at his job?"

"Naw. Ain't got enough sense to saddle a horse. I'm fixin' to git rid of 'im."

But the damage had been done, Sean thought in disgust, regretting his decision to bring Kate to the ranch before getting decent clothes for her first. She had come through a harrowing experience, could have lost her life, and he'd just wanted to get her home. He'd even thought she'd have the sympathy of the Shamrock servants and cowboys. Instead, they had followed the bad example set by the senator and his wife.

Clothes influenced people's first impressions, especially government officials. In a pretty dress, Kate could have walked in and commanded the respect due her. Still, Bonham might have recognized her anyway, depending on how close he had been when he saw her.

Sean reached down, pulled a blade of grass, and stuck the stem in his mouth. "I suppose we'll know more when we eat tonight."

"Think you can trust Kate to keep her mouth shut about you and the colonel and Stone Wolf?"

"I trust her." Sean stretched and stuck his hands in his back pockets. "I'll see you tonight?"

"Got a few things need doing, son. I'll see you tomorrow."

"Malachi, I'll see you tonight when we eat."

"Aw, now, Sean," Malachi said, shaking his head, "I ain't a party man."

"Tonight you are."

"I just ain't comfortable bein' around that jug-butt senator and his beak-nosed wife."

"I'm sympathetic, but not enough to say you can stay away. Besides, I need an unbiased opinion about what's happening. Something besides my own gut feeling."

"I'm a ranch foreman," Malachi argued, not meeting Sean's eyes. "Foremans ain't supposed to hobnob with senators."

"Tonight we're making an exception. Besides, when've you ever been just the foreman? You've had a hand in everything that affects the Shamrock since before I was born. When you get right down to it, you are the Shamrock."

"Below the belt, son," Malachi said, squaring his shoulders, but a faint smile belied his words.

"Then you'll come?"

"It's that or quit, and I ain't of a mind to hunt for another job. Guess I ain't got much choice in the matter."

"I don't suppose Bonham said anything about seeing me with Stone Wolf's band?"

"Naw, reckon not. Musta not seen ya. I don't think he coulda kept it to hisself. Talks all the time. Just like a damn guinea hen."

Sean shoved away from the rail fence. "See you when we eat, Mal."

"What if I ain't got a clean shirt?" Mal asked slyly.

"I know where you can borrow one."

At a brisk knock on the door, Kate walked sedately to answer it. At the sight of him all decked out in dress-up clothes, his face clean-shaven, his hair slicked back and tied with some kind of a band, she felt her heart skid into a backward flip.

Sean's eyes widened, and for one barely perceptible moment Kate thought he would kiss her. Of their own volition, her lips parted in invitation. She put out a hand to balance herself. If, at that moment, he'd asked her, she'd have followed him wherever he led—not a pleasant revelation, but seductive and provocative. She reminded herself that she couldn't live with a man who was half white, half Indian.

She intended to have the rules placed on the table, and now was the time to do it. "Good evening."

"Aye, lass, looking at you, it is that."

"Sean, I don't know my place. What am I? Servant? Whore? Wife?"

"The clothes might have changed, but you're still my wife."

"At Stone Wolf's ceremony, I was never consulted about marrying you. You did not ask. Nor did your grandfather ever question."

"Kate, I thought we were past that. After the night in the sheepherders' cabin, I had begun to hope—nay, to think—everything would be fine."

"You saved my life."

"And so I did, but what does that have to do with your question? Your place is beside me."

Kate rolled her eyes. "None so blind . . ."

"No more such talk tonight." His face was a mask. "We've a fine dinner awaiting, Kate. We'll sit at the table and eat with perfectly balanced cutlery, drink from delicate crystal glasses, and wipe our mouths with fine linen. And we'll tell ourselves on the sly how wonderfully nice it is to be among civilized people."

She wasn't sure where he was going with the conversation, whether he was making fun of her or the senator, his wife, and the people they'd brought along with them. At the moment she didn't want to find out. She wanted to sit at the table as he suggested, watch the people around her, and try to make sense out of all that had happened, including her place in the household and Anna's impudent behavior. "Right, and I'm hungry." When he held out his arm, she placed her hand at his elbow. "And while I'm at it, I'm impressed with the Shamrock."

"The Shamrock is a combination of Irish lace and cowboy homily. Tonight you'll dine with government dignitaries. You'll converse with a state senator. He lives in Dallas. He's pompous and overbearing and looking for donations."

"He brought his wife, don't forget, because I can't seem to be able to."

He scowled. "Aye, she's with him. Two of a kind, they are."

Kate was close enough to smell a lotion familiar to young men of fashion in her hometown, those who made it to church. Very nice, but too expensive for most of them. Tonight she'd met Sean, Texas rancher, and she wasn't sure how to respond. After all, she'd seen him only as Grayhawk, Comanche warrior, and Sean, the piano-playing Irishman.

"The senator's wife . . ." She hesitated, wondering if she'd read more into his words than he intended. "What can you tell me about her?"

"Well, not much more than you probably observed for yourself. She has a pinched face from looking down her nose. She wears ugly colors and thinks she's the height of fashion. She keeps the senator jumping."

"And you don't like her?"

"And you won't either, I think."

She turned a troubled look on him. "I hoped things would be different tonight. But it isn't important what I think."

"Kate Hartland's thoughts are important to me, even if they concern the weather."

"The weather?"

He grinned, laugh lines furrowing about his mouth. "Do you foresee a storm, my Kate?"

Was he bringing up the weather to remind her of their night together? Did he anticipate spending another night in her bed? "I'm not a weatherman," she said, making no attempt to keep the coolness out of her voice. "But I don't foresee a storm."

"Katie, Katie. Why do you have such trouble trusting me?"

Tears stung her eyes, and she blinked them back. He read her well, and God knew that she wanted to trust. She also wanted to find her place, a future singing—not in a saloon, but in a reputable opera house or stage. Here in Sean's fine home she was an outsider, and she already dreaded the evening.

Sean greeted his guests, the senator and his wife and other lesser members of the state government, introducing Kate as they moved along, calling her Kathleen. Parties of this kind were a bore, but the colonel had laid out the plans. Sean would host the politicians, wine them and dine them. Privately he wished his annoying guests were somewhere besides the Shamrock.

Once again he cursed his bad luck that the senator and his cronies had arrived earlier than expected. Several days earlier, as a matter of fact. No doubt they never missed an opportunity for a free meal and a night's lodging—more, if the host proved congenial.

By bringing Kate home with him, he had arbitrarily thrust her into the Comanche–white conflict. He had made known to Stone Wolf that if Kate's time with the Indians ever reached the outside world, her life would become unbearable. He hadn't considered that her torture would begin at the Shamrock. Not from the servants. Guests, yes. The present company bent with the wind, and hatred of the Indians got votes. But Anna . . . her hypocrisy was written in her face. If he let her go, she'd alert the county and the whole Texas panhandle, as well. And poor Kate . . .

No, never poor Kate.

His Kate could be discussed from hell to breakfast, but her chin would still be up at lunchtime. Tonight he'd baffle the guests, and maybe even Kate herself, with all the attention he'd give her.

He picked up the thread of conversation that swirled around him as he and his guests chatted in the parlor before dinner. "How are things in Austin, Senator? Any new legislation that would affect the Shamrock?"

"Not as I remember, Mr. O'Brien . . . Sean. When I get back there I'll ask my secretary. She'll remember. I'll have her send a note." The senator turned his attention to Kate, his gaze hovering barely above her cleavage. "Reckon you're glad to be home, Miss . . . Miss Kate."

"Yes, I am, Senator, extremely glad." She didn't look at Sean. "It's nice to be home among one's own people."

The senator held her hand, smiling affably until his wife elbowed him in the side. "You know my wife, Ophelia Maud.

People who know her call her Maudie. That includes me, I reckon." He laughed. "I'm kind of a joker, you might say."

Sean agreed heartily.

On his left, the good senator's wife Ophelia Maud sat ramrod straight, her gaze narrow and piercing, her cheeks puffed out like the feathers of a ruffled hen. Kate smiled. "Ophelia Maud. An unusual name, Mrs. Platt. From one of Shakespeare's works, isn't it?"

"My good mama's name. The Maud part. I'm not sure where they got the Ophelia. Guess they thought it was pretty." She looked toward her husband for confirmation. "Different."

"In Shakespeare's play, Ophelia goes mad." Kate continued to smile and shake her head. "Crazy as a coot."

Sean tried to hide his laughter. "Kathleen's an Irish name, and the lass sings." And Kate's words, soft or cutting, could slide easily from her beautiful, moist lips, and woe to the recipient, he thought. He needn't have worried about protecting her from the likes of Ophelia Maud.

The senator nodded enthusiastically. "Well, it would sure be fine if the little lady sang for us. After we've had the meal, o'course."

Sean brushed a tendril of hair from Kate's cheek. "If she wants." He took her arm. "Shall we lead the way in?"

The table was set with a white linen cloth, gleaming silverware, thin bone china, and sparkling glassware. Two servants stood well back from the table, ready to assist if needed, while a tall, thin man served the food. Anna, in black, her hair drawn tightly into a coil atop her head, stood by, determined the meal would be a success. Her face said it wasn't every day that a senator and his family came to the Shamrock.

Sean led Kate to the head of the table and held the chair on his left for her. "You're lovely, Kathleen," he said, loudly enough for those near to hear.

He took his place and picked up his napkin. "I'm told the pheasant is good. Shall we see?"

There were murmurs of appreciation, the ladies speaking across the table to each other, and occasionally to the men on either side. After the diners had mellowed from wine and food,

Sean directed remarks to Kate. "How did you like the wine?"

Before she could answer Ophelia Maud spoke loudly enough for her voice to carry all the way to the end of the table. "Miss Hartman, I understand you spent time in an Indian village as a captive."

"Yes, Mrs. Pratt. I was a prisoner in a Comanche camp."

"Platt. Ophelia Maud Platt. Pretty women find favor with the Indian braves, I suppose." She gave a knowing glance to the woman across from her before turning back to Kate. "You seem to have survived quite well. I confess I've always believed a Christian woman would rather take her own life than endure a fate worse than death such as you've experienced. And I just know I'd have killed myself before it could happen to me." Ophelia Maud sniffed and smoothed her hair back from her brow. "Yes, I'm sure," she said virtuously, "that I'd have taken my own life."

Other wives of the group nodded in agreement, some vigorously, others piously, and like coyotes awaiting the kill, they leaned forward to hear every single word Kate would answer.

Kate looked pointedly at Ophelia Maud's thinning hair. "The homely captives as well as the comely ones were courageous. Not one of them killed herself."

"Well, I . . . dear me," Ophelia Maud said, and placed her hand at her sagging bosom. "Finias would never let such a thing happen to me, would you, dear?" Not waiting for an answer, she gave Kate a chilly nod. "So I'll have to take your word, Miss Hartman."

Kate bestowed her most beatific smile. "That's extremely kind of you, Mrs. Pratt."

"Well, is the little lady going to sing?" Finias boomed his question. "About time, ain't it?"

"I'm a little tired, Senator. I'm sure you'll forgive me."

At that point Sean stood, and the diners reluctantly followed. Again seeming like hungry coyotes, they had circled the victim and been deprived of the kill. Finias Platt looked daggers at his wife and the other guests, while disgruntled wives and disgusted husbands murmured to each other. "Gentlemen," Sean said, his eyes betraying his boredom, "shall we retire to the library for a smoke?"

"Fine idea, Sean," the senator said, turning once more to give his wife a baleful glance. "Yessir, a first-class idea."

Sean was confident that Kate could hold her own with women like Ophelia Maud, women who were bent on devouring her, but he feared that tonight was only a beginning. Kate had been gracious only because she chose to, the mark of a lovely lady. Underneath, he knew she was seething. "The ladies may enjoy the parlor." He left the head of the table and turned to take Kate's arm and lead the way.

"Nice going, my Kate," he whispered. When he glanced down, he was amazed to find tears in her eyes. "Don't let these people bother you," he said. "They're vultures. The whole lot of them."

She blinked rapidly and made a wry attempt to smile. "It's almost like my arrival at Stone Wolf's camp. These women did everything but pinch and hit me. Not a friendly face among them. Given half a chance, they'd spit on me."

"I suppose, and I sympathize, darlin'. If you want, tell them good night and head upstairs."

"And have them think I'm afraid?"

He almost chortled. "They could never think that after you gave Ophelia Maud her comeuppance."

"I had no idea my own people would turn against me. After all, I had nothing to do with getting captured."

"The good senator is a poor excuse for a leader, but his wife is a poor excuse for a human being." He hadn't the heart to tell Kate that many women, too many, would receive her with the same ridiculous rhetoric.

He heard Kate directing the women to comfortable chairs, and turned thoughtfully to join the men. Seeing Kate go into the parlor was a little like the description in the good book about a man who went into a lion's den. In this case, a very courageous woman had braved the stares and insults.

Even Finias had been taken aback by his wife's attack. But what of tomorrow? What kind of a life could Kate expect if she left the Shamrock? Where did he fit in? As her Indian brave? Perhaps her Irish benefactor? Or would she let him in at all?

Upstairs in her room after dinner, Kate brushed angrily at tears that insisted on falling. Why was she crying when such women existed everywhere? Mama collected such women like saltcellars, making the Hartland home a gathering place. Papa called them monsters, even to Mama's face. Her mother had been as mad as a hornet, her red hair no redder than her face. She said Papa had no regard for people with class.

Kate wiped the tears. Thank goodness her papa had known the difference, and had shown by example what he thought of Mama's heartless old-biddy friends. Sean O'Brien was like Papa.

Like Papa? Heaven forbid. Sean O'Brien was as much Comanche as he was Irish. She had seen him dancing to the beat of the Indian drums, throwing himself around like a whirlwind. Remembering, she almost smiled.

Chapter Eleven

After a restless night of tossing and turning, Kate found sleep when she moved to the window seat and the thin cushion on top. Heaven forbid that she'd grown accustomed to the Indian way of sleeping on the ground. The mattress was simply too soft for her to sleep well. She had to admit that she missed sleeping with Sean.

Her long bouts of wakefulness, broken only by short catnaps, had given her time to think about what she was going to say to Sean. In the morning silence, it was easy to hear when his bedroom door opened and his booted feet touched the gleaming wood floors.

She faced him in the hallway outside her room. He was dressed in Levi's, a blue cotton shirt, and a wide-brimmed hat. The clean, manly scent of him hit her almost like a blow. He smelled good, like soap and warmth and strength.

"Sean, we need to talk."

"Aye, lass, and what would you be wanting to talk about this early in the morning?"

Hugging the borrowed nightgown around her, she bit back

her frustration. "I must have a job, Sean. And clothes. I appreciate this nightgown, but I can't wear a Sunday dress or a nightgown during the day." She bristled at the harsh look that came over his face. "I don't think I'm asking too much. I want to work."

"You misunderstand, darlin'. I have no problem with what you're saying. It's that you have clothes. They're in the wardrobe in your bedroom. Anna should have told you."

"Anna didn't tell me. And I did find some clothes, but I certainly didn't assume they were mine." She gave an exasperated sigh. "When did you have time to buy clothes for me?"

He moved uncomfortably. "Katie, darlin', I told you I had McDougal at the trading post order them. Malachi had one of the boys pick them up. I knew that you'd need clothes. And you won't be needing a job."

Choking back her fury, she faced him squarely. "From the moment I met you, you've turned my life into turmoil. You forced me to stay in the Indian camp, brought me to the ranch looking like a filthy Indian woman, and dumped me headfirst into a snakepit. Now you tell me you'd bought clothes for me before we left Stone Wolf's village. You tell me I don't have to work." Her eyes narrowed. "You've planned my life, and without a word from me."

"But, Katie—"

She was close to shouting. "I'm in charge of my life!"

"Keep your voice down, Kate. Do you want the whole house to hear?"

Opening her mouth to give him a fresh volley of angry words, she recognized her folly and clamped her lips shut. She absolutely refused to give Mad Maud any additional fuel for her gossip team.

With effort, she lowered her voice. After all, he couldn't have known how awful his guests would be. "The dinner party was a horror."

"I'm sorry, lass. Mrs. Platt wasn't the soul of kindness."

Thinking about the Platts and people like them made her head ache. "Hire me until I can save enough to buy my own clothes and find a job."

His eyes turned a stormy gray. "Would you feel better if I put you to weeding the garden? Or maybe you'd rather clean horse dung out of the stables?"

She folded her arms over her breast. "What does it pay?"

"Bloody hell, Kate. You're my wife. Stone Wolf made it so. And my wife does not have to clean horse barns."

She whispered because she thought there was a chance she'd explode. "I'm nobody's wife."

"But . . ." When he spoke again, his words were gentle. He smoothed a knuckle down her cheek. "Didn't the night at the cabin mean anything to you, Katie?"

The fire eased out of her, and she answered him in a similar voice as truthfully as she could. "It meant something. I don't know what. Yet."

Outwardly satisfied, he nodded. "And the clothes?"

Damnit. He'd waltzed around her with his tender tone and charming words and led her right where he wanted her. The clothes hanging in the wardrobe were lovely. She'd looked them over but thought they belonged to somebody else. "At this point I don't have a choice."

He leaned a shoulder against the wall and didn't meet her eyes. "Did you find the underthings? Underwear? In the chest?"

Now he was rubbing salt into the wound. "I'm a guest, for God's sake. I don't rummage through drawers." She'd lifted the lid of the chest a bit, enough to see that it contained some personal apparel. "Well, maybe a little. Just to see . . ."

He burst out laughing. "Aye. And I understand." Straightening, he lifted his hat and ran his fingers through his hair. "You feel you need a job. I need a woman to oversee the servants. See that the house runs smoothly. Greet any guests who come, expected or unexpected. Someone I can trust."

Kate considered his offer suspiciously. "What's the pay? I may prefer mucking out the horse barn."

"Before we set an amount, let's wait to see if you like the job and how much work is involved."

"What about Anna?"

Shrugging, he looked down at her, lifted a strand of her

glossy dark hair, and watched it curl around his finger. "What about Anna?"

"She's not going to take kindly to this arrangement."

"Katie, I'm the boss of the Shamrock, except for Malachi, and he bosses everybody." He grinned. "Even me. As for Anna, she'll take orders from you if I say so. As will the other servants."

The change in her relationship with Anna should stir things up, and Kate had a fleeting moment of exultation. Common sense told her she'd have to act quickly if she were to be the boss. Establish early on that Anna no longer had complete control over the way the house was run. Until Papa died, Mama had had servants. She'd taught her daughters well how to a household. When Milton came, he didn't receive a salary large enough to support household help, and, as Kate remembered it, Mama hadn't seemed to mind. She had two daughters to do the housework and had gained a higher social position in the town as a preacher's wife. Kate couldn't believe she was thanking her mother for anything, but she bowed to her mother's expertise in delegating work. "We'll give it a try."

All smiles now, Sean lowered his head and brushed her lips with his, a quick kiss that lasted only long enough for her pulse to jump about like a circus clown. Triumph flashed briefly in his eyes before he lowered his head to repeat the kiss. "Once our house guests leave, and you don't have to spend all your time entertaining them, you can start. Aye, Katie. You'll be fine at the job."

"What of the people who come and find out I lived with the Indians?"

"No worry there, Katie. Look how you handled the occasion with Ophelia Maud."

There were too many Mad Mauds, she thought uneasily.

Sean glanced up from checking Midnight's hooves when Malachi emerged from the barn carrying a pail of oats. "And it's a good day I'm wishing you, Mal." He would appreciate a good day for himself, Sean thought wryly. If anybody had told him he'd be faced with a set of problems equal to his present ones, he'd have questioned their sanity.

"Yeah." Malachi set the pail down and took cigarette makings from his pocket. "Not much wind."

Sean ran a currycomb over Midnight's back, now and then giving the big black an affectionate pat. "You know, Mal, after seeing Kate ruffle Mrs. Platt's feathers last week, I relaxed a bit."

"I'd say Miss Kate held her own."

"You saw how the women followed Ophelia Maud's lead."

"Yeah, I noticed. It's a shame, but Miss Kate'll be looked down on until she's married. For some reason marriage has a way of purging a woman of sin." Malachi shook his head at the truth of his words. "Ophelia Maud made me want to throw up. Course, she always does, even on my good days."

Sean backed up against Midnight's side. "Wherever Kate goes, it will be the same."

"She ain't leavin'!"

"Aye, if I don't give her a job."

"Now, ain't that just like a woman? Women in general, I'm speaking of. What job would she want here? Cain't see her cookin' or sweepin'."

"I took a chance, Mal. From what I can tell, when her father was alive, the Hartland family lived well. They had a comfortable home with servants." Sean couldn't keep back a smile. "Now the Platts and their party are gone, Kate's going to take over the job of running the Shamrock. Everything—servants, meals, garden. All of it."

Malachi gave a short laugh. "Way I figure it, you've jest piled heaps of fire on yore head."

"After the way Anna acted the first night the Platts were here and since, I hope she quits."

"Not a chance, Sean. Anna ain't gonna give up easy. The money's too good. You know the guy I was telling you about? The blabbermouth? Seth Bonham? Well, a interesting thing, Sean—him and Anna have got to be real good friends. Sometimes behind the barn."

"That's good to know, Mal." Sean slapped Midnight on the rump and watched him gallop around the paddock. "After we eat today, I'm heading for the canyon to get my horses. We'll

213

be needing them for fall roundup. The Ghost took over Midnight's place with the mares. Be interesting to see whose foals arrive in the spring."

"Both them stallions please the ladies. And that's a fact."

"Lucky stallions. Don't suppose you'd like to go with us after the horses?"

Malachi's eyes lit up. "Might. Sure as hell might."

"Get your gear together and pick out three or four boys to go along. We'll spend the night. Probably two." He glanced toward the main house, anticipating what kind of battle waited for him. "It's a few hours to noontime, thank God."

"Reckon I'll eat with the boys today, son. Cowboys are loud, but I've a feelin' today the meal will be quieter than in the dinin' room. 'Specially with Anna and Miss Kate and that little Afton." Malachi laughed and took off for the barn, pausing once to look back over his shoulder. "Why don't you marry the girl, Sean, and make an honest woman of her? Besides, it's time you started thinkin' about a family."

"What makes you think I haven't?"

Malachi wheeled and stared at him. "I'll be damned."

The noon meal took place at twelve o'clock sharp. Sean's father had established the time, Juanita told her emphatically, and Kate knew she was supposed to honor it. "Who decides the menus?"

The cook's round, good-natured face broke into a smile. "Anna. And she ain't had a first thought in thirty years."

Preparing menus was something Kate had learned well from her mother. She decided to introduce a new dish at lunch. Over the past week she'd encouraged the servants to bring their problems to her, but not Anna. One or two had become friendly. Some remained hostile.

With suggestions from Kate, Juanita had food on the table and a smile on her face. "Reckon it's ready, Kate. Folks around here ain't never had chicken cooked like this. And 'fore I forget, Sean says Coleridge and Afton eat at the table with ever'body what's here. Reckon you cain't imagine how surprised folks was when a black man set down." She laughed. " 'Specially that spoiled kid, Afton."

Kate pondered her words as she went to welcome Sean and the guests who'd managed to get there in time to eat. The table soon filled. A lawyer friend of Sean's and a cattle buyer from around Chicago were guests. Coleridge and Afton sat side by side, Coleridge a bit uneasy when he looked at Kate. Sean had told her how they came to be here, and knowing a little of what he was experiencing, she smiled at him. She was rewarded with a generous smile in return. Afton sat like a hungry puppy, her eyes fixed attentively on the food.

Kate waited uneasily for Sean to recognize that a new dish had found its way to the table, but his attention was directed to his discussion with the guests. She unfolded her napkin and laid it across her lap, delaying her first bite until she saw his reaction. He appeared surprised, tasted, chewed, then nodded and smiled and went back to talking with the cattle buyer. The lawyer's satisfaction was evident. Kate buttered a small piece of bread. The first hurdle was over.

"Mama came from Virginia and knew how to make chicken taste good without frying it," Afton said, after cutting a sharp glance at Kate. "I didn't know Indian women knew how to cook anything but buffalo meat. Didn't think they knew how to make soup like this either."

Kate spoke before Coleridge had an opportunity. "I'm not sure Indian women know how to make this particular dish, but they make other dishes that are very good."

With a tilt of her chin, Afton gazed straight ahead. "Indian women are infidels. That's what Mama said."

Kate smiled, adding easily, "To Indians, I suppose, whites are infidels."

"Pooh. I'm no infidel, and Coleridge isn't one. Slaves don't have souls, so they aren't infidels either."

Coleridge continued to eat, his impeccable manners never more evident. "Excellent meal, Miss Kate."

Instinct told her to overlook Afton's hurtful words, that Afton was, after all, only a child. Smiling and ignoring Afton, she thanked Coleridge as graciously as he had addressed her.

"Sometimes a change of menu . . ." She looked up in time to see the malice in Anna's eyes. "Sometimes a change is called for."

"Cole's going to say whatever you want him to." Afton looked first at Anna and then at Cole. "After all, he's just a slave."

Sean's heavy sigh told her he'd heard, and that Afton's argument was an old one. Kate waited for Sean to speak. When he said nothing, but appeared engrossed in whatever the cattle buyer was saying, she decided it was up to her to educate Afton. "President Lincoln doesn't consider Cole a slave. He made people like Coleridge free."

Afton looked at Anna for approval. "But Cole doesn't belong to old Lincoln."

Annoyed, Kate hoped to take the sting out of the child's words. "He belongs to himself. Coleridge is his own man now."

Afton shook her head. "He belongs to me. He's a nigra. He's black."

Kate was appalled at such opinions from a small girl. Obviously the child had learned her prejudices from a system that included her parents. Kate's eyes met Sean's.

His hair had been tied back with some kind of black band that hid its length. His sharp features, a mix of Indian and Irish, had never appeared more prominent. By white standards, his dark skin and straight hair were more Comanche. His eyes, his smile, his laughter—all Irish. His honor? A mixture, she supposed, of white and red. But why didn't he speak now to this obnoxious child?

She didn't have long to wait.

"Properly, Afton, the word is Negro." Sean smiled at the little girl. "And the Civil War settled the question of slavery. The United States does not condone slavery. And by the time you're a young lady, color will no longer matter."

Afton looked down at her plate. "Mama said . . ." She glanced from him to Cole and saw Cole frown. "Yes, sir," Afton said meekly.

In Cole's place, Kate thought, she would have been shouting her anger from the housetops. Since her stay at Stone Wolf's camp, her intolerance toward Indians had changed—not enough to forgive them, but now she could be more objective, admit they had some good points. After all, her intense feelings had come from Papa's murder. No comparison could be made with Afton's mulishness. Anybody could see that.

"Perhaps you'd like your dessert now, Afton?"

Afton's petulance had been replaced with sullenness. "No."

"I suspect the rest of us would like ours." Masking her displeasure with courtesy, Kate signaled Anna, who wore the same sulky expression. "You may serve now."

"I've changed my mind," Afton said. "I'll have my dessert, too. Mama said table talk should be comfortable."

Sean took his time, then wiped his mouth and smiled at Afton. "And we want good manners at our table. Remember, Cole's no longer a slave. He didn't ask to be a slave. It was forced on him. Please don't mention it again."

"But," Afton said, her eyes rebellious, "he's black. Anybody can see that."

"Afton," Cole said gently, "I suggest you listen to what Mr. O'Brien says."

Afton looked down at her plate and whispered grudgingly, "All right."

Sean turned his attention to his dessert. "I'm leaving for a few nights. Not sure how many. I have horses in the canyon, so I'll be taking some of the boys to help bring them to the Shamrock. Malachi will go."

When the meal was over, Sean and the guests excused themselves and walked down the hall to Sean's office. Kate heard the door close and gave an inward shudder at what lay ahead. Anna made no secret of her dislike, and many of the other people in the household, victims of Anna's sharp tongue, behaved the same way.

"We'll do fine here," Kate muttered when she was alone. "Despite this gargoyle looking over my shoulder."

Later, when she saw Sean and the men getting ready to leave, she hurried to the corral. "Good-bye, Mal. Good-bye, Sean."

Sean kissed her good-bye on the mouth. "Miss me, lass."

She watched them out of sight, until she could no longer see Sean's western hat. She missed him already.

With Malachi beside him, Sean and his riders rode northwest toward the Palo Duro, making good time, sleeping around a campfire that night. The next morning they traveled up stream, with Sean leading the way to the ravine he called his canyon. Here his herd grazed, raising their heads when they saw him and his men approach. At Sean's whistle, the Ghost whinnied a greeting and trotted toward him.

At the same time Sean spotted another rider, a young man from his looks. Immediately Sean knew why he was there, and anger welled in him. A stranger had dared to encroach on his pasture. In Texas, a man was hanged for stealing just one horse.

Sean eased his hand down to the gun in his holster. No point in taking chances with a horse thief. "I'm O'Brien from the Shamrock spread."

"Andy Bennet." He waved an arm toward the horses. "These mustangs are mine. I found them first."

Malachi spoke up before Sean could answer. "They wasn't lost, son."

"Mean you left them here?"

"Reckon so," Malachi said, turning his eyes on Sean. "This man owns them."

"You that Irishman the piano player in Tascosa spoke about?"

"What did he say?"

"He said if gittin' the horses didn't work out for me, I ought to see a Mr. O'Brien about a job."

Malachi laughed, enjoying himself. "It shore didn't work out, son."

Bennet nodded woefully. "Just my luck. I thought I'd found a bunch of wild horses. Planned on taking 'em to sell and getting enough money to start a little spread." He attempted to smile past his disappointment. "Even figured on taking a wife."

Recognizing that the man was neither a threat nor a horse thief, Sean found himself in sympathy. After all, he had a similar problem; the difference was that he couldn't convince his wife to stay. "The girl live around here?"

"No, I met her on the stage coming from Missouri."

He'd probably met a young whore, new at the job and looking for work in one of the frontier towns. A shame, since young Bennet seemed a nice enough sort. "Where was she going?"

"Tascosa. Pretty as a speckled calf. Red hair." Andy Bennet's smile spread over his freckled face. "We hit it off right away. She was going to see her sister. Said she sang at the Gilded Lily."

Sean gave him his full attention. "Did she meet her sister?"

A worried look furrowed Andy's brow. "Naw, her sister didn't sing there no more, but the guy that owns the place, he gave Maureen a job. Said he'd help her find her sister."

Sean knew before he asked, but he wanted confirmation from Andy Bennet's mouth. "What's the girl's last name?"

"Maureen Hartland. Right pretty name. Her sister's name's Kate."

"Does Maureen sing at the Gilded Lily now?"

"I don't think so," Andy said, wrinkling his face in study. "That piano player—name's Joe as I recollect—said she didn't." Andy paused, his eyes registering his sadness. "And I said, 'How long's she been gone?' "

Sean waited impatiently for Andy to continue, but Malachi jumped in with, "This Joe, what did he say, boy?"

"A few days, Joe said, and then he went back to playing the piano. I asked him where, and he just shook his head and kept playin'. When I asked him if the owner knew where she was, Joe said it was prob'ly best not to ask. Joe mentioned something about Comancheros, and then he shut up and wouldn't say nothin' else."

Malachi's weathered face showed his concern. "Whatta you think, Sean?"

Sean knew he had to do something quickly, or somewhere a Comanchero would exchange Kate's sister for rifles, after he'd availed himself of the merchandise and shared her with his comrades.

His mind engaged in angry planning, Sean began slowly to

create a strategy. "Mal, if you and the boys will help, we'll rescue Maureen."

Inhaling deeply, Andy nudged his horse a little closer. "Mr. O'Brien, mind if I tag along? I hung around when this guy Boggs offered Maureen a job. I didn't like his looks, but Maureen was determined. She said she knew Kate was in Tascosa. Kate wanted Maureen to come to where she was. Seems Kate had sent her a hundred dollars."

Sean knew about the hundred dollars. He also knew about Boggs and the Gilded Lily. Boggs was evil, vicious. Thank God Kate had gotten away. Now he had Maureen to worry about. He wheeled his horse around. "Mal, you hurry back to the Shamrock. I need you to look after things while we're gone. I hope this doesn't take long, but we may be gone awhile. Tell Kate not to fret; we'll find her sister."

He beckoned Andy. "This is what I want you to do. You're in charge, and the men here will help. As soon as you get the mustangs rounded up, herd them up the stream in the Palo Duro Canyon and hold them until I send word." He described in detail what was expected. "And after we get Maureen, I'm going to kill Boggs. I'm going to skin him and stake him out for the ants."

Staggered by the news Malachi brought with him, Kate peppered him with questions. "Where did Sean go?"

"Don't rightly know, Miss Kate. He left and that's the last I seen of 'im."

"But he must have told you something. Which direction did he take? Did he go toward Tascosa?"

"Miss Kate, Sean didn't go to Tascosa. I think he'll prob'ly look for a Comanchero camp. He's a good tracker. He was taught by the Comanche and they know how to read sign. Besides, he can take care of hisself. He don't want you worryin' none. He can handle it."

Kate paced outside the barn door, wondering what course she should take. The country was so big, so many miles of barren prairies, so dangerous. How could she help? What could she do? She studied the events, mulling each one in turn. The idea popped into her head from out of the blue.

"Mal, I'm going to Stone Wolf's camp in Tule Canyon. Stone Wolf wasn't planning to move back to the Palo Duro until after the first frost. I'll ask him where Sean might be."

"Aw, now, Miss Kate, Sean wants you to stay here and wait. You know," Mal said, his tone wheedling, "to meet yore sister when him and her gits back. Besides, who's gonna look after the house?"

"Anna." She smiled at him. "Unless you want to."

"I warrant you're teasin' me now, Miss Kate. But if you're dead set on going, at least wait until morning. Why, it's nearly dark now. You'll have trouble finding your way. For all we know, Sean may be heading back with Maureen right this minute."

"Boggs hates me. He'll use my sister to get even with me." And sell Maureen into Mexico, she thought, her anxiety close to panic. She simply had to do something.

Kate told Malachi good-bye and marched toward the main house, her shoulders straight, her chin mutinous. She supposed she should wait until morning, but patience had never been one of her strong points.

How dared that slimy Boggs take her sister!

In her room, she searched the wardrobe for pants and a shirt, something comfortable, for she fully intended to ride astride. She chose warm clothing for traveling at night, boots, and a rabbitskin cap. Then she went downstairs in search of a slicker and met Anna walking toward her, her felt slippers making no sound on the shining floors.

"I'll be leaving in the morning. I'd appreciate your taking over as housekeeper again."

Anna tried unsuccessfully to hide her satisfaction. "Of course. I'll speak to the servants."

The woman was sure of herself, Kate mused, and she supposed that by the time she returned, she'd have to start over at winning the confidence of the servants. She could count on Juanita remaining loyal to her. In the kitchen, Kate found Coleridge peeling potatoes. He stood and waited for her to speak.

"My sister has disappeared, and there's a possibility she's

held by Comancheros. Sean has gone looking for her. I'm so scared for both of them." Kate tried to swallow around the lump in her throat. "I don't know where he's looking, but I plan to go back to the Indian camp where I was held captive. I'm acquainted with the chief there. I'll ask for his help."

"Is that wise, Miss Kate?"

"I'm known at the camp," she said simply. "I think Stone Wolf will listen to me. And call me Kate. Or Kathleen, if you're uncomfortable with Kate."

Coleridge bowed his head slightly. "Then I'll call you Kathleen." Laying his knife down, he wiped his hands on a towel. "I'll go with you."

"That won't be necessary. I can—"

She was interrupted by a cry behind her. "You can't go, Cole."

"Miss Afton, we're indebted to Mr. Sean for giving us a home. He needs our help now."

Afton stamped her feet. "You can't go. You're my slave, and I say you can't go."

"I have to go with Kathleen, Afton," he said gently, but firmly.

Tears trailed down the girl's face. "You won't come back, Cole. Mama said given half a chance, slaves always run away."

"I promise."

Sobbing, Afton held out her arms. "Please, Cole. Take me with you."

Cole held her, one hand stroking her hair. "Honey, I'll be back, but Mr. Sean and Kathleen need me, and you're safe here."

Moved by the scene, Kate shook her head. "There's no need for you to go, Cole."

"There's a need, Miss . . . Kathleen. Mr. Sean would never forgive me if I let you go alone. I'll get my gear."

Briefly she'd considered waiting until morning, but Cole's offer made the decision easy. "Don't suppose you have a slicker?"

Cole smiled showing his white teeth. "I have indeed. And I know where there's another."

They left the house and Afton's sobbing to go in search of

Malachi. He helped saddle two horses and waited until they mounted to give directions. "I ain't sure you're doing the right thing going into Tule Canyon, but I understand why you have to go. Reckon I'd go with you, but I'm needed here. Be careful."

Kate leaned over to shake his hand. "Thanks, Malachi. We'll be back with Sean and Maureen."

"Hope so, Miss Kate. I rightly hope so."

They put the horses to a brisk walk, riding side by side when they could. Knowing how Cole must feel at meeting Indians, Kate spoke confidently, assuring him there was no danger in going to the Indian camp. "I know Stone Wolf, the chief, and most of the people in the village. You and I will be welcome."

Several hours later, and following Malachi's directions, they came to the canyon and the entrance they sought. Kate led the way down, turning occasionally to check on her companion. A black void awaited them. Even the air was cooler, and the smell of vegetation and cedar rose to meet them. The hair on the back of her neck stood up, and she thought of Cole. Riding into the canyon would be a new experience for him. And he was no doubt remembering the massacre of the wagon train. Kate was impressed with his courage. "We've a way to go, Cole. I think we'll be there by morning."

A harsh voice came out of the darkness, and two big hands grabbed for her. "I wouldn't count on it, gel. Me and Riley got other plans for you." He yanked the reins from her hands and called to his companion. "I got this one, Riley."

Kate fought hard. She clawed and kicked and did her best to bite the hands that held her. She scraped her fingernails down the man's face and heard his grunt and curse. Her hands came away wet, and she knew she'd drawn blood. Now was the time to keep her head. A knee to the groin. A kick in the shin. She would go for his eyes.

But he was ahead of her. His hands found her throat.

Gasping, she gurgled at Cole. "Ride, Cole, ride. Get help."

"Shuddup." The man's hand shot out and connected with her cheek. "Jest shuddup." He yelled at Cole. "I don't know who you are, man, but I got a gun on the gel. Come after her and I kill her right off."

"Run, Cole; get help. Go while you can!"

Fighting Riley off, Cole argued first with her and then with the man. Kate could hear thuds and grunts in the exchange of blows. She heard Cole's curses, and for some ridiculous reason, she found them comforting. Again and again the sound of fists connecting with flesh came to her ears, and then the noise of a body hitting the ground. Moments later she heard the squeak of leather, the squeal of a horse, and retreating hoofbeats.

"Sumbitch got away, Morse, and just when I got hold of my knife." Riley spat in disgust. "That nigger plum got away."

"Bonham's gonna be mad as hell when he hears about it."

Kate worked at calming her nerves and waiting for her heart to stop pounding. Who was Bonham? Where had she heard the name? Then she remembered the smirking cowboy on the day of their arrival. "Mr. O'Brien will hear about this. He'll come after you with his men and his guns."

"Listen to her, Riley. She's scarin' me plumb to death." The man Morse held her hard against him and fondled her breast. "She scare you, Riley?"

"Hell, yes. I'm peein' my britches, I'm that scared."

Morse tightened his hands around her throat, cutting off her air. Oh, God, he was a madman intent on killing her. Gasping, she fought with all her strength. "Let me go." She gagged at his fetid breath. He held her with arms of steel and attempted to kiss her. Twisting her head, first to the right and then to the left, she avoided his mouth.

"Let me alone, you . . . you criminal."

"Oh, Riley, we got us a feisty one."

"We got orders, Morse. Don't nobody touch the gel. We're s'pose to get her to the Comanchero camp as soon as we can." He mouthed an oath. "Otherwise we'd both have us a go."

"Who says we cain't? Bonham?"

"Bonham says Boggs been lookin' for this woman. He's already got her sister. Holdin' her for bait. Boggs knowed the Irishman was sweet on this one, so Boggs sent Bonham to the Shamrock. And by God, she showed up. Ain't that lucky?"

"Bonham works fer Boggs? Reckon if'n it's Boggs givin' the orders, we'd better listen," Morse said reluctantly. He kneaded

Kate's breast. "What'd Bonham do? Send word to Boggs?"

"Damned if I know, but prob'ly. Bonham's been watchin' her fer days. He rode like hell to get word to me soon as her and that nigger rode out. Warn't no problem to meet 'em here."

Kate's heart sank. Boggs intended to get even by selling her and Maureen to the Comancheros. Chills went down her back. She struggled, doing her best to break Morse's grip by biting him. She knew she'd lost the battle when Riley tied her hands and lifted her to the back of her horse.

Perched behind a rock above the canyon floor, Hawk waited impatiently for word from Little Crow. He'd lost precious time going to Stone Wolf's camp, but he needed help from his mother's people. Little Crow had volunteered, saying he knew where the Comanchero camp was located in the Palo Duro. Kate had saved his son, and Little Crow would not forget.

"Why isn't Little Crow here?" Andy asked, turning to look behind him. "That Indian could have been here sooner if he'd started in Mexico."

"He's putting together a war party. Takes time." Every inch a Comanche, Hawk had donned leather pants and the jacket Kate had made for him, and placed a leather band around his head. His face was cold and impassive. He thought and reasoned like an Indian. Now and then he could feel Andy's quizzical gaze. "Something the matter?"

"Mr. O'Brien, you look an awful lot like an Indian."

"I am an Indian."

"Yeah, I reckon so," Andy said uneasily.

What, Hawk wondered, would his new friend do if he indulged in a war whoop? "I'm not as much Comanche as Little Crow."

Andy gave a wan smile. "Right glad we're friends, Mr. O'Brien."

The moon had made a silvery appearance and lit the prairie enough for them to see the terrain. Hawk pointed. "There they come. Look closely and you'll see the dust."

"My God," Andy whispered, "there's a bunch of them. Are you sure they're friendly?"

"As sure as I am that the wind will blow tomorrow."

When Little Crow rode up, Sean nodded. "My brother has honored me." He spoke in the language of the People.

Little Crow moved his head enough to acknowledge the familiar greeting. "Little Crow's spy says the Comancheros wait for Boggs."

Boggs, that son of a bitch, had bargained with the Comancheros to hold Maureen captive for him.

Hawk could feel Kate's anger all the way from the Shamrock. "Did the spy say where they keep the prisoners?"

"In the corral by the cliff."

"Fine. Which cliff?"

Amusement crossed Little Crow's face. "Come. I'll show you. Leave white eyes here."

Hawk looked at Andy. "It's time."

Andy gazed into the darkness. "I'm gonna marry Maureen. It's like she was already my wife. You can recognize her by her red hair. I'll bring the horses as soon as I can." He looked at Hawk for confirmation. At his nod, Andy jumped, his boot finding the stirrup. "I'll ride back as fast as I can. From the southeast."

Little Crow led the way and Hawk followed. They stopped several times to watch. On the canyon floor half a dozen wagons had been drawn together, their wagon tongues down, burros and mules grazing nearby. Men sat around a campfire, smoking and passing a bottle. Hawk couldn't hear what was being said, but he could imagine their impatience. For good reason, thieves were never patient.

"We'll ride over to that crest and wait for Bennet and the horses."

"My brother is lazy or maybe crazy." Little Crow's voice held laughter. "We will crawl."

After circling to a spot where they were better able to see, Little Crow signaled a stop. "Look close. Do you see the woman?"

"Not yet."

"We should sleep."

Hawk nodded in agreement. Hidden as they were, their best

bet was to wait for morning. He couldn't disappoint Kate by failing to rescue her sister. Kate had paid a high price to see that Maureen had a better life. So far her money had bought little but heartache. "Crow, you take the first watch. I'll take the second. We'll be able to tell more when the sun comes up."

When the sun's rays hit the canyon rim, Hawk was wide awake. He had seen no activity until the Mexican patron climbed out of a wagon and began shouting orders. Immediately the Comanchero camp came awake. Little Crow slithered over to Hawk and pointed toward the east.

Three riders galloped into the camp, followed by two Comanchero lookouts carrying rifles. Two of the newcomers were men, the third a woman. Her wrists were tied, but she clung desperately to the saddle horn. Hawk shuddered at what she must have gone through, and quickly made up his mind. The woman would be rescued along with Maureen and any other prisoners who might be there.

From a distance, the woman appeared young. Her shoulders slumped with fatigue, and even when the men halted the horses, she still gripped the saddle horn. Hawk suspected she was hungry and cold, for it was doubtful her captors took much interest in her comfort. Where had these men found her? He didn't have to ask what they intended to do with her.

Little Crow pointed at a man who'd emerged from the lead wagon. "The boss's name is Martinez."

The patron spoke rapidly and with many gestures, at last motioning toward a rock wall. The sun had started its climb up the eastern sky, and Hawk leaned forward for a better look. An adobe hut, almost hidden by shadows, backed up to the base of a cliff. Leaning indolently against the fence, his boot hooked over a rail, his rifle butt down, a guard yawned and stretched.

Hawk pointed toward the hut. "Prisoners?" At Little Crow's nod, Hawk whispered out of the side of his mouth, "I'll crawl closer. If the guard sees me and raises a ruckus, don't wait for Andy and the mustangs. Signal your braves, and we'll storm the bloody hell out of them."

He lay on his stomach and inched forward. The dry buffalo

grass scratched his face and hands, and where his fingers dug into the ground to move him forward, the skin soon turned red and bloody. Easy, easy, he told himself. Any sign of movement would alert the guard and anybody else who stood watching.

Stopping, he watched attentively as two men struggled with the new captive. Her black hair, tangled by the wind, snarled about her face and shoulders. Kicking and screaming, she tried to break free. She was about the size of Kate, and the woman's pants shaped her hips the same way as Kate's. Hawk's breath rushed out of his lungs. His heart burst into a hard and relentless hammering.

Kate. His Kate was being herded toward the prisoners' hold.

Cursing, one of her captors backhanded her. She staggered, almost falling, her startled cry ringing in his ears like the call of a trumpet. One day, Hawk promised silently, he'd kill the bastard.

The man Little Crow had identified as Martinez stood beside his wagon, his gaze fixed on the east. There, a line of horses and riders filed into the canyon by way of a trail from the rim. Even at a distance Hawk recognized Boggs.

Kate had been brought here on Boggs's orders. No doubt Maureen had been brought for the same reason—revenge. Hawk knew he could get no closer until Andy brought the horses. First they needed a lay of the land, a plan for storming the fence where the prisoners were. Dimly he heard Martinez screaming for the men who held Kate to hurry up.

"Put her in the blockade. Maybe she can shut them kids up. I cain't stand hearin' them cryin' for their mamas. Every time we get young'uns, there's a howl. 'Nuf to drive a man crazy. Boggs is on his way, and he don't take kindly to the wailin'."

The man who held Kate waited until the gate had been opened; then he loosened the ropes on her wrists and with a curse shoved her to the ground. There were cries from inside and then silence. Was she cold? Hungry? Had they hurt her?

Hawk vowed vengeance. He'd kill every Comanchero. Martinez. All of them. He'd start with the men who'd captured Kate.

And Boggs. He'd save Boggs for last. He'd watch him grovel and beg, and then he'd kill him slowly.

Blood boiling in his veins, Hawk eased back to where Little Crow waited for him. "If somebody doesn't beat me to it, I'm going to kill Boggs. That bastard's going to die."

Chapter Twelve

Stunned, inert, Kate sprawled on the hard ground. For several seconds she couldn't remember where she was or how she had gotten there. She rolled to one side and ran her fingers over her jaw, winced, and then brushed gingerly at the dirt on her cheeks. Her abraded wrists were raw and bloody, and she flinched at her broken fingernails.

Cole had gotten away, and she prayed fervently that he'd made it back to the ranch. If Malachi could alert the marshal, or get up a posse, or find Stone Wolf's camp to get help—

She was out of her mind. Malachi could never ride safely into the Indian camp, even if he knew where it was. Stone Wolf's braves would have his scalp. As for the Comancheros, Sean's foreman would meet a terrible fate if he rode against them.

Maureen! Had the Comancheros hurried her south into Mexico? Kate vowed that if she got out, she'd spend the rest of her life seeking vengeance on Nathan Boggs. She knew beyond a doubt that he was behind her capture and Maury's—and the lowlife would surely pay. As for Bonham and her captors,

230

Morse and Riley, she'd think of something appropriate. For the present she was helpless, but she had no intention of remaining so.

Sean had gone in search of Maureen, possibly toward the Canadian River, and there was no assurance he even knew this camp existed. Of one thing she was certain—the Comanche knew of this meeting place, and if they were aware, perhaps there was a chance Sean would learn of it. She hoped that before setting out to look for Maureen he'd go first to ask Stone Wolf his advice.

Before she gained her feet, she scanned the cliffs. They were in a canyon. But which one? The Palo Duro or the Tule?

She rose painfully and brushed at the mud on her clothes. It was then that she heard the faintest of sounds. When it came again, she recognized the whimper of a child. Ignoring the guard's lascivious look, she walked unsteadily across the yard toward the miserable hut that served as a shelter. Like most cabins in the area, the hovel backed up to a cliff wall. The door was partly open, hanging dejectedly by one hinge. She hesitated at the door, peering into the murky room.

Sickened by the odor of defecation and vomit, she put her hand to her nose to close out the smell, and hoped desperately she didn't have to stay here any longer than it took Sean to find her. She'd told herself he'd come so many times since her capture that she'd convinced herself he would.

After her eyes adjusted to the dark interior, she saw the small huddle of humanity that stared back at her with big, frightened eyes. "Can any of you speak English?"

"Kate! Oh, Kate!" Maureen bolted out of the corner and flung herself at Kate, wrapping her arms around her. "Oh, Kate," she said, crying and laughing at the same time, "I knew you'd come. I just prayed and prayed. This is a terrible place. Can we leave now?"

Kate held her sister tightly. God, what had those awful men done to her little sister? When she could trust herself to speak, Kate placed her cheek against Maureen's and whispered, "Maureen, honey. I'm here."

She stroked Maureen's filthy hair. Gone was its silky feel. Her clothes were in tatters, her feet bare. Tears streaked the dirt on her pretty face. She plucked nervously at her clothing. Kate wanted to kill Nathan Boggs.

Promising they would likely be out in no time, she crooned reassurances. She couldn't imagine what Maureen had already been through, but it wouldn't hurt to keep up her sister's hopes.

"Maury, honey, we're prisoners. This is a Comanchero camp. But we won't be here long. I have a friend . . ." Kate hesitated, wondering the best way to tell her sister about Sean. When he found this Comanchero stronghold, he would come as Hawk. "There's a man I know who'll soon have us out of this dreadful place."

Despair returned to Maureen's face. "You're a prisoner, too. Oh, Kate," she sobbed, "I prayed you'd find me and take me home."

Kate tightened her arms around her sister. "Stop crying. If my friend doesn't come soon, we won't wait. We'll get away on our own. You and I together, we'll find a way. Now tell me who brought you here."

"Nathan Boggs at the Gilded Lily." Maureen whimpered, and then broke into tears again. "He said you were gone, but that you'd be back. He said I didn't sing as well as you, but he'd hire me in your place."

"And then what?" Kate wasn't sure she wanted to hear the answer. "What happened next?"

"He . . . tried to force me, Kate. Threatened me over and over with what would happen to me if I didn't do what he wanted. When I refused, he said he'd give me to some terrible men. He said they would put me in a whorehouse."

Kate continued to stroke Maureen's hair. Her heart ached at hearing the pain in her sister's voice. "How did you get away from home, honey? I thought you had decided to marry Verlin."

"Verlin's nice but I couldn't bear to marry him, so when I found the hundred dollars Mama had hidden, I ran away. I wanted to be with you, Kate. I stayed with a wagon train leaving for California and then took the stage to Tascosa." A wistful smile curved Maureen's lips. "I met a man. His name was Andy Bennet. He liked me. I know he did, Kate. He said he did."

232

Maureen was so vulnerable. So gullible. Kate gave her a gentle shake. "Did he learn that you worked at the Lily?"

"Yes. He was there when Mr. Boggs hired me. And then Andy left. I'll never see him again. And," she said sadly, "he'll never want me now."

"One thing at a time, honey," Kate cautioned, wanting to bludgeon Nathan Boggs to within an inch of his life. "Tell me about Mama and Milton."

"Mama hid the hundred dollars you sent, so I guess she was afraid Milton would get it."

"Why? What happened?"

"Milton lost the church. The members brought in somebody else to be their pastor. Nobody wanted anything to do with Milton. A man, a member of the church, threatened Milton. He said Milton insulted his daughter. That Milton put his hands on her."

"So Mama finally had to face the truth."

"Yes, she was all torn up about it."

"Did Mama ever mention me?"

"I think she was sorry you were gone. I felt bad for her."

Her sister could always be counted on to show sympathy, and Kate found herself sharing the feeling. She'd grown up since being away from home, and now she had a better understanding, not only of her mother but of other people. She loved Mama despite her silly need to cut a figure in the town's society. Mama had thought that since Milton was a man of God, he'd assure her such a place among the wealthy.

Papa had been different, Kate thought sadly. He laughed at the women Mama wanted to be like, calling them a bunch of old biddies. He was educated, a hard worker, and never let anything interfere with his fun or his love for his family. He made money, and then more money, but he stoutly refused to be a part of the tea-and-crumpet scene.

He had been so important to his daughters, especially Kate, and she had adored him. Following Papa's death, there had been nobody until Hawk came into her life.

She hugged Maureen again. She'd be strong for her sister. Papa would expect nothing less. Maureen, the lovable little nitwit, had never been able to do for herself. "Maureen, honey, don't give up. We'll get out of here."

Looking at it squarely, Kate admitted wryly, this time she'd been presented with a sky-high predicament. She not only had her sister, but little children, some as young as five or six, to care for. One little sad-eyed Mexican child whimpered for her mother. "Señorita, give me drink, *por favor*."

A small boy reached for her hand, his black face almost lost in the gloom. "I'm berry hungry, ma'am."

All of them were hungry and dirty, and all of them pleaded to be taken home to their mamas. Kate hugged, patted, and prayed. She ached at their misery, and lied a little, saying they'd soon be going home.

Hawk would come, she told herself, desperately hoping it would be soon, and that what she'd told the group of captives would be the truth. She gently freed herself from clinging hands, sat down among them, and pulled one of the smaller children into her lap. Crooning, she rocked back and forth. "A man is coming and he'll bring his friends and we'll leave this place."

A scared little voice came from behind her. "You promith?"

"I promise."

She chided herself for being as trusting as the children, but she had to believe that Hawk and Stone Wolf's braves would come hurtling in and wipe out this beastly camp.

The place where they were held, the small, evil-smelling shed, would not keep the children from freezing when cold weather came. Of course, she didn't know how long Boggs or Martinez would hold them. "Maury," she asked gently. "How long have you been here?"

"I've lost track. Mr. Boggs had some men come in the night. They put me on a horse and we rode . . . ten miles, fifteen miles. A long way." Maureen gave a negative shake of her head. "We stopped at a stream and Mr. Boggs—"

"For heaven's sake, Maureen, don't dignify a snake by calling it mister."

Maureen cringed and tears welled in her eyes. "I . . . I called him Mr. Boggs when he turned me over to some ugly men, one he called Martinez. And both of them laughed."

"I imagine they did," Kate said dryly. "What happened then?"

"Mr. . . . Boggs said for Mr. . . . for Martinez to wait for word from him. He'd soon have another woman to send along."

Kate ground her teeth. Without having to give it a thought at all, she could name the other one.

Little ones hovered about her, getting as close as they could. Some of them called her Mama, and she answered. When they put out their small, grubby hands, she forced back tears and tried to comfort them all. A girl of about sixteen or seventeen, almost a woman, sat hopelessly in a corner apart from the others her eyes on the floor. "What's her name, Maureen?"

"Dorcas. Martinez uses her. He hurts her."

Boggs should be hanged. No, he should be turned over to the Comanche, who were adept at killing slowly.

"Has she cried?"

"I don't think so. She just sits staring at the ground."

"See if you can draw her into the circle. We must not leave anyone out, Maury."

Maureen rose obediently and crossed to where Dorcas hugged the wall, her thin body wedged into the corner. Trying to make herself smaller, Kate mused sadly, so the man who'd used her would not see her in the gloom. Dorcas shook her head at Maureen's coaxing.

Setting aside the child in her lap, Kate got to her feet and moved to where the young girl sat. "Dorcas, we've been brought here against our will. The men who captured us are evil and mean. They hurt us. But none of it, honey, is our fault."

"The man does bad things to me."

"I know," Kate said gently, "but that doesn't make you bad."

"A girl at home was used by some men, and nobody would even speak to her. If I go back, people won't have anything to do with me."

Kate felt like crying. She took one of Dorcas's hands and squeezed it between her palms. There were many Ophelia Mauds in the world. "Your mama and papa will be so glad to see you. They'll hug you and hold you, like I'm going to do. Come sit in the circle, honey. We want you to."

Velda Sherrod

At first Dorcas refused, but with Kate's urging she reluctantly joined the group. "I'll help with the children."

She had to think of a way out, Kate mused, for all of them. She couldn't bear to think of leaving the children. Absently singing and humming, she comforted with pats and caresses while contriving, rejecting, and plotting. She looked around for possibilities.

Inside the dismal excuse for shelter, pale sunlight showed through the cracks. A cliff behind the shack was evident from a rotted-out corner. A small person could crawl through the hole in the wood. And if one could escape through it, maybe eight could. Gradually a plan emerged. Slowly, dimly, the scheme came into focus. But first they must wait for darkness.

In the meantime, the children had to have food and water. How long had it been since these little ones had been given anything to eat? Her anger escalated to fury. She'd have a word with the guard dog. He'd leered at her and pointed his gun at her heart, but she was reasonably sure he wouldn't shoot. He worked for Martinez, and his boss gave the orders.

Holding the hands of two of the children, she walked outside, glanced around, and spotted the guard. "Look, jackal, these children are hungry. They have no food or water."

The guard slouched against the stockade fence, his gun slung loosely over his arm. "Now, ain't that too bad. And who you callin' jackal, lady?"

"Any blackguard who'd let little children go hungry," she said, raising her voice, "after stealing them from their homes."

"Don't blame me. I didn't steal 'em. I work for Martinez, and he said to watch the stockade. That's what I'm doing. And so far, he ain't said nothin' 'bout feedin' 'em. You either, lady."

"You go tell that poor excuse for a man that I said to bring food for these children, or they won't last the night." She turned loose one of the children, stepped closer, and put a finger in the guard's face. "Go."

The guard showed his surprise, grinned, then whistled at one of the men walking around with a rifle over his shoulder. "Hey, Mac. Tell Martinez these kids are whinin' for something to eat. And tell him to send some water." He undressed Kate with his eyes. "Now, you see, honey. I can be nice. And I could be real nice to you."

Her gaze bored into his. "You could never be nice enough."

"But what if I insisted? Like layin' you down right here and seein' what happens." He slapped his thigh at his joke. "Yessir, might be real interestin'."

"The last man who tried is singing tenor at camp meetings."

Snarling, the guard grabbed for her with his free hand. "Yeah, but I cain't carry a tune, 'specially when I ain't got no music."

Kate backed out of reach. "Here comes a drone with the food."

"What the hell's a drone?"

She almost laughed. "One of Martinez's peons. He waits for Martinez to give him directions. Martinez feeds him, and in return the drone does what he says. Just like you."

The guard squinted at her. "I ain't no drone, lady. Martinez pays me."

"To hold a gun on little children? Real dangerous work you're engaged in."

His face took on the color of bricks. "You got a smart mouth for a whore."

"Not a whore, guard. A woman trying to care for children. Give me the food."

He gave her the bag of bread, then turned back to take a pouch of water from the man he'd called Mac and gave that to her as well. He mumbled a curse. "Shut up and git yore butt back in there with them screamin' kids."

With the food and water in her hands, Kate laughed and threw a glance over her shoulder. "You'd probably be a pretty good sort if you ever decided to get away from Martinez. But then, who'd tell you what to do?"

The guard sputtered, but before he could answer, Kate hurried back inside the shack. "Give the children water first, Maury. I'm sure their throats are dry."

Maury did as she was told. "Do you really think we can get out, Kate?"

"Things are bad, but they could be worse. We're alive. And

I think I've figured a way to get these children and ourselves out of here."

"Those men will find us, Kate. You know they will."

"Stop sniveling, Maury. If you don't cry, maybe the children won't." She handed out bread. "Eat your food, children, and be quiet. Then I want you to take naps."

Naps! Who could sleep at a time like this? Kate almost laughed out loud at her own orders. But the children did as they were told, and the sun finally began to slide behind the cliff. Kate knew she had to hurry. Boggs would be sending them south, probably tomorrow, and if she, Maury, and the children were to get away, it had to be tonight.

Kate waited until the children had all fallen asleep before crawling toward the hole in the wall. If she hugged the cliff face and gained the big boulder, she could be there as each child crawled through and came to her. Maury would come last. They'd sneak upstream, wading to hide their tracks, and when the children got tired they'd find some kind of shelter.

Pain centered in her chest. The plan was flimsy, full of holes, and almost surely doomed to failure. She wanted to pound the wall in frustration. Nothing else came to mind—and they had to try.

"Maury," she whispered, motioning her sister closer, "see the big hole in the corner?" At Maury's nod, Kate outlined her strategy. "Later, after the guard is drowsy or sleeping, I'll climb through and wait at the big rock. See the big boulder on the left? You can send the children through one at a time."

"They'll catch us, Kate. I just know they'll catch us."

Exasperated, Kate glowered at her sister. "Do you have a better idea?" When Maury shook her head, Kate pointed at the hole. "We have to try, Maury. If we don't try, not all the children will live. We have to hope the guard will not think to watch a couple of women and a bunch of children too closely. Do you understand?"

"I understand," Maureen whispered fearfully, looking toward the door.

Kate wondered if she was expecting too much of her sister, but she had to depend on somebody, and her sister was an adult. Kate and Maureen sat next to one another on the dirt floor until darkness had fallen completely. Then they gently woke up the children. Kate hugged each child and promised they would all be out of the place very soon. She nudged Maureen. "Watch me as best you can. I'll signal; then I want you to send the children one by one. Don't start with the smallest or the oldest. Pick one in between and let the others watch. When that child reaches me, send another. The smallest. One at a time, remember." Maury's white face gave no assurance the directions would be followed.

Dorcas scooted over until she was directly in front of Kate. "I'll do it the way you want."

"Did you hear what I told Maureen?" At the girl's nod, Kate put an arm around her. "Good. I know you can do what I ask."

"Yes, ma'am."

"Can you keep the children quiet?"

"Yes, I can do that."

"Good girl. Maury will come last, and before her, you."

"I'll come last." Dorcas pointed at Maureen. "She can be before me."

"I'll go now. Watch for my signal."

Kate made herself as small as she could and wiggled through the hole. Hugging the ground, she inched herself forward. She listened for voices, men searching for her. When none came, she crept on. It seemed forever before she gained the protection of the rock. She touched it. Unshed tears burned her eyes. She was free. Now for the children—

God, she couldn't believe what was happening.

A herd of wild horses stampeded through the camp, followed by Indians, whooping and howling like the very demons of hell. The mustangs surged through the camp, scattering the Comancheros in all directions. The Indian warriors who rode in behind the wild horses overturned wagons, set fire to tents, tore down the stockade fence, and headed for the shed.

Through it all, Kate could hear the terrified cries of the children. She had failed, and she couldn't stop her tears.

* * *

Howling his anger, Hawk rode in behind the wild mustangs, joining Little Crow's braves in trampling, setting fires, and chasing any man on the ground with gun and arrow. Hawk reined Midnight toward a man whose main objective was to get out of the way. The great horse knocked the Comanchero to his knees. He gained his feet, only to be bumped again, this time to his back. Each time the Comanchero tried to rise, the horse rammed him. Hawk took grim satisfaction in the game.

"*Madre de Dios*, Comanche. Let me up."

Speaking in a harsh, guttural tone, Hawk asked the question that burned in his brain. "Boggs?"

The Comanchero's eyes widened in recognition. He pointed at a tent. "Boggs. He's got a woman with him. Now let me up."

If Boggs had Kate, Hawk intended to roast him over the fire. Guiding Midnight with his knees, Hawk slowly, deliberately backed the man to the very edge of a campfire. "One move for your gun, *hombre*, I push you into fire. Then," he said, pulling his lips back from his teeth in a vicious snarl, "then, *hombre*, I keel you. Slow. With tomahawk. Cut nose first. Then ears."

His voice weak, his teeth chattering, the Comanchero pointed. "There. That tent to the left."

"Louder, *hombre*. You speak with pale voice."

"That tent, in the name of the Mother."

Satisfied that the man spoke the truth, Hawk backed his horse up. "Thees Boggs. Get him."

Keeping his eyes on Hawk, the Comanchero eased away from the fire and staggered toward the tent where he'd pointed. Hawk followed, allowing Midnight to stay at the man's heels. "Faster, *hombre*."

"He won't find me, savage. I'm at your back and I'm holding a gun." Boggs walked out of the shadows, tugging at his pants. "Who sent you to raid this camp?"

Hawk turned his head to look behind him. "Martinez, he send."

"Lyin'. You're lyin'." Boggs screamed as if he'd been stabbed. "Dumb savage. Martinez runs this place. He ain't crazy enough to have his own camp raided."

"Martinez," Hawk insisted. "Keep prisoner women—self."

"The hell he is. We made a bargain. The two women he's holding go south. Into Mexico." Boggs licked his lips. "I'm gonna see they make it to a whorehouse. I'm gonna sell 'em."

At the word *whorehouse*, Hawk kicked his horse in the flank and Midnight leaped forward, but not before Boggs got off a shot. Hawk felt the bullet graze his arm. His gaze bored into the saloonkeeper. He threw his tomahawk and heard the satisfying sound of the weapon finding a target.

Behind him, screams, shouts, and the sound of death reached his ears. He whirled and dodged, zigzagging toward the stockade. Several of Little Crow's braves had pulled the fence down and were waiting for directions. Hawk threw himself from his horse and ran for the door. Inside the hovel, the smell of human excrement was staggering. The children, a small huddle of misery, cried and clung to each other. A woman cowered among them.

His heart sank. She was not Kate.

Slowly Hawk became aware of Andy beside him, peering through the gloom at the small faces of the children, but seeing only the woman.

"Maureen!" Andy opened his arms.

Crying hysterically, Maureen launched herself into them. "Oh, Andy, Andy."

So this was Kate's sister, the one Kate had sold her virtue to save. But where was Kate?

Hawk placed a hand on Maureen's shoulder. "Maureen," he said, as kindly as his anxiety permitted, "where is Kate?"

She shrank from his touch and shook her head, her face buried in Andy's chest. "Gone. Gone."

Devastated, Hawk continued to look around, finally realizing his search was futile. He moved closer. "Where? Where did she go? Please tell me."

"Answer him, honey." Andy tried to force her head up. "Where's your sister?"

"Gone." Maureen muffled her reply against his shoulder. She pointed at a hole in the corner of the shack. "Through there."

"I'm Dorcas." The voice came from the shadows. "We planned to escape. Kate was going to go first, then wait at a rock for me to send out the children. We rested until it was dark; then Kate wiggled out. I had just gotten Amos ready to go when we heard all the commotion in camp.

"You're sure she made it outside? That she got away?"

Maureen broke into fresh sobs. "We never had a chance."

"We know she got to the rock," Dorcas said, her eyes going from one man to the other. "We could see her."

Hawk looked into the young-old face, into eyes that had seen too much horror, experienced too much pain "How old are you, Dorcas?"

"Sixteen. Seventeen in July. I was to guide the children to her." Whispering, she turned to Andy as the only white man present. "If you take her, will you take me, too?"

Hawk motioned her to him and watched as she reluctantly sidled closer. "Nobody will hurt you, Dorcas. One of the Indians will carry you out. Don't be afraid."

"But you're an Indian, and Indians hurt people, too."

Hawk smiled at her, recognizing that the paint on his face must be frightening. "Yes, an Indian. But tonight Indians are your friends." He smiled at her. "Instead of the cavalry, the Indians have come to rescue you. We're here to take you out of this place."

The girl turned her gaze on Andy. "But you're not an Indian."

Nodding, his arms still around Maureen, Andy looked at her. "Naw, and I reckon I wouldn't have believed it either, that there's some good Injuns. But it's true."

Baffled at the turn of events, Hawk stooped to see through the hole in the corner. He could tell where she had broken some of the rotten wood to make a space big enough to allow wiggle room for a body as small as Kate's. Rain started, a drizzle blurring his vision. He had to find her. "Dorcas, where were you going once you got out?"

"Kate said she knew of a place. We were going to take the children there. It was a cave, she said, where Indians and Comancheros wouldn't go. She said that in the daytime we'd hide."

"What about food?"

Dorcas held up a pitiful sack of bread. "She said we'd give it to the little ones to keep them from crying."

The pain in his chest intensified. His Kate had tried to rescue the children. He could not do less. "Andy, keep the children together until Crow's braves can rescue them."

Once outside, he recognized that the sound of battle had changed. The Indians still circled, but the Comancheros had rallied and crouched behind rocks, their rifles pointing and belching fire. Hawk whistled to get Little Crow's attention. Once Little Crow reined his pony back in his direction, Hawk ran toward him. "Crow, get the children out of here. Tell Stone Wolf that as soon as I can find Kate, we'll take them off his hands."

Andy came up behind him, herding the children, his arm still around Maureen. "What about us? Do we go with the Indians?"

"Follow Little Crow." Hawk took his eyes from the woman in Andy's arms and met Andy's gaze. "Try to stop her crying; then maybe the children will stop, too."

From atop his pony, Little Crow looked around and back to Hawk. "Your woman?"

Hawk shook his head. "Gone," he said. "She escaped about the time we arrived. She was attempting to rescue the children. I don't know whether she got away, or one of Boggs's gunmen found her. But I'm going to find her. And then I'm going to kill the son of a bitch who captured her, if it takes the rest of my life." He threw himself over Midnight's bare back. "When I do, I'll head for the camp."

As if she'd given him a map, he knew the direction Kate had taken. She'd go to the cave where they'd spent the night and watched the stars. It was there they had seen the Comancheros' meeting with Boggs. Hawk hated thinking of her scrambling around in the dark of the canyon, of the wild animals she might face.

He thought of them as a team, he and his beautiful Kate. There were times when he wondered if her strength was a limitation, that some inner fire goaded her to reach a goal, and, once it was begun, she couldn't give up—even when the odds were against her. In these grim surroundings, his Kate had wanted to save the children. She had worked out a plan.

243

As soon as he saw the children on their way, Andy assuming responsibility for Maureen, and Boggs dead or damn near, he'd find Kate. It shouldn't take long. He was sure she'd follow the stream up the belly of the canyon. With a little luck, she'd recognize the place to climb the cliff, and, once there, she'd be secure until he could be there with her. He'd tell her how brave she was, and how the children were safe with Stone Wolf's people.

First things first. He had to find her. He wheeled his horse in time to meet the bullet that knocked him from Midnight's back. He landed hard, struggled to rise, staggered, and fell to his knees. "Kate. I have to find Kate. Bloody . . . hell, Crow . . . take . . . the children . . ." He tried to speak, but the world rocked around him, and he sank into a dark void. The ground rose up to welcome him.

Miserable at the turn of events, Kate watched the fight from behind the boulder. No longer making their unholy shrieks and screams, the Indians snatched the children one by one and rode toward the prairie. Even the children were quiet. They were probably too afraid to cry. She couldn't see Maureen, but Dorcas—brave, staunch Dorcas—fared no better. The courageous young girl rode astride, clinging to a garishly painted Indian whose sole purpose appeared to center on getting her out of camp. Kate shuddered at what awaited the girl. The night had become a nightmare, and in her torment Kate looked frantically for Maureen. Whose camp were these Indians from? She prayed they weren't Quanah Parker's braves.

A burst of gunshots reminded her she had to run, to get away while she still had time. She needed to get as far from the camp as she could. If she were lucky, the rain would remain light, but heavy enough to wash away her footprints. She stumbled down a trail toward the bosom of the canyon, and to freedom.

Boggs would never give up looking for her. She hoped he'd been killed or taken prisoner.

She'd find the cave. Hawk would come, she knew he would, as soon as he found she had followed him from the Shamrock.

The ground grew more slippery, and she stumbled along,

falling and scrambling toward a safe place. Now and then she stopped to listen. Hearing nothing, she continued putting distance between herself and the Comanchero camp. Her heart ached for Maureen and the children. They'd gone from victims of the Comancheros to captives of the Indians. She thought of Boggs and her hatred grew. If she had the opportunity, even the slightest chance, she'd point a gun at Boggs's chest and pull the trigger. The man didn't deserve to live.

Sanity returned, and with it a clear head, reminding her that whether he deserved to live or not, she could never kill him. Papa had taught her well. Taking a life, any life, would be wrong, including the lives of Indians.

She'd bet that if Papa could look down from whatever mansion he occupied in heaven and speak about it, he'd say Indians were human, and life was sacred. No doubt he would have respected Hawk, even knowing Hawk's relatives had killed him. She believed the same way. It was hard to imagine that Hawk would ever harm anybody. Not even Ophelia Maud. Of course, he might want to spit in her ear.

Her rejection of his ancestry had become vague and indefinable, as though it had never existed. She tried again and again to go back and pick up the threads of her distrust, but never once had he failed her, even in facing danger to search for Maureen.

The picture of him, his sinewy muscles straining under his sun-bronzed skin, his gray eyes laughing into hers, the curve of his sensual mouth, was indelibly stamped on her mind. She remembered his easy gallantry, his lighthearted teasing, the way he bent his head toward her to listen, to smile. It was good to think about him, better than wondering why life had plummeted her toward this night.

And through it all, she felt guilty. Her own bigotry galled.

Walking, running when the trail allowed it, Kate pushed on until her legs and feet ached, until her body was bone-weary. She stopped to rest occasionally and at such times tormented herself by imagining all kinds of animals leaping from the shadows. No night sounds came from the blackness, no snarling or rustling in the underbrush. The farther she went, the less she feared the Comancheros, and the more she thought of wild animals, but if the birds had sense enough to hide, perhaps the animals would also.

At one point she lurched into a plum thicket. She ate as many ripe ones as she could tolerate without throwing up. She worried about the baby. Would this ordeal affect the child she carried? She had never thought of herself as a mother, and she harbored deep misgivings at telling Hawk he'd soon become a father. He'd press her to stay at the Shamrock. Would she want to leave? If not for herself, for the baby in her womb? She'd leave the answer to that question until another time, a time not devoted to saving her own life.

When she could no longer force herself to take another step, she curled under a shallow rock overhang, hoping for respite from the drizzle. Thankful to be out of the rain, and too tired to move, she leaned wearily against the rock wall and contemplated spending the night.

A low, menacing growl came from nearby. Hawk had warned her that mountain lions were in the canyon. Remain still, she warned herself, too frightened to do otherwise. Barely breathing, she listened intently. From a distance came the beat of horse hooves and the muffled sound of male voices.

She heard the animal jump from whatever perch it occupied, crash through the brush, and splash downstream. She'd traded one terror for another. Boggs knew she'd escaped and was looking for her.

In no hurry, the two men rode single file. "I told Boggs and Martinez the damned Injuns lit out for the prairie, takin' all the captives with 'em. But Boggs wanted to make sure."

"Boggs took a bullet in his arm. Wonder who the hell he's lookin' fer? She shore must be somethin'. Why would he think she'd be in the damned canyon?"

The first voice spoke again. "Likely jest hopin'. I seen them two women. Both of 'em's purty."

"Aw, hell, Murdock. A sixty-year-old whore'd look purty to you."

The man called Murdock laughed. "When I git my pay, I'm headin' south. Maybe goin' as far as San Antone. Some of them señoritas is beautiful. Last time I was there, I fell in love nearly every night."

"There ain't nobody in this here canyon but us, and I'm fer goin' back."

"Yeah. First trail leadin' to the rim. Man could run into a panther down here. Be on top of the cat 'fore he knowed it. Ever hear one scream?"

"Once. And I ain't wantin' to hear it again."

Kate heard the men turn their horses and return the way they'd come. Soon their voices were indistinct, eventually fading away altogether. Cold and cramped, she leaned her head back. She had no intention of sleeping, but closed her eyes to rest. When she awoke, dawn had appeared weakly through low, scudding clouds. She scraped the mud from her boots before shivering her way to the stream. Dipping her hands in the water, she rinsed them, cupped her palms, and gulped thirstily. The chill was numbing, but it helped stop the roiling in her stomach. After a while the nausea receded and she could lift her head.

The last and hardest leg of the journey lay before her, and she forced herself to take the first step. Several hours later and dead tired, she peered through the gray gloom at remembered landmarks. Ahead she could make out the narrow gorge and the tall cliffs that rose on either side of it. She had walked all night and half a day, countless miles.

She stopped often to listen, but heard only the twittering of small birds—tomtits, Papa had called them. Water dripped from rocks and trickled down to join the muted gurgle to the stream. Sparse evergreens, stunted by shallow roots, clung to the cliff walls. The climb upward began when she rounded the curve in the creek and saw the faint trail.

She couldn't fail now, not when security awaited her near the top. Taking a deep breath, she started the ascent.

Chapter Thirteen

Hawk awoke to rain in his face, and the startling awareness that he was cold and wet and lying in a puddle of water. He tried to rise, and got as far as his knees when a sharp blow to his side laid him flat, followed seconds later by a slam to his chest. He got almost to his knees again before he sank once more into a vague and obscure darkness, where Kate waited in the shadows. He tried to call to her, but the only sound he heard was his own agony.

A bludgeoning pain broke once more through his consciousness. The toe of a boot made another contact with his ribs, and Hawk forced himself to lie still. Acute understanding came abruptly, and he turned slowly, laboring to see more clearly the mocking face that looked down at him.

Boggs. Damn his eyes. Hawk had been sure he'd killed the son of a bitch. Instead Boggs had shot him. Where was Kate?

Raucous laughter accompanied the saloonkeeper's next strike, and Hawk fought to stay conscious. He knew in the deep recesses of his mind that Boggs planned to kill him, but first the man wanted knowledge of Kate's whereabouts. She had refused him, laughed at him, and the saloonkeeper's vanity couldn't abide the insult. Boggs sought vengeance.

Hawk had plans of his own.

Squatting beside Hawk, Boggs gave an evil laugh. "Thought you seen me die, did you, savage? You miscalculated. Who put you up to raiding the camp? Quanah? Maybe that damned Irishman? Or did you figure to take the captives to Mexico yourself? They'd bring a fair price. Buy lots of pretties. Much whiskey. Especially the women." Hate blazed in his eyes. "Where did your braves take them?"

Hawk squinted at his tormentor and muttered a Comanche oath.

"I know you speak English, you damned renegade. You lost the mustangs. We shot 'em. Now answer me. Where are the women?"

"No sé, gringo."

Knowing bitter and miserable defeat, Hawk lay still. Kate had run to the cave and expected him to come for her, and here he lay like a trussed-up turkey. A lucky shot had knocked him from his horse, but not before he'd seen Little Crow and his braves ride out with the children. He wondered about his men from the Shamrock. None of them had seen him fall from his horse. Andy Bennet had seen him shoot Boggs. Except Boggs didn't die. He lived to take Hawk prisoner.

Hawk moved his bound hands upward and raked them across his shoulder. His fingers came away slick with blood. As nearly as he could tell, the bullet had barely creased him, drawing blood and hurting, but doing no permanent damage. Nothing to worry about, he told himself, knowing it had to be true if he was to find Kate. He anticipated the next agonizing thrust of the boot and absorbed the blow without flinching.

"Look, Comanche. You and me can make a deal. Tell me where they took the women, and I'll let you up. I'll get one of my men to cut the ropes. You'll be free."

"No sé."

Boggs screamed in frustration. "You speak English. English, you hear." He turned to the man nearest him. "The damned Indian won't talk."

"Them Comanche can take a lot of punishment, boss. I knowed one that didn't even make a sound when we set him on fire."

"Get him away from the Comancheros. Take him to the canyon meeting place, the one below the narrow gorge. Make sure he stays tied up. Soon as I can get away, I'll come. Better take some food. I may be a couple of days. I don't want nobody to know I had a hand in seeing how much pain this big Injun can stand."

Hawk knew the place they planned to take him. As well as he knew his own name, he was certain Kate would be at the cave above them. She would look down from her high perch, see him bound, and watch the men torture him. What would she do? He prayed she'd stay hidden, but the woman who had risked her life to save the children was capable of anything— even challenging Boggs.

"Still not talking, savage? Well, we'll see."

Hawk lay motionless until Boggs turned away; then he worked at loosening his bonds. Whoever tied them had done the job well. Prepared to take whatever punishment Boggs would inflict, Hawk closed his eyes.

Fatalism. A Comanche warrior knew he carried his fate in his spear, that an enemy's arrow could find his heart. He accepted what life had to offer, not asking more, but less. To die young in battle to escape old age, that was a Comanche warrior's dream of the future. Hawk had no such philosophical bent. The woman he loved depended on him to come to her. He would not fail her. And he would not die.

After lying in the rain for hours, Hawk was thrown over the back of a horse like a sack of potatoes. However uncomfortable he might be, he dreaded even more being closer to Kate. If he could count on her staying hidden . . . He couldn't bear to think of Boggs getting his hands on Kate. Hawk almost groaned.

Revenge bounced around in his head.

He had visions of communicating with Stone Wolf, and willed his grandfather to hear. Stone Wolf had been known to intercept wayward thoughts, thoughts that penetrated the air and found their way to his camp. Whether that would happen today and his grandfather would hear, Hawk could only hope.

The men traveled at a trot, one leading the packhorse, making the trip arduous and miserably uncomfortable. Hawk tried repeatedly to hold his head so it wouldn't bang against the horse's flank, but eventually he had to close his eyes to the inevitable—give in and let his face slam against the horse's side. Despite his misery, he had no trouble hearing his captors' conversation.

"Boggs said he'd be here sometime, and to keep the redskin bound up. If I had my way we'd kill the bastard."

"Yeah. Too many of 'em. Reckon in the long run that's what we'll have to do. Kill 'em. All of 'em."

"I'm fer that."

The talk filled Hawk with dread. If too many men thought like these two, the peace plan he and the colonel had begun would be no more effective than the smoke from a peace pipe. Hawk winced against the pain in his shoulder. From the feel, the wound was still bleeding. Constant pounding had his head aching, and thirst and frustration had dried his mouth. He worked at detecting where they were, and how much farther they had to go to the meeting place. All too soon he recognized landmarks that had long been part of his childhood. Places he knew as well as the back of his hand, but their familiarity aided little in easing his frustration.

Inside him was a great anger. When Kate needed him most, he was unable to protect her. He swore at his impotence, not caring if the men heard him, if they understood the language of his people. How could he possibly take care of Kate when he was trussed up like a Christmas goose?

Kate had a head start. Had she reached the cave?

After the steep climb to the mouth of the cave, Kate was too fatigued to do anything but lie down in the dry, sandy entrance and stare at the gray sky. She let her mind wander to Hawk. Where was he? He had no way of knowing she waited here. But when he learned she was gone from the Shamrock, her heart said he'd come.

Cold, miserable, and hungry, she closed her eyes. She'd almost relaxed when she remembered the snakes. Bolting upright, she glanced around fearfully. She had no intention of checking to see if any were spending the night. Cold weather caused reptiles to hole up in a cave, Hawk had said. Well, it was cold enough.

She looked behind her and noticed scratch grooves furrowed into the rocks. Bobcats. She tried to still her trembling. There were bobcats in Missouri. Papa had told her about them, even showed her where the cats sharpened their claws. What could she do if a cougar came to claim his den?

She remembered the notches made by the Indians, little steps down to the canyon floor. She could hardly bear to look at them, and she'd never, never be able to use them, even to get away from a wild animal. Like the legendary Indian maiden, she'd have to jump.

A glance at the pale sun told her it was late afternoon—four o'clock, or close. Exhausted, she tried to clear her mind enough to rest, and finally dozed. She awoke to the sound of voices coming from the canyon floor.

Easing to her stomach, she wriggled close enough to see over the ledge and down to where two men had dumped a third. An Indian man lay helpless while his captors talked between themselves. After a few minutes, the men retired to a scrawny copse of mesquite.

She turned her attention to the Indian lying on his side, his helplessness wringing a burst of sympathy from her. She continued to watch as he attempted to make himself more comfortable. He was bare-chested, his black hair bound by a strip of leather. His face was painted in stripes of white and black. Bigger than the men who held him, he nevertheless lay quietly, biding his time, she was to think later, waiting for a chance to escape. She couldn't take her eyes away. When he moved, she gasped.

Oh, God. Hawk. They had Hawk. The men held him captive, tied like a calf ready to brand. Tears burned her eyes. What could she do? How could she help? She continued to stare at the scene below her. Was Hawk looking up? Did he see her?

She gave a brief lift of her arm. Had she seen an answering movement? She repeated the signal, and again saw the small raising of his bound hands.

Beyond where Hawk lay, the two men sat around a fire and shared a bottle. They laughed loudly at times. Other times they swore, their curses clearly audible. Her hand brushed against the dent in the rock, a handhold for a person descending the rock cliff.

As if she'd been burned, she drew her hand back quickly.

When she could get her feelings under control, she tried hard to think objectively, logically. How many years had Indians used these steps to escape attackers, stopping only when an unhappy Comanche maiden flung herself over the edge, inadvertently putting a stop to using the cave? If the climb down scared hell out of them, blaming ghosts was as good an excuse as any to decline using them.

Like a moth to a flame, Kate's gaze was drawn back to Hawk. What bitter irony. She and Hawk could see each other, yet she could do nothing to free him. If she struggled down the trail she'd used coming up, his captors were sure to see her. However, the cave mouth was not visible to them, nor the Indians' escape route.

Tension built within her. Her mind slid over the options, raising the hair on the nape of her neck. The steps. No, no, absolutely not. She hated heights. Her foot might slip. What if she had a rush of nausea? What if the men saw her? What if . . .

Oh, God.

To stop her trembling, she looked around her. She had nothing to cut the ropes. Nothing. She stopped thinking of her fear and started wondering what she could use as a knife. There had to be something.

Shale!

Shale was everywhere. She'd run into the slippery rock on her way up, and had cautiously eased across it. As she looked around for a nearby source of the mineral, she refused to let herself think about climbing down the nicks in the rocks.

She couldn't do it. Couldn't. Absolutely could not.

Poor Hawk. He must be grinding his teeth, wondering what

she would do. She was sure he had thought of the steps. Lying down, she wiggled her body toward a shale outcrop, and chose and rejected pieces until she found some with sharp edges. She put the rocks in her pocket, just in case they should come in handy. Sliding backward until she was sure she was out of sight of the men, she crawled to the edge of the cave and signaled Hawk. She could see a slight negative movement of his head, which she chose to ignore.

She patted the shale at her hip. If his bonds were thick, using the shale to cut them would take forever. It might not even work. It had been a ridiculous idea.

She could see the small slits cut in the rock. It was a long way to the bottom. God, she couldn't climb down using those little toeholds. Nobody could, except maybe a damned Indian. Hawk couldn't expect her to. How did he ever get himself in such a predicament anyway?

With every cell in her body protesting, she crept forward until she could reverse her body and put her legs over. Her right boot found the first chink. She clung to the ledge, perspiration beading her forehead. She'd taken the first step. From there it was one step down. Then another. And another. Nothing to it, she told herself over and over.

Then why was she so scared?

Partway down, her foot slipped. Too terrified to scream, she hugged the cliff and searched frantically for the next small crevice. When her foot found the step, it took several minutes for her to get her terror under control. She had clutched the rocks so tightly her fingers bled, and she had to wipe the slippery blood on her shirt. When that no longer worked, she rubbed her fingers in sand and dust that had collected in the cracks to give her fingers purchase. Fatigue and strain threatened with every move. When at last she reached an outcrop wide enough to support her, she oozed herself onto it to rest.

Refusing to look down, she watched a great bird catch a wind current and sail above her. It would be nice to fly, to sail over the canyon. To not be afraid.

Eventually she looked down at Hawk.

* * *

Hawk watched his woman scale the cliff. His heart stopped. Fear and panic dried his mouth. Bloody hell, he couldn't breathe. Above her, heavy clouds threatened, and he thought despairingly of the flood they had escaped with only minutes to spare. Surely fate wouldn't send such an ordeal again. She had made it halfway down, and he could see the weariness etched her in her face. When she'd slid over the cliff, and her intention to descend the rock face became evident, he'd died a thousand deaths. He couldn't watch. He had to watch.

He wanted to shake her until her teeth rattled.

He wanted to hold her in his arms.

Frowning, he glanced frequently at his abductors. If they saw Kate, they'd forget him, or more than likely kill him and ride away with Kate. She'd be a prize delivery to Boggs, and bring a few dollars to their pockets. As tension built in him, Hawk felt the muscles contract across his stomach. He was mad at her. He was mad for her. He was losing his mind. How could she do this to him? Make him sweat every step of the way down that bloody cliff? And then what? Another bloody scheme to make mincemeat out of his mind?

Oh, God, she'd slipped. One foot dangled. He couldn't look, but he couldn't take his eyes from her.

Every moment he expected one of his captors to sidle over to check his ropes. And then the man would see her. She wouldn't stand a chance of getting away. All he could think was of the danger she'd put herself in. And how scared he was for her. If she fell now, his life would end. Nothing worthwhile would ever be his again.

He didn't know how much time elapsed. It could have been minutes or hours before she gained the ground and smiled her heartbreaking little smile.

Bloody hell. A man could only take so much.

Ignoring him except for a smile and a nod, Kate sat awhile to stop her trembling, and to quell the nausea that rose unexpectedly. Being pregnant had its drawbacks, especially when one needed to climb down a cliff wall with nothing to hold on to but imagination and a few rocks that jutted out just enough to provide handholds. She swallowed a bubble of hysterical laughter. No doubt the baby was as scared as she was. Knowing Hawk must be wild with fear, she dared not look at him.

Giddy with relief, she fought desperately to keep her mind clear. She'd come this far. She could face the next hurdle. She'd beaten the darkness with little grace time, but enough light remained for her to be visible. Scooting silently to a spot behind a mound of tumbleweeds, she considered a move as absurd as her last one. Maybe this idea would work also.

Not twenty yards away, her man lay on his side, his head propped on a rock, his face furrowed with strain. She gave him a little wave and mouthed, "I'm coming."

He glared at her.

Kate pulled the bristly tumbleweeds apart until she had enough to conceal her body. Inch by inch, she crawled toward him, edging the tumbleweeds ahead of her. The wind shifted and tugged at her cover, but she held on stubbornly. She'd covered half the distance, and only hell itself could make her stop.

She could almost hear Hawk grinding his teeth.

Boggs's henchmen were easily heard now, and she paused to listen. They were so sure they were the only ones within a hundred miles.

"It's gonna git colder. Wind's out of the north."

"Time o'year for it, I reckon."

"Thet Indian's gonna be mighty uncomfortable with no more clothes than he's got on."

"The bastard can freeze to death for all I care."

Kate listened in horror to their callous conversation. If she didn't free Hawk soon, he'd freeze. Or Boggs might arrive. Either way, he wouldn't stand a chance. The men made no attempt to lower their voices, doubtless thinking they were completely alone.

"Think one of us ought to keep watch?"

"Nah, Slim. Nobody knows he's here but you and me and Boggs. Maybe a few coyotes."

"S'pose coyotes knows how to untie ropes?"

Slim laughed uproariously. "No, sir, them varmints don't

know nothin' but to kill cattle and howl. 'Fraid thet redskin's out of luck. Cain't count on no hep from nobody, not even a damned coyote."

The men talked at length about the weather, the Comancheros, Boggs. "Boggs said he'd pay us good to take care of this Comanche. I don't know what he thinks is good, but I'd say fi' dollars would be in keepin'. Whatta you think, Packer?"

"Yeah, 'bout right, I'd say. Too bad we ain't got the woman. We'd have us some fun, and hope Boggs waited a while to show."

"Naw. Not me, where that woman's concerned. Boggs shore wouldn't like it, and he's got long arms."

"Say we found her and took a few turns on her, how in hell would Boggs find out?"

"You ain't thinkin' good, Packer. The gel's got a mouth. Don'tcha think she'd tell 'im?"

"Martinez said all Boggs wants is to have 'er hisself. When he's done with her, he's gonna sell 'er to the Mexicans. Martinez said thet. Don't make no sense to me why we couldn't have 'er first."

"Well, we ain't got 'er, so there ain't no use puzzlin' 'bout it."

"Yeah. Might as well git some sleep."

"We could git out of the drizzle, if we moved ourselves over to thet big boulder. The one with the scooped-out place on the front."

Panic washed over Kate as the men got to their feet and headed in her direction. She carefully pulled the tumbleweeds about her, flinching when the nasty little needles stung her bruised and bloody hands. If Packer and Slim saw her, she'd be on her way back to Boggs.

From Hawk's agonized expression, she knew she feared the same, but the men passed him by with hardly a glance. They were at her back now, and even if she were ever so careful, the prickly tumbleweeds made turning her head to watch them an ordeal. What were the ruffians doing, for heaven's sake? Why was it taking them so long? Surely by now they were down for the night. When she started again, Hawk frowned.

"Be still," he mouthed.

257

Afraid to move, she lay quietly, awaiting Hawk's signal that it was safe to crawl again. When it came, she had almost given up hope that the men would ever sleep. She worked at disentangling herself from the tiny barbs on the tumbleweeds, finally giving up in disgust to wait for a better time. When she reached Hawk, she could feel his tension.

"You shouldn't have come, darlin'," he whispered. "Scared the bloody hell out of me."

She went to work on his bonds. "I had to come," she said simply. When she saw his wound, she wanted to cry. "I've got some shale. That's all I could find to cut the rope. It will take a long time."

"Aye, lass, we must hurry."

They didn't talk, and Kate noticed that Hawk glanced often at the men. They had found a spot partially protecting them from the cold wind and the threat of rain, then had proceeded to fall asleep. Their fire had long ago fizzled out, and they hadn't bothered to start another.

Kate worked at cutting the ropes until she ached all over. Now and then she had to hold on to the tumbleweeds to keep them from rolling away. Hawk tugged at the ropes. A few fibers gave way, then a few more. They were making progress.

His bonds finally fell away, and Kate waited for Hawk to cut the ropes on his ankles. "Hurry," she whispered.

He nodded, and after a few more strokes he was free. Crawling beside her, he pushed the tumbleweeds to hide them both. When they reached the darkest shadows, he stood and motioned to her to do the same. He led the way quietly. "We'll take their horses," he whispered.

Kate quelled her uneasy excitement enough to answer, "We will?"

"Aye, lass, we wouldn't want to show partiality by taking only one."

Stealthily, using the language of the Comanche, Hawk approached the horses, gentling them with his hands. He adjusted the stirrups on the saddles, all the while continuing his soothing monotone.

To Kate's amazement, the horses stood quietly. Now she understood why the Comanche were successful horse thieves. They were not only master horsemen, but they communicated in a language horses understood. He swung into the saddle and lifted her behind him. Holding the reins of the second horse, he nudged them into a walk.

"Hold on to your man, darlin'. You saved his life. The Comanche say now he belongs to you."

"Fine sentiment, Comanche, but concentrate on getting us away from here."

When they were out of range of the sleeping men, Kate asked against his back, "Hawk, why am I not riding the other horse?"

"If they had awakened and given chase, we might have been separated. I couldn't go through that nightmare again. When you began the climb down the rock wall, I nearly went out of my mind."

"Nothing to it actually," she said airily. "One step at a time, until you reach the bottom."

"Nay, darlin'. Don't joke. One slip, one misstep . . . Bloody hell, Kate, a man can stand only so much."

She waved airily, mimicking his speech. "Sure, and you're right, Irish. But 'tis nothing. The climb down was a breeze. I'll likely do it again sometime."

"Such words make me cringe." He urged the horses into a gallop, then reined them up a trail toward the canyon rim and onto the open prairie. "We don't want to be caught near the Comancheros' meeting place, in case any are still there, but it lies between us and Stone Wolf's camp, so we circle."

"What about Maureen and the children?"

"Little Crow and his braves have taken them to Stone Wolf. I saw them ride out before a shot knocked me off my horse. Another shot grazed my head. Another hit my shoulder."

Suddenly the whole scene back at the Comanchero campsite made sense. Little Crow and the other braves in the tribe had ridden to save her and the other captives. Hawk had been injured and captured trying to rescue her and Maureen. Kate's heart swelled.

"When I get the chance, I'll thank Little Crow." She pondered her change in attitude. She would be forever grateful to Stone

Wolf's braves for saving Maureen and the children. She was sure her father would be appreciative if he were alive. And much more forgiving. Despite Little Crow's treatment of her—taking her prisoner, his silly courting—she had to admit he had risked his life for her sister.

So had Hawk.

Kate touched his arm. "You're bleeding. Is it painful?"

"Nay, no broken bones, but where Boggs's boot connected gives me a bit of a twinge."

"You may have broken ribs. When we stop, I'll take a look."

"Katie, darlin', I'm alive. My wife risked her life to save me. I'm a lucky man."

His wife. He made it sound almost like a benediction, not a curse, as she'd always thought of it. And he was her brave. Brave in more ways than one, until she insisted on looking at his wounds. "We must see how badly you're hurt, Hawk, and this is a good place to stop."

"Nay, Katie, darlin' . . ."

"Here." She made a move to slide over the horse's rump. "Right now."

Sighing, Hawk drew up the reins. "We need to hurry."

Kate motioned him to sit. When she saw all the blood, she wanted to cry. "Hawk, I need to clean the wounds. Thank God, we're here by the stream." Using her hands to palm the water onto his bruised and bleeding skin, she cleaned as best she could. An inch to the right or the left, and he'd have died never knowing she carried his baby. She shut out the devastating thought and choked back her tears. She'd have to deal with telling him, but not now.

Gently, she washed away the grime, lightly caressing as she went. As was the case when she touched his body now, her pulse went soaring. "You're squirming," she said, crossly. "These wounds aren't life threatening. Besides, a Comanche brave should be able to handle a little pain."

"Ah, Katie love, 'tis not the pain. My body recognizes your touch and responds. As for the tender ministrations, I'm thankin' you. For sure, I'll soon be well."

"Not if you don't be still."

Hawk sat quietly while she finished, and then they quickly got back under way. They circled south toward Tule Canyon before Kate mounted the second horse.

"Is the horse too spirited?"

She shook her head. "I can handle him. I must say he's a little harder to handle than my horse, Barney. I bought Barney from a stableman in Tascosa when I ran away from Boggs. I wonder if I'll ever see Barney again."

"I've lost Midnight as well. Too fine an animal for the likes of a Comanchero. Someday I'll get him back. As for Barney, I'm sure Little Crow counts him among his herd."

"No doubt."

He turned to grin at her. "Little Crow and his braves stormed the camp to rescue Maureen. Would you challenge him over a horse?"

"I'll have to think about it."

Hawk burst out laughing. "You drive a hard bargain, my Kate. Perhaps you'll change your mind when we get to Stone Wolf's camp."

They rode the remainder of the night and for the entire day following, coming at last to Tule Canyon, a distance of fifty miles or so. The Indian village occupied both sides of the stream, the tipis dark shadows in the moonlight. Hawk halted his horse. "We'll spend the night in our tipi. Stone Wolf retires early. I'll meet him tomorrow."

"When will we find out about my sister? And the children?"

"Tomorrow. The camp has settled in for the night."

Kate looked around them. "Are we waiting for the lookout to see us?"

"Aye, lass. I wouldn't want an arrow in my back."

Several minutes later, having signaled their presence, Hawk guided them to the tipi. "You're safe here, darlin'."

Dismounting and rubbing her backside, Kate limped to the entrance. "Seems like forever since we left here. If you weren't here when the village moves, what would happen to your tipi?"

"Pia would take care of it." He stretched a buffalo hide over the floor and motioned her to lie down near the banked fire. "Pia must have been expecting us."

"How could she've known?"

"Several ways, my Kate. She might have guessed. Little Crow could have told her. Stone Wolf may have mentioned it."

"How would Stone Wolf know?"

He gave her a long look. "I'm not sure. Perhaps from the wind."

Tomorrow she'd ask him what he meant, but for the present, she was too exhausted and too hungry. "As much as I dislike it, tonight I'd settle for pemmican."

"No pemmican, darlin'," he said tenderly. "But I promise you'll eat first thing in the morning."

Pemmican in the morning! Along with morning sickness.

She sighed. It was not a combination to which she was looking forward.

"Shall I help you off with your clothes?"

Kate almost shivered with desire at his husky suggestion, her exhaustion quickly forgotten at his invitation. "I wouldn't mind." She said, holding out her arms to him.

He skillfully removed her garments, his fingertips gently caressing her skin as he completed the task.

When he, too, wore nothing she molded her naked body to his and could feel his heart hammering like a drum against her breast. Before sleep could take her, passion blossomed under Hawk's skilled hands. He covered her mouth with his, caressing her breast, murmuring his thanks, seductive words, luring her deeper and deeper into the wild, turbulent, delicious world of his making.

Hawk stared unseeing at the hole in the top of the tipi. The night before, he had loved Kate with his heart and his body, and she had responded, her fiery nature finding release in his arms. Even so, with the intuitive knowledge of a man loving a woman, he had recognized a hesitation, a reluctance to give of herself totally.

He knew without being told that the core of her prejudice remained between them, that she was fighting it. Whether she was winning or losing the battle, he couldn't say. He remembered the satin feel of her, her moist acquiescence, her sounds of pleasure, and longed to make love with her this morning. What he wanted above all was to be loved and accepted by her. She had risked her life to save his. Such daring delighted the Comanche. Such courage would impress his father. Hawk gazed bleakly at the wall of the tipi. Kate loved him, but rejected his ancestry. If she chose to view him as an Indian, he would rise to the honor.

His mother, his grandfather, his mother's sister were one blood; his own had been mixed with the Irish. The Comanche called him brother. The whites would call him a breed. He'd wrestled with himself for too long. No more would he hide his identity beneath a cap and a brogue. If Kate could not look beyond her heritage, she could leave him. He would hold his head high and bid her farewell.

She made his face shine with her presence. She brought spring to his breast. Her smile brought joy to his life and laughter to his lips. But always in the night, when she lay willingly in his arms, she denied him her heart.

The time had come. He would no longer disclaim his blood. The mission he and the colonel had hoped for was somewhere in the future. From this day forward, he'd be the man he was born to be, walk proud in that knowledge. He'd bloody well hide his regret at being alone.

Without looking at Kate, Hawk made his way outside into the early morning. He greeted the day without enthusiasm, and stood watching the village come alive before heading toward Stone Wolf's tipi.

What would he tell his grandfather? That he refused to further ingratiate himself with whites, even when it spelled failure for the plan he and the colonel and Stone Wolf had envisioned? Would his grandfather understand that he was honoring his mother with such an announcement? Would his Irish father accuse him of forsaking his pledge to peace?

Once outside Stone Wolf's lodge, Hawk called softly, and was answered and bidden to enter by the younger of his grandfather's wives. "Good morning, Grandfather."

Stone Wolf puffed his pipe. Without looking up from where he sat cross-legged on a colorful buffalo robe, he motioned

Grayhawk to sit. "My grandson's thoughts are heavy. He does not rest in his mind."

"I've come to ask after my wife's sister, Grandfather. Little Crow and I and his braves made a raid on a Comanchero camp. We found the woman, and Little Crow brought her back to Stone Wolf's village."

"Has my grandson spoken with Little Crow?"

With a small shake of his head, Hawk answered in the negative. "Not without first speaking with my grandfather."

The old man puffed his pipe. "The woman is here."

"And the man? I saw them leave the Comanchero camp, Grandfather, a young white man who would claim the woman as a wife. They rode out following Little Crow and a young girl."

"They are here. Little Crow took the girl to Pia." Stone Wolf smiled. "Also the children."

"My mother's sister has her hands full," Hawk said, his face strained. "Grandfather, I have forsaken the plan we pledged with the colonel. When the whites learn I am Comanche, they will turn from me." Including his woman, Hawk reflected, anger in his breast. "But I can no longer hide my heritage. I will walk proud with my mother's people."

Stone Wolf glanced up, gave a short puff on his pipe, and nodded. "My grandson speaks as a man. He is Comanche."

"Why, Grandfather, do you suppose my mother's people accept me, but my father's people will not?"

His grandfather shrugged. "Some whites *pukutsi*."

"Crazy, yes," Hawk said, searching for something in their conversation he could use to calm the storm in his breast. "Not my father."

"Not all whites speak from both sides of their mouths. My grandson should not measure all by few."

"I'll be fair, Grandfather, but the time has come. I will no longer hide my face."

Hawk waited to be dismissed. When his grandfather ignored him and went back to his pipe, Hawk backed out of the tipi. He wanted to find Little Crow. He hadn't long to wait before Little Crow found him.

"My brother is safe," Little Crow said.

"My brother is also safe, and for that my heart is glad."

"And your wife?"

Fearing Little Crow could see into his heart, Hawk made a point of looking beyond his friend. "She's in my tipi."

"What do you think? Maybe Little Crow will take the girl. A Comanche warrior needs four wives. Two quarrel. Three wives, two gang up. Four? Just right."

Hawk had no desire to be drawn into an argument about the number of wives a man should take. He had enough trouble convincing one to marry him. "The girl's name is Dorcas, Crow. What does Dorcas say?"

"Your wife will tell me," Little Crow said, his stance saying he wouldn't take no for an answer.

One more thing to give him a headache, and he already knew Kate's answer. "We'll see."

Little Crow crossed his arms over his chest. "I would like to make the maiden my wife now."

"I'll speak with Kate."

Nodding, Little Crow waited. "The braves say Boggs is dead."

For a moment, disappointment clouded his mind, and Hawk was disgusted with himself. He'd wanted to kill the man himself. With no further words exchanged, Hawk left his brother. He dreaded telling Kate that Little Crow wanted Dorcas.

Kate was not in the tipi. He found her on her knees at the stream. She didn't look up. "What are you doing here? Where's Maureen?"

"She's safe. Still asleep, I would guess."

"Thank God."

"Little Crow says one of his braves killed Boggs. I'll talk to the brave."

"I'll go with you."

Hawk picked up a rock and skipped it across the water. "The brave pitched his tent at the end of the far village and up on a ridge. You'll slow me down."

"I guess I slowed you down at the Comanchero camp. And I slowed you down when I climbed down the cliff. And when I used shale to saw those damned ropes, I guess that slowed you down." Tears threatened, finally breaking free to trickle down her face. "I don't think you're very fair."

Hawk sighed. She was so touchy these days. "Katie, darlin', wait a minute. I'm not sure I'll go. If I do, it will be after we leave for the Shamrock." The moment had come. He had to ask. "As a favor to Little Crow, will you speak to Dorcas? He wants her for his wife."

She wiped her tears with her palms and stared in disbelief. "Me? Little Crow wants me to speak to Dorcas. For him?"

Chapter Fourteen

Kate couldn't hide her astonishment or her horror. "Hawk, Dorcas has come through hell. I can't imagine she'd want to marry anybody. It's too soon. She's too young. She'll be horrified at the thought of marrying Little Crow. Absolutely revolted."

"I insisted he let Dorcas answer for herself. I'm merely passing along his request, lass. I know you will give it your full scrutiny."

"Don't hand me that Irish blarney. You don't want to tell your lecherous friend he's a dunderhead."

Hawk lifted his hands in protest. "Nay, darlin', 'tis a wrong you're doing me. I but said I'd ask you to speak with Dorcas on the subject. I'm no matchmaker. But I give you leave to invite her to the ranch. Little Crow or the Shamrock."

"Thank goodness she has a choice. But if my speaking to Dorcas is a way for me to thank Little Crow for leading his braves to attack the Comanchero camp, then I'll do it. I won't give her encouragement. In other words, Little Crow should be prepared for a refusal."

"You'll speak with her. That's enough. And I will have kept my word."

"Dorcas will thank him for saving her from the Comancheros. But to be his wife? Forget it. The girl is probably sixteen. No more than seventeen."

"Little Crow is good to his wives. And he's a good hunter. He seems to think that will be enough."

Kate showed her disgust by lifting her hands palms up, at the same time rolling her eyes toward the sky. "Then let's get it over. Afterward we can make plans to get her home to her family."

With a nod, Hawk walked to the door of their lodge. "Katie, I've hardly had time to say hello to you since we've been back in Stone Wolf's camp." He grinned. "The time we've had, my mind was on other things."

A smile threatened, and Kate shooed him out. "Go get Dorcas before I decide differently, and tell Little Crow he has more women than he needs."

"He says four is better than three."

"And I suppose five would be better than four."

Hawk choked on his laughter. "Nay, lass, not Little Crow. Quanah? Aye." He disappeared from sight, and Kate sighed. She'd spend time with Dorcas, explaining that while Little Crow had shown great courage in rescuing her and the children, Dorcas was in no way obligated to become wife number four. Besides the girl had been so abused in the Comanchero camp, she'd be appalled at Little Crow's proposal.

Ready to stand up for her young friend, Kate remembered how frightened she'd been of Little Crow's advances. She supposed she'd always be wary.

When Dorcas appeared at the tipi entrance, Kate hastened to embrace her. "Dorcas, come in. Have you rested after your wild ride?"

Dorcas nodded. "I'm rested, and I'm not hungry. Little Crow's oldest wife gave me all the food I wanted. She also gave me a skin to put over me so I wouldn't be cold at night."

"Good. You were so brave in the Comanchero camp. Taking care of the children the way you did. Word in the camp here is that you're still comforting the little ones."

"The Indian women are kind to children, Kate. It surprised

me." Dorcas played with the fringe on the skirt. "Little Crow's wife gave me this dress."

Surprised at her young friend's serenity, Kate studied her and wondered how to lead into the big question. She fully expected Dorcas to scream. "Dorcas, Little Crow wants you as his fourth wife. Can you imagine that?"

After a long wait, Dorcas answered, "I think I would like that."

Kate couldn't believe what she'd heard. "You aren't really considering becoming his wife?"

"In Mustang Valley, where I live, people would think it was too bad the Comancheros got you. Or feel sorry for you that you'd lived with Indians. But they'd look down on you. Like you did it on purpose. The Comanches raided a settlement near us and took a girl, Mary Ellen. When she was rescued, nobody, 'specially the women, would have anything to do with her. People treated her like dirt, a whore, so after a while, Mary Ellen turned into one."

Remembering Ophelia Maud, Kate agreed. "Some people are like that. And life isn't always fair. Generally I think people are good, but some are bad and influence their neighbors."

"I'm glad you're here, Kate. And I'm glad I'm here, too."

"You don't have to go with Little Crow. He has three wives already." Kate remembered Little Crow's courting strategy. "Besides, you're white and he's an Indian. You can go with us to Hawk's ranch. You have a choice."

"Little Crow has been kind to me. And he made his wives be nice to me. His first wife liked me right off. I don't think she likes his other two. But I do. Why do you suppose Little Crow likes me? He has to know Martinez bothered me."

"Because . . ." Kate worked at finding an answer. "It must be because Little Crow recognized how courageous you were. How you looked after the children. Indians admire bravery."

"It will be better for me here than at home. I know how Papa and Mama would feel. I liked Mary Ellen a lot. When she came home, Papa and Mama wouldn't let me have anything to do with her. Like it was Mary Ellen's fault. Some people said her folks thought she should have killed herself. Even after she

269

came home, they told some neighbors they couldn't understand why Mary Ellen didn't put a gun to her head."

Kate understood. Dorcas preferred life with the Indians to returning home to the brutal reality that would await her. From her own experience, Kate knew how cruel people could be. Hadn't she herself experienced the same ugliness at the Shamrock?

"Don't be hasty, Dorcas. Give yourself time. When you reach a decision, come talk with me."

Dorcas had no hesitation. "I've made my decision, Kate. I'll stay with the camp and be Little Crow's wife."

When the girl left, Kate allowed herself to cry. Dorcas had witnessed too much cruelty, observed too little sympathy, and although the girl knew her family loved her, she also knew they would never again accept her. Dorcas had made her choice. Who was to say it was not the better one?

Hawk arrived and motioned Kate outside. "Little Crow wants to know Dorcas's decision."

"Why doesn't he talk to Dorcas?"

Hawk lowered his voice. "Crow's afraid the answer is no. He hopes I'll ask you to encourage Dorcas. First time I've ever seen the warrior worried."

"Tell him"—Kate hesitated—"tell him he won't be disappointed."

Surprised, Hawk raised his eyebrows. "Who can understand a woman?"

He left to share the news, and Kate could hear him talking to Little Crow outside the tipi. Their voices were too low for her to distinguish Little Crow's tone of voice, but she supposed he was happy. Indian culture was difficult to comprehend. The marriage, if the travesty could be called such, was an example. But the union made as much sense as the stand Dorcas's family would take.

When Hawk returned, his face showed his doubt. "Kate, I'm not sure if this marriage is a good idea, but despite his headstrong ways, Little Crow seems to care for Dorcas. It's not what we would want for her, but it may be better than what she'd get at home. He's offered me five horses," he added ruefully.

"Little Crow is the lesser of two evils," Kate said bluntly. "I can't believe that, given half a chance, Dorcas would have agreed."

"Aye, lass, but Dorcas is practical. She feels cared for. In time, she may grow to love her new family."

"Miracles happen." Her eyes narrowed. "Did you accept the five horses?"

"It wasn't up to me. Stone Wolf said ten. The horses will be added to his herd."

"Why?"

He shrugged. "It's the Comanche way."

Kate ran her fingers through her hair, which was still damp from her bath at the stream. This was only the second day they had been back at the camp, and strangely enough, she felt at home. The morning was filled with the usual sounds: small boys shouting to each other, their mothers talking as they moved about their chores. The smell of wood smoke drifted in through the tipi entrance. The familiarity of the scene was comforting, but she worried about what she planned to do. Her nausea had passed, leaving her pale but determined. She dressed as carefully as her one pair of pants and shirt allowed.

Today she would pay her respects to Stone Wolf, to thank him for sending his warriors to rescue Maureen and the children. Possibly Hawk would thank him, too, but courtesy demanded she appear before the chief as well.

The flap to Stone Wolf's tipi stood open. Outside, his wives were busily engaged in women's work, which included one wife carrying heavy loads of wood from near the camp. The cookpot was already smoking, and the other wife, whose name Kate could never pronounce, was stirring it. The chief was nowhere in sight.

When she greeted the women, they smiled and pointed toward the stream. Kate mouthed her thanks. She found Stone Wolf staring into the water. She stopped several feet away and waited until he motioned her forward.

Using her faulty Comanche and the chief's limited English they managed to communicate; their conversation an odd mix

271

of the two languages. "This woman would speak with the great chief."

Stone Wolf nodded gravely. "The chief will listen."

"This woman would thank Stone Wolf and his braves for saving the children."

"Children make the chief's heart glad."

"When will the great chief see they go back to their families?"

The chief met her eyes. "The children will stay here."

Kate couldn't believe that Stone Wolf of all people would refuse. "But they need to be with their folks. They're little and lonely for their mamas and papas."

"They are Comanche. Their mamas and papas are Comanche."

"But—"

"The Comanche are good parents. They will not beat the children. They will teach them the Comanche way."

Wanting to stamp her feet, Kate put up an argument. "But Stone Wolf, the children are white."

"The children are Comanche now. We will talk no more about it."

Bowing her head to the inevitable, Kate hid her anger and dismay. She wanted to argue, to shout at the old man, but her command of the language was too limited to make much of an impression. Besides, she was reasonably sure the result would be the same. Stone Wolf had been rigidly molded by tradition and culture. He had allowed his braves to follow Little Crow against the Comancheros. Little Crow had brought back children. Stone Wolf had spoken. The subject was closed.

Afraid she'd cry at the injustice of it, Kate stared at the ground. "This woman would go now."

"When my grandson is born, bring him."

"But the child may be a girl."

"The leaves say it will be a son."

"The great chief is wise. The earth tells him much."

He shrugged. "The earth says there is great danger ahead."

Shocked and trembling, she had to ask. "Who will be in danger? Hawk?"

He shook his head and turned back to the trail leading to his tipi. "The wind does not tell."

Kate stared after him. She had admitted she was pregnant to the chief and the child's father still had not been told. Who was in danger?

Long after Stone Wolf was out of sight, she pondered their conversation. How did he know she was pregnant? She didn't believe he had ever bought Hawk's explanation of why she should be given to him instead of going with Little Crow. Yet Stone Wolf had been so positive she was carrying Hawk's child. And who was in danger? Did the old man actually receive messages from the wind? Did leaves speak secrets?

She refused to believe such nonsense, but Stone Wolf knew her condition, and she hadn't even told the child's father.

Blast! And blast again.

She couldn't ask questions of Hawk without being questioned in return. Namely, why did she take so long to wash her face in the stream? Why she was so irritable in the mornings?

Why she hadn't told him she carried his baby?

At the present time, she needed all her faculties working in fine order to figure how she should tell Hawk about his coming fatherhood, and how she would have to deny him. She'd have to explain so he would understand that the baby would have Indian blood; therefore he would be subject to the same hatred as a full-blooded Comanche. That she had the baby's future to consider.

Hawk listened as Kate told him of her visit with Stone Wolf. The meeting was a deep and painful disappointment to her, evident in her eyes and voice. "Stone Wolf's mind is made up. He refuses to give the children back to their parents."

"I can't change him. There are conditions in life that have to be accepted, Kate."

"I'll never accept this . . . this unforgivable . . . stand he's taken." Tears trickled down her cheeks. "What can we do?"

He refused to be swayed. As much as he wanted to please her, circumstances dictated otherwise. Once Stone Wolf had spoken, nobody crossed him. "As matters stand, nothing."

"Hawk, there must be something."

"Lass, Stone Wolf will no longer listen."

"But—"

"Bloody hell, Katie. Don't you think I'd do something if I could?" He walked to the front of the tipi and looked at the sky. "Before the snow falls, Stone Wolf will take his band back to the big canyon."

"Will that be soon, do you think?"

"Aye. Soon. The Palo Duro will protect the village from winter blizzards."

Kate nodded her understanding. "Will the Comancheros still trade with Stone Wolf's braves?"

"Aye. As long as the Indians bring them barter. The Comanchero meeting places are usually scattered and transient. With Boggs and Martinez dead, their men will look for new leaders. And the leaders will trade with anybody."

"Were any braves killed from this camp?"

"One. According to Little Crow, Two Bears caught a bullet when we rode in. He was young. The raid on Martinez was his first battle."

Distressed at hearing of the young brave's death, Kate's pain savaged her heart. "He lost his life saving Maureen."

"Two Bears was young. The young are reckless."

"Maureen seemed to think after being a prisoner of the Comancheros, Andy wouldn't want her."

Hawk shrugged. "Andy is a good man. If he loves Maureen, and I think he does, what went before won't matter. Don't take on that worry, Katie. One worry at a time is enough."

She looked past him to the small fire. "No worries would be better."

She had changed to a borrowed dress, one of Pia's, made of antelope skin. The outline of her body inside the too large garment was both provocative and seductive. In the time since he had known her, she had matured. Her slender frame had filled out, her breasts fuller, her hips rounded.

"The Comancheros have Midnight. I plan to get him back."

"What about Barney? Have you ever mentioned my horse to Little Crow?"

Hawk looked at her as if she had sprouted bat-wing ears. "You really don't expect me to demand your horse back, after what he did for you?"

Her eyebrows went up, and then she smiled, her heartbreaking little grin that tore at his gut. "Now that you mention it, I suppose it would be presumptuous. Why don't you give him our thanks?"

"Bloody hell, Kate, he has Dorcas," Hawk said testily. None of their conversation had been what he had planned. The truth was, Kathleen Hartland had a way of disarming him. All she had to do was smile at him, look longingly at his mouth, and ask a favor. To deny her made him uncomfortable, as if he were being unfair, as if he didn't want to give her the whole bloody world. "I can't ask Crow right now. He'll be busy seeing that Dorcas has her own tipi."

"I'll forget Barney, Hawk. But I miss him. I haven't had a horse of my own since I left Missouri."

"When we get back to the Shamrock, I'll get a horse for you. One you'll like."

"I wasn't thinking right when I asked you to get Barney back from Little Crow."

Hawk didn't bother to answer. He had already made up his mind to see if Crow would sell Barney.

Kate could hardly wait to talk to Maureen. There had been so little opportunity for them to spend time together since escaping the Comancheros and arriving at Stone Wolf's camp. Since Dorcas seemed destined to be with Little Crow, the children had divided their affections between Maureen and Pia, but Pia, perhaps because of her age, satisfied their need for security. Pia seemed always to be surrounded by the children, the little ones touching her, clinging to her.

She shouldn't have been surprised, Kate thought, the suggestion of a lump in her throat, the Indian woman had experience caring for new members of the tribe. She fed, comforted, and talked to the children in her language. In addition, Pia had been kind to Maureen. Looking after the children together, the two had become friendly, Pia encouraging the girl, and Maureen shyly showing her appreciation.

Hurrying toward them, Kate embraced her sister, holding her close and babbling once again about how glad she was they were all safe. "Maury, I was so frightened for you, honey. And for these children. I'm glad you're with me now. Hawk will make sure we're safe here. At the first opportunity, we'll be moving on."

"What will become of the children, Kate?"

Kate found it difficult to meet her sister's gaze. "They're Comanche children now."

"What?" Shaken by the announcement, Maureen stared wide-eyed. Then, much to Kate's amazement she nodded her head and said, "Perhaps that is for the best, most of these children are orphans with no home to return to. Pia will see they are well taken care of."

As Kate returned to Hawk's tipi after visiting with Maureen, Pia, and the children, she pondered her sister's words. Would the children be happy here with the Comanches?

Kate thought of her former life, at home, at the Lily. Then of the time she had spent with the Indians. As she had lived in their community, she had become happier and happier. In fact, the past had started to fade almost without her realizing it.

Almost unconsciously, Kate rested a hand on her stomach. What would the future hold?

The cold autumn day had progressed to a steady rain. Kate was bored staying in. Because of having to hide her nausea and to pretend everything was all right, she took her frustration out on Hawk. "Books. I never realized how awful a rainy day could be without something to read."

He frowned and went back to working feathers into an arrow. "Not if one stays busy."

"What kind of busy? I've done everything I can think of."

"Kate, think on this. We're leaving here."

She hurried to where he sat cross-legged on the floor and sank to her knees beside him. "When? It's raining."

"This canyon is closer to the Shamrock than where the tribe

will spend the winter, so I figure now is the time. The rain won't stop us. Why don't you rest now? We will leave early tomorrow."

Kate worked at appearing cheerful and cooperative. The trip would be cold and miserable, and she had no idea how long it would take to get to the Shamrock. Above all, she never let herself forget that she had the baby to consider.

"I could fill the parfleche now, except that we have nothing to put in it. A little jerky is all."

"We'll ask Pia."

"Yes, I suppose we could do that." She had become increasingly sensitive to the times she fell short as a good wife. "When the rain slacks off, I'll go talk with her. Ask her for some leftover food."

Hawk looked up in surprise. "You make it sound like we're beggars."

"Well, aren't we?"

"Katie, darlin', sometimes you're a bit crotchety. I'm doing what you want. What else is bothering you?"

It was the perfect time to tell him about the baby, but she hadn't made up her mind of the course she should set. She had the baby's welfare uppermost in her mind, as well as Maureen's.

"Worry about Maureen and Andy makes me difficult. I'll try to do better."

He laid aside the arrow. "Are you sure that's all?"

She was cornered. She could tell the truth and cause more problems for everybody, or she could stall. "What makes you think otherwise?"

"You've only been this way for a short while. Or maybe it just seems that way." He picked up the arrow again. "I'm a bit on edge myself."

Kate stretched out on the buffalo skin. "I'll take your advice and rest awhile."

"A good idea. You've begun to look a little tired these days."

"Seems like we always get caught in the rain."

"Aye, but this time we've no reason to fear anybody. Boggs is dead. Your sister's safe. We'll soon be back at the Shamrock."

He lay down beside her. "I think I'll join you, since it will be the last time before we get to the Shamrock." He nuzzled her cheek. "Katie, love, I'm amazed that you're more beautiful each day."

"I've learned to recognize Irish blarney."

"Nay, darlin', 'tis truth you're hearing." He caressed her thigh, and when she didn't brush his hand aside, he cradled her face. "Kiss me, Kate."

Her arms went round his neck, and she lifted her face so he could find her mouth. He tenderly caressed her breast. "Katie, one more kiss, one more touch, and I'll never be able to stop."

"So . . . ?"

He let out a lusty sigh. " 'Tis a lovely thing we've begun, my Kate, but we'll have to wait for the finish. I must alert Andy to our plan to leave."

"You were nice to provide him with a tipi."

"Cost me a deer and two rabbits."

"Andy will thank you." She scrambled to her feet. "I'll go with you."

"Anywhere?"

She was slow in answering. "Maybe."

By the time dawn streaked the sky over the canyon, Hawk was preparing the pack animal and saddling Kate's horse. Andy and Maureen appeared down the trail, leading their horse, prepared to ride double.

"We've a few things left to do," Hawk told them, smiling. "Won't take long. Kate's not quite ready. She's a bit slow this morning."

He looked toward the stream where she knelt, taking longer than usual to wash her face. He'd met with Stone Wolf earlier, told him of their plan to leave, and received his grandfather's approval. "Take care of your wife and bring my grandson to see me," he'd said.

Hawk chided himself for not telling Stone Wolf the truth, that Kate was not pregnant, nor had she been when Little Crow brought her to the camp. But he hated to see the disappointment in the old man's eyes. What was more, his grandfather's loyalty to the colonel's cause was a tenuous one, and Hawk had no desire to jeopardize it by angering the chief. The mission was important enough to Da that he'd risked sending his son to see the project succeed. Hawk faced the truth squarely. The country wasn't ready. There was no middle ground. The golden mean was yet to be.

He intended to tell the colonel at their next meeting he was tired of hiding his ancestry. He was proud of his blood, and wanted to be honest and up-front about being part Indian.

When Kate made her way toward them he called impatiently, "Time's wasting."

"Who cares?"

"Why are you so irritable? I've done all the work."

"And so you have." She nodded at Maureen and Andy. "Seems everybody but me is ready to ride."

Shadows smudged her cheeks. Her face was pale. He opened his mouth to tell her she was delaying the trip but changed his mind. Maybe she hadn't slept well. He didn't want to start an argument before they'd left the Indian campground.

He cupped his hands for her foot. "I'll give you a lift up."

"Don't bother."

"Katie, darlin', why are you so testy this morning?"

"That's just the way I am."

"Kate," Maureen chimed in, "you didn't used to be. Papa said you always woke up singing."

"I suppose it's the long ride ahead of us." Kate's long face disappeared when she looked at her horse. "You got Barney back for me."

"Aye, and it cost me three horses. When I get to the Shamrock, I'll cut out three mustangs and send them to Little Crow. He's getting a bargain."

Kate's pleasure at getting her horse was worth the effort, even if it was short-lived. He picked up a soft deerskin poncho and threw it over her head. "For the rain," he explained. "Without a saddle, Kate, you're in for a long, uncomfortable ride. Your backside will get very uncomfortable."

"I can handle it."

"You've had a little practice, but not for a two-day trip."

"Then I'll learn. Just don't worry about me."

"Worry about you! Ha. That's all I've done since I've known you."

"I can't be somebody other than who I am."

Neither could he.

This journey was the end and the beginning—the end of his dual personality, possibly of his relationship with Kate, and the beginning of a lonely life without her. She came eagerly into his arms, bringing no declaration of caring, no commitment, and, he was certain, harboring ideas of leaving the Shamrock. Now that she had Maureen with her, all else would be forgotten.

"Kate, rein your horse to follow mine. We've a way to go. Andy and Maureen can come last."

They passed massive boulders and high cliffs. The stream bed narrowed, and Hawk paused to get his bearings. "I dislike this trail. It's little used. The path is wet and could be slippery. Your horse will follow mine, so all you have to do is hold tightly to his mane."

He waved to Maureen and Andy. "Don't stay too close. You'll get mud in your face from Kate's horse's hooves."

"Hold up, Hawk." Andy dismounted and walked toward him. "May not mean nothing, but I'd swear I heard somebody following us. Once, I was sure I saw a man." Concern clouded his face. "Suppose it was an Indian?"

"I doubt it. Indians can hide in plain sight," he said, and added drolly, "you may have noticed. I'm part Indian."

When Andy didn't smile, Hawk shrugged. Boggs was dead. Martinez was dead and his Comancheros scattered. Possibly Andy had seen somebody, but even if he had, it was doubtful the man meant harm.

Nevertheless, Hawk looked back often.

Chapter Fifteen

On the third day after leaving the Indian village, Sean led the tired and hungry group on the last mile of the trip to the Shamrock. Kate had tried unsuccessfully to engage him in conversation, but his usual Irish good nature was missing. Their welcome home came from Malachi and several of the riders, the cowboys shuffling their feet and grinning. Smiling, Cole stood nearby holding Afton's hand—or, Kate thought, perhaps it was the other way around.

Kate remembered her first reception at the ranch, and thanked her stars she knew what to expect with this arrival. She was certain Anna had made her position secure by convincing the servants that their loyalty should lie with her. Kate gave her head a mental shake. What could be worse than the fear and squalor of the Comanchero camp? She could handle Anna, as Papa would say, with one hand tied behind her.

A surreptitious glance at Sean, and Kate saw a different person, a successful cattleman instead of a Comanche brave. He'd shed his Indian identity along with his breechclout. He met her eyes with a question in the depths of his gray ones and waited for her to break the silence.

Velda Sherrod

"I'm glad to be back, Sean," she said, making an effort to hide her fatigue. "I'd like to thank the riders for helping."

He nodded and turned to address his foreman. "Figure a way to reward the men, Malachi. Some money. A little whiskey."

Malachi waved his hand to include the riders. "Them's good boys, Sean; they'll be grateful."

"Loyal and dependable, I'd say." Sean saluted the men. "Thanks."

He returned to his conversation with Malachi, and Kate was sure Sean had forgotten her. Instead he swung out of the saddle and walked over to help her down. He lowered her slowly, letting her body slide down his hard frame. She knew at that moment what he was thinking, even though he'd spoken little on the trail, had even ignored her much of the time. She had to admit that none of them had been eager to talk. They had ridden miles, grateful at night to ease their tired bodies to the ground, eat, sleep, and be ready to go the next morning.

Sean's behavior had shown her a side of him she'd never seen before. Withdrawn, speaking only when called upon to give directions, he'd used as few words as possible. Had something happened to his work with the colonel? Wasn't he glad to be back at the Shamrock? He hadn't smiled once.

Not so with Maureen. She bubbled with happiness. Andy had helped her dismount, and now Maury had her arm linked through his. "Andy rode to save me, Kate. Wasn't that brave of him?"

"Makes you a hero, Andy," Kate said, smiling at the young man. "Maureen told me how you met. How you rode the stagecoach together."

"Glad she told you 'bout me, 'cause I'm gonna marry her." He looked lovingly at Maureen. "If she'll have me."

They all heard Maureen's joyful laugh. "Oh, Andy, I'll marry you. I prayed so hard you'd come back for me."

"Will you go to Montana with me?"

Her heart in her eyes, Maureen snuggled closer. "You know I will."

Lost in the moment, Andy continued to look at her until something alerted him to the folks around them. His face turned red. "We'll talk about it some more tonight, honey, when we're by ourselves."

Their happiness was beautiful to see, Kate mused, making up her mind quickly on what she would say to Sean later. The time had come to tell him all the things she carried in her heart. He'd be hurt, but perhaps she could make him understand. She moved to Sean's side and rested her hand on his arm. "I've something to talk to you about."

"All right. And I've got something to tell you, but it will have to wait for another time."

Did he have an inkling she carried his baby? She didn't want to wait to find out. "What is it, Sean?" He didn't answer. She might have known he'd make her wait until he was ready to talk.

Near her, a winning picture was playing out before her eyes. Malachi had his hand on Cole's shoulder, his rancor toward the black man forgotten. "Here's another good man, Sean. Rode into that bunch of Comancheros like he could take 'em by hisself."

"Afton and I have been treated so well at the Shamrock, I had to help, Mistuh Mal." His face reflected such agony, as if in remembering, he lived the pain all over again. "When Miss Kate and I rode to the canyon together, and those terrible men pulled her from her horse, she kept yelling for me to ride for help. I didn't think I could leave her in the hands of those reptiles, until I realized what she was telling me was the only way. I rode as fast as I could back to the ranch. Then Mr. Mal, the riders and I gathered up Mr. Sean's horses and the rest you know."

With praise being heaped on Cole, Afton lifted her chin a trifle. "Cole does all right for a slave. Papa taught him."

Once more Kate had a desire to swat the little girl's bottom. A sideways glance at Sean showed that his face had darkened. He spoke softly, but his tone said he intended that she should listen well. "Afton, Coleridge is not a slave. And you're old enough now to mind your manners. Never again, in my presence anyway, say anything about being a slave. God only knows why he allows you to behave so."

Velda Sherrod

Cole knelt beside Afton. Kate had no idea what he was saying to his small charge, but she hoped he was giving that little baggage a piece of his mind. Cole ushered Afton away quickly before she could say anything else.

The servants waited at the entrance to the ranch house, and Kate introduced Maureen and Andy to everybody, noting the sullen faces of the servants. They were back in Anna's line of defense, their less than friendly faces turned in her direction. Kate nodded to them. She'd deal with them later.

Kate glanced at Sean, and when he said nothing, she instructed Maureen to follow her upstairs. Surprising nobody, her sister was hesitant to leave her lover. "Come along, Maury. You can see Andy later. You'll be in the bedroom next to mine."

On their way up the stairs, Maureen gasped at her surroundings. "This house is so beautiful. Nobody in our town has a house like this, Kate. Not even Verlin. His house is dreary." She gushed on, frequently bringing Andy's name into the conversation. At last she stopped. Embarrassment pinkened her cheeks. "Kate, when I was with the Comancheros, I wasn't . . . I know you worried and wondered about me. Kate, I'm not pregnant."

"I'm glad," Kate said, smothering her relief. She could remember that not too long ago—or maybe it was a hundred years—her sister would have been embarrassed at speaking the word *pregnant*. After Mama had married pious Milton, she had taught Maureen and Kate that the word was not used in polite company. No doubt Milton had influenced Mama. Papa would have laughed at such a stand. "You're lucky. It could have been different."

"I kept telling the men I was having my woman's time, Kate, and they believed me."

"Some men have distorted ideas about that, I've heard. Did Andy ask if they assaulted you?"

"No, but I told him what I did to keep them away. He said if they had hurt me, he'd have hunted them down and killed them. He said even if they had used me, he'd want me just the same. That it wouldn't have made any difference." She hugged herself. "Andy's wonderful. I was so scared, Kate. I'm not brave

284

like you. There were times I wanted to die, and then I'd think of you and Andy."

Trying to smile, wanting to cry,Kate turned toward the door. "I get frightened, too. And I'm glad the men didn't bother you. I'd hate to think how much more terrible it could have been. But now you have Andy." She had to wait to hear the rest of Maureen's tale. She was too tired and too close to tears. "Honey, I'm going down now to see about getting bathwater brought up. You can rest awhile."

She walked quietly down the hall. Maureen was stronger for having been through such an ordeal, but at such a terrible price. She had matured, and no doubt Andy's love had helped. Love seemed to change people.

Kate met Sean at the foot of the stairs. "Hawk . . . I should say Sean. I forget sometimes which one to use."

"Does it bother you?"

"What if I slip up and call you by the wrong name at the wrong place? Spoil the plan you and the military man are working on?"

He shrugged. "Don't worry about it."

"Thanks for saving Maureen from Boggs."

"Glad I could help."

Blast, he wasn't helping now. "You've made Maureen happy. She has Andy, and he wants to marry her."

"You're biding time, lass. Are you saying good night?" He waited, his eyes a stormy gray. "Well?"

"I have Maureen to think of, Sean."

"So we aren't sleeping together."

They had been so close at the Comanche camp. Now there was a world between them. "Sean . . ." She stumbled over the words. "Thanks for saving me from Boggs."

"I promised to protect you. Stone Wolf married us."

"But he's an Ind—" She bit her lip. "What I meant to say is . . ."

His brow went up, and he finished for her. "He's an Indian? So am I."

"For a while," she said lamely, "I'll sleep in my bed. I wouldn't want Maureen to think wrong thoughts about us."

"Maureen hasn't had a thought that didn't include Andy Bennett in her bed."

"Maureen will make him wait until after they're married." Kate searched his face uneasily. "That's the proper way."

His relentless gaze drifted down. "Aye, and now it's proper you'd be wanting." His interest in her body gave way to a look of indifference. He shrugged. "Since when?"

She watched him walk away from her, her insides a scramble of emotions. Where once her world was a dangerous place, now it simply loomed barren and uneasy. She walked slowly down the hall. In the kitchen she met Anna giving Juanita instructions for the next meal. "Anna, I'll direct Juanita from now on. For the present, please see that the boys bring up hot water for a bath."

Not waiting for Anna's surly reply, Kate retraced her steps to the stairs. She had to tell Sean about the baby. On the stairs she had lost her courage. The timing had just seemed wrong. She thanked her stars the morning sickness had gone. She was surprised Sean hadn't mentioned that she'd put on weight.

Had he noticed the changes in her body, figured out the reason, and waited for her to tell him?

She hadn't confided in anybody, and only Stone Wolf knew for sure. He had said the leaves told him she carried his grandson in her womb. With the approach of winter, the leaves would soon be gone. What would tattle to him next? Sagebrush? Maybe a stray buffalo?

When the time came that she apprised Sean of her condition, he'd want to know why she'd waited so long to tell him. And when he found out, he'd never let her go until the baby was born. And he'd insist on keeping the baby. She wanted to cry.

She would, she decided, take it slow for the next few days, until she was sure of her decision. Until she was on firmer ground, and her emotions were under control. She had Maureen to think about now, but her own feelings kept intruding. She had to use caution and keep a cool head. The baby's future was at stake.

Back in her bedroom, she stalled at undressing in front of Maureen. Her condition would be obvious. "If you need anything, let me know. Your bedroom is next door. I'm sure you're tired and wanting to bathe and rest."

"Yes. But first I want to tell you how wonderful it is to be with you, Kate. Thank you for all you've done."

"Many people are responsible. Most of all Sean."

Gazing at her sister under the glow of the bedroom lamp, Kate was impressed once again by how much Maureen had changed. The eyes that once looked out of that innocent face carried a different message now. She was no longer a child, but a woman who'd endured too much of the dark side of life. Not old enough to become cynical and no longer fearful, Maureen spoke what was on her mind. "Are you in love with him?"

"Yes, I'm in love with him." There, she'd admitted aloud that she loved him.

"He loves you. I can tell. He's so kind to you. Looks after you. Look how he joined with the Indians to rescue us and bring us here to his ranch. He did that for you."

The longer Maureen talked, the more uncomfortable Kate became. "Yes."

"He was friends with the Indians. And they did what he asked. And they all rode into the Comanchero camp whooping and hollering. My Andy was with them."

Kate longed to tell the truth, that Sean was an Indian—and look what the Indians had done to Papa. Besides, if she and Sean married, as long as they lived she'd be hiding his dual personality. And what if she slipped and said something that would betray him? "The Indians trust Sean. They're his friends. With me he has been generous and kind. I'll always appreciate his concern."

Soon the worrisome problem of Sean's paternity needed to be addressed. The baby would be part Indian, and she'd live in fear that someone would find out, that the baby would be in danger from some unscrupulous white man. Or grow up in a place with women as biased as Ophelia Maud. If she took the child away, to another city and state, nobody would ever know.

And it would break Sean's heart.

*　　*　　*

Velda Sherrod

The days since they'd been back had not been the best ones Sean had ever known. He worked like one of the hands; the harder the task, the quicker he was to take it on himself. He rode out early and came back late, too tired to do more than bathe, eat his supper, and climb into bed.

Juanita had told him Kate had assumed the responsibility of running the house, leaving Anna disgruntled and vindictive, pouring out her venom to the other servants. The cook also mentioned the upstairs maid being tired of Anna's sly insinuations. Sean wasn't sure what he intended to do about it. Anna had been with the Shamrock most of her life, her mother before her doing the same job, and both had been welcome employees. It was one more bloody thing to worry about.

The sun jumped over the horizon, announcing the beginning of a new day. The household was stirring. He'd exchanged a few words with Juanita and downed a couple of cups of coffee. Not wanting to tarry, he'd thanked the cook and hurried outside. He planned to head somewhere, anywhere, to get away from his disturbing thoughts. He saddled his horse, wishing he had Midnight back in his corral. Who had his horse now? He prepared to heft himself into the saddle when a polite but firm voice stopped him.

"*Mistuh, suh.* Sean." Cole's voice came from the barn. "Sean, could I have a word with you before you leave?"

Sean paused, surprised and a little irritated at having to delay his escape. "What's on your mind, Cole?"

"Suh, I would address a matter, one I've kept secret. But the time has come to speak."

"Aye, lad, but you're a bit serious for early morning. Has something happened?"

"It's about Afton."

Sean couldn't hide his surprise. He'd never expected to be approached by Cole about a subject as delicate as Afton. "What about Afton?"

"I know," Cole said earnestly, "that she appears unruly at times."

"Aye, I can testify to that," Sean said, wondering what that had to do with him. He wasn't the girl's father.

288

For the first time Cole appeared to have trouble expressing himself. "You see, suh, I'm aware she's peevish, and a little petulant. And I also know you're a bit impatient with such behavior."

"Right on both counts." Where in the world was the conversation headed? What the child needed was a strong hand to guide and remind her, and a few strong words to shut her up. But that wasn't his job. In fact, he didn't even want to discuss it.

"Afton suffered a great loss, Sean. Seeing her parents killed was a terrible experience for her."

"I'm sympathetic, Cole, but that doesn't mean she should continue to insult everybody around her. Especially you."

"I know, suh," Cole said, lowering his eyes. "The truth is . . . the truth is—"

Impatient to get on with whatever bothered the young black man, Sean interrupted. "The truth is, Cole, you don't want to reprimand her."

"I love her mightily, and she hasn't always been this way. I'm all she has, and she's terrified she'll lose me." He met Sean's gaze with a direct look. "And she's all I have."

"That's your business, Cole, but perhaps a bit of advice is in order. You're a free man. Stop her from abusing you. Why are you so subservient?"

"Not subservient. I understand her." He paused. "You see, she's my sister."

At a momentary loss for words, Sean fumbled for something to say. All he came up with was an inane question. "Your sister? But she's white."

"We had different mothers. Mine was a slave. Our father treated me like a son, and his wife, Afton's mother, hated me."

"Does Afton know?"

"Perhaps I'll tell her someday. I think her attitude is improving." He looked hopefully at Sean. "Would you agree, suh?"

Sean decided it wouldn't hurt to lie a bit. "Aye, I seem to have noticed a change."

The strain went out of his voice, and Cole smiled. "I'm glad

289

to hear it. Very glad indeed. I wouldn't want her to be rude to you or anyone else."

Rude! Afton was a spoiled brat. A mess. By way of dismissal, Sean put his foot into the stirrup. "I appreciate your gesture, but why are you telling me this?"

"You see, Sean, if anything should happen to me, I'd appreciate your taking care of Afton. Here at the Shamrock she'll have someone to look after her."

Sean was touched by Cole's confession. "I understand. I'll honor your wishes."

"I hoped you would." Cole bowed his head. "Thank you, suh."

The black man hurried away, no doubt glad he'd made his confession, Sean mused, preparing once more to ride out.

Malachi's raspy voice stopped Sean yet again from settling into the saddle. "When a man owns a ranch, he's supposed to talk to his foreman, unless," he said, sarcasm coloring his words, "unless he's too damn busy getting away by hisself."

Mentally cursing his luck, Sean dismounted. He'd hoped— nay, wished—that this morning he'd not have to talk to anybody. He'd already had an uncomfortable conversation with Cole. "Morning, Mal. I didn't know you were up yet," he said slyly, knowing he'd get a rise out of his foreman. It was a game they played going back to Sean's childhood.

"Been up a while, son. Not like some folks I could name."

"Nay, Mal, I wanted an early start. Thought I'd take a look at that windmill in the south pasture."

"Nothin' wrong with the blamed windmill. Way I figure it, you ain't wantin' to talk to nobody, and that includes me."

"You're maligning me, Mal. I'm an industrious rancher."

"Aw, hell, son. I've knowed since you got back from saving the girl that you had something on your mind."

"You're right," Sean said, brushing his hand across his horse's shiny neck. "Give me a few days."

"Yeah, reckon I can do that. There's another matter. The senator's gonna be here the day after tomorrow. He sent word."

Sean met Malachi's announcement with a snarl. "Bloody

hell, Mal, they barely got home, and now they're coming back?"

"Right about them headin' back. Wrong about them ever going home. The senator's out stumpin' the state. Soon as he feeds himself good at your table, he'll go home and mess up the government."

"How many are coming?"

"Six we know of."

"Now Ophelia Maud will have Maureen to cluck about."

"Might ought to cover up 'bout Miss Kate's sister."

"Anna would never let that happen. I don't know what I'm going to do about Anna, Mal."

"Yeah, she's a handful now that Miss Kate's here."

"What do you think I ought to do?"

Malachi kicked at the low rail of the fence. "Guess it'd be kinda hard to let her go, seein' as how her mama raised her here. You might want to talk to Anna. Miss Kate, too. Maybe something can be worked out. This is different, o' course, but when one of the boys gets a burr under his saddle, I just ask him to kindly get his ass off the range."

"I don't suppose you'd want to . . ." At Malachi's quick shake of his head, Sean nodded. "I figured you wouldn't."

"But the way I see it, Anna ain't what's botherin' you."

Sean leaned against his horse. "Mal, I'm prepared to tell everybody about my Indian blood. I'm tired of hiding my identity. The raid on the Comanchero camp proved that the mission the colonel and I have been working on can succeed. Indians and whites helping each other. As of now, I'm taking myself out of the picture. I've sent word to the colonel, and I've told Stone Wolf. Besides, the Shamrock riders saw me dressed as an Indian. They'll spread the news."

"Naw, that ain't right, son. We ain't got a rider that's not loyal. I told 'em not to mention the rescue to nobody off this spread."

"What about Bonham?"

"Sean, we jes' plain run him off. One of the boys—Gus, I think it was—said loud enough for Bonham to hear that it looked like nobody else was gonna kill the son of a bitch. Guessed it was up to him. Next mornin' Bonham was gone."

"He had a hand in Kate's kidnapping. I'd like to string him up to a cottonwood."

"I reckon," Mal said complacently.

Now there was the senator. The more Sean thought of entertaining the Platts, the angrier he got. He absolutely refused to spend another minute listening to Ophelia Maud brag about being a senator's wife. "Send word that we're not in a position to entertain. We've become more selective."

"Naw, son, I don't think that's best. Better to have the goodwill of a yeller dog than to wait for it to bite you. I'll jes' tell 'em this ain't a good time for visiting."

"Tell him I'm tired of feeding him and his gossipy, self-righteous wife. Tell him no more campaign donations." Sean warmed to his words. "Tell him he's a fat, pompous pig. And his wife is a fat homely pig."

"I ain't mentioning nothin' to him 'bout free meals, donations, him being fat, or his wife being ugly."

Fuming, Sean knew it was best to let Malachi handle the problem his way. They lapsed into silence, but Sean recognized the symptoms. Malachi had something else on his mind. Sean waited, thinking the day had already headed for hell in a wheelbarrow. "Anything else on your mind, Mal?"

Malachi took his time, rolling a cigarette, licking the paper. "Well, me and some of the boys seen where some riders held a meetin'. Looked to be about five, maybe six."

"How do you know they weren't from the Shamrock?"

"You ain't dealin' with a boy this morning, Sean. I can read hoofprints good as the next man."

"What are you saying? That we've got rustlers?"

"I ain't sure. I'll tell the boys to be on the lookout." Malachi lifted his hat and ran his fingers through his hair, what he had left of it. He opened his mouth to speak and then shut it.

"While you're at it, and the first chance you get when he isn't wrapped up in Maureen, ask Andy Bennet if he'll take a look in the canyon valley where we kept the horses," Sean said, his eyes on the horizon. "If Midnight got away, he might have gone back hoping to find the mares."

"Already done it. Bennet said he'd get on it. Seemed right happy to be asked."

Sean reached for the reins. "Anything else?"

"I been doin' some thinkin' here of late. 'Bout Miss Kate."

Every nerve in his body sprang to attention, and Sean glared at his foreman. "What about Kate?"

"She's lookin' a little peaked-like of late."

Sean studied his foreman. From childhood he had learned never to take Malachi's words lightly. "Kate was worried about her sister. You think that could be the reason?"

"Reckon that would do it." Malachi leaned against the fence. "Maybe."

"What else could it be?" Sean's sharp tone surprised even himself. "Have you noticed anything for sure? If you have, tell me."

Malachi shook his head. "I don't know that anythin' is wrong. I was just checkin'."

Was Kate ill? To him she'd never been more beautiful. He'd have to keep an eye on her, which was about as close as she'd let him get. No doubt she was tired from the horseback ride.

One thing he knew: he'd gone as far in pursuing her as he intended. The rest of the way was up to her. He'd done everything he could to make her happy. He'd used all his skills, the ones he'd prided himself on, in making love to her. He'd come when she needed him. He'd led the charge to rescue her sister. Of course, she'd done her part, climbing down that rocky cliff. She'd been kind to his people, saved Little Crow's son from strangling. And she was wonderful to love—like no one else. But a one-eyed man could see that her heart was never involved. There were times in the past when she looked at him with shining eyes, her body pliant against his, reveling in his caresses, but those days were gone.

She didn't have to tell him she was leaving. He already knew. And it made him want to fight with her. Pick a quarrel and go a few rounds. But one thing had to be done. He'd thought about it all the way from Stone Wolf's camp. He would no longer hide his ancestry. He was half Indian and it was time the world knew it. He'd do the honorable thing and be true to himself and to his mother. His father would know soon enough that his son no longer intended to play the game of go-between, hoping to bring whites and Indians to the peace table. And Kate would soon know of his intent to reveal his ties with Stone Wolf. What would she say?

He glanced toward the kitchen door in time to see her walk toward the garden. The sun shone on her hair, streaking it with strands of red, and he marveled all over again at her beauty—and how much she'd matured since the night she'd come to his hotel room, her sumptuous breasts more enticing, her hips slightly wider. Given the anguish and suffering she'd been through, no woman could remain a girl.

Bloody hell! Would he ever stop wanting her?

Sean adjusted himself in the saddle and, without a backward glance, kicked his horse in the flank and raced for the prairie. Maybe he could outrun his feelings.

Kate went about her duties, taking the reins from Anna and ignoring the woman's sullen looks. It hadn't been easy, but she'd begun to see improvement in her relations with the servants. Little by little the house had begun to adjust to her management. Soon she'd be leaving and Anna would have her old position back.

Disgruntled at such thoughts, Kate made her way upstairs to her bedroom. Maureen had continued to blossom since their arrival at the Shamrock. Andy made no effort to hide his feelings. He adored Maureen.

Soon they'd be leaving for Montana. Kate wasn't sure how much money Sean had given him—loaned him, Andy insisted—but from the shine in Andy's eyes, the amount must have been substantial.

With a sigh, Kate changed into her nightdress. White and full and chaste, the gown hid her barely rounded belly. She turned back the covers on her bed before blowing out the candle. Moonlight, ephemeral and pale, filled the room. She slipped between the sheets and closed her eyes. Determined to sleep, she forced herself to lie quietly, but the longer she lay there, the less likely sleep seemed.

Down the hall two doors, Sean would be in bed. She'd heard him climb the stairs, his steps slow as he passed her room. First he would have pulled off his boots with a bootjack, then unbuttoned his shirt and pants, and last he'd have removed his hat. Unmindful of the cold nights, he'd sleep naked. Thinking of him now, she tried to remember Papa, the horrible way he'd died, but his face no longer came into focus. All she could see was Sean's fine gray eyes frowning at her.

Reaching a decision, she rose and, before she could change her mind, went barefoot into the hall. She refused to keep news about the baby from the child's father any longer. Looking both ways to make sure no one saw her, she paused only a moment at the entrance to his room. Her heart began a drumroll, and before her nerve failed, she turned the knob. She closed the door behind her and stood waiting for some sign he'd heard her.

The covers of his bed had been tossed aside, and moonlight bathed his naked body. She couldn't be sure he was awake. He made no move to cover himself. "It's late. Is something the matter?"

She couldn't just blurt out the reason she'd come without first leading up to it. "I've come to tell you I'm grateful. To thank you for what you've done."

"Is that the only reason you're here?" He lowered his voice. "If it is, you could have told me earlier. This morning at breakfast, or tonight at dinner. Besides, you've already mentioned it, and so has your sister."

"I thought"—she cleared her throat—"it needed to be said again."

"There's no need for you to be grateful, but since you've said it," he said, his indifferent gaze raking her body, "you can go back to bed."

"That wasn't the only reason."

He leaned forward on his elbow. "And what is that other reason, Kate?"

For the life of her, Kate could think of only one thing. She wanted his arms around her. "We haven't had a chance to be together, and I thought you might be . . ."

295

"I might be what?"

She wanted to say she thought he might be lonesome for her. "Actually, I wanted . . ."

"For God's sake, Kate. Say whatever you came to say."

The conversation wasn't going at all as she'd planned. "I . . . Maureen has her own bedroom here, and I thought . . ."

"You thought Andy might be spending his nights there. And you want me to talk to him. To stop him."

"No," she whispered. "I didn't come for that."

He continued as if he hadn't heard her. "As far as I'm concerned, that's their business."

"I agree."

"Then why are you here?"

"You said you had something to discuss." She looked away, down at the floor, and then back at him. "I've something, too."

"Don't let me stop you. As if I've ever been able to."

"I'm going to have a baby."

His surprise quickly became genuine delight. He chuckled and rose quickly, his naked body beautiful in the candlelight. "Ah, Katie," he said, drawing her against him. "Such wonderful news, lass. Makes me glad all over. And you're more beautiful than ever. How long have you known, darlin'?" he asked tenderly.

The question she'd dreaded. How could she explain to him so he'd understand? She clutched at her nightgown, her fingers drawing the fabric into a ball. "I knew before we left Stone Wolf's camp."

A puzzled expression spread over his face, and then the truth hit him. "Were you waiting for me to find out for myself? Or did you think to hide under a buffalo robe?"

"I needed time to think about it."

"What could be more important than telling a man he was going to be a father?"

"Sean, the baby has Indian blood." She spoke quickly, almost gagging on the words. "If he grows up here, whites will look down on him. You know that."

He stared at her as if he couldn't believe what he was hearing. "I'm an Indian, Kate. You have trouble facing that fact."

His lips curled in scorn, and his voice became scathing. "Like Ophelia Maud."

"Truthfully, I'm only thinking about the baby." She turned tortured eyes up to his. He just had to understand. "Our son will be looked down upon. Despised."

"Not by the Indians," he informed her bluntly.

The man was blind. Oblivious to the truth. Her anger rose along with her voice. "He'd have only one place to go—Stone Wolf's camp."

"A hell of a lot better than some of the places I've seen. Boggs's saloon being one."

Kate had the grace to blush. "I wouldn't have been there if I'd had another place to go."

"There are other Boggses, Kate, men waiting for a chance to come after you."

"Mama's no longer living with Milton. I'll go home to have the baby."

"Home? That surprises me." Harshness turned his voice raspy. "What if the child is a girl, and your mother marries another preacher? Doesn't the girl need a father's protection?"

"Stone Wolf said it was a boy."

"Aye. He believed my lie that you carried my baby."

"I told him the truth."

He pivoted and snarled, fury straining his face. "It's all right to tell someone else, but not the father?"

"Stone Wolf is the only one who knows, besides you, of course."

"Am I'm supposed to applaud?"

Tempted to blast him, Kate clamped down on her temper. She had never seen him so difficult, so obstinate, so pigheaded. "He said the leaves told him."

"I wish a leaf, a blade of grass, even a bloody buffalo chip had told me. The mother certainly wasn't up to it."

He had a point. Struggling desperately to hang on to her shrinking determination, she drew a long, shaky breath. "I wanted . . . I didn't want him to face people who'd hurt him."

"Nobly spoken," he said, his voice laced with sarcasm.

"You'd have our child grow up with the same intolerance as the Mrs. Platts of the world."

"No. No, I'd never want that."

"I'm tired of wondering what you want, Kate. But I know it isn't me."

"What do you want to do about it?" she asked, a tremble in her voice.

"I'm going to help you find a place other than the Shamrock. A safe place. I want my child close by so I can be a father to him."

Kate felt the room whirl about her. Not to be with Sean . . . not to know his love . . . She couldn't bear the thought. Her eyes filled with tears. "I suppose deep down I've tried to blame you for something you had no control over. Now I've begun to think more clearly. In trying to protect the baby, I've hurt you. I've heard the slur in Mrs. Platt's voice. I've seen the disdain in the eyes of the servants. I've behaved shamelessly."

He tipped his head back and closed his eyes. "At one time or another we've all been hurt. And at one time or another we all act shamelessly, Kate."

Hearing him speak her name was like the promise of a caress. "The only excuse I have is that I was thinking about the baby."

The anger slowly left his face, exposing his pain. "Kate, when you climbed down the cliff you were in terrible danger. If you'd fallen it would most surely have killed you. If the Comancheros had seen you, they'd have killed me and taken you back to Boggs. You weren't thinking about the baby. You were thinking about me. You risked everything for me."

"I had to do something," she whispered, wondering if the ache in her heart matched his.

If she were to leave the Shamrock, his words would forever haunt her. How blind she'd been to her own true feelings. How unfair she'd been to Sean. "I wasn't thinking. . . ."

"When you started down, I thought I'd lose my mind. Every step you took, I died a little. Don't you see, darlin', I need you the way I need air to breathe, water to drink. Living without you would be hell. I can't bear to lose you." His voice broke. "I love you Kate."

He loved her. The most precious words a woman could hear from her beloved. She could no longer deny her heart or the plea in his eyes. She loved him. They would raise their baby to be a just man, a good man, wherever he chose to live when he grew up.

Forced to confront her prejudices, feeling shame for having harbored them, one by one she laid them aside. The time had come to stand up for what was right and just. She had lived with Indians, earned their respect and a place in their society. Their ways were not her ways, but she respected their right to live the way they believed. Whatever Sean's background, she wanted to be at his side the rest of her life. He had never failed her, had placed his own life in jeopardy for her. He was her baby's father. Most of all, she loved him.

"I love you, too, you . . . Indian."

"You're sure my kinfolks won't matter to you?"

"I'm sure, but there is one other thing."

He looked at her doubtfully. "What thing?"

"I want to go to bed with you. If you want me."

"If I want you?" He grinned and held out his hand. "Wanting you is a permanent condition with me. Come to bed, Katie."

"I mean I want to make love with you tonight. You think we might . . . ?"

"Aye, we might make love." He stared down at her, smiling, the haunted look gone from his eyes. "And I suspect that we will." He kissed her, lifted her in his arms, and placed her lovingly on the bed. " 'Tis a fine thing to know you love me and want me."

"Aye, laddie, I want you," she said, laughing at her own attempt to mimic him. "I came here to seduce you, but you knew that already, didn't you?"

He chuckled dryly. "A man can hope." His smoldering gaze dropped to her lips, and a tender smile crossed his face. An

299

instant later his mouth found hers. He trailed his lips across her cheek, gently caressing her breast, all the time murmuring words of endearment.

She delved into the sweetness of the moment. When she rode the crest, he traveled with her.

Chapter Sixteen

Malachi leaned his weight against the corral fence. "Them riders I told you 'bout, the ones holdin' their meetings on the Shamrock range, well, one of our boys found another place they got together. Closer to the house this time, there where the creek swerves to the west. I ain't likin' it, Sean."

He didn't like it either, Sean thought, wondering what business such men would have on his ranch. "Probably a few drifters figuring on grabbing a Shamrock steer."

"Could be, I reckon. And I hope you're right."

Sitting atop the fence, Sean watched the caravan crawl across the prairie toward the Shamrock. The senator and his hangers-on had arrived complete with biases and baggage. "Thought you were going to send word to the senator not to come? That his timing was bad."

"I did. Sent Charlie soon as you told me. He got back sayin' the senator had to come on. They had no place else to go."

"Why didn't you tell me?"

"I figured there was no use tellin' you. All you'd do is get mad and dread it. Whatcha call worry, son. And there wasn't nothin' you could do about it."

"I suppose not."

Ophelia Maud would have gotten her second wind and would be poisoning her arrows to take aim at Kate. If Ophelia became too aggressive, Kate would, he was sure, meet her halfway. "They'll soon be here, Mal."

"I ain't blind."

"More wagons this time. More people."

" 'Pears like. Guess the senator's campaign ain't goin' too good. Might be he's afraid he ain't gonna get hisself reelected."

"He won't get my vote this time."

When the travelers rolled into the yard, Sean took his time jumping to the ground and walking to meet them. The senator was predictable. He'd come for another donation for his campaign fund. "Good day, Senator."

Always the jovial guest, Senator Platt stuck out his hand. "And a good day to you, Mr. O'Brien. Seems like this place gets prettier ever' time I come."

"Nice of you to say so, sir."

"It's the truth. Didn't I say that not five miles back, Maudie?"

Busy with the driver, Ophelia Maud could only nod. "Don't drop the bags to the ground, Alexander. Handle them carefully. Easy, I said."

Simpering, she turned to greet Sean. "Mr. O'Brien, how very nice of you to have us again. We do love coming here."

"An unexpected pleasure, Mrs. Platt, from such illustrious visitors," he said mildly. "And undeserved, I might add."

"Oh, no, Mr. O'Brien, the senator and I are just regular people. Some folks treat us like aristocrats. Even royalty, you might say. It can be embarrassing." She smirked and patted her hair, waiting for him to agree. "They do, Mr. O'Brien. Can you believe it?"

"Some things are hard to believe, Mrs. Platt." He smiled benignly. "And I'll remember not to treat you so. I surely would not want to embarrass you."

"You're so nice, Mr. O'Brien," she said, clearly unsure whether to be pleased. She looked around her. "The woman who spent time with the Indians. I've forgotten her name. Is she still here?"

"Yes, she's still here."

A frown crossed Ophelia Maud's face. "Is that so? I would have thought she'd be back with the savages. As I said the last time we were here, most women—and I do sincerely believe this, Mr. O'Brien—under the same circumstances, most women would have taken their own lives."

Interested, Sean stepped closer. "Is that so? And why do you think such an action necessary, Mrs. Platt?"

"Really, Mr. O'Brien, I hesitate to answer the question here among these people. Some of them are quite young." Her pious glance included all within listening distance. "But I suppose if they don't hear it from me, they'll hear from someone not so . . ."

"Discriminating, Mrs. Platt?"

"Yes, yes, discriminating. The very word I was searching for. I'm glad you understand. The woman, what with being around Indian braves and all . . . Well, you know what probably happens in such cases."

"I'm not so young, Mrs. Platt, please tell me. What do you think might have happened?"

She leaned toward him and whispered conspiratorially, "It's a delicate subject, Mr. O'Brien, but she probably went from one tipi—that's what they live in—to another."

"And . . . ?"

"Well, you know, sleeping with all the warriors. Must be just terrible. Like a . . ." She searched for a word, finally whispering, "Like a woman of the night. No decent woman could endure that. Don't you agree?"

"Considering that the woman in question was not responsible for her capture, it hardly seems fitting that she kill herself. Most people want to live."

"I doubt a man could understand, Mr. O'Brien, how horrible that would be to a virtuous woman."

The senator entered the conversation. "Now, Maudie, us men ain't so dense that we cain't understand. And I reckon that a good woman would feel that way. Ain't that right, Sean?"

Murmurings among the guests brought a wry smile to Sean's lips. "Death before dishonor, Senator. Right, Mrs. Platt?"

"Oh, you do understand, Mr. O'Brien. I was sure you would, being from across the waters."

"We Irish try to be understanding of our womenfolk, but it isn't always easy. Especially in matters of this kind. But we try, Mrs. Platt. We try."

Sean turned his attention to the men present. He shook hands all around before directing them toward the house. "I'm sure you'd like to rest awhile. Especially the good woman."

"Yes," Ophelia Maud said, and placed a delicate hand on her breast. "I am a trifle weary. It is a long trip across the prairie. So many inconveniences. And always the threat of Indians."

"Of course, Mrs. Platt. No doubt the men in your party felt a grave responsibility. Decent women have to be protected at all costs, and if worse comes to worst, protected against themselves." He turned to shake hands with others present, figuring he and Ophelia Maud had covered the subject of Indians.

He reminded the party they had some time before dinner, saying whatever appropriate words he thought necessary. Relieved to be spared more conversation with Ophelia Maud, he watched them march toward the main house. He glanced around him, searching for Malachi.

That good man had gone into hiding. He found Mal smoking a cigarette in the hay barn. "You do such a good disappearing act, you ought to be a magician." Sean glowered at his foreman. "You see the wagons and carriages, and when I turn around you're gone."

"They circled you like Herefords around a water tank,' Mal said, chuckling. "I didn't have no time for chitchat, son. I had things that needed lookin' after."

"Then why were you hiding behind these hay bales?"

Malachi turned a surprised look on the hay. "Truth to tell, I just noticed that hay, and was reminded them cows might need a little more feed to get them through the winter."

"Perhaps you could postpone that thoughtful action until tomorrow. In the meantime, we'll be eating a little later than usual. I'll have to tell Juanita we're having guests. She and Kate can take it from there. So you'll have time to get ready."

"Now, Sean, I got no business at that table. A foreman's

s'posed to eat with the boys in the cook shack. Besides, I lose my appetite around that Orphelyer Maud."

"I'm counting on your being there, Malachi. I'd appreciate it. As a favor to me."

"In that case, I'll clean up. But I'm tellin' you, Sean, it's like wearin' a hair shirt."

"A little penance never hurts anybody."

Grumbling, Malachi headed toward the bunkhouse, stopping a few feet later to defend himself. "Ain't done much sinning lately. Not enough to repent for, but I'm thinkin' about changing that."

"With that plump little widow in Willow Grove?"

Malachi retraced his steps and put his finger in Sean's face. "You leave Louisy out of this. She's a nice woman."

"I didn't say she wasn't nice. I asked if you were going to sin with her."

Removing his hat and running his fingers through his hair, Malachi grinned. "Thinkin' 'bout Saturday night. If'n she's a mind, o' course."

"Well, this isn't Saturday. So put on clean clothes and be ready to eat with the guests. Royal guests," he amended. "Texas nobility."

"You're makin' me sick to my stomach. Hell, I might even throw up."

Kate pushed the curtain aside and watched the scene below her window. "Maury, here comes that odious senator and his equally unpleasant wife. Sean didn't mention anything about their visiting."

Hurrying forward, Maureen brushed past Kate's shoulder and knelt by the windowsill. "Maybe they'll be nice tonight. I hope Andy doesn't say something they wouldn't like. He's like that. Not always careful."

Kate thought about being careful and decided she was like Andy. "Tonight should be interesting then." She looked at her sister, beginning with Maureen's hair and moving on to her feet. "We need to look our best tonight. Suppose I do your hair first. We'll wind some ribbons into it."

"Andy likes my hair. He said he likes redheads. And you know something, Kate, his mother had red hair. Before she died, of course. Not as red as mine, or as pretty, he said."

"A coincidence for sure, honey. Before we start getting ready, I'll run down and talk to Juanita about the meal."

She took the back stairs to avoid running into a guest, but ran into Cole on his way to the kitchen. "Cole," she said, smiling, "how is Afton feeling?"

"She's all broke out with chicken pox, Kathleen. She itches."

"Get Juanita to give you some cow's cream. Then rub it over the spots. It will help the itching part. Chicken pox is contagious, so we need to keep her away from other people. Maureen and I had the disease when we were little. Tell Afton I'll look in on her in a while."

"She'll like that."

"Have you ever told her you're her brother?"

Cole showed his broadest grin. "I told her. And Kathleen, I think the child was glad, she was so afraid I'd run away, even though I assured her over and over that I never would."

Kate's eyes sparkled. "And what did she say?"

"She said, 'Just don't get uppity because we're kinfolks. If there's one thing folks can't stand, it's an uppity nigra.' "

Cole laughed and Kate joined him. "I'm sure that's a load off your mind."

"Not really, Kathleen. People will say our father used the black women on his plantation. Which isn't true. My father loved my mother and told her so. In my presence."

Kate walked to the kitchen with him. "Afton is lucky to have you."

He went about the business of explaining his need for cream to Juanita. "And I would appreciate it."

"We've got what you need right here. I just took the cream off the top. It's still cool. I fetched it from the wellhouse myself."

Juanita's kitchen always smelled good, like spice and sweet cakes and seasoned vegetables and roasting meat. Her fresh-baked bread made Kate's mouth water. The big Mexican woman smiled happily. "At the same time you take the cream, Cole, you can take a jelly roll up to little Afton."

"Good. She's a little cross right now."

After Cole left with his cup of cream and the roll, Kate arched a brow. "I'd say Afton is cross most of the time."

"She's doing better. Getting to be a sweet little girl. I prayed to the Virgin to take her in hand. Looks like she did."

"I've yet to see this miraculous change, but I'm glad for Cole's sake."

"Kate, Cole understands that little girl better than I understood my children. He told me Afton was trommer . . . He used an English word I don't know."

"Traumatized?"

"Something like that. He said seeing her parents killed by the Indians did that to her. He loves her, y'know."

Kate couldn't meet the cook's eyes. "I know."

She and Afton had both suffered losing loved ones to Indians. Afton was a fighter and doing her best to handle her loss. She didn't always behave admirably, nor was she always kind, but who was? Juanita had no problem overlooking the child's exasperating ways, and made excuses for Afton's imperious behavior with Cole. The cook seemed to understand instinctively that Afton would have to overcome some of the things she had been raised to believe and the losses that she had suffered.

Kate hoped that Afton would overcome her biases, just as she herself had. Kate hated to think how rigid in her prejudices she had been. But she also knew firsthand that personal experience was the best way to combat false notions about other cultures and races. And in Sean's household Afton would certainly be exposed to more open-minded beliefs.

She and Juanita discussed the evening meal, adding up the total number of guests and deciding on a menu. Then Kate went in search of Anna to make sure the servants were assigned certain posts.

"I've given the orders. After all, I've been doing this for a long time," Anna said impatiently. "I don't need somebody telling me what to do."

"I am sure you have," Kate said as patiently as she could. "But there's always the chance you and I might see things differently. For example, don't send Lena to help Mrs. Platt get dressed."

"But she's a senator's wife."

Kate smiled. "An elected official is paid by taxes collected from people like you and me. If his wife requires help to dress, the senator can pay such a person to accompany them."

"Whatever you think," Anna said, miffed. "But after all, she is a—"

"I know. She's a senator's wife. Would you send the boys up to my room with hot water?" She smiled.

Satisfied that everything was well organized for dinner, Kate went back upstairs. Her room was empty, and Kate surmised that her sister had gone back to her own bedroom to rest before dinner. Maureen's happiness shone in her face, turning the girl into a beauty. As for herself, Kate thought, observing her figure in the full-length mirror, she intended to look her very best tonight.

Sean greeted his guests graciously, if not warmly. The truth was, he wished them out of his sight. After what he planned for this night, he suspected he'd no longer be plagued with a return visit. They had gathered in the large parlor in preparation to go in to dinner. Kate had not yet appeared and he gazed upward, looking expectantly toward the top of the stairs.

Still dazzled by the knowledge of his coming fatherhood, Sean felt himself smile involuntarily. Learning that he would soon have a child of his own had only reinforced Sean's belief that publicly embracing his heritage was the best way to honor his family. And he believed that his father and the colonel would understand as Stone Wolf had. He would continue to work towards peace between the Indians and the whites, and by living openly as a half-breed he would make his life an example of how a balance could be achieved between the two worlds. Some people would stick by him and others wouldn't, but he planned to lead by example. The success of the rescue mission proved that he could get the Indians and the whites to work together on a limited basis. He had great hope for the future before him—especially now that he would share it with the woman of his dreams.

The woman who suddenly filled his vision.

Kate stood with one hand on the banister, hesitated, then saw him waiting for her. Giving him a beautiful smile, she started down. She was dressed in a shimmering black gown that molded to her bosom and left her shoulders bare. The neckline dipped in front to expose a tantalizing hint of the valley between her breasts. About her waist she'd secured a broad scarf of gold, draping it in front, a daring coverup of her condition. Her hair had been swept back from her face and fastened on top with a jeweled clip, then left to cascade down her back. Her slender throat gleamed white like alabaster. She was, he decided for the hundredth time, perfection.

Behind him he heard Ophelia Maud's disgruntled snort. The man standing next to him whispered, "My God."

And Maureen's squeal said it all. "Oh, Kate's so beautiful."

Mutterings continued as she descended gracefully, smiling at the guests and offering her hand to him. Sean bowed and kissed it. "You're quite the loveliest woman I've ever seen."

"When have you been off the range, rancher?"

Laughter welled up in him. Kate could always be counted on to help keep his feet on the ground. He threw a surreptitious glance at the senator's wife, observing the scathing looks that she cast at Kate. "Beautiful, isn't she, Mrs. Platt?"

"Beauty's skin-deep," Ophelia Maud said loudly enough for Kate to hear. "Just skin-deep."

"But how would you know that in Miss Hartland's case?"

"We've spoken about it before, Mr. O'Brien."

"You'd have her dead, Mrs. Platt?"

"Well, as I've told you before—"

"It seems a pity to deprive one so beautiful of life. And by her own hand? Nay, Mrs. Platt, it would be a sacrilege."

"Blasphemy, Mr. O'Brien."

Sean watched as Kate ended her conversation with one guest and extended her hand. "Mrs. Platt, I'm sorry I wasn't present when you and your party arrived. I hope you will forgive me." Her tone said she wasn't sorry at all. "I trust you've found everything to your comfort."

If the senator's wife expected a curtsy, Sean thought, hiding a grin, she could forget about it. Kate's good humor had relieved her of any ungraciousness, and he was uncommonly glad she wasn't given to the vapors. A glance at Ophelia Maud's face told him she might need a little hartshorn.

"We're comfortable," Ophelia Maud managed, her lips drawn tight in disapproval.

"I'm glad, Mrs. Platt."

Before the scene changed to something less polite, Sean grasped Ophelia Maud's arm. "Shall we go in to dinner, Mrs. Platt?"

With the senator and Kate following, Sean led them into the dining room. He waited for his guests to be seated. The senator remained standing. "Something the matter, Senator?"

"A nigger is sittin' down at the table preparin' to eat with me."

When Cole started to rise, Sean motioned him to remain. "Coleridge is my friend. Why would I deny him a place at my table, Senator?"

The senator clearly welcomed the challenge. His voice increased in volume sufficiently to fill the halls of Congress. "Texans fought the war to keep niggers in their place, and their place ain't eatin' with white folks. Niggers eat in the kitchen."

"It's really not done, Mr. O'Brien." Ophelia Maud smirked at her friends for confirmation. "Why, I still have a nigger maid at home, and a black yardman. They know their place."

"And you pay them now, I'm sure."

"Oh, yes. Of course, we don't have to feed and clothe them anymore, thank goodness. And if they get sick, they can take care of themselves."

Sean nodded. "Freedom bears a price." He sat and then leaned back in his chair. "Coleridge remains, and I hope the rest of you will. Shall we eat?"

Sean watched the senator quickly battle between his desire to make a point by leaving the dining room and his hunger. Grumbling, he sat. Immediately conversation erupted into nervous dialogue. Kate had instructed the servants well, and they served the delicious dishes silently and efficiently. Once the food was in front of them, the guests turned their attention to eating.

When he was sure everybody had finished, and knowing the time was right, Sean rose. "I have an announcement to make, one that may affect the way you feel about me and about visiting in my home."

A few voices protested, saying they couldn't imagine anything disrupting their friendship with Sean O'Brien. He was well known and his hospitality was unequaled anywhere in the panhandle of Texas.

"I thank you for those brave words, but you'd better hear what I have to say first. I'm a half-breed. Part Irish, part Comanche. I'm proud of my ancestry. I refuse to hide either kinship any longer." He waited for the suddenly shrill voices to subside. "My father, an Irishman from Country Mayo, Ireland, married the daughter of a Comanche chief, Stone Wolf of the plains country. Perhaps some of you have heard of him. I am Stone Wolf's grandson. My Indian name is Grayhawk."

"Well, O'Brien, that's a real damn surprise."

"Does it bother you, Senator?"

"Hell, yes. We ain't Indian lovers."

"Whatever you think is right, sir. But the time will come when the fighting will cease. I hope the hatred will also."

"Now, ain't them fine words!" Boggs strode into the room, accompanied by five men with their guns drawn. He sidled to where Kate sat very stiffly, her face pale, her eyes straight ahead. Wrapping his arm around her throat, he drew her roughly back against his chest. "Thought you might like to know, savage. I'm taking this one back. She ain't going to like what I do to her. Then I'm giving her a one-way trip to Mexico. By the time I'm finished with her, she'll fit right in with them other whores."

"You can't do that," Maureen whispered. "Please don't do that."

"What the hell? I ain't wanting you," Boggs said furiously. "Nobody would want you. Always blubbering."

"You son of a bitch, that's not so," Andy said in a growl, starting for Boggs.

Without taking his eyes off Boggs, Sean stopped Andy with a sharp command. "Stay where you are."

Boggs's men raised their guns menacingly, and Boggs laughed, showing his teeth and gums. "Better listen to 'im. My men are trained to shoot."

Sean struggled for control, his rage barely leashed. Impossibly, Boggs was alive. He'd never wanted to hurt anybody as much as he wanted to pound this man to a pulp. His voice never wavered. "Boggs, get your hands off her."

"What are you going to do about it if I don't?"

"I'm going to kill you. This time I'll make sure you're dead."

"I'm hard to kill." Boggs chortled. "You're finding that out now. But we've chatted enough, savage. Reckon we'll go. And I'm taking this whore. Couldn't keep her out of my bed."

"Turn her loose, you sorry excuse for a man." Sean clenched and unclenched his fists, his anger again reaching dangerous levels. He considered rushing the man, but Kate's life was at stake. Boggs would kill her. "Kate wouldn't have anything to do with you. Wouldn't come to your bed for a few cheap beads, so now you want to get even."

"That ain't so. And I heard what you said. Goin' around pretending to be an Irishman. You're a damned Comanche Indian." Boggs tightened his arm around Kate. "And she's a thieving whore who took up with you. She stole a valuable piece of jewelry. Left town owing everybody. She stole a horse, and that makes her a horse thief. And she's going to pay. So back off. I'm taking her."

Ophelia Maud whimpered. "Let him take her, Mr. O'Brien, before he shoots us all."

"And if you were in her place, Mrs. Platt?"

Boggs laughed loudly. "Lady, you ain't in danger." He turned back to Kate. "This one will earn her keep in a whorehouse, doing what she knows how to do best. When she was at the Lily, men said she knew moves they'd never heard of. And she never got tired. Worked cheap, too, so I guess she liked her job. Why, I could tell you stories—"

Maureen's screech filled the room. Sean watched spellbound as she hurtled from her chair, seized the carving knife from the meat platter, and rushed toward the saloonkeeper. Boggs's men stayed rooted to the floor, too surprised or too unsure of where to point their guns to do anything but stare.

"Liar, liar, liar." She drove the blade to the hilt into the saloonkeeper's soft belly. "I hate you." Her screams turned to sobs. "I hate you."

All eyes were on the man whose arm gradually fell from Kate's throat. Boggs clutched his stomach and stared at the blood that streamed through his fingers. "That scared rabbit stuck . . . She stuck . . ." He slumped to his knees and tried to speak. His eyes rolled back. Gasping, he sprawled on the floor.

In two strides Sean was at Kate's side. He gathered her in his arms. All he could say was, "Thank God, thank God."

Boggs's men slunk out of the room. Soon their horses could be heard galloping out of the yard.

And Ophelia Maud fainted.

Dawn swept the prairie with pale gray clouds. The senator's caravan prepared to pull out, and the senator had no trouble expressing himself. "O'Brien, we won't be back this way."

"I'm sorry for last night's unpleasantness."

"The night had a few other surprises," the senator said pompously, his thumbs in his vest pockets. "More than my wife and me can accept. Indians and niggers at the table? Eating with white folks?" He shook his head. "We can't do that. And that other nasty business. That man threatening to kill your—My wife has a delicate nature, O'Brien. She'd stood all she could."

"We understand your wife, Senator. And we sympathize with you."

"And that business about you being an Indian—that was a real surprise. A lot of folks are gonna know about it. I'll see to that."

"I was sure you would, Senator."

Kate interrupted, her voice carrying her conviction. "Sean's surprise announcement is not the only one, Senator. You see, I'm Sean's wife, Grayhawk's wife. We were married in a Comanche wedding ceremony. And I'd like to add that I love him with all my heart."

"In the sight of God, young woman, that makes you an Indian. And no court anywhere will recognize your marriage."

Ophelia Maud's voice rose above the din. "I knew it. I just knew it."

A smile swept across Sean's face. "My wife is wonderful."

"Wait." Kate held up her hand. "I've other news. Sean and I are having a baby."

His voice husky with emotion, Sean smiled down at her. "I love you, my Kate."

She chuckled. "I know."

Sean shifted to encircle her waist and to address the departing visitors. His glance included Anna. "If our revelations are too much for you to accept, then have a pleasant trip."

With Andy and Maureen, Kate and Sean watched the senator and his entourage wind their way across the prairie. Kate sighed. "They're gone, thank goodness. The senator has a load of prejudices. But he has Ophelia Maud to help him. She'll always consider me a fallen woman."

"Forget that dreadful woman, Kate. We know you're wonderful." Maureen escaped Andy's arm long enough to kiss her sister's cheek. "So strong and brave."

Kate let the tears slide down her cheeks. After last night, she knew Maureen was also strong and brave. Maureen had grown up. Her sister was no longer a frightened rabbit, afraid of her shadow. She'd make Andy a good wife. Kate watched them walk away. They planned to leave soon for someplace in faraway Montana.

Maureen no longer needed her. Maureen had her Andy.

Sean must have sensed her tug of sadness. He brushed a tendril from her face and eased his knuckles down her wet cheeks. "I love you, beautiful lady. Go upstairs with me," he said, tenderly, "and I'll make you forget all the unpleasantness."

"Does that include the odious Ophelia?"

"She's first on the list."

"Good. I wanted to spit in her ear."

Laughing, he smothered her with kisses. "That's the way with you Comanche."

"I love you, Sean."

His words were soft against her hair. "Aye, 'tis the luck of the Irish."

Theresa Scott
Eagle Dancer

Bound and helpless, the blue-eyed prisoner is an enemy of her people. One who is going to die. But his powerful gaze tells Hope his spirit is strong, and suddenly she knows this man has a part in her future.

Baron's will to live had fled during the Civil War, during an act so unforgivable he's been punishing himself ever since. He doesn't want mercy at the hands of his captors, but he is granted a second chance by an old woman and a beautiful Lakota girl. Can a sacred ritual and a loving heart make him whole again, give him the right, at long last, to take Hope?

___4899-X $5.99 US/$6.99 CAN

BRIDE OF DESIRE

THERESA SCOTT

To beautiful, ebony-haired Winsome, the tall blond stranger who has taken her captive seems an entirely different breed of male from the men of her tribe. And although she has been taught that a man and a maiden might not join together until a wedding ceremony is performed, she finds herself longing to surrender to his hard-muscled body.

___4474-9 $5.99 US/$6.99 CAN

Dorchester Publishing Co., Inc.
P.O. Box 6640
Wayne, PA 19087-8640

Please add $1.75 for shipping and handling for the first book and $.50 for each book thereafter. NY, NYC, and PA residents, please add appropriate sales tax. No cash, stamps, or C.O.D.s. All orders shipped within 6 weeks via postal service book rate. Canadian orders require $2.00 extra postage and must be paid in U.S. dollars through a U.S. banking facility.

Name_____
Address_____
City_____State_____Zip_____
I have enclosed $_____ in payment for the checked book(s).
Payment <u>must</u> accompany all orders. ❏ Please send a free catalog.
       CHECK OUT OUR WEBSITE! www.dorchesterpub.com

Savage Honor
Cassie Edwards

Shawndee Sibley longs for satin ribbons, fancy dresses, and a man who will take her away from her miserable life in Silver Creek. But the only men she ever encounters are the drunks who frequent her mother's tavern. And even then, Shawndee's mother makes her disguise herself as a boy for her own protection.

Shadow Hawk bitterly resents the Sibleys for corrupting his warriors with their whiskey. Capturing their "son" is a surefire way to force them to listen to him. But he quickly becomes the captive—of Shawndee's shy smile, iron will, and her shimmering golden hair.

___4889-2 $5.99 US/$6.99 CAN

White Dove

SUSAN EDWARDS

White Dove was raised to know that she must marry a powerful warrior. The daughter of the great Golden Eagle is required to wed one of her own kind, a man who will bring honor to her people and strength to her tribe. But the young Irishman who returns to seek her hand makes her question herself, and makes her question what makes a man.

Jeremy Jones returns to be trained as a warrior, to take the tests of manhood and prove himself in battle. Watching him, White Dove sees a bravery she's never known, and suddenly she realizes her young suitor is not just a man, he is the only one she'll ever love.

___4890-6 $5.99 US/$6.99 CAN